Baby Angel

Carla Donn

Contents

one

The sky is incredibly gloomy despite it being a very exciting day for her. The ash color clouds and dimly lit natural lighting weren't matching her mood. The passing cars were vibrant, but not as vibrant as they would've been had the sun been shining bright into the sky rather than hiding behind the clouds. On top of everything else, it was raining. The sound of light rainfall hitting the car reminded her of the days she would sit in her childhood room, sketching the scenery. Even though it was extremely gray and gloomy, her smile rests upon her lips.

Her gray noise canceling headphones are on her head as she sits in the passenger seat, quietly listening to her Rainy Days playlist. Aurelia drowns herself in music on days like this. Sometimes, the music helps her determine how she feels for the day, and on good days, it gets her creative juices running for another painting she wants to finish. That's one of many of her goals this year. Finish all the unfinished canvas tucked away in the trunk of her mother's car.

A tap on her shoulder causes her to pull her headphone off and turn around in her seat. "Yes?"

"I wish you look a bit sad," Her mother tells her, wiping the tears under her eyes carefully so she wouldn't ruin her makeup she spent hours on before they left the house. "You're going to be leaving us for months, but you're sitting comfortably."

"I am comfortable." She says, making her momma hit her shoulder.

"Ouch!"

"Sean! Do you hear how she's talking to me!" Her mother says dramatically, pushing her father's shoulder from the backseat as he drives.

"I heard her, babe." he laughs before glancing over at his daughter with a smile before shaking his head.

Aurelia laughs quietly, covering her face so her momma won't notice that they're laughing at her.

"She has never lived without us before! How can she sit comfortably right now!" Her momma expresses as she sniffles softly.

Rolling her eyes, Aurelia pulls her headphones back on, listening to one of many of her favorite songs. Her mother is being really dramatic. She's behaving as if Aurelia will never return home ever again. This is her first year at, one of her top picks for college. Shouldn't her momma be happy that she decided to enter the tough world of arts? Maybe she's concerned that she won't make it far with it. The art world is hard, especially when she wants to showcase her unique paintings to the world. Sure, every artist is unique, but eventually they all blend together. But she refuses to blend when it comes to her artwork. Aurelia is shooting to stand out.

"Aurelia!" She hears her mother say her name loudly.

"Momma!" She says back, pulling her headphones off once again. "Can we please not do this? You knew I was leaving today, why are you crying like this?"

"My only child is leaving me and you want me to be happy?" Her mother sniffles. "That's cruel."

"Yes," Aurelia sighs. "I want you to be happy for me."

"Honey," her father backs her up. "College is an exciting milestone! We should be glad she wanted to go to college. Imagine if she decided to work a random nine to five for the rest of her life and not do what she loves to do? That would be more heartbreaking than her moving into a dorm room."

Aurelia holds her father's hand, gracing him with one of very few toothy smiles that she does. Looking back at her momma one last time, she holds her hand out. As her mother squeezes her hand, she smiles warmly. "Please stop crying. Let's make this a very happy moment. Okay?"

Her mother fans her eyes before nodding her head. Aurelia laughs quietly as she turns around, pulling her headphones back over her ears.

She never expected her mother to cry so much. Her mother, Lauren, spent most of her time at the hospital. Even then, Aurelia understood that her mother was important, being the head doctor. Although her job is important, Aurelia saw her less than she saw her father. Her father, DeSean, worked as a tenth grade biology teacher, and he was home more. Therefore, they spent more time together. Now that she thinks about it, that's probably why her mother's so emotional.

To her, it must seem like time flew so fast. Her baby, Aurelia, is no longer her baby but a new adult. A new adult that's off to college.

Aurelia dreams of having her art work displayed in her very own art gallery. Her passion for creating unique works and understanding the history behind all works of art in the world grew over the years. When she was nine, she remembered seeing The Son of Man by René Magritte in a cartoon she was watching. Of course the cartoon was one of those educational ones, where every episode focused on something different. It was all she had to watch since her parents never really showed her anything else, but the picture looked so peculiar to her, and she just couldn't take her eyes off. Her father used to tell her that's when she really started loving art, but it was a bit later that she really became serious about it.

Aurelia was about eleven when she started drawing with her number two pencil and notebook paper. Starting with lines and circles, seeing how she could make them look different each time. She kept doing that for hours a day, after homework and chores. When her art teacher, at school, gave her class paint and a blank canvas, Aurelia just fell in love.

Her emotions would just travel through the wooden handle, and pours out through the bristle of the paint brush. When she finally realized she was down, her art teacher's face looked so shocked and surprised.

"This is honestly so beautiful," her art teacher uttered to her. "I'm so shocked by your details. It's like I can feel what you feel. Excited. Passionate."

Aurelia remembered being so surprised that her art teacher knew how she felt. She understood her art piece. Her words sent waves through her heart. It gave her enough confirmation that she wanted to do art for a living. She alway envisioned herself as another Picasso, but of course, that's just her dreaming unrealistically. Again. It's not a crime to fantasize about it though. The dream isn't impossible.

Aurelia looks down at her phone and smiles when she sees a message from the group chat that she and some of her closest friends set up before they all went their separate ways to different colleges. Sabrina, the oldest—oldest by five months—got into Harvard, and her journey to be a neurosurgeon.

Aurelia and the rest of the friend group wasn't surprised since she always had the best grades and studied a lot more. Cameron decided to go to a university out of state as well. He decided to go down the language branch, study different languages. He was never good in the math classes, but he excelled everywhere else.

They were sending messages, asking Aurelia if she made it to the campus yet. Smiling ear to ear, she looks up from her phone, getting excited as the car pulls into the crowded neighborhood with student housing, which isn't that far from the main campus. She gives them a quick response before pulling her headphones off and looking at the small house that seems to be two-story.

"Did they give you your roommate's name?" Her father asked her as she put her phone in the front part of her overalls and her headphones in her bag.

"Uh," Aurelia nods her head. "Their name is Jackie. They told me I got pulled from the waitlist, so I got chosen for student housing. My room-mate is a year older. I think they're in their second year?."

"Are they a boy?"

Aurelia rolls her eyes and sighs before opening the passenger door. "Yes, I took the survey and said I wanted a boy for my roommate, so they paired me with one."

Her father playfully pushes her making her push him back while laughing.

"Stop the shenanigans and go open the door." Her mother scolds them both while taking one of two of Aurelia's luggage from the trunk of the truck.

"Hold on, momma." She tells her as she looks around to see a few other people in the neighborhood moving in. "I have to call my roommate to see if she's inside."

Just as she finds the contact, a car playing loud music pulls up right behind her mother's truck. Her parents shared a perplexed look, but she took the courage to approach the car. As she approaches, four people get out. Three girls and one guy.

The guy was tall, but not taller than her dad. He was wearing a gray hoodie, with university on the front, and jeans; a standard college guy outfit. He was tan, not an orange tan, but a light bronze tan. His hair was as dark as his eyes, giving him a very intimidating aura. Once they meet gazes, Aurelia carefully turns her eyes to the other three girls.

"Aurelia!" Jackie smiles and hugs Aurelia tightly, making her stiff a bit at the sudden hug.

"I'm Jackie! Your roommate for the year!" Jackie greets before turning around to properly greet Aurelia's parents.

"I'm Genesis and this is Abby, we're Jackie's friends." Aurelia nods her head politely, but smiles awkwardly.

"Nice to meet you." Aurelia looks at her parents and Jackie before the older girl turns towards her.

"Let me show you the place," Jackie finally looks at her. "Babe, can you show her parents around downstairs?"

"Oh-" her parents said at the same time before laughing a bit, but they were just as confused as Aurelia.

"We're fine. Aurelia will be the one living here, so she should know the layout." Aurelia's mother tells her before holding onto her father's arm.

Jackie nods her head and pulls Aurelia towards the steps up to the door. She hands her a key to the dorm, and smiles before unlocking it. Inside the dorm, at least on the first floor, was really clean. The kitchen, dining, and small living area was all very clean. So far, Aurelia wasn't regretting accepting Jackie as her roommate.

"So basically, this is our closet," Jackie points to the door on the left the moment they walk into the home. "You can put your coat and jackets here. You can also store your umbrella and other stuff like that in here."

Aurelia noticed how weirdly friendly she is, but it could be that she's just happy to have a roommate. Jackie grabs her hand and leads her upstairs since the bottom floor was an open concept. Everything could be seen without having to look around fully. She probably does all that on her own.

"Here's the bathroom," she smiles and pushes the door open the moment she sets foot on the last step. "Our room is right here."

Aurelia looks around the bathroom, nodding her head slightly before following Jackie to the bedroom that's small. It wasn't too small. There's enough walking space, and there's a small desk for each side of the room. Jackie walks over to the closet, pulling the doors open.

"The space is pretty big. You get the right side of the closet and the right side of the room." Jackie smiles. "And we're done. I hope you enjoy your time here!"

Aurelia smiles and nods her head. "Thank you for the quick tour, you seem busy."

Jackie crosses her arms and giggles. "Yeah, I almost forgot about you. We were at this small event for freshmen. When you are done settling in, maybe you should head to the main campus after."

Aurelia laughs a bit and nods. "We'll see. Thank you for the tour."

"Of course!" Jackie says walking out of the room with a smile.

Naturally, she followed behind her, meeting her parents back at the truck while Jackie walked to the car she came in with her friends.

"Remember what I said, good luck settling in!"

As the group leaves, Aurelia smiles genuinely at her parents, despite their concerned expressions. Her mother looks like she is on the verge of tears, but of course, before that happens, Aurelia grips her luggage and her mother's hand.

"Come on, help me." She laughs, that excitement never leaving her face as she leads her mother to the room upstairs.

"Aurelia," her mother's voice cracks. "Are you sure this is what you want? That girl seems very wild. Nothing like you."

Aurelia tilts her head as she sits her luggage by the ladder of the loft bed. She turns to her mother and crosses her arms. Her mother is right. Jackie is the total opposite of her, but she's sure the girl is like that because she was in a rush to get back to her friends. Besides, she didn't mind the idea of only seeing the girl occasionally. She is the type that likes to stick to herself, unless it's with her closest friends.

"Roommates aren't supposed to be exactly like me, momma." She explains with a reassuring smile.

"Yeah. Well, she could at least have the decency to help you settle in some more."

"Momma." Aurelia sighs and starts to dig in the bag her mother brought up with her.

Inside were cleaning wipes, so she could wipe down the desk and the railing of the bed. Aurelia just wanted to be sure everything was clean before she started putting her stuff away. As her mother and father help her situate everything, Aurelia couldn't stop thinking about the information she was given about the event they were holding for freshmen. Though it sounded exciting, it wasn't really her kind of thing. Parties scared her. Even when Cameron dragged her and Sabrina to one every other weekend.

She remembered at one of the mystery parties Cameron dragged them to an older guy repeatedly tried to make passes at her. Aurelia tried her best not to sound too dismissive or reject him nicely. The man didn't leave her alone until Cameron protected her by pretending to be her boyfriend. However, the way Jackie spoke about the event, it's obvious a campus thing they do with freshmen every year, so maybe she should go.

"Look at her," her father murmurs to her mother. "It's like she's all grown up."

Aurelia turns around to look at her parents, smiling sadly.

"It's time for us to go." Her father smiles and kisses the top of her head. "Make sure you call us every other day."

"No! Everyday!" Her mother hits his arm before kissing Aurelia on the cheek.

Aurelia follows her parents back to the truck, kissing them both on the cheek as a last goodbye. Of course, she would see them again, but it was time to live on her own, spend her new left, her new journey at the school of her dreams. Grabbing her bright yellow easel, she waves to her parents as they drive away, down the same road they came into the neighborhood. Smiling down at her easel, Aurelia turns around on her heels and begins to walk back to the house, closing the doors right behind her.

The girl carefully makes her way up the concrete stairs pushing the front door open and closing it with her foot. Aurelia walks over to a generally empty spot in the living area to set her easel up. Once everything is perfectly set up, she pulls her phone out of her pocket and facetime her best friends. After a few seconds of waiting, they both answer, almost at the same time.

"How is it?" Sabrina asks right away, making Aurelia laugh.

"Better than I expected."

"What about your roommate?" Cameron asks her as she takes a seat on the couch, sinking into the cushions. "Is she cool?"

"Yeah. She's different, but she does give off that party girl vibe. Kind of like a female version of you Cameron." Aurelia explains, pulling her attention to the ceiling as she talks to her friends.

Sabrina hums softly. "Do they have orientation?"

"That's not until tomorrow, but..." Aurelia looks at her screen seeing that both of her friends seem very busy on their end, especially Sabrina.

"But?" Cameron repeats, looking down at the camera. It seems like he is driving somewhere.

"But Jackie, my roommate, said they do a big event for freshmen and I should come." Aurelia didn't seem very convinced, and she definitely didn't know if she should go since she's socially awkward and can't hold a conversation for more than ten minutes before going to short single-word answers.

"First day of that college girl life and you already saying no to a way of making other friends besides us." Cameron shakes his head while Sabrina rolls her eyes.

"Just ignore his annoying ass," Sabrina laughs. "If you don't want to go, you don't have to, Relia."

Aurelia shrugs and sighs.

She honestly was still debating, but it wouldn't hurt to just look around, get a sense of the people, maybe talk to other freshmen that could possibly live nearby or taking the same classes. Cameron was somewhat right, she should definitely try to use this event to connect with some new people. Aurelia loves her friends dearly, but maybe having friends in the present would help her feel less intimidated by the simple fact that she will be alone. Chasing her dreams.

"Fine." Aurelia sighs again.

"Yes!" Cameron cheers. "Our baby is growing up, Brina!"

Sabrina shakes her head and laughs softly. "I see. Tell us how it goes. Okay?"

Aurelia nods before ending the call with her friends. She walks up the stairs, deciding to freshen up just a little bit. She didn't want to change into other clothes, she just wanted to make sure she looks decent enough to blend in the crowd rather than stand out. She was only going to have some conversation, or possibly meet new people.

Of course she just hopes it goes well.

□

two

<hr>

In the canvas of dreams, artists are the weavers of hope, threading the tapestry of the good that lies hidden within our most cherished aspirations.□

▼

▲

□

The closer she got to the main campus, the louder the music could be heard. They really were throwing some form of event for the freshmen. Aurelia, deep down, did not trust Jackie's word. She is a complete stranger. She doesn't really know her, but it wouldn't hurt to get to know the person she will be staying with why she attends this school.

Walking up the flight of stairs, she got chills as she took a glance around the place. There were so many people. One thing for sure, she did not do well with big crowds. However, if it was a small group of three she would be perfectly fine. For the most part. Putting her hands in the pockets of her overalls, she walks towards Campus statue. The statue of its founder. Even in a place like this, full of people, Aurelia somehow loses herself in the art rather than the music and people.

"Aurelia, right?" A voice speaks close to her ear, causing her to flinch before looking beside her.

It was the same guy that showed up with Jackie. Now that she thinks about it, she doesn't know if she ever got his name. That was besides the point, here he is now. In front of her looking taller now than he's beside her rather than a few feet away from her.

"Uh," Aurelia nods her head slowly. "Yes, I don't think I got your name though."

The male smiles big, showing off his pink gums and pearly white teeth. His laugh was monotone, much like his speaking voice. The man is attractive, like a stone sculpture of a man, a god from Greek mythology. Though she didn't have a type, she could definitely say he gives off an approachable vibe the moment he speaks. Despite his size, he wasn't that intimidating.

"Aiden." He tells her nodding his head in a certain motion, as if he's indirectly telling her to follow him. "Jackie's boyfriend."

Aurelia makes a small 'o' with her lips before nodding her head. That made sense to her. When they first showed up at the house, she did hear Jackie call him babe, but she didn't think anything of it. She was too nervous and awkward to be as energetic and talkative. These are the times she wished her best friends were here. They would've helped her warm up in an environment like this one. Unfortunately, they aren't here. So she needs to start doing these kinds of things on her own.

"We are at the tattoo booth." He tells her as she walks alongside him.

"Tattoo?"

"I know, I know," he laughs. "What kind of school allows a tattoo booth?"

Aurelia nods her head laughing quietly. "I get it's art and we are at an art university, but they allow people to buy tattoos?"

Aiden stops at the popcorn stand and buys a small cup of popcorn. "You're right on the nose. The school doesn't allow people to get actual tattoos at events like this."

He tosses some popcorn in his mouth, before offering her some. Aurelia smiles kindly and shakes her head politely at the offer.

"They're temporary school related tattoos. You know the logo and shit." He explains as he continues to walk. "A guy, who used to attend this school, opened his own tattoo parlor not too far from here, a few months ago. I heard he asked the school if he could promote his parlor at this event, so he's here along with a few other people that work there, selling temporary tattoos of the school logos in their art style."

Aurelia just nods and listens, looking at the different food trucks and stands. Along with small games to win small school merch; a t-shirt, hoodie, sweatpants, and a lot of other items. The event is cute and it seems fun. Of course, as always, she was worried for nothing.

"That seems fun."

Aiden shrugs his shoulders, stopping by a recycling bin, tossing his empty popcorn cup inside. "I guess. Jackie's just up there, you see that black and purple tent?"

Aurelia stands on her tippy-toes trying to look over the crowd full of people. This caused the tall male to laugh at her before shaking his head.

"You'll know it's the tent when you make it to a crowd full of girls and when you hear indie-rock music playing." He explains before another guy walks up out of nowhere.

"Yo! Aiden we need to talk about Tony's surprise party." The stranger says. Wrapping his arm around Aiden's shoulder.

"Yeah, yeah." He says. "See you around, Aurelia."

Aurelia stands there for a second to wave goodbye. Though she didn't know who that stranger was, she could tell that Aiden is part of a larger friend group. Large than a group of four people. There is nothing wrong with that, but four people could be too much for her. She doesn't know if getting to know her roommate friends is something she will try to do, but she wouldn't mind getting to know Jackie. She is her roommate, so it's only natural.

Turning around, Aurelia carefully makes it through the crowd. It was a scary large crowd, since many people were spread out everywhere, but this event must be one of many that they throw for the students that attend the university. It's great to know that her current school has its students in their best interests. As she gets closer to the tent, sure enough, the crowd switches from all sorts of people to one demographic. Women or feminine presenting people.

Uttering a small 'excuse mes' she could see Jackie standing off to the side of the tent, drinking from a can with a straw. Aurelia makes her way over, already wishing she walked slower. Had she walked slower, maybe she wouldn't have found herself stepping into an argument.

"It doesn't make any sense," Abby crosses her arms, trying not to frown, but trying, resulting in her frowning so hard anyone would've stopped and asked if she's okay. "All these people came to see him, and him only, and he didn't show up?"

"You're mad that he didn't show up," Genesis rolls her eyes. "Everyone else isn't thirsting for just him. All the other tattooists are attractive as well, Abby."

"Oh, shut up." The shorter girl frowns. "At least I'm not thirsting after a crackhead who ditched town-"

"Aurelia!" Jackie calls her name loudly, causing Genesis and Abby to look at her.

"Sorry, did I interrupt something?" She asks as Jackie hugs her again, making her tense up like before.

"No, lovely. We were just waiting for this booth to clear up to get tattoos." She smiles widely, making Aurelia return a small smile. "How did you know I was here?"

Aurelia laughs awkwardly, "Uh, Aiden? He showed me the way. I just got here."

Abby and Genesis turn towards each other and continue to have a conversation, while Jackie smiles at her, as if she doesn't hear her friends arguing behind her. Honestly, Aurelia was so distracted by the bickering, it made it hard to focus on whatever Jackie was telling her. Art clubs? Painting studio? Community art center?

"You're mad that he didn't want to sleep with-"

"Hey!" Jackie finally turns around. "Can you two shut up! The man isn't even here and you two are getting your panties in a tangle!"

Aurelia cringes at the choice of words, turning her attention towards the small crowd of girls nearby that heard her whisper-shouts at her friends. Aurelia clears her throat and touches Jackie's arm.

"I'm going to head over to one of the food trucks," Aurelia lies. "I'm a bit hungry."

Jackie tilts her head at Aurelia before turning back to Abby and Genesis. "See what you two did? You made my roommate uncomfortable."

"No, no. It's okay." Aurelia tries to reason Jackie so they wouldn't draw more attention to them.

It Hasn't even been a full day since she has been here and the friend group already seems like too much for her. Aurelia gives Jackie one more forced smile before the woman returns it and nods. As she turns around to leave the three, she takes a deep breath and before walking away. When she's far away enough, she lets out the breath she has been holding before slowly walking through the crowd.

Even if they were making her extremely uncomfortable, Aurelia still wanted to check out the rest of the event. It was meant for the students like her—freshman. As she gets to the stand talking about different art studios on campus and people running exclusive clubs outside of campus. This had to be what Jackie was trying to tell her but her friends were being rude.

"Welcome!" The guy beside the booth smiled. "Are you interested in the brochure to show you all the locations of the studios here on campus?"

Aurelia smiles and nods her head.

The guy hands her one before repeating the same thing to the group of three standing beside her. There were a lot of studios, some even allow you to reserve a solo space. This is nice.

"Well look who decided to grace us art seniors with his presences." The guy who just gave her a brochure chuckles before greeting someone.

Aurelia turns her head, looking at the person he's talking to. Woah. Was all she could think of. Long curly blonde hair, stopping just above his shoulder. Ink covering his skin. Everywhere. His neck, torso, arms, but none on his face. It was still a lot more on him than she saw on anyone else.

"Don't do that," he laughs and hands the other guy from before a sheet of paper. "I had to edit something and print it out. That's why I'm late."

"Don't worry, Elijah, your team seems to be promoting your parlor pretty well. Though because you didn't show up, we got a lot more people show- ing up to our stands than they were last year." The other male chuckles before walking behind the stand. "I know a person that can make you a good flyer, but thanks for the formal request."

Aurelia turns her head away as the stranger, Elijah, glances in her direction. She pretends as if she was looking at the open spots in some clubs. Though she would never join one, she had to act as though she wasn't listening in on their conversation.

"I mean this place helped me a lot, so the least I could do is follow the rules. Just because I used to be a student here, doesn't mean I want special treatment." Elijah laughs, walking closer to the booth, causing the group of friends on the other side of her to whisper to each other.

"Ladies, ladies." The man behind the stand calls them. "I get he's walking art, but please refrain from crowding my stand if you aren't interested in anything here."

Elijah chuckles quietly before turning towards the group. "I don't mind." He shoots them a wink causing them to laugh softly before walking away.

"Of course, you don't." The male shakes his head.

Aurelia rolls her eyes before laughing to herself.

"Here," the guy gives Elijah a white card. "Heather is a good digital artist here, she doesn't charge an arm or leg for services."

"Thanks. See you around Sunny." Elijah says before walking in the direction of the tattoo teng.

Aurelia sighs lightly, grabbing a pin from Sunny's stand. "Thank you for the brochure."

The male smiles and nods. "Anytime. I'm the head of the art Major around here. My email and contact number is on there if you need anything. A gig? Or maybe the right people to sponsor your artwork? I prefer if you email me first before calling."

Aurelia nods again before walking away. As much as she wanted to go back to the dorm, she was hungry. She walks to the food truck line, wanting to get something small and light. The line wasn't too long so she didn't mind waiting.

"They said Elijah here? Should we just come back?" The guys in front of her tell each other before they both agreed before walking out of the line.

"Aurelia!" She turns to see Aiden approaching her.

He greets the person behind her and drapes his arm around her shoulder, making her look up at him. "Hey."

"What are you doing here? They are about to start the performance." He tells her, causing her to smoothly step from under his arms and walk forward as the line gets shorter.

"I think I'm just going to eat and head back to the dorm." She tells him, his expression almost looking disappointed at her decision to leave.

Aiden nods. "What did you want?"

Aurelia looks at the menu and shrugs. "Maybe the hamburger?"

Aiden grins and walks to the front of the line. She tilts her head, her eyes widened with horror as he walks into the truck, grabs her a tray with fries and a hamburger. He grabs a water bottle and bottle lemonade before coming out of the truck with everything.

"Thanks Josh! I owe you." He tells the guy before walking towards Aurelia with everything.

"Here."

"Aiden. You didn't-" she digs in her pocket for money, but he stops her.

"Just take it. I know the guy who runs the truck, it's cool." He winks at her before handing everything to her before taking a step back.

"See you around, Aurelia." he waves before he runs up to his friends who were pushing him around laughing.

She doesn't understand why he was being so nice to her when this was his first time meeting her. It didn't click in her mind why, but she's sure it's because she's his girlfriend's roommate and he wants her to feel comfortable at the university as well with him and his girlfriend friend group. Aurelia wasn't planning on having a closer relationship besides roommates. After today, how her friends were acting, she's not sure she could keep up with all of that.

Aurelia looks around, finding a clear spot on the stairs, right next to a guy wearing a big black hoodie, scrolling on his phone. It was clear he wasn't going to talk to her, so that was good. Now she can eat without anyone bothering her or asking questions. So much for the first day being smooth. Last time she listened to her parents. It may have been smooth sailing for them, but it has been the opposite for her so far.

"Fuck." The stranger beside her suddenly blurts out before sitting up shoving one of his bluetooth earphones in his ear, before playing something on his phone.

Aurelia could tell he was having a bad day, considering the tone of his voice and the way his hoodie is covering his face, as if he's hiding. Maybe hiding from the people. She should've thought of that, but she didn't unfortunately. Her best friends would beat her ass if they found out she was closing her shell up after they spent all of middle and high school trying to break her out of it. Which they did, for the most part.

The male beside her digs into his duffle bag, grabbing his empty water bottle out. He sighs loudly before tossing the bottle back into his bag. She did have a water bottle, but Aiden also grabbed a lemonade for her, so she didn't mind giving the water away. Swallowing the food down, Aurelia grabs the water bottle and hands it to the hoodie person. He slowly turns to look at her, his glare almost making her flinch away.

Surprisingly, he takes it, uttering a small thanks before opening it and drinking it.

She smiles at him. "You're welcome."

Standing from the steps, she begins to walk down the stairs, getting ready to walk home. The walk back wasn't bad at all, but she wished that she at least told Jackie she was going back. Knowing the campus wasn't that far from where she would be staying for the rest of the year, she knows that things could and would get better if she just find people who are interested in the same things that she's interested in and found a good small group of friends.

Aurelia had to make this work. SHe begged for her parents permission to attend this school the moment she got accepted. This was her dream college, and she's going to make sure she makes it the best year.

The moment she makes it to the dorm, she calls her best friend, telling them everything. The whole argument and even how her roommate bought her dinner even though she didn't ask him to.

"Is he attractive?" Sabrina asks, causing Cameron to sigh loudly.

Aurelia laughs. "I guess he is, but that's my roommate's boyfriend, and I don't think I have the confidence to mess with someone's boyfriend."

"Good." Cameron says. "I'm sure you're going to find a single guy who's as boring as you are."

Aurelia gasps dramatically. "Art isn't boring."

Sabrina laughs at them both. "I got to go, I got class bright and early tomorrow. I'll text you two later."

Cameron says goodbye, leaving just her and him on the call. Aurelia and he talked about different things, like the hours for classes, when they should have group calls so it wouldn't interfere with their schedules for the year.

"I'm proud of Aurelia." Cameron suddenly says, making her smile. "Brina and I thought you were going to follow one of us to the end of the planet, but we're glad you branched off on your own."

"I'm proud of myself too." Aurelia nods, agreeing with her best friend. "I'm sure I can do this on my own. I just need to find the right people, and not my current roommates and her friends. I need my own here."

"I'm sure you'll find them," he tells her. "Just be careful. A city like the one you're in is big, which means it's not one hundred percent safe to be by yourself in. Call us if you ever need someone to talk to. You know we got you."

Aurelia smiles and nods her head. "Thank you, Cam. I needed to hear that. Especially now. It'll give me some more courage to do this on my own."

"Talk to you tomorrow, Relia."

Once the call ended, Aurelia sent her parents a goodnight text and got ready for bed. It was weird, considering that Jackie wasn't back and the night was getting later, perhaps she was staying with her friends for the night. She didn't mind since she preferred the quiet anyway. She wonders what tomorrow will bring her, hopefully something better than what she experienced today.

□

three

Uncertainty is the threshold of possibility, a canvas yet to be painted.

Aurelia holds the yellow basket she would be using for her bathroom necessities close to her body. As she walked around the bathroom section of the store, she had her noise canceling headphones on her head, blasting her favorite chase atlantic song. Of course, everywhere she goes she must have music playing. Before she left for college, her friends and her created a playlist for almost every occasion. Holidays, bad days, good days, even moods. At the time it was a stupid idea. Sabrina, Cameron, and she made about fifty different playlists that were over thirty hours long. Now that she thinks about it, she's quite grateful that she made them. At least now she knows she wouldn't be deprived of her favorite songs. Her mother and father were never big fans of the music she listens to, despite telling that she listens to everything, including the stuff they deem as old folks stuff.

"What you know about New Edition?" Her father laughed when he walked into her room a few months ago.

"I listen to their music," Aurelia smiled as she turned around in the stool, holding the paintbrush in her hand after turning the volume to the music down on her phone. "I don't know much about them as people though."

Her father sat on her bed that day, and told her all about the boy group that had shaken up the eighties and had the hearts of all the girls during that time. The memory makes her smile as she continues to walk along the isle, listening to her productive playlist because she needed to do a lot before her first class, which is late in the day. How she wanted it to be.

Aurelia dreamed about walking around the beautiful city during the day, and studying hard during the evening. She has never been an early bird, so doing early morning classes were going to make her miserable at school she deem as her dream college.

Her mother almost had a heart attack when Aurelia told her she would be doing afternoon and night classes. She went on how it would be dangerous, especially when she's alone with no friends who's doing the same schedule as her to walk with her. Of course, her mother is right, it's more dangerous at night than during the day, but it's not like she has class everyday of the week. Besides, Aurelia knew she could take care of herself, she has a few things to protect herself if it comes down to it. She checked the neighborhood before deciding to attend her dream college, but even if the only crime that has been reported in the area of her dorms are break-ins, she still made sure to think about everything before accepting the acceptance letter.

Her form is located only a few blocks away from campus security. Her campus is a bus ride away from the police station if she ever needs to report something, and she has her dean and guidance counselor if she needs help with anything more. Aurelia is set. Her mother, and her friends, don't need to worry about her. She has everything under control.

"Body Scrub..." She murmurs to herself, picking up the body scrub with cocoa butter and other natural ingredients.

Hygiene is a big thing for her. High school traumatized her. When she was a sophomore, she forgot her feminine hygiene bag at home. Even then, Sabrina couldn't help her. She had everything she needed in that bag, but she left it. It left her high school self no choice but to walk around the school building smelling like sweat and chlorine, since she was swimming then. Everyone whispered behind her back, and the boys at the school made inside jokes about her, even though it was the first and only time that happened to her. Now, fast forwarding to the present, she plans to maintain her hygiene routine as she did when she was at home.

"So you're going to avoid me?"

Aurelia's music wasn't blasting, so she could still hear the people around her muffle conversation, so when she hears the male voice, it causes her to turn her head to the source of the voice. She couldn't tell completely, but the man did seem really familiar. The closer he got, the more familiar he seemed. As he pushes his cart in her direction, her eyes widen as she notices he is walking right at her, and it seems like he is on the phone, so he isn't paying attention.

Of course, like any normal person in this situation, she steps to the side quickly, and stops his cart with her hand so no else would be put in a situation where they have to deal with someone who's on their phone and not paying attention to where they are going.

"The fuck," He says looking at her, but his expression changes quickly before he realizes the situation.

"Andrew, I'll call you later."

He definitely looks familiar.

"No, I'm not avoiding the conversation-" The male sighs before turning away from her, pressing hsi phone closer to his ear. "Andrew, I just bumped into someone, just give me a few minutes and I'll call you back. I promise."

"Because you distracted me!" He whispers shout on the phone. "Look, I'll call you later, okay?"

Aurelia didn't mean to stand there that long. She would've appreciated an apology, but it wasn't as if she was waiting for one. The girl could've easily told him to pay attention next time and moved on, but of course her curiosity got the better of her. The only reason she stood there was because he looked familiar. She always had a curiosity problem, according to her best friends.

"Don't look now," Cameron whispered in her ear the day they went out joy riding before Sabrina left for college. "I'm sure that dude over there is looking at Brina."

Of course, Aurelia turned her full body around, and stared the man down, making Cameron slap his forehead before pushing her towards the back-seat door of his jeep.

"I told you don't look, and you turned your entire body. Damn, Relia, you suck at this discreet shit."

Aurelia remembered being so confused about what she did that night, but she could tell from her standing right here in front of the man that almost rammed her with his cart, that she definitely had a curiosity problem.

"Hey," the male says, walking up to her smiling widely. "I'm sorry for bumping into you... I wasn't paying attention."

That was a lot easier than she expected to be.

"It's okay." She says, not making direct eye contact with the man. "I stopped it just before it hit me."

"That doesn't mean anything," He chuckles. "I should've been watching what was in front of me, so for that I'm sorry."

Aurelia smiles a bit before clearing her throat. "It seems like you were on an important call, so it's fine. Really."

"If you say so." the stranger laughs, leaning against his cart as he tilts his head, squinting his eyes at her.

She knows that she saw him somewhere before, and it had to be recent. His curly blonde hair sits in a low bun as he stands in front of her. His gray brown eyes roamed her body, head to toe. Aurelia shifts, showcasing that him staring at her for so long is making her uncomfortable.

"Have I seen you somewhere?" He asks. "Are you a student?"

Aurelia tilts her head before she realizes exactly who the man is. The guy. The tattoo guy that everyone was going crazy for at the event two days ago. She couldn't remember his name, but she did remember the impact he had on people. Especially the people who were only there for him and the people that worked for him.

"I go to the college not too far from here," she tells him, knowing that he used to be a student. "I think you were at the events they held for the freshmen."

If she didn't recognize him she would've said no and went about her day. He didn't seem like a creep either, so she made a quick judgment so she wouldn't seem weird or awkward for not responding to him too fast. Perhaps that was her overthinking as she always does, but she knew how to get over these. Cameron told her to focus on one thing, specifically the topic or person right in front of her so she wouldn't overthink too much and become overwhelmed.

"Oh!" He snaps his fingers. "You're a freshman, you were at my old mentor stand. Art Major?"

"Art History," she tells him. "Well, I still paint, but I want to change my major for next semester. I didn't think you would remember, It was like two days ago."

"I have a good memory." He chuckles. "You got it all figured out, huh?"

Aurelia nods seriously, and takes a small step back. "You seemed busy, and I should go. I have a lot of things to do after this."

The stranger smiles and pulls his phone back out. "I see," he hums, nodding his head as a smile covers his face.

"Sorry again for bumping into, maybe whenever we bump into each other again, I can take you to get some coffee?"

Aurelia flinches and nervously clears her throat as she holds the body scrub in her hand. "No. No, that's okay. It was nice meeting you..."

"Elijah."

"Right. Nice meeting you, Elijah." She laughs it off a bit before turning on her heel and walking away from the man while holding the items she grabbed close to her chest.

It was weird and he came on strong. Even if he is attractive, she does not know him. Now everything in her is hoping she doesn't run into him again, but given the circumstances, she might actually run into him again.

As she walks back to the dorm, she talks to her best friend about how. It seems like Sabrina was the only one she could talk to since Cameron was too busy to get on a group call with them. Besides, she needed at least one of them on the phone with her so she could make it back safely.

"So this man asked you out and you said no?"

"Yes." Aurelia says. "Well, I didn't say no I just didn't take him up on his offer because I don't know him at all."

"I see." Sabrina hums into the phone. "So, you said no."

Aurelia laughs a soft yes into the phone. Sabrina was always the girl everyone wanted to talk to in high school, but of course, she was more focused on getting out of high school rather than having a high school relationship. When guys talked to her back then, she would reject them and tell them about her. Sabrina used to talk her up, and sometimes it worked, but most times the guys were only interested in her best friend. So now, when she told her about Elijah, the tone in her voice suggests that she wanted Aurelia to step out of her comfort zone, and start talking to guys without her wingwoman around to help her out. Although that sounds easy, Aurelia definitely prefers getting to know someone before trying to pursue something with them. She's more old fashioned and traditional when it comes to the steps of pursuing someone she's into.

"Your first week hasn't officially started and guys are already hitting on you," she laughs quietly, Sabrina must've been in a study room. " I heard the guys at prestigious art universities are quite creative in the romance department."

"Well, I wouldn't know." She hums. "I'll let you know when I find one of those guys, because so far, the only guy who has been throwing strong and weird signals is Aiden."

"Aiden?"

Aurelia sighs as she waits at the bus stop. This bus would take her just a few blocks away from her neighborhood. That way she could walk comfortably without feeling too nervous, since the evening is turning darker.

"Yeah," she looks down at her white converse. " My roommate's boyfriend, he's been oddly friendly, but I show him that my reaction and actions are simply friendly."

Sabrina sighs. "I hate men sometimes. You should tell her."

"Well, he hasn't really flirted with me or anything. His actions just seem really generous?" Aurelia explains as she waits for the bus. "If it gets out of hand, and I mean he's out right flirting with me, I will tell Jackie about it."

"Good because he's being weird, he's lucky Cameron isn't there, he would've called him out." She tells her, causing them both to laugh. "I won't hold you too long, love. Let me know when you get back to the dorm, okay?"

Aurelia agrees before ending the call with her. After waiting for five more minutes, the bus finally shows up. She gets on and stands next to the exit since she wouldn't be there that long. As she stands there quietly, she plays her music, mouthing lyrics slightly as she bobs her head a bit to the song. Once her stop comes up she gets off of the bus and begins to walk back to the dorm.

When she gets there, she could hear the loud music playing over the music that's playing through her headphones. Aurelia turns the music off, unlocking the dorm door and walking inside. The moment she's inside she sees Jackie's friends on the couch laughing while watching something on one of their phones. They haven't noticed her yet, but judging how Jackie, an unknown man, and Aiden are all occupied smoking in the tiny kitchen they had in the dorm.

Aurelia's eyes widened, feeling uncomfortable. Jackie should've told her she was having a guest. Coming home to this would make anyone just as uncomfortable as she is right now. A few more steps inside, Genesis looks up from the phone, her smile slightly fading as she puts the lollipop back into her mouth before looking at the phone again.

"Jackie, your pretty roommate is back." Abby calls out, tossing the popcorn in her mouth before looking at the phone again.

Jackie turns around, fanning the smoke from the weed they were smoking away. "Aurelia! Shit..."

Her roommate walks towards her after handing the blunt to Aiden. Of course the tall, Ken-like, guy takes the rolled up stick and takes a long drag before turning to look at Aurelia. She shifts a bit as she pulls her headphones from her head to her neck. The male winks at her before he waves slightly, greeting her with the nod of his head first. He then takes another hit and passes the brown stick to the unknown man in front of him.

"I'm sorry about the smoke, does it bother you?" She asks, her eyes glossing over with regret as her hands come out in front of her, rubbing Aurelia's arm in a consoling way. As if she's trying to get her to understand or convince her to accept her smoking. In general, her tone seemed a tab bit manipulative and she didn't like that.

"It is bothersome," Aurelia tells her truthfully. "Can't you just smoke outside? The back yard is small, but it's enough room for the three of you to smoke."

Jackie's eyes twitch a bit before she covers her face with a huge smile. "Of course, lovely."

Genesis and Abby's stifling laughter made Aurelia clear her throat a bit before stepping around Jackie. The two were mocking Jackie's tone and the words that she said to her, but that wasn't her business and she wasn't going to pay too much attention to them.

"You look nice," Aiden tells her just before she walks up the stairs. "Are you going to bed?"

Aurelia looks at Jackie, who was now too occupied with talking to her friend to see her boyfriend compliment her right in front of her unknown guest.

"Thank you," she tells him quietly, before clearing her throat again. "And no. I have a bit more to do before I go to sleep. Why?"

"I was just wondering," He chuckles. "I was going to get everyone to leave just so you can sleep. It'll be pretty rude of us if we were to stay if you're trying to get some sleep, right?"

Aurelia nods her head to agree before looking at Jackie again, who's finally staring at them. Her face twists up in confusion as Abby and Genesis make it look as though they are shocked. Eyes widen and mouths in a thin line.

"I should get back to what I was doing. Thanks for the chat."

"Of course," Aiden says with a smile before turning back to the stranger. "Pass it over, Sean. Stop hogging it."

Aurelia walked towards the stairs and made her way up. She has to get her shower basket perfect and ready before she's able to set up her desk. She wanted to set up her area for her paintings downstairs, but Jakcie's company is downstairs and she didn't want to intrude on them just to set something up, so she will wait for tomorrow to fix it up.

Despite the second red flag, Aurelia was honestly giving Jackie the benefit of the doubt. She knew that they all must be hanging out because classes are about to start up again for them, so they are spending the last couple of days partying and hanging out. Hopefully, they are out together instead of hanging at the house with her friends.

"Hey."

Aurelia flinches as she looks up from her basket and sighs softly when it was just Aiden.

"Hey, Aiden." She says smiling a bit before returning to the task at hand; organizing the things in her basket.

"So, I know you're a freshman and all," he says, standing in the threshold of the room door. "And I typically don't invite freshmen to the parties I host, but do you want to hang out with us tomorrow? It's one of our good friend's birthdays tomorrow, and it would be nice to have my girlfriend's roommate there."

Aurelia tilts her head and slides her basket under her desk neatly. "Why would that be nice? Wouldn't it be weird since I don't know them? Besides, I'm not good with parties."

She avoided Aiden's eyes, it's a bit hard for her to hold eye contact with people she barely knows for too long.

"This could be a good opportunity to get to know us though. Especially when you're Jackie's new roommate, and I can tell you're way different from the last girl, now she was-"

Jackie enters the room behind him. "Aiden?"

Aiden turns around and smiles. Even from the side, Aurelia could tell that smile screamed guilty. She's trying to figure out what he's acting so suspicious for.

"I was just telling Aurelia about Tony's surprise party we're throwing to-morrow night." He tells her while looking at Aurelia.

Jackie tilts her head and crosses her arms before looking at Aurelia. "No offense, but she doesn't even know Tony, why would you invite someone he doesn't know."

"I'm just trying to help her get familiar with our friends, so she wouldn't feel uncomfortable every time she comes home to all of us here." Aiden tells her, making Jackie sigh.

"I don't know. Aurelia, do you want to come?"

Aurelia looks at Aiden and then at Jackie, her extroverted roommate who looks more uncomfortable and unsure than her. She did mind, and she did not want to go.

"No. I'm not comfortable with that and I have things to do." She tells her, causing Jackie to look at her boyfriend and pats his chest.

"There's your answer. She doesn't want to so we aren't going to try to force her to. Okay?" Jackie smiles at Aurelia before leaving the room.

Aiden watches her leave before walking over to Aurelia. He grabs her sticky notes and one of her pens before writing something down. He takes the note off and sticks it on her hand before walking backwards slowly.

"Just in case you change your mind." He winks at her before leaving the room.

Aurelia looks at the phone number and sighs. This doesn't feel like it would be a good idea, more so a good idea for him to be this friendly towards his girlfriend roommate. Maybe she should go, but only if she has time.

☐

four

In the dance of creativity, anxiety becomes a partner, but art leads the way, turning each fearful step into a graceful expression.

Aurelia takes a small step back, observing her small corner she set up downstairs for her easel. She had all her unfinished canvas leaning against the wall and a tiny shelf for all her brushes and paint. Even though it's small, it was perfect for her. She could wear her headphones and quietly paint without disturbing Jackie whenever she needed to study or do homework.

As she turns around to clean up the cardboard boxes, Jackie and Abby walk through the door, talking excitedly. Once the two see her gathering the cardboard, Jackie approaches her with a smile before tossing her bags, from shopping, onto the couch.

"Do you need help?"

Aurelia looks up and returns a small smile. "No, I got it. It's just one box. Thank you for asking."

"You? Offering help? That's a first." Abby comments as she plops down on the empty spot of the couch.

"Shut up! I help out all the time." Jackie walks around the couch, leaving Aurelia to gather her boxes, break them down, and store them in a spare closet for whenever she needs to move again.

"The party starts at ten, but Aiden wants us there by seven to decorate." Jackie says as she pulls different dresses from the bag, trying to pair it with the bright neon colored jacket she had.

Although she just wants to mind her business, it was hard to not listen in on them when they were the only people in the current area of the home. Aurelia cleaned her mugs and ceramic plates she made way back in a pottery class she took for a couple months. She remembers when her sudden burst of creativity and passion to do art happened, she begged her parents for months to take a pottery and ceramic class.

She loved the class, even though most of the people were there because of the teacher. Sure he was good looking, but good looking in the eyes of fourteen year old girls and guys who attended the class. Aurelia truly was there for knowledge, that grown man wasn't on her mind at all, besides his words and advice. He used to use her pieces as examples of textures and smoothness when he was teaching most lessons. However, those were the days when she was younger and still exploring.

"OH MY GOD! JACKIE! HE'S BACK!"

Abby screams, causing Aurelia to cringe at the loudness and subtly slide her headphones on, but not to play music just to drown some of her noisiness out.

"Who?" Jackie questions still looking at the different clothes combinations with this jacket in her hand.

"Who?!" Abby says loudly, even Aurelia's headphones couldn't drown her out. "Did you just ask me who?! Jackie, Andrew is back! Omg! Omg!"

"Andrew? I thought he wasn't coming back until next week? You know when classes start." Jackie says, still staring at herself in the mirror, smiling as if the bright neon yellow jacket would match the neon purple skin tight dress well.

"I guess he's finally clean! That means he must be the surprise guest that Sean wouldn't shut up about." Abby comments scrolling through her phone.

Aurelia slowly walks back to her corner and carefully places the current artwork she was working on on the easel. She tries to not listen to them, but even with the low music, they were still speaking so obnoxiously loud.

Abby grins mischievously. "Make sure you hide the pills tonight, we don't want him to relapse at Tony's party!"

Jackie glances in Aurelia's direction before kicking her friend. She must've assumed she didn't see her, but the kick caused Abby to wince just as loud as her speaking voice.

"What the hell, Jackie!"

"Don't joke about that! You and Sean are the ones who got him hooked on them." Jackie scolds.

"No, we were all doing them, but not how he was doing it. Andrew ruined himself. He was the reckless one popping them whenever he had a chance." Abby stands up after rubbing her shin.

"Can we not talk about this? I'm sure my roommate doesn't want to hear this." Jackie comments walking around the couch pulling Aurelia's headphones down making her flinch away.

"Sorry!" Jackie laughs softly. "Do you want to help me pick an outfit out? It'll be a lot of help since my best friend would rather look at gossip than help her desperate friend in need."

"So fucking dramatic," Abby walks out towards the front door with her face practically glued to her phone. "I'm going to call Genesis and Nicolle to let them know."

Aurelia watches the taller girl leave before turning to look at Jackie. "I wouldn't be much help either. I'm not that good with fashion."

"But your color theory knowledge can come in handy, right?"

Aurelia shrugs and turns around. "I guess so."

Jackie smiles and pulls Aurelia from her spot on her stool. She wasn't too uncomfortable with her asking for her opinion. In fact, she was willing to help if it means she gets to have the night to herself, that is, if she decides not to show up. It's so clear that Aiden is overly friendly, especially when she's practically a stranger to him, and he doesn't realize he's also still a stranger. She appreciates the man trying to make her feel welcome and comfortable, but she has no interest in sharing the same friend group with people who joke about their friend's addictions, hit each other, and degrade each other out of spite of one another. That's not a group of friends she can handle.

Cameron and Sabrina were her closest, and only, friends. They took care of her socially, now she got to do these things on her own. She would've never gotten to step out of her comfort zone had they not pushed her past her limit and tested the water with a lot of things. They understood that she's a lot different than them, and instead of judging her they treated her like everyone else.

"Okay, darling! What do you think of this jacket and this dress?" Jackie asks her, pressing the same two pieces of clothing against her body, probably hoping it would look different if she pressed harder?

"Green and Purple compliments each other," Aurelia tells her, avoiding eye contact with her. "And the two colors go well during the summer time."

Jackie looks impressed, her smile actually looking more genuine than it did when they first met.

"But?"

"But I think the jacket looks tacky." Aurelia looks at her face for a second, watching her smile fade slightly before it widens again. "I think the dress alone really compliments your complexion, if you still want to have that neon green-ish color, my best advice would be accessorize? With a purse or shoes?"

Jackie is silent for a second before she crosses her arms. "You're really blunt. Jeez."

Aurelia's eyes widen before she shakes her head quickly. "Sorry, I thought you would appreciate my honesty more. I really hate lying to people."

Even though her roommate tried to brush it off with laughter, Aurelia could tell she didn't appreciate her honest opinion.

"You could've lied... just a little bit. But, thank you for the honesty, darling." Jackie smiles before she sits on the couch.

Aurelia clears her throat to speak but before she does, Aiden and Abby both walk through the front door. "Changing plans, Andrew isn't coming."

"Why not? He's our friend, babe." Jackie says, standing again, greeting her boyfriend with a kiss.

"We never really fuck-" Aiden stops himself, glancing at Aurelia, giving her small grin before clearing his throat. "I mean, we haven't seen him in a while and things change."

Aurelia didn't understand why he looked at her after saying it. It's clear this friend group is flawed and full of fake disingenuous people.

"Oh please," Abby rolls her eyes and grabs her bag full of clothes. "You never liked Andrew because before he showed up all the girls wanted you."

Jackie grins. "And I got him."

"Probably why all the bitches flocked to Andrew." Abby comments, making Aurelia's roommate frown. "What? You one jealous hateful ass bitch."

"Abby? Seriously?"

Abby shrugs, making the tension in the room rise. Aurelia is starting to feel uncomfortable in this place, she's almost considering going on campus. Perhaps, talk to someone about getting a switch or something.

"Who's Andrew?" Aurelia asked, causing everyone to look at her.

"No one." Aiden smiles, pulling away from his girlfriend to talk to her. "Well, our ex best friend, he went away for a while so now he's back. I'm glad you don't know who he is."

"Why do you care?" Jackie questions. "She can be interested in him if she wants. Why are you glad she isn't?"

Aiden winks at her before turning around to face his girlfriend. "Babe, I'm just glad she's one of few people in this damn school that haven't either fucked or want to be fucked by Andrew."

Aurelia awkwardly clears her throat. "I'm going to go upstairs and finish unpacking. I hope you all have fun at your party."

As she walks towards the stairs, Aiden's heavy steps could be heard behind her. "Wait, you aren't coming?"

"I don't know Tony, and clearly this day seems really special." Aurelia turns to look at Aiden, but she could tell from the corner of her eye, Jackie was not happy with Aiden.

"It doesn't matter," Aiden smiles, stepping up on the bottom step to talk directly to her. "Just come because I'm asking. I want to get to know you."

Abby scoffs. "US? You mean you want her to get to know us? Right?"

Jackie grabs her boyfriend's arm, pulling him down to her. "Leave her alone. She does want to go. I thought we already established this."

Aiden wraps his arm around Jackie and sighs. "I guess it can't be helped, huh?"

"Thanks for inviting me though, I appreciate it." Aurelia smiles a bit.

As she continued her journey up the stairs, she could hear the light bickering again, causing her to sigh through her nose and close the door gently. She sits at her desk and puts her head down. Being around them for half a week causes her exhaustion. She's not sure if she could spend a full year here with Jackie. All this is just way too much for her.

Aurelia pulls her phone out her pocket and scrolls through social media, seeing what her friends are up to. She smiles as they post their new friends they met, happy that they are fitting right in. Even though she's happy for them, she wishes it was that easy for her. Granted, she's not really trying. She spent these last few days preparing for the school year, and pushed away a toxic group of friends in the most polite way she could.

Maybe she could just browse the neighborhood.

"Hey."

Aurelia lifts her head and sees Jackie walk in the room, holding the dress in her arms.

"Hi?" She says, unsure about her being in the room with her.

"I'm sorry I haven't been a good roommate." She confesses, looking down at her feet. "I promise things are a lot less chaotic when the school year starts. We just want to have as much fun as possible. Being a student here is difficult as it is."

Aurelia nods her head. "I kind of figure that's why you all are always here together. I just really appreciate it if you at least give me a heads up. I live here too, and it gets uncomfortable sometimes."

Jackie smiles and nods. "I know. I genuinely apologize. How about we go to one of my favorite cafes before I get ready for the party?"

Aurelia smiles at the offer and nods. "I would love to. Thank you."

Jackie places her dress on her bed and pulls Aurelia to her feet. The two lock arms and head downstairs. The physical contact was a bit uncomfortable, but it wasn't that bad. She was just happy Jackie finally is taking notice of her actions. That in itself makes her see Jackie's character, especially when her friends are not around.

This side of her is nice and bearable.

□

five

In the palette of emotions, anxiety creates the dull hues of the world, creating a intense painting of the blank canvas of the soul.□

▼

▲

□

Aurelia is sitting at her easel, looking at her unfinished artwork. She could hear the giggling and laughter from upstairs, where Jackie, Abby, and Genesis are getting ready to go. She has overheard enough of their conversations to know that this party is supposed to be Aiden's biggest one he has ever thrown for any of his friends. The girls would even joke about him liking the guys in the friend group more than the girls, but knowing them for the past two days, she's sure they weren't joking and those were words branching from their true thoughts and feelings about Aiden.

She doesn't understand why they would want to go out and party together when it's clear they do not like each other as much as they try to lead on. And for whom?

Aurelia's friends, back home when she was in high school, only ever fought over small childish things. Like who's hogging the blanket and who's turn is it to host a sleepover. It was never as serious as who's sleeping with who, and who popped what pill. They were never like that, and despite being Aurelia's best friends, Sabrina and Cameron had other friends besides her; giving her friends time away from each other so they won't get sick of each other earlier on. So when they went out again, it was always safe and fun, never hostile and uncomfortable.

However, her time with Jackie wasn't as she assumed it would be. Even though she preferred the comfort from the student housing, Jackie somehow gave her enough convincing to actually go to this unknown cafe with her. It wasn't a bad idea. The both of them didn't have any time to talk to each other since she moved into the house, and Jackie really didn't help make things easier by creating an uncomfortable space for her by inviting her friends out of nowhere. So this trip was necessary, at least to her.

The cafe visit wasn't a bad one. The light browns and wooden accents were very pretty. The subtle whites and green colors were the pretty shade for that cozy vibe. The place sparked a bit of inspiration in her, but of course, she couldn't get distracted at the moment. That doesn't mean she doesn't plan on coming back, but alone this time.

"Here's a good spot." Jackie took a seat and Aurelia followed.

Just like any normal visit, they sat and chatted over a cup of coffee, well tea for her, since she really didn't like coffee. Aurelia had expected Jackie to spend their time together gossiping about her so-called best friends, but she was surprised. The older woman decided to actually get to know Aurelia. Asking the meaningful and fun questions, rather than the obvious questions. This also meant Aurelia got to know a bit more about Jackie—as well as Aiden.

"We were childhood best friends," Jackie smiled before taking a sip of her iced americano. "But when we got to college, I finally worked up the courage to tell him how I felt."

Aurelia nodded her head, not sure what to say as she sipped her dragon fruit iced tea.

"It's funny because our parents already knew we would get together. My mom and his mom are best friends. They're already visualizing our wedding." Jackie told her with confidence, but now that she knew this information it made her wonder if it's really all sunshine and rainbows with them.

"Well That's not about you though," Aurelia commented, swirling her straw around as she sat there quietly, staring at Jackie's face, but not directly into her eyes. "I mean, it is about your relationship, but Aiden isn't my roommate, you are. Tell me about you."

Jackie looked confused before she shrugged her shoulders. "Not much to say. I'm a theater major but of course, my parents really wanted me to continue my classical music study, but I told them no. I wanted to follow Aiden to this school so I picked my passion. Theater."

Aurelia almost cringed in front of her after hearing that she followed Aiden to a school just because she wanted to be with him. If she would've said something like that to one of her friends, they probably would beat her down until she made sense, but not literally. Going off to college was encouraged by her parents because they wanted her to make her own path and discover herself. It was one of the main reasons why her friends made sure she decided to go off to a different college rather than follow them.

"Aiden is my whole world," Jackie told her before sipping her coffee. "Without him, I think I might go crazy. That's probably why I get so jealous when he talks to any girl."

She was sure that comment was directed at her, but it's not like she's talking to Aiden for a long time. Most of their conversation ends right when it starts. Not to mention that Aiden makes no effort to hide his flirtatious ways, and Jackie didn't care to acknowledge them but only when he's actively trying his hardest to flirt with her. He also seemed very stand-offish with Jackie but that's only when she was around.

After they talked a bit more about Aiden, they made their way back to the dorm because Jackie's friends told her that she needed to hurry back so they could get ready together.

Now as she sits in the living room of the student home, painting away at her canvas, she wonders how long Jackie would be out and if she would bring Aiden back. If so, she needed to make sure she avoided him as much as possible. Jackie made it clear she isn't very fond of girls talking to her boyfriend. It wouldn't be very hard either, because she plans on keeping things one sentence only with the male from now on. Especially after knowing what kind of romance trope he and Jackie are in, she wants no part in that.

"Finally!"

Aurelia flinches slightly at the loud voice of Jackie, causing her to slowly pull her headphone off and turn around to see what's going on. Their eyes only met for a second before Jackie avoids hers all together. It seems like she didn't take her advice about the jacket, now that she has it on, it definitely looks tacky like she feared. So much for her honest opinion. Aurelia looks past her seeing her other best friends, Abby and Genesis dressed in similar neon colors, descend from the stairs.

Jackie stands in front of the tall mirror just off the side of the stairs. She looks over her appearance, adjusting the jacket a bit and swirling some of the curls that have already fallen. Judging from the frown growing on

Jackie's face, Aurelia's sure it took her a while to do the style with the curling iron. "Ugh, why is it so hard to maintain curly hair."

"When you have straight hair," Genesis comments, pushing her auburn hair around, adjusting her wavy hair. "Curls won't stay, but if it's natural a little styling will make it look twice as pretty. Right, Ariel."

Aurelia wasn't sure who she was talking to, but when she turned to look at her, that confirmed things. "Aurelia. Not Airel."

"That doesn't even remotely sound the same, dumbass." Abby says to Genesis making her shrug her shoulder, but Jackie quickly shoulder bumps her.

Genesis rolls her eyes and smiles fakely. "Sorry Aurelia, I didn't mean to get your name wrong."

Aurelia could tell she is being fake, but she just nods her head and puts her headphones back on. Since she has been nosey since she got here, she didn't bother turning music on, but she did resume on her unfinished canvas.

"I look so good," She could hear Jackie tell herself.

"Yes, I'm sure Aiden would be the only man to turn his eyes." Genesis rolls her eyes.

Jackie sighs. "He's the only pair of eyes that I want on me. Unlike someone."

"What's that supposed to mean?" Genesis scoffs.

Jackie laughs this time. "We all know you're wearing this tight neon yellow two piece to get all the guys attention. No wonder you pulled it from the shelf."

"Is it so fucking wrong that I want to look sexy?" Aurelia could tell from the tone of her voice that things are getting serious.

"You can look sexy, but we all know you just do this for attention."

Genesis tone gets higher. " Well at least I get attention, your man barely shows you attention. Especially when a pretty girl that's just his type comes along-"

"Would you two shut up! Let's just take a picture and go." Abby shouts, causing Aurelia to put her paintbrush down and pull her headphone off. She stands up from her seat and looks at the girls, nervous that they might be frowning or close to throwing a punch, but of course, like a one and off switch they weren't doing that at all.

Abby's demand triggered all the girls to pull on fake smiles, posing in the mirror together. It's honestly unbelievable but they made it look like they actually like each other. Aurelia just walks to the kitchen, putting the kettle on the stove, to make some tea. She could see where she was standing in the kitchen that the trio was cuddling up to each other, as if they weren't just at each other's throats a few seconds ago.

"Okay one video, let's just say happy birthday Tony." Genesis says, causing Aurelia to shake her head slightly, leaning against the counter, crossing her arms.

"One, two, three-!"

The three say happy birthday to Tony all together before breaking away from each other. Jackie looks upset, resulting in her turning away from Genesis. Abby is the only one smiling while her two friends just look in the opposite direction from each other.

"Can you two just stop this shit and move on?" Abby complains, putting her phone in her bag. "You both are attention whores. There. Now let's go, Aiden is literally outside waiting for us."

Aurelia could feel herself take a deep breath as she sees the trio walk towards the front door. Once they are gone, she just sighs out loud. The home is finally quiet and now she can have the rest of the night to herself. The kettle begins to whistle, making her turn the fire off and take one of her mugs, the ones she made, down from the cupboard. Aurelia also grabs the lemon, chamomile honey box tea down and puts one packet in her mug. She pours the hot water in the cup and carefully puts the kettle down.

Aurelia is a paranoid and nervous person generally, and she could tell when something doesn't feel right. After that big spat between Genesis and Jackie, she's sure Genesis was referring to her. Sure, she could be overthinking it, which is a big problem she tends to have, but it just didn't make any sense for her to say that with her in the room.

Trying to shake the thought out of her head, she picks her mug up from the small area of the counter, and walks over to the couch where her laptop is sitting on the accent table just a few inches away from the couch. Aurelia sips her tea carefully as she sits down, of course it was good, but even with the peace and quiet she feels uncomfortable. Has she really grown to the loudness of the house already? She sighs and puts her mug down before pulling her phone from the front part of her overalls. She calls Cameron and waits for him to answer. After the first ring, he picks up.

"Hey," he answers tiredly. "What's up, Aurelia?"

The guilt washes over her. "Did I wake you up? I'm sorry."

Her best friend laughs deeply. "Don't worry about it, I need to get up anyway. So, what's up?"

Although she still feels bad, she really needs to talk to someone, especially after everything she has learned from Jackie and her friends. These are things that she wants to share with her best friends.

"I feel so uncomfortable." She tells him honestly. "I'm trying to stick it out until after the first month of classes start, but I don't know if I can handle being around them."

"Woah..." His voice was laced with concerns, completely pulling the tiredness from his tone. "Slow down, Relia. Deep breath, like we practiced before."

Aurelia calms down, taking deep breaths like he taught her the night before he was off to his dream school. She remembers staying up all night, trying to prepare herself for his departure. That wasn't a good idea. It caused her to have the worst panic attack in her life. Aurelia wasn't ready to let another one of her best friends go.

When Sabrina left, Aurelia cried for days, not leaving her room and only coming out when Cameron wanted to make her feel better. Even when she left, she still had Cameron to lean on and cry to. He was what kept her from losing it. When it was his turn to leave, it unfortunately ended with her panicking in his bedroom during their last sleepover. Cameron was so scared that night, until he quickly realized what was happening, resulting in him helping her through her panic attack, and teaching her different breathing techniques. They helped her a lot after that day, and after he left.

"I want to give Jackie a chance," She tells him slowly, enunciating her words. "But, for some reason wherever she's around her friends, her behavior shifts and it's weird energy between us and her friends."

Cameron sighs. "So she's fake?"

"It appears that way," she comments. "Like she seems so genuine when she asked me to go to the cafe with her, but when her friends are present her personality does a three sixty. Even today it seems like they were trying to check me? Or drag me into their toxic friend group."

"Aurelia, my best advice is to talk to the head of housing. Let them know you are uncomfortable so you can just move into a dorm room." He suggests before the sound of running water fills her ear. "Truefully they sound really fake, but personally I'd ignore them or keep myself so busy that I only have to see their face in the morning. I just hate burdening people. However, that shouldn't matter for you, you should definitely talk to the head of student housing or talk to Jackie and let her know how you feel. Even if she is fake, you can at least tell the head of student housing that you tried to reason if the situation doesn't get better."

It was a good suggestion, but maybe she should talk to Jackie, and this time lay it on her as thick as possible.

"I have to get ready for student hall, it's a bit late for you right? I'm three hours ahead, right? It's like seven right?"

"Seven is not late!" Aurelia laughs before drinking her tea since it cools down a bit. "But okay, I'll text you in the morning, hopefully Sabrina can call me later tomorrow. I think I'm just going to shower after I get my official schedule for Monday."

"Alright love, sleep well, talk to you tomorrow! Also consider what I said, don't just allow yourself to be uncomfortable." Cameron tells her before they end the call.

After talking to Cameron, Aurelia felt a bit better about how to approach things. She was going to talk to Jackei tomorrow, letting her know how things are going to be, and compromise with her so she doesn't feel uncomfortable anymore. As she walks to the kitchen to clean up everything, she can suddenly hear music playing out of nowhere. As she dries her hands, she walks back to the living area, looking around for the source of the music. Once she walks towards the stairs, the music gets louder, but it wasn't coming from upstairs.

Aurelia looks at the accent table just beside the full body mirror and sees that it's a phone sitting behind the fake plant. She carefully picks the phone up and sees the caller ID. When she sees Aiden's name with a heart beside it. She didn't want to be nosey, and she was just going to leave it alone, but if it's Aiden, then maybe he could return the phone to the person it belongs to. It couldn't be Abby's phone, she saw her walk out with it, and it can't be Genesis' phone because it has a heart beside Aiden's name, so it leaves one person.

Jackie.

Answering the phone, she presses the phone to her ear. "Hell-"

"Genesis! Where did you go? I thought you said that Andrew was coming? Are you fucking him or something? Was my dick not enough for you tonight?" Aiden aggressively answers the phone, not allowing her to even speak, but unfortunately she ends up hearing things that she clearly wasn't supposed to hear.

"O-Oh...uh.." Aurelia takes a deep breath. "I guess Genesis left her phone here?"

She closes her eyes, smacking herself on the forehead for even deciding to answer the phone.

"Aurelia?" Aiden's tone is clearly full of shock, even with the loud music blasting on his end, there wasn't any hiding that specific sound. "Shit... uh.."

"Just... When you see Genesis, let her know she left her phone." She tells him, hanging up the phone, putting back where it was internally cursing at herself before walking up the stairs after gathering her laptop and phone.

She knew she would have to come back down because she needs to clean up the paint and other things downstairs, but she had to calm herself down from what she just heard and done just because she wanted to be nice. Genesis and Aiden are sleeping together and Jackie doesn't know about it? She just brought more of their bull crap onto herself.

"Why did you answer the stupid phone..." She mumbles to herself as she put her laptop on the charger before sitting in her chair at her desk.

After a few minutes, her phone ringtone fills the empty room, making her groan before answering it. "Hello?"

"Hey," Aiden's voice fills her ear, making her cringe a bit. "I know I said somethings... but don't take that seriously and don't tell Jackie... please."

"Aiden..."

"Look, how about you come down, have a few drinks and have fun? That way you can give Genesis her phone back and we can forget all about this." He speaks over her, trying to ignore the obvious concerns hidden in her voice. "Just for tonight, and I promise I'll talk to Jackie so you won't have to worry about keeping anything a secret. Okay?"

Aurelia nibbles at the skin of her thumb trying not to have a panic attack over the phone. "I just don't want to get mixed up in all of this. I don't even want to show up, so please, don't call me. Thank you."

She hangs up and blocks Aiden's number. It was the right decision for herself, and she was going to talk to the head of student housing to get a new roommate, or even a dorm room of her own. She doesn't even know if she could look Jackie in the face after hearing just a sentence of secrets from a three second phone call.

□

six

Even in her darkest moments, a blank canvas has the power to reveal its true colors without the need for a paintbrush in motion.□

▼

▲

□

Aurelia waits outside on the steps of the house, staring at the time on her lock screen. Only an hour has passed and she knows that Jackie isn't coming back any time soon, especially after her conversation with Aiden and what she heard. The male probably makes sure she doesn't come back, but Aurelia needs to talk to her. Her mind couldn't rest with the secrets and thoughts on leaving without at least trying to explain the situation to her roommate and causing her distress.

She wants to call her parents, but that would defeat the purpose of her wanting to go to school a state over, away from them. Aurelia remembers her father telling her that college is best experienced with independence.

"Exploring the campus, talking to people, and being completely away from parents are a few things that make college life fun." Her father told her as he helped move her things to the car a few days ago. " I know your momma is worried sick about sending you off, but just know I trust you. I trust that you can and will make the right decisions, ladybug. Make your own path for your life, we can only take you so far."

Aurelia remembered crying in her father's arms after he told her that. He knew she was nervous because this would be her first time officially being alone. Of course she had experienced other incidents where she was alone, making her own decisions and being independent when she was in high school. However, this is the real world. Aurelia is fully aware that she needs to grow up, and part of growing up is handling issues like this without being too anxious or nervous about it.

Aurelia stands from the step she is sitting on and grabs her tote bag. Nothing was inside it beside her pepper spray, wallet, phone, and her headphone. She had planned on just pulling an all-nighter at the local twenty-four library not too far from her dorm to avoid Jackie, but that's not going to cut it. Running away isn't going to solve anything, she needs to tell Jackie now, at this moment.

As she walks away from the house, Aurelia dials Jackie's number, wanting to ask her where the party was and if she could talk to her. There's just no way she would unblock Aiden's number, she was way too familiar with guys who use their charms and good choices of words to manipulate.

Though, during the days she has come across guys like him, they were always guys from high school. Unfortunately, their manipulative ways weren't always directed at her. Most of the time they were directed towards Sabrina, but fortunately, they had each other's backs and always pulled each other out of anything that didn't feel right. Like the one time a guy from her high school was at a party, and he kept wrapping his arms around Aurelia's shoulder, making her feel more uncomfortable than she already did being alone. Sabrina had stepped away to go to the bathroom, but the guy was nice at first, talking to her normally, but it turned uncomfortable and pushy when he started crossing boundaries: putting his hand on her shoulder and waist. When Aurelia finally said stop, he didn't take that for an answer. Which caused Sabrina to help her the moment she got back from the bathroom,

Those days were easier for Sabrina to pull Aurelia out of any situation because she never really talked to any guy, long enough before they started to show their true colors. However, Aurelia found it very difficult to pull Sabrina away from guys, because she's a socially awkward person so the moment one thing goes south it ends with her panicking which is the thing that ran those guys away. Good thing Sabrina was able to handle things herself, but Aurelia still wished she helped her a bit more.

That didn't matter though.

Those memories weren't going to stop her from going to that party and finding Jackie to talk to her. She wasn't going to talk about the house situation, but she will tell her what she heard over the phone. Keeping secrets like that eats at her conscience until she breaks, and she doesn't want that.

"Hello?" Music and laughter could be heard along with Jackie's voice. "Aurelia?"

"J-Jackie, where is the party? I need to talk to you about something." Aurelia is blunt, straight to the point.

"Seriously?" Jackie laughs on the other end with the sound of the music getting quieter and she could hear her voice better now. "Can't it wait? Don't get me wrong, I would love to talk but right now?"

"It honestly can not wait, Jackie." Her tone is urgent. "I overheard something that I think-"

"Aurelia! Did you change your mind!" Aiden's voice could be heard on the phone with Jackie laughing in the background of the call this time. It was then she knew that Jackie allowed Aiden to take her phone.

"Can you give Jackie the phone back, Aiden?"

Aiden sighs, there wasn't laughter and music blasting in the call. She knew it, she knew his entire tone changed because no one was around him anymore. He sounds a lot more annoyed this time. "Look, I know what you heard is shocking, but let's just talk before you go to Jackie with this."

"Why should we?" She challenges easily, stopping her walk to the bus stop. "I just want to talk to Jackie about what you are telling me to hide."

"I'm telling you to keep it to yourself because It's not something that should be brought up again. Look, don't misunderstand okay? Genesis and I slept together once and I already told Jackie about it. I was drunk and dumb. I want you to keep it to yourself because I don't want her to get upset over it again." He explains. "Okay, how about you come down, so we can talk in person. Doing this over the phone like this will make her more jealous."

Aurelia takes a deep breath, not falling for a thing he's saying, but she did want to get there and tell Jackie anyway. "Fine. What's the address? I'll come."

"Good. Good." Aiden utters with a sigh of relief coming through the phone before he tells her the address.

Aurelia puts the direction in her phone before hanging up on the man. She walks towards the bus stop and waits for the bus there. Though her heart was pounding, she was determined to let Jackie know the truth. That's the only reason she's going, maybe after she tells Jackie it'll help them develop some relationship with each other so she wouldn't have to leave and burden a lot of people, including the university.

It took her about fifteen minutes to get to the street where the party was being held by bus. It also took her five minutes to walk to the house they were having the party at. Even as she continued her walk along the sidewalk, the closer she got to the house the louder the music got. There were people crowding outside. This would probably be the first and last party she attends while she attends the school. Without people she's comfortable with she's not sure if she could just go to any party alone.

"Yo!" Some guy shouts before pushing someone else to the ground.

It was getting chaotic, but lucky some of the guys surrounding the area broke it up before it escalated. However the shouting caused her heart to race and she was starting to regret coming to this place already. As she carefully walks past a lot of drunk, sober, and barely drunk people she gets to the front door. Aurelia didn't have time to catch her breath as she takes a couple of steps inside the house, where the music gets louder the further she walks in. Everything is overwhelming to the point where her head begins to hurt and her eyes start to shake as she glances around.

Finding an area that's relatively empty, she takes deep breaths, trying to calm herself down. She also tries her best not to draw too much attention to herself. Some people already noticed her when she walked in because she's the only one who's not recognizable, and a freshman. Aurelia pokes her head out the open window for a moment, feeling rather nauseous after breathing so much. After a minute or two, she sticks her head back inside, finally calming herself down enough to continue on the path to finding Jackie before Aiden finds her.

"Aurelia?"

Too late.

"You made it," he laughs, wrapping his arm around her shoulder making her flinch but of course, because he is so loud everyone looks at them. He leads her to another area, it looks like a living room, but she couldn't tell because there's no furniture. "I thought you changed your mind again."

He finally lets her go and grabs a large bottle of alcohol and pours it in a highlighter green cup alone with some unknown bright yellow liquid that looks like juice. Aurelia knows what he's doing, but unfortunately for him, she doesn't drink.

"Are you having fun-"

"Where's Jackie?" She asks him right away, causing him to laugh as if it's so funny that she asks about his girlfriend's whereabouts. "Is she upstairs, the bathroom, or-"

Aiden turns around with two cups and hands her one, and she stares at him before shaking her head. "No. I don't drink."

"I know Aurelia, you're a freshman here so it's clear you are " he rolls his eyes, and pushes the cup closer. "This cup only has the mango juice. Promise."

Aurelia frowns a bit and grabs the cup, sitting it on the table before turning on her heel to look for Jackie herself. Her nerves were practically all gone, they are most likely still present because of a lot of people staring at them.

"Hey, hey," Aiden holds her wrist and pulls her to an empty room. "Can you not cause a scene, Aurelia?"

"I won't cause a scene if you tell me where my roommate is." She counters, watching the male jaw clench before he looks away.

"You are one stubborn person," he utters. "Come on."

Aurelia was ready to argue with him this time, but he gave in, just like that. "Really?"

"Yeah." He mumbles, opening the door to the room they were in and walking out. She follows behind him closely, so she wouldn't get lost in the crowd.

As the two of them walk through the house, he takes her down to the basement, which he had to unlock the door for. It is weird considering everyone is upstairs, but she slowly started to realize why it was separate. Upstairs is a different kind of party, people dancing on each other, passing bottles around and tossing white and pink pills in their mouths. The sight alone made her nerves.

"There he is!" A non drunk guy walks up to Aiden before looking over at her. "Ah, is this cutie another birthday gift for me?"

As he walks closer, making her take a step back, Aiden stops him and shakes his head. "She's with me, which means she's off limits. Where's Jackie, Tony?"

"How come you always get the cute freshman." Tony complains before rolling his eyes. "I wouldn't be like this if you tell me what the hell this surprise Sean has been talking about. I'm trying to be sober enough to remember the shit."

Aiden crosses his arms. "I've been trying to find Sean and Genesis since you showed up so we can get this surprise over with. So where is Jackie?"

Aurelia could tell he is getting annoyed with the mention of the surprise just from the way he's avoiding eye contact with Tony this time.

"Well," he glances at Aurelia again, making her avoid eye contact with him. "Last time I saw her, she was upstairs setting the music up for later or something like that."

Aiden nods his head and looks back at her, before nodding for her to go first. Not arguing with him, she walks up the stairs, gripping the door knob to open it, but he puts his hand over hers causing her to stop in her tracks. She shivers uncomfortably when she feels his breath just inches away from her ear.

"Whatever you plan on telling her, just know," he tells her in a low tone. "You can just let it go right now, and we can both pretend that none of this happened, yeah?"

"No." She says firmly pushing the door open, just to be meant with Jackie and Genesis standing in front of her.

"Aurelia?" Jackie looks at Aiden and then at her again. "What are you doing here?"

Aurelia steps out of the doorway of the basement door and clears her throat. "I'm here to talk-"

"Aiden, why is she here?" Jackie completely ignores her and grabs her boyfriend's wrist. "You know what, save it for later, I have to get Tony, Genesis decided to just do something else for Tony since Andrew didn't show up."

"Do what?"

"She's a dancer too," Jackie says. "Besides, I'm sure Tony would prefer her dancing over Andrew's anyway, she's a woman."

Aiden shrugs his shoulders. "I could care less at this point, but you would think because he's friends with Tony as well he would show up for his birthday at least."

Genesis steps up this time. "Don't talk about him when he's not here, he's probably dealing with school stuff."

"You really think they'll let him back into this school after getting so fucking high in the dance hall? Please, Genesis, don't act so fucking stupid."

Aiden frowns before his girlfriend, Aurelia's roommate groans out loud before storming down the basement steps.

"See what you did?" Genesis says turning on her heel before storming off in the opposite direction.

Aurelia shakes her head, finally realizing coming to this party to talk to Jackie was pointless. She barely acknowledged her when she said she had to talk to her. She should've just followed her first mind and avoided her until she talked to the board of student housing, and asked about moving to a different house or even a dorm room. Now she's at a party with the dysfunctional friend group she wanted to avoid from the very first moment she met them.

"Whatever." Aiden walks away leaving Aurelia to find the exit herself to go home.

The task sounds easy but trying to get past the drunk people was impossible, and she didn't want to push people. SIghing in defeat, she takes a spot on the wall and waits until some people clear out. It reminds her of all the times she did this when Sabrina and Cameron convinced her to go to a party in high school, but even if she stuck to a wall they made sure to stick by her side. Being alone like this isn't the best feeling and dealing with a toxic friend group is annoying as it is.

"Not your scene huh." A stranger says close to her ear as Genesis tells people to clear the middle of the room.

Aurelia looks to her right, seeing an oddly familiar man in a black hoodie, the hood covering his face, but it is pushed back enough to get the side profile of the man's face. If her night wasn't so bad, she would acknowledge how attractive this stranger is, but she could care less about how good someone looks right now.

"No. I prefer to be alone with a small group of friends I trust."

He laughs quietly while sipping from his drink. The stranger glances over at her as the loud music starts playing, causing her to hold eye contact with him for a second before he pulls his attention back to Genesis who was getting everyone to quiet down.

"Surprise Tony!" Genesis smiles seductively at Tony, as the music starts up and the crowd gets hyped up, cheering her on as she takes the room's attention. However, not everyone's attention. Aurelia is more interested in the person who seems the most normal out of everyone who's here, his presence alone makes everything and everyone else blurry and muffled. As he turns his gaze back to Genesis slowly, he tilts his head slightly, drinking from his cup slowly.

Her heart begins to race as she slowly peel her eyes from the stranger, watching Genesis put on a performance.

After she finishes, she looks over at the stranger, he leans over to her. "Let me let in on a little secret," She could feel his breath gazing over her ear, making her swallow hard. "You can't trust anyone here, Angel."

"I found that out the hard way." He tells her before he pushes himself off of the wall, unzipping his hoodie off, revealing the white beater underneath and his tone arms covered in tattoos. He turns towards her, tossing his hoodie in her arms before he opens his arms wide enough to catch the people around attention.

He pulls his gaze away from her to the person who was beside him. He nods at them before walking backwards in the crowd, when he gets to the circle, Genesis was already in Tony's lap, showering him with happy birthday kisses.

The people around start to get chaotic and begin murmuring as they see the male, the stranger who captures everyone's attention without uttering a word. However, the space he opened for himself coincidentally led a path right to the front of the crowd. She steps forward, taking advantage of getting away from the dark corner and to the front of the crowd. Aurelia didn't know why, but she wanted to see what he was planning on doing, it's not like the night can get any worse for her.

"Andrew?" Genesis calls out, causing the crowd to get wild the moment they hear the name of this stranger.

So this was him?

The man that had Jackie's friend group in shambles.

He looks around before his eyes land on hers again. A familiar man, Sean, walks up to greet the stranger, but his eyes never leave hers. Andrew nods and Sean instantly runs over to the stereo to change the song that was long done. As the music started, Sean and Andrew got into character instantly, it was as if the music took over his body.

Though both men were there dancing, Andrew had his eyes on her, and she couldn't look away either. After a stressful night, she needed this small moment to enjoy art. The art of dancing. Andrew's moves were slow and sensual and the crowd was loving it. The only ones in the room that weren't happy at the moment were definitely Jackie and Aiden.

When the dance is finished, the people at the party begin to crowd Andrew, but before that happens, he quickly walks towards her grabbing his hoodie and rushes out of the house. Aurelia watches the people follow him out, making her finally have a clear line out of the suffocating house.

Even if the dance was only a minute long, that minute made her appreciate the dance, mostly because it was sexy, something she hadn't seen anyone do that close to her before. Although that was truly the best part of the night, despite this Andrew being a complete stranger. He was the only one who didn't seem fake, and it made her wonder more about what he said to her.

However, that could wait, her thinking about those words could wait. She just wanted to get home before Jackie did, but judging how angry she looked, she more than likely wasn't showing up to the house, which was perfect for her.

□

Andrew & Sean's dance (for the people who want a visual.)

https://youtu.be/IIwvDgfBPyc

seven

☐ Sometimes an artist needs to step out of their comfort zone to get in the zone. ☐

▼

▲

☐

Aurelia gathers the papers from her second class, putting them neatly in her folder before pushing it in her tote bag. As expected, the first week of classes were only syllabus reviews. She wasn't expecting much, but going over the same copy and paste documents for the academic classes was exhausting. The last class for, which wasn't until another two hours, was her art class with a popular artist teaching the class. Specifically someone she has been following since she started high school and admired.

"Hey," someone calls out to her as she walks out of the room. "You're Aurelia right?"

Aurelia tilts her head, she has no idea who this person is, but they somehow knew her name. What is even more odd to her, is the man kind of looked a lot like Aiden, but he had longer hair with a lot of tattoos and piercings.

"Uh, yes?"

The male smiles politely. "I'm Adrian, I saw you at the orientation event last week at the tattoo tent."

Aurelia makes an 'o' shape with her mouth as she continues to walk with the male right beside her. That explains how he knows her based on appearance, but that doesn't explain how he knows her name. That alarmed her a bit.

"I know this is weird," he laughs awkwardly and stops walking to dig in his bag for something. "I'm an art major as well."

She watches him closely as he fishes for something in his bag. It has given her a few seconds to look him over. His dark brown hair really suited his face, especially with the grunge aesthetic he has going on for him. Even if he's Aiden's brother or twin, he is the complete opposite of him. Just from the little interaction, his personality is far better than Aiden's. Once he finds what he was looking for, he pulls the list out and looks it over before handing it to her.

"Sunny, the head of our department gave us, the seniors, a task to welcome all the freshmen as an assignment." He chuckles as he switches bags and pulls a cute little rainbow bag. "I have to give out these welcome bags to every freshman."

Aurelia couldn't help but laugh before smiling widely. "This is cute. Did you make it?"

He shrugs his shoulders and nods. "Most of it from the dollar store, and it's not too much stuff."

She smiles and pulls a pen out of her bag and signs her name for him.

"Here you go," she hands him the paper back. "Thank you for the welcome bag."

Adrian puts the paper back and shakes his head. "No problem-"

"Yo! Adrian!"

Aurelia's smile slightly fades as Aiden, Jackie, and Tony walk up to them. They haven't talked to each other since the party, which was two days ago. Jackie had spoken to her when they were at the dorm, but it wasn't to have a full conversation. It was only if she was asking her about when she'll turn in to sleep or when she won't be coming home. She wasn't sure if her showing up to the party made her upset with her, or just seeing her beside Aiden that night bothered her a lot. She honestly didn't know, but things are kind of tense.

"I see you found my twin," Aiden grins, squeezing his brother close, but Adrian pushes him away. "I know he's not as hot as me but... you know we are identical."

Adrian rolls his eyes and stares at Aurelia. "I'll see you around."

Everyone watches Adrian walk away, making Aurelia wonder about their story, but she would rather hear it from him than his brother and his friends.

"I fucking hate him." Aiden mumbles before wrapping his arm around Jackie. "He thinks he's all high and mighty because he's Elijah's bitch."

Aurellia couldn't believe her ears. It's like whenever she's around them, they bring their negativity along with them. She looks at her bag and smiles before turning on her heel to walk away from them, but she could hear running behind her.

"Hey, Ariel, wait!" Genesis calls out, making Aurelia sigh mentally before turning around to face her.

"Aurelia." She corrects her, making Genesis tilt her head from confusion before nodding.

"Right, anyway," she crosses her arms after pushing her hair over her shoulder. "Since when did you know Andrew? His video at the party, with him and Sean dancing in front of you is becoming a hot topic on campus."

"I don't know him," she tells her truthfully. "I just happened to be standing next to him before he started dancing."

Genesis tilts her head and sighs. "Andrew isn't the type of guy you happen to just stand next to."

Aurelia is mentally rolling her eyes at this girl. The way people talk about this man, putting him on this godly level is overwhelming enough, but her trying to belittle her because she didn't get a chance to talk to him, is even more overwhelming. On top of everything else, she gets name wrong all the time.

"Well, I guess when you see him, you can ask him yourself." Aurelia lingers there for no more than three seconds before turning away from her to walk to the nearest cafe that's close to the main campus.

She wants to text her best friends, and look at the gift bag Adrian took the time to put together for all the freshmen in the same department. As she waits at the bus stop, she puts her headphones on and plays some music as she waits for the bus. She could call a lyft, but the money her parents transfer into her account is only for emergencies.

Aurelia knows how well off she is, but she doesn't plan on relying on her parents for too long. She has been looking at the jobs available on campus and ones near campus to pay for things that she wants at the moment.

Once the bus pulls up, she uses her phone to pay digitally and stands in the front until the bus stops right in front of the cafe she wants to go to. It wasn't the one Jackie took her to, it was one she had been considering sending an application to since it's a bus trip away and they are hiring for the night shifts. Since she has all afternoon classes, working late wouldn't be a problem for her.

As she walks in, the line to the front counter is long. Aurelia listens to her music, looking over the cafe menu above the counter. She didn't want anything sweet, so she planned on having the unsweetened peach tea with salt bread. When she looked around at the cafe, she could see that everyone was sitting and chatting, some had to be from her college. Once the line moves, she takes a step forward.

"Couldn't we have a lunch break at a restaurant or something? Why did we come here?" she hears someone complains a tab bit louder than her music.

Aurelia smoothly looks over her shoulder to see a group of five walk into the cafe. They all had the same style, but all five were very different.

One had a green buzz cut, his features strong and attractive, making him look intimidating but she could tell by his smile he was far from it. Beside him was a girl around his height, her arms tatted up and two piercings in one ear. As the line moves, she turns around for a moment. She wants to wait a few seconds before observing the group further. After ten seconds passed, she turned around slightly again, getting a good glimpse of a pretty natural ginger, with brown smooth skin, and the guy next to her, the one complaining, was a lot different from everyone else, but his style was the same. Grunge. Based on his appearance, Aurelia could tell he had albinism.

Although they all seem like an interesting bunch, amongst the five, only one of them was familiar.

Elijah.

The attractive blond who she seems to be running into a lot lately—By chance, of course.

"We can't leave Justin and Amaya alone for too long," the blond, Elijah, says as he scrolls through his phone. "Besides, it seems like Adrian is going to be late, so why not buy everyone something."

"Did we all need to come then- ouch, Grace what the fuck?"

"You're causing a scene," Grace warns, nodding in Aurelia's direction. "See, even the pretty girl can't enjoy her music because of your loudness."

Aurelia wanted to turn her head, but what would be the point? They already caught her staring. Elijah raises his head slowly, frowning lines between his thick dark eyebrows as he glances around for the girl his friend is talking about. The moment they make eye contact those frown lines from before disappear and his lips that were in a straight line slowly curl into a big smile.

"That she is," Elijah utters deeply as he walks in front of everyone and takes a few steps towards her. "Hi again, Aurelia."

She slowly pulls her headphones off and smiles a bit before nodding.

"Elijah, remember?" He asks just as the guy, who was complaining before, steps up right behind him.

"I thought all your groupies knew your name." He snickers, causing Grace to yank him away from Elijah.

Groupies?

The generalization bother her, and that word in itself made her want to turn around and-

"Ignore him," Elijah sighs. "He associates every person I talk to as a groupie. I just wish he would knock that shit off."

Aurelia nods a bit again before she turns around a little to take another step forward since the line is moving.

"Anyway," he takes a small step to the right, so he could stand facing her. "I see that we ran into each other again, how about we make small talk and get to know one another, yeah?"

"What for?" She questions, tilting her head before taking a small glance at him.

He grins, his mole just above his top lip moving upwards with his pearly teeth on display. His blond hair is in a half up and half down style, making him a lot more attractive than she honestly remembers.

"Ah, so she does speak. Hear I thought you were keeping that pretty voice of yours to yourself."

Thump.

Aurelia shyly adverts her gaze elsewhere, causing the male to grin before the woman from before stepping in between them.

"Stop flirting with everyone you see."

"I'm just being nice, Grace." he chuckles quietly. "Besides, it doesn't seem like she minds me flirting just a bit, right?

The attention made her panic a bit, causing her to quickly step to the counter, since it was her turn to order.

After ordering what she wants, she takes her receipt with her order number on it and quickly finds an open table to sit at. Aurelia sits her things down and turns her attention outside the window, not wanting to make eye contact with the man. Just when she thought she got away, a few seconds after ordering, the man takes a seat in front of her, making her swallow down air.

"I have a strong feeling that you're avoiding me," Elijah says, raising his eyebrow while folding his hand out on the table. "Do you not wish to talk to me?"

Aurelia awkwardly avoids his eyes looking down at her phone as if she's changing the song. "I just... don't know you?"

"Then let's start over," he suggests calmly, not in a pushy way. "I'm Elijah and you are?"

She looks up from her phone, and in that brief moment, the moment their eyes gaze into each other for three seconds, Aurelia holds her breath until she looks away again. She places the bag she got from Adrian on the table and clears her throat.

"A-Aurelia. My name is Aurelia." She gathers enough courage to look at Elijah, watching him closely as he just stares at her. "What?"

"Your name is beautiful." he compliments. "Hm... is that latin?"

Aurelia slowly nods her head as she looks away from him again. "It's my great grandmother's name, but I don't know much about her."

Elijah hums gently before the girl, Grace, walks up to their table and taps it. "Come on lover boy, leave her alone."

"Grace, please," Elijah groans playfully. "If you keep this act up, I'm going to assume you want me all to yourself."

"You wish, Elijah." She rolls her eyes before looking at Aurelia, who is observing their behavior as they interact with each other.

"You know," she leans down to whisper to Aurelia. "He's pretty but he's a man whore."

Elijah grins and shakes his head. "I can hear you, Gracie, I'm sitting right here."

"That you are." Grace crosses her arms. "Why don't you go over there with the rest of our friends and leave her alone."

The man who was complaining before also walks towards the table, sliding into the spot beside Elijah, forcing him to scoot over before smiling at her. "I'm Abel, the more... hotter and charming guy of this friend group."

"Oh brother..." Grace rolls her eyes again before joining the other friends at the table to the right of her.

"Oh wait a minute," Abel points to the bag. "That looks a lot like the bags Adrian stayed up all night putting together. You must be one of the freshmen from the art department at that school."

Aurelia eyes slowly glances over towards the bag. "I haven't... looked through it yet."

"He didn't do much, but I know he said that it would make it count since this is his last year or something," Abel rants before turning towards Elijah, who had been staring at her this entire time, which made her feel very uncomfortable. "Speaking of that school, I saw a video of Andrew today, it seems like he didn't lose his touch."

As Aurelia looks at Elijah, his facial expression changes again. She was really good at reading people's faces, being a good observer, but she couldn't quite grasp what emotion he was feeling after hearing Abel bring up Andrew. Did he have a problem with Andrew too, just like everyone else did?

"He's not living with you, right?" Abel pushes, clearly not reading the room. "Did you two even-"

"Yo, Abel!" The guy with the green hair, from their circle, speaks up from the other table. "Pipe down. Stop interrogating him."

Abel shrugs. "I was just curious since I saw him on the video."

"Number two ninety?" The person at the counter calls Aurelia's number, causing her to excuse herself softly.

It was good that her number was called, the tension between them all made her really uncomfortable, but not like how Jackie and her friends made her feel the first week she got to the house. The discomfort came from her being in the middle of something she didn't quite understand but everyone else did. Even when she didn't know what was happening, she still understood from their reactions and responses to Abel that it wasn't something that should be talked about out in the open. By the time she got her things, the next number was called, causing Elijah and his friend group to get up and leave.

Aurelia sighs in relief as she watches them walk in her direction as she walks back to the table. She could finally have some alone time before her class. However, as she sits back down at her table, Elijah turns around, pulling his phone out his pocket.

"Can I... get your phone number?" He asks her, making her instantly shake her head.

"No," she turns him down. "I don't just hand out my number... I hope you understand."

Elijah tilted his head, but he didn't look upset, just curious. Was he expecting her to say something else?

"Interesting." He says before putting his phone back into his pocket. "I hope to see you around, Aurelia."

With that, she watches him and his friends leave the cafe together, giving her time to breathe. That was the first time, in a while, that she was able to hold a conversation, kind of, with people other than Cameron and Sabrina. Though she was able to talk to Jackie and her friends, it didn't really feel like how she just felt with these guys, it felt a lot more safer, as if she wasn't being watched and judged for everything she says or does.

It did make her a lot more curious about them though, because this is the second group to talk about Andrew. It made her wonder more about the strange man. She only held a small conversation with him before he started to dance, but since more than one person has brought him up, she wonders what truly happened with him. But of course, like anyone else, she does not know him and doesn't plan on asking him about his personal life. It was silly for her to even be curious.

Aurelia sends a quick check in message to the group chat with Sabrina and Cameron before looking through the bag Adrian has given to her. There were a lot of art supplies, and two bags of gummy bears. She thought it was a good welcome bag. It did make her feel quite welcome, but if Adrian is super nice, she never expected Aiden to be his twin brother. Aiden is the complete opposite, and it was obvious who was the more approachable one out of the twins.

She just hopes she can find a small group of close friends of her own. One she didn't have to over hear drama or get caught in an uncomfortable situation with. She wanted to feel less lonely.

Aurelia takes her tea and begins to drink it slowly after putting her headphones back on and listening to one of her playlist she had made from before.

eight

In life, like interpreting art, perspectives differ. Yet, as artists grasp their creation's truth, those intimately involved in a situation often hold a deeper understanding of its reality.

▼

▲

☐

Aurelia takes a deep breath, staring at the blank canvas in front of her. She was under a lot of pressure, and seeing the girl to her right and the person to her left just, sketched away overwhelmed her.

"Remember, don't think about it," Arthur, the famous artist who decided to spend his off season teaching at her university. The same artist she became so obsessed with when she first started high school. "If you spend time thinking, you take away the time you have to feel. Just put your pencil to the canvas and sketch."

Nibbling at her bottom lip, she slowly begins to move her pencil across the blank canvas. Two medium sized circles. They were perfect circles, a skill she perfected when she took her first art class. However, she couldn't move any further than that. Her thoughts were slowly creeping in, making her hands shake.

"Simple."

Startled, she turns her head towards her teacher, Arthur, the man with paintings that could make a blind person cry. His work is amazing and here he is, eyeing her sad excuse for a beautiful piece. Aurelia knew she had other pieces, ones she would be more than confident enough to show him, but this, this wasn't her, this was not her best. After uttering the most heart crushing words about her unfinished, barely started, work he walks away, eyeing the other students in the class work.

Aurelia swallows down nervously, looking down at her hands before closing her eyes. Here she thought art history was going to be tough. Something told her to wait until the next year to sign up for this class, but she knew she wouldn't be able to be guided by the best. Arthur is the best, having him mentor her was the only reason she really wanted to be accepted at the school.

"Don't worry," the girl beside her whispers. "I took his class two years ago when he was teaching Australia, and freshmen never make it up to this point. So clearly you have some talent."

When the girl turns back to her work, Aurelia just sits there and sighs before bringing her pencil back to the canvas. After the class is over, Aurelia takes the large blank piece of paper and puts it neatly in her large bag. She could see a lot of the students asking him questions, and even joking around with him. She knew she was the first freshman to ever be accepted in one of his classes, but she could tell the other artists were on a whole other level compared to her.

"Think of those pieces as final exams," Arthur announces to everyone as people stuck around and others pack up. "Fail to impress me and yourself, you failed this class."

Aurelia sighs and gathers her things before making her way towards the door. She quickly walks out of the room, bumping into someone right outside.

"I'm sorry!" She apologizes quickly, helping the person pick their papers and art tools up.

"It's fine, Aurelia." Adrian says, making her look up at him. "I wasn't paying attention."

She shakes her head and stands up, putting the papers in his hand. "I wasn't either."

Adrian looks at the door as students finally begin to leave the room. He gently holds her upper arm and pulls her to the side, so they wouldn't be in the way. "I heard his classes are tough, but I'm more surprised that you passed the applications."

Aurelia lets out a long sigh before nodding her head. "After today, I'm not sure if I'm ready for this class."

Adrian laughs and shakes his head. "It's only the first day, I remember my ex girlfriend's first day and she was kind of like you. Ready to give up before giving it another shot."

He looks away from her, putting his art tools in his bag as he speaks. "I'll just tell you what I told her. Art is suggestive, and there's no such thing as good or bad art here. The only person you should want to impress is yourself. If you impress others, think of it as an accomplishment for finishing another art piece."

"Those words are really meaningful, Adrian."

"Well," he shrugs. "I guess they were."

Aurelia takes a good look at his sketches as he tucks them in the bag as well. "Are you studying ceramic and sculpture?"

Adrian grins at her and raises an eyebrow. "Couldn't resist taking a peek huh?"

She looks down ashamed. "I did... just for a second though."

"Well, if you're curious, then yes." he smiles at her before nodding for them to walk together. "Even though it's not something my parents wanted me to do, my uncle introduced it to me before he passed away when I was only five."

"I'm sorry," Aurelia says, causing him to shake his head. "Don't be, he was an asshole sometimes, but when he wasn't, he was teaching me hands on what it was like to mold clay and sculpt out different things using my hands. Besides, he took care of me most of the time, since my parents were more interested in my brother's soccer dream."

Aurelia could tell that talking about his family is bothering him, though she never asked, she did kind of trigger the topic by asking the question.

"If it makes you feel better," she speaks softly, and cautiously so the topic will be subtle. "My mother is a doctor and my father is a teacher. No one in my family expected me to be interested in art, let alone art history."

"Ah," he chuckles. "Right, Art History."

"What?"

He shakes his head as he laughs. "You just... remind me of my ex so much."

Aurelia looks away, feeling both shy and uncomfortable. Uncomfortable because she didn't want to be compared to his ex, or compared to anyone at all. However, she is shy about it. Aurelia is being herself and if that was enough to make him laugh as he is now, it made her really shy that she was making, hopefully, a good friend.

"Don't worry," he tells her, making her look at him again. "Even though things ended horribly, I would never talk down about her to you. She's honestly not worth mentioning since—actually nevermind, just all the good things I remember about her I see with you. If that makes sense."

"Well, at least they are all good things." She jokes a bit, causing him to laugh himself.

"Sorry for comparing you to her," he says softly as they exit the main campus building together. "But you're good people, It would be cool if we hang out more. That way you could have better company than my brother and his friends."

Aurelia stops walking holding her bag close, causing Adrian to look back before clearing his throat. "Sorry, I shouldn't have said that. Especially when they're your friends."

"No," she shakes her head. "You're right. I do need better company than them."

She looks down, not sure if she should talk about anything involving them, but this is Aiden's brother, his twin brother. It wouldn't be wrong to tell him about his brother's behavior, and all the things she heard coming from his mouth, right?

"They aren't the nicest people," she continues, watching the older male tilt his head before sitting on the stone that was near the bench. "I only find myself around them because Jackie's my roommate. It's truly exhausting being in that house with her."

"Have you talked to the board of student housing?"

Aurelia shakes her head. "I don't want to make a big deal out of it, and recently we haven't really been talking."

"That doesn't mean that it's better, it just means she's being petty... as usual." He sighs before digging into his pocket. "Here, if you ever need to get out of that house and just hang out, call me."

Adrian writes his number on a sheet of sticky note paper and passes it to her. "I know how annoying my brother and his friends are. I also know what lengths they go to make people's time at this school miserable."

"Thank you Adrian, I appreciate it. I just haven't gotten the chance to talk to someone face to face. It just seems like everyone loves them as people and refuses to acknowledge their flawed personality." She quickly realizes that she's talking about his brother as well. "No offense... of course."

Adrian stands up and shakes his head. "The only thing my brother and I share is a face and blood," he comments. "I could care less what happens to him and what people say about him. He's an asshole."

Aurelia looks at her smartwatch and holds her hand over her stomach when it embarrassingly growls loud enough for Adrian to notice. He laughs quietly before clearing his throat.

"I was going to make my way to work," Adrian says, pretending as if he didn't hear her stomach practically begging to be filled. "There's a sandwich place just next door you can go to."

She smiles at him and nods. "Lead the way."

Adrian walks towards the parking lot, causing her to quickly realize he has a car, something she wanted to get, but then realize that she wanted to wait until her sophomore year to beg her dad for one. Her commute to campus and her house would be shorter which would give her more time to sleep and paint. As she placed her art bag in the backseat of his car, she was surprised by the cleanliness of the car. She also noticed that it smelled nice, so her ride to the sandwich place was comfortable.

When she gets out, Adrian locks his car and puts his keys in his pocket. "After you're done eating, just come next door. I'll unlock my car so you can get your bag."

"Alright," she nods. "Thank you again, Adrian."

"Hey, we're friends now," he playfully pushes her. "Now go eat, I heard their turkey and ham sandwiches are the best in the city."

Aurelia laughs at his antics and nods. "See you in a bit."

Adrian walks into the tattoo parlor, where he works, and she walks into the sandwich place next door. It was great that there wasn't a line, but it was still really crowded. Aurelia walks up to the counter and orders a turkey sandwich with a bottle of lemonade.

Once they hand her the lemonade and sandwich, she sits down at the table closer to the door and right beside the window. She puts her headphones on and plays her favorite Sherrionn song, in her calm playlist. As she eats, she checks her email, one being from the head of the art department asking to meet with her two days from now. She sends a formal and quick email back from her phone and places it down.

Tryna get you close, yeah..

She hums along to the song quietly before she takes a sip from her lemonade. Aurelia looks at her watch, noticing she had a few messages from her group chat. As she goes to look at her messages, she gets a call from her mother. Aurelia quickly answers her mother's call, switching device usage so she could put her phone up to her ear.

"Yes."

"Hey baby, how's the first week going?" She asks, making her smile.

"It's fine momma, but I thought you said that you would call at the end of every week." She could hear her mother sigh dramatically, causing her to laugh silently.

"I couldn't wait, I wanted to know what my baby had been up to. No boys I hope."

"Momma, please..." she groans embarrassingly. "I hardly have the time for boys."

"Good. I can't wait to see you when the holidays roll around. Don't stay up too late and make sure you eat."

"I know momma, I'm not a kid anymore." She covers her face.

Her mother sighs sadly. "I'll talk to you in two days, okay?"

"Talk to you then, momma. I love you."

After her mother says it back, the call ends, and Aurelia proceeds to look at the group chat. It seems like Sabrina is going to a dinner party with her roommate and asked about hers and Cameron's opinions on her outfit. Aurelia told her that the colors were great but she could go with a neutral color shoe. Cameron responded right after saying that he was heading to class but the outfit looked good.

Aurelia started to realize that her friends are in fact becoming busier, so having people like Adrian will help with killing time and build a good friendship with him. As she finishes up her sandwich. She adds Adrian's number to her phone number to her contact, sending him a quick message so he knows it's her.

She stands up from the table, and tosses her wrap in the garage on the way out the door. She walks next door, already overwhelmed by the semi crowded place with people talking to each other.

"Ah, we meet again!"

Aurelia pulls her headphones off and smiles politely. "H-Hi."

Grace walks around the front desk and crosses her arms. "I'm assuming that Elijah's charms bewitched you and you're now back for more."

She shakes her head quickly and crosses her arms. "No. I'm actually here for Adrian. He told me to come here after I finished next door. I could call him."

"I'm kidding girl," she laughs, holding her hand. "Adrian is setting up in his booth, I can go get him for you."

Aurelia nods and waits patiently for Grace to come back, after a few seconds Adrian walks up with one glove on his hand and the other with his keys. He smiles at her and points his car key at the window, opening the car from the inside. He looks at his watch and curses quietly before tilting his head.

"It's a bit late," He says, looking at her. "It'll be pretty fucked up of me to make you take the bus when I brought you here."

Aurelia shakes her head and crosses her arms. "No, it's okay. I can just take the bus-"

From the corner of her eye, she could see two people walk up to them. She could tell from his tall stature and the golden blond hair that shined, due to the building across the street windows reflecting the sunlight in the dark-ish place, that the stranger approaching is indeed Elijah. A small brief memory of the group of friends talking about Adrian being late for work appeared in her brain. It made sense on why he was present, this was his parlor.

"I can take her," Elijah says, causing Aurelia to swallow nothing down, in hopes it would help the moisture in her mouth as she observes this attractive man. "She can just tell me where she lives, unless she does not wish for me to take her."

Aurelia clears her throat and slowly turns her head towards Adrian. "I really don't mind taking the bus."

"Ouch," Elijah disrupts her train of thought once again. "Is being in the same car as me repulsive, Aurelia?"

Adrian tilts his head and looks at Aurelia. "You know him already?"

"Who doesn't?" Grace adds on, standing behind the desk right in front of the entrance, leaning forward as if the scene playing out in front of her very eyes is the most entertaining thing in the world. "He is the Elijah. Man with the long wavy hair, pretty blue hazel eyes, and a smile that would kill a puppy."

"That's a bit graphic, but I appreciate it, Grace." He winks at her, not Grace, the one announcing all of this, but at her the quietest in the room.

He loved it. Elijah loved the way Grace described him. Aurelia quickly realized that he loves the attention. So as Grace strokes his ego some more, it makes her see a lot more than she wanted to when dealing with the man.

"I met him... a few times but we didn't talk that long." Aurelia explains to Adrian.

"And each time she turned me down," he announces to everyone in the area, including the unknown girl that walked up to them alongside Elijah. "Can you believe that, Adrian?"

Adrian rolls his eyes and groans from annoyance.

"Just, it's up to her, if she decides to go, don't mess up my car." Adrian turns to Aurelia after handing Elijah his car key. "I'm sorry for not being able to take you, my client is waiting for me in the back. I'll text you later or something."

"Don't be sorry, I'll see you around later." Aurelia tells him softly, before making small contact with Elijah before walking out the door.

She could hear Grace whistling as she walked away, but that didn't stop the handsome man from following her out. "Wait a moment, love."

Elijah stands in front of her, blocking her path to the backseat door to Adrian's car.

"Just let me just... take you home." His tone sounds as if he's pleading for her to say yes, causing her to cross her arms.

"This is the first time a woman turned me down... at all." He chuckles, leaning against the car slightly. "Did I offend you?"

"No." She answers, making him tilt his head. "You didn't offend me... I'm just a tab bit intimidated by your extrovertness."

She decided to be honest with him. His personality type is intense. Cameron and Sabrina were extroverted, but they were also introverted at times which is why Aurelia clicked with them so well. Not to mention, he's extremely attractive, which means that everyone will flock to him every time they see him. It was bad enough that people think she's somehow connected with Andrew simply because that very night he happened to dance in front of her.

"I can tone it down this whole car ride," he suggested. "If it means I can spend most of it getting to know you better."

"If I say yes-"

"Yes!" He cuts her off, making her smile stretch on her face before she laughs at him.

She covers her smile, calming down her laughter as she notices him staring at her intensely. "I didn't get to finish, and you just agreed?"

"I'm a risk taker, baby." He winks before opening the passenger door for her.

The name has her stunned, she stares at him before sliding into the passenger seat. Aurelia didn't know why it shocked her, she had been called baby by Sabrina and even Cameron, but why did her heart race and her throat dry up when he said it?

"So," he slides into the driver seat, putting his seatbelt on. "How about you start by telling me something about you."

"About me?"

"You're an art major," he says. "I used to be an art major at that school. The best in fact. Made the school pull their hair out when I turned that million dollar contract."

"Turned it down?"

Elijah glances over at her with a smile before focusing on the road. "Is that so shocking?"

"No one turns down money these days." She speaks softly.

"Well," he shrugs. "I'm from a well off family, I didn't need the money, and besides my passion was elsewhere. Not making paintings for the rich every time they wanted it."

"Art is supposed to be fun," he continues, his eyes still staring at the road ahead. "That's what I was doing it for, but everyone, mostly the head of the art department, was calling me an art prodigy. My work deserves to be seen by millions."

Aurelia listened to him and thought back to the piece she could barely start in her class. It didn't feel fun for her, but maybe it was because she was nervous.

"Is that why everyone loves you?"

He laughs and sighs after. "I may be loved by many... but I don't just share my love with anyone."

She smiles at that, but she didn't know why, was it because he said that to ease her mind? Or was it because he wanted to showcase his true self rather than his rumors.

"So, oak road or evergreen?" He asks her. "Your place?"

As he looked at her, she could feel her heart bumping against her chest and her mouth becoming dry again. "Oak... Oak Road."

Elijah chuckles to himself before turning back to the road, quickly making it down the narrow street way. Aurelia points to the house, realizing there's a bunch of people in their front yard and music playing. She could tell just from the look of everyone outside that the party just started.

Again, Jackie didn't tell her before time and she hasn't been considerate of her.

"Thank you for the ride... Elijah." Aurelia says, grabbing her bag from the back before exiting the passenger side.

This was getting annoying, and Aurelia doesn't know if she could contain her thoughts this time to spare people feelings. She plans on letting Jackie know tonight or she will be heading to the board first thing the next day.

"Hey," Elijah gets out of the car, causing people to look at them. "I can go in with you."

"That won't be-"

"Aurelia!" Aiden calls her name, coming down the stairs with Jackie trailing right behind him.

As he approaches her, Elijah finds time to step beside her, making Aiden glare at him for a half second before replacing it with a face smile.

"I see you brought company."

□

nine

There are two sides of every artist; an artist full of passion and an artist full of madness. Both aren't afraid to showcase their beauty through a blank canvas.

▼

▲

☐

Aurelia couldn't believe that Aiden was worried about Elijah and not about her, his girlfriend's roommate. The one who also lives in the home he and his girlfriend keep throwing parties at. She was livid, but she didn't know if getting mad and yelling at them would solve anything. She just wanted to keep the peace, but why keep the peace when Jackie and Aiden are being really disrespectful when she has done nothing but respect them and their lifestyle without causing trouble since she got to the house.

"What a surprise," Aiden grins fakely, sipping his drink from his cup, not taking his eyes off of Elijah. "Elijah decided to join the fun, everyone!"

He announces to everyone on the front lawn, who cheers before getting back to the party. Aurelia looks up at Elijah, who holds no expression as he stares at Aiden as the male steps closer to them.

"Should I get you a drink," Aiden says lowly, but not low enough so Aurelia couldn't hear. "Or should I get you a small red bag with his favorite pink and white pills."

Elijah jaw clenches before he shakes his head. "I'm here to make sure she gets inside safely, but I can see you and her... haven't changed even after the incident."

Aurelia turns her attention to Jackie, who's quietly standing there. "Why are you throwing parties? I have class and a lot to work to do. The least you could've done was told me that you were having people over? I thought we respected each other enough to understand that much."

Aiden wraps his arm around Jackie. "Now, now, Aurelia. The party just started, how about we go inside and chill, but I would appreciate it more if you leave your unwelcome guest outside."

She was offended.

"All these people, including you, are unwelcome guests! I live here too in case you two forgot!" Her voice is firm, but not once did she raise her voice to them. "This is just disregarding me and how I feel at this point despite me being very respectful!"

Elijah gently holds her upper arm, pulling her back slightly. She looks at him and pulls her arm from his hand, and looks at Jackie again. "What is your problem?"

Jackie just rolls her eyes and turns on her heel. She's choosing to walk away from Aurelia's genuine question, frustrating her. All she's trying to do is get to the root of the problem, and she's being childish about it. Petty.

"This isn't even surprising. This is how Aiden operates." Elijah shakes his head, causing her to look at him, but Aiden takes another step forward, frowning a bit.

It was obvious that he was upset—no he was far more than that. His eyes were already bloodshot, and his lips were in a straight line. He shakes his head and tilts it slightly while holding the cup in his hand.

"Are you serious?" The tone of Aiden's voice is low and threatening. "You think because my brother bends over for you that you can talk down on me? Fuck. That."

Elijah scoffs from disbelief before turning to look at Aurelia, who is so distraught and annoyed to care about what they have against each other. The blond male takes a deep breath, his face full of concern as he just smoothly ignores the man's words in front of him.

"Look," Aurelia turns to Elijah. " I know this is where you live, but these people aren't really safe. Especially with alcohol and drugs involved."

"Hey!" Aiden takes his hand and shoves Elijah's shoulder. It wasn't like a hard shove. It looked more like a warning shove, one that would definitely cause a fight if no one walks away from it. "Stop being fucking weird and leave her alone."

Elijah jaw clenches before he just laughs to himself, but she could tell from his eyes that he wasn't amused in the slightest. "You know, I'm not going to give you the satisfaction, goodnight Aurelia."

She watches the blonde walk off with one hand in his jean pocket while the other stays close in a tight fist as he walks around the car. Aiden jeers, taunting him as he gets into the car. She could tell Elijah wanted to turn around and say a few words, but it was very mature of him to just be the bigger person. She didn't want him to fight someone like Aiden, especially when it's obvious that he's under the influence of drugs and alcohol.

"You know Aurelia," Aiden slurs his words as he finishes whatever is in his cup. "You're really hurting my feelings."

"What?"

"First Andrew," he tosses the cup to the ground pulling a bag out of his pocket out in the open. "Now you show up with that fucking guy, in my brother's fucking car?"

Aurelia's face twists with a frown as he tosses two pills in his mouth, swallowing them dry.

"I don't even know Andrew, and Elijah only gave me a ride in your brother's car because he was working and couldn't drop me off himself." She explains truthfully to the intoxicated man.

"Do you like him better or something?"

She sighs. "I didn't say that, I barely know him, but from the little time we spent together he seems like a really nice person."

"What does he have that I don't, huh?"

She took a deep breath before shaking her head. The scent of the alcohol made her subtly cover her nose, trying not to let the smell bother too much, but it was hard.

"Look," she says firmly while pushing at his chest while covering her nose for a second longer before pulling her hand away. "You're clearly under the influence, Aiden, you should sit down and drink some water or something-"

"So you're looking down on me too?" He shouts, causing a few sober and non drunk people to look in their direction.

"Down on you?" She questions his question. "Aiden I barely know you, and if I did, I would never look down on you. Just sit down somewhere and drink some water-"

"Fuck off!" He swats her hand away before he lets a small scoff out under his breath.

She watches the man turn on his heel and walks away, stumbling only slightly as he pushes his way through the crowd in the front yard. Aurelia just shakes her head, not really in the mood to go after him.

She had no reason to.

Aiden showcases nothing but red flags to her, and he doesn't have any shame in doing so. She doesn't want to hang around them, and all of this just solidifies her decision. Jackie forced her hand, leaving her no choice but to get the board of student housing involved.

Aurelia knew she should've listened to her gut and Cameron, her best friend. Even he told her to go to them to see if she could get a dorm room or even move into another house with a different student. The only reason she didn't go the first time was simply because she wanted to give Jackie the chance to change. With only the first week of actual classes, Jackie didn't change not one bit.

Holding her things close to her body, the young woman walks past the dancing and chatting people in the front yard, trying to make her way up the smooth stone stairs.

There were people standing in front of the door. Her eyes held annoyance, she's sure of it because it takes one look before the three in front of the door move out the way. Aurelia takes another deep breath, trying to calm her nerves. Without hesitation, she forces her way in the front door.

"Ouch!" An unknown woman and her friend glares at Aurelia while hold-ing her arm. "The hell?!"

It was only then she noticed that she hit the girl standing behind the door with the door. Aurelia utters a quick, unapologetic apology, since they were the dumb ones to stand directly behind the door.

"Excuse me." Aurelia pushes past them, trying to step fully inside.

The front yard wasn't as crowded as it was inside. Unknown people sit-ting on their couch chain smoking, passing a brown stick around while watching something on the television mounted on the wall. She didn't understand how they were watching anything with the music blasting so loudly. As she walked around the couch, the crowd somehow led her towards the kitchen. The layout of the house's first floor was an open concept, so the kitchen wasn't really separated from the living area.

She didn't even mean to get to the kitchen, but maybe it was a blessing. She got to see random people using her mugs, the same mugs she made back when she took those ceramic classes forever ago. One was being used to drink out of while the other was being used as an ashtray. Aurelia didn't even think about it, she takes her mug from the random man and pours his liquid inside the sink. As she allows the hot water to run in the mug she turns and snatches her other mug from the stranger, causing her mug to fall on the floor, breaking into pieces.

"Who the fuck is this?" The two men laugh at her before walking away from the kitchen, with three others following behind them.

Aurelia knows how pathetic she looks, scraping up her mug pieces in her hand at a wild party. She knows how out of place she looks. That didn't matter though. She didn't care about that. She knows she looks more pathetic putting up with Jackie and her friend's crap this entire time, simply because she doesn't want to cause problems.

This is the last straw.

"I did say not to trust anyone, Angel." She hears a familiar voice over the music. "Especially not them."

Aurelia looks up and over her shoulder seeing Andrew staring down at her, in a similar outfit the night of Tony's party. Only this time he had gray wash jeans on and his oversized black hoodie and white tank top underneath. He wasn't afraid of accessories either, but he didn't go overboard. Two chains around his neck, small hoop earrings, and a few rings on his left hand.

Andrew takes a long drag of the weed from the brown rolled up stick, puffing smoke into the air before squatting down beside her, causing her to swallow hard before turning back to her broken mug.

"I'm not in the mood," she tells him, as she scoops up the last pieces of the mug and puts it in the sink with the other mug.

"Great." She murmurs to herself, rubbing her forehead with the back of her hand.

"You can always get another one, Angel." He says close to her ear making her snap her head in his direction, her annoyance covering her face.

He's so close, but not too close. She had a lot of room to breathe.

"There's no replacing this one." She tells him, her eyes roaming his face before meeting his eyes.

He stares into her eyes for a moment, a grin covering his lips, before he looks over her shoulder into the sink. She follows his gaze, trying to see what he was looking so intently at.

"It looks like a cheap mug you can find anywhere, Angel."

"I made this." She tells him, offended by his comment.

He whistles and holds his hand up in defense before smoking the stick in his hand again with a grin covering his face.

Sure.

The mug was a bit lumpy, and slightly uneven. She didn't care. It was a mug she made when she first started taking Ceramic classes. This mug especially was her first mug she ever made. Even then she thought it was horrible, but it still felt good to keep it because she was proud of herself for finishing it. Now, the mug is broken, completely broken, irreplaceable.

"You know," Andrew speaks again. "I was shocked to see a girl like you hang around people like Aiden and Jackie."

"What's that supposed to mean?" she crosses her arms, turning to face him.

"You aren't the type of girl they let around them, so if you're actively participating in parties like this, I clearly misjudged you." He tells her, making her roll her eyes subtly before looking away from him, trying to scan the party for Jackie so she could talk to her.

"I don't hang out with them, and I just showed up because I live here." She is annoyed and there is no point in hiding it. "I just need to find Jackie so I can talk to her."

"Talk?"

Andrew laughs, causing her to look at him, admiring the tattoos on his neck. They weren't covering his neck, just small tattoos here and there. He is slightly taller than she is, but he wasn't super tall so she didn't have to strain her neck to look him in the eyes.

"There's no talking with someone like Jackie." He tells her, leaning against the kitchen counter, still smoking the stick in his hand, puffing the smoke into the air.

Aurelia couldn't help but stare. He's an attractive man. There's no denying that, and now that she thinks about it, he's a picture perfect bad boy. That's the only way she could describe him. Perhaps it's because it's very rare for her to find any man attractive, so when he's the second man she has come across, of course she'll believe even the smallest things like smoking weed is sexy.

"Why do you say that," she asks, pulling her eyes away from him when he turns his head to look at her. "I'm her roommate. It shouldn't be difficult to have an adult conversation with her."

Andrew laughs again, causing her to glance over at him before rolling her eyes. She turns around and begins to walk towards the direction of the stairs.

"Wait," Andrew says, hoping over the small island in the kitchen to stand in front of her. "I wouldn't go up there."

Aurelia frowns a bit. "My room is upstairs. With the rest of my things, and this is my home."

Andrew chuckles. "It's funny that you still think Jackie will give a shit about this being a shared home."

She crosses her arms. "And it's funny that you chose to hang out with people who you seemingly don't trust."

His smile begins to fall from his face, and his gaze darkens.

"Looks like we all got jokes tonight, why don't we ask your so-called untrustworthy friends about–" she steps back against the wall just off from the living space. She resists the urge to flinch as he leans forward, leaving very little space between them.

His facial expression held no emotion. It's like the words she spilled from her lips snatched his playful and confident behavior away.

"Don't talk as if you know me, Angel." His voice is low and close to her ear. "I hate it when people assume shit about me."

Aurelia swallows down nervously and quickly steps away from him. She could tell from his anger that she did say something to make him upset, but she didn't think she said something false. This is the second time she has seen this man, and the second time it was at a party Jackie and her friends have planned and thrown.

Without saying anything, she quickly walks up the stairs, walking towards her room door. The same room she shares with Jackie. As she opens the door, she gasps loudly, covering her mouth as she sees Sean and Genesis. She was on her knees in front of him, and it only took two seconds for the both of them to notice her. She quickly closes the door and rushes to the bathroom, panicking. Once the door is locked, she slides to her knees, taking deep breaths just like Cameron taught her.

Sean was sitting on her bed. Her bed. All this is too much. Way too much for her. She can't handle this kind of lifestyle. Jackie had no respect for her or her things. Her mugs were used, and one ended up breaking. Her room and bed are being used for sexual activities. This is beyond disrespectful.

Aurelia's breathing isn't working, her heart is still racing from panic. She wraps her arm around herself and counts backward from ten. As her heart slows down and she finally is able to bring her panic down, a twist of the doorknob makes her raise her head. She slowly looks up at the doorknob seeing it jiggle before someone bangs on the door.

"Hey!" Jackie's voice fills the semi-quiet bathroom. "Other people have to used the fucking bathroom! Take the sex to the bedroom or something!"

Aurelia quickly stands up, unlocking the door. Once she snatches the door open, Jackie's surprised expression covers her face. She didn't give her roommate a chance to protest or say anything. She grabs the older woman by the wrist and yanks her inside behind her.

"What the fuck?" Jackie shouts just as Aurelia slams the door close and locks it again. "Move, Aurelia!"

"No!" She says, her voice slightly raised. "Not until we talk!"

Jackie rolls her eyes again, crossing her arms. "There's nothing to talk about, now move!"

Aurelia stares at her in disbelief. "Really? You really don't want to talk about how disrespectful you have been towards me? I respect your lifestyle and your space but you can't respect mine?!"

"Respect?" She raises an eyebrow. "You seem to know how to respect my space but not respect me when it comes to my boyfriend."

Aurelia is stunned. "What?"

"Yeah," she unfolds her arms and steps into her face. "You showed up at Tony's party after preaching about not wanting to come, and the first thing you do when you're there is be all over my man? So, fuck off Aurelia!"

Aurelia couldn't believe her ears and what she was hearing. Jackie is being this way because she's insecure? Disrespecting her and her things?

"Are you serious?"

"Very." She says firmly crossing her arms again. "I saw how close you two were! And I already told you about my love for him!"

Her hands were shaking and her heart was racing. She could tell from Jackie's face that she was very serious with accusations she was putting on Aurelia. However, she was far wrong. False.

"I was there for you, Jackie! I wasn't there to be with Aiden!" She tried to tell her without raising her voice, but it was hard since she was being unbelievable at the moment.

"You really think I'd believe that?" Jackie says. "Aiden literally told me that you begged for the address! You wouldn't leave him alone that night!"

Aurelia shakes her head and laughs from disbelief. "I'm not doing this with you, not now. Tell everyone to leave."

"No."

She pulls her phone out while shaking her head. Aurelia wasn't going to sit here and argue with her. This is it.

"What are you doing?"

Aurelia ignores her and puts the phone up to her ear. Once the operator on the other side answers routinely.

"911 what's your emergency."

Aurelia calls the police because there's no winning with Jackie. There's no reasoning with her. Everything she explains Jackie has a rebuttal. So, she decided to call the police to end the party.

"Hello, operator," she begins to speak, watching Jackie's face twist with anger. "I live in one of the student houses near the college of arts. One of the student homes is throwing a party and I've been told there are illegal substances present. I would've called campus security but drugs seem to be a lot more serious."

"Can you give us the name of the street?"

Aurelia gives her the address and ends the call afterwards. Jackie frowns deepens, stepping in her face. "You fucking snitch!"

"You left me no choice." Aurelia argues before Jackie bumps past her and unlocks the door, storming out and down the stairs.

After taking a few deep breaths, Aurelia takes a step out of the bathroom, her things in her hand still. She looks downstairs hearing Jackie telling everyone to leave because she had snitched on them all.

"You should get out of here." Aurelia looks to her left to Andrew leaning against the wall. It was almost as if he was listening to their conversation.

"Why would I leave? I live here! And I called them!" She tells him.

Andrew pushes off of the wall and takes her wrist. She protested but the male did not let her go. He storms down the stairs and opens the back door practically pushing her through the threshold. She yanks her hand from his grip, making him sigh from frustration.

"If you stay they'll just arrest you." He tells her, shoving his hands in his pocket. "Just because it's your house and you called, doesn't mean they won't arrest you. It never means that."

"How would you know-"

"You're not this naive, Angel, are you?" he shakes his head. "It doesn't matter, just trust me and go to one of the local libraries around her for an hour or two before returning."

He tells her, it's like his anger disappeared completely.

Aurelia didn't trust him, but she also didn't want to risk the possibility of her getting arrested. She wasn't naive and she knew exactly what he was talking about. Her calling the police and mentioning drugs probably caused a lot more problems than she thought.

"Would they even show up?" Aurelia asks, watching Andrew shake his head.

"Most likely, no." He explains to her while everyone inside becomes more and more chaotic to leave. "They might think you're just a drunk college kid playing a prank. But... that's rarely the case."

Aurelia wasn't going to take any chances. The young woman gathers her things, specifically her bag with her laptop and other electronics in it. She also had her bag with her practically blank canvas inside. She didn't want to risk the chances of that possibility. Afterall, she was the one to call.

"Come on," he ushers her to follow him. "I know a library around here you can wait at."

"Why are you helping me?"

He grins and turns to face her with both hands in his jean pocket. "To sleep with you."

Aurelia's face changes from a confused expression to a horrified one.

"Relax," he laughs as he starts walking out the back gate of the house, holding it open for her. "I'm kidding, unless... you want to fuck?"

"No thank you." She shakes her head and continues to walk down the alley, which seems to be the right way considering that he didn't tell her it was the wrong way.

Andrew laughs again, a sound she's now somewhat used to.

"You aren't ugly," he compliments. "And now that I have a better view of your body... I would definitely fuck you."

"I would appreciate it if you stop talking now," she mumbles, trying her best to ignore his comments. "And refrain from announcing what you would and want to do to me. I'd rather not hear that, thank you."

"God!" He laughs again, holding his hand over his stomach as they walk further down the alley. "You're so interesting...I'm intrigued."

Aurelia looks at him one last time before she continues the walk in silence. This night was another one that she could put in her book of hated nights. She was going to make sure she set a meeting up with Jackie and the board of student housing. She needed a new roommate or a new place to move to. She couldn't stay there with Jackie anymore.

She couldn't put up with their toxic behavior anymore.

□

ten

In art, each brushstroke is a heartfelt note, resonating with the melody of passion. Breathe life into your canvas, let every stroke be a dance of emotions, and watch as your masterpiece becomes a connection between the soul and the palette of life.▯

▼

▲

▯

Aurelia yawns softly as she waits patiently in the meeting hall, where the campus board holds weekly meetings. Except today. Today the board meeting hall is closed, but she is there to ask for the head of student housing. After everything that happened two nights ago, she's not sure if she could stay in the house with Jackie any longer.

When Andrew walked her to the library, two nights ago after leaving the party. He told her to just stay there for an hour or two, just in case the police did show up. She found him more interesting that he walked her all the way there, and then left his phone number. Even though it was her second time meeting the man, he didn't pull her away too much. His vulgar jokes, and his overly confident personality really does make her nervous, but not in a bad way. Aurelia wants to step out of her comfort zone, and sometimes being around someone who's the complete opposite of her can help drag her out of her bubble.

However the man is unpredictable and after just spending a few minutes with him, she noticed he gets angry rather quickly. Aurelia also notices he can turn it off just as fast as he can turn it on.

"You're playing hard to get," he told her as they got closer to the library. "Lucky you, I like chasing what I can't have."

She rolled her eyes at the man and turned to look at him. "Well... aren't you desperate."

"Careful, Angel." He grinned before he turned his attention to the sidewalk ahead.

"That's not my name, you know." She told him, watching the man just double his shoulders and tilted his head to the right.

"One night with me," the grin still plastered on his face. "You won't even remember your name, Angel."

She rolled her eyes and continued to walk, almost forgetting about everything that just happened not too long ago. Even while spending only a few moments with him, she could tell that he had a way with words. It could be mistaken as manipulation, but it's truly a charm she definitely can say she noticed about him. In simpler words, he's distracting.

"Aurelia." She told him, causing him to glance at her before nodding his head. "I prefer that name when I'm with strangers."

"Strangers?"

He laughed and stepped in front of her, causing her to walk right into him. Her forehead grazed his chin just slightly before she took a step back. Andrew leaned against the brick wall of the small department store just off the corner of the crosswalk. He tilted his head and raised an eyebrow.

"Well," he took his index finger and traced the edge of the pocket stitched on the front of her jean overalls. "Considering this is our second time meeting, I would say we are a lot more than strangers, Angel."

Aurelia swallowed hard before she cleared her throat. "I'm sure you used this on a lot of girls, but this doesn't work on me."

"How would you know?" He sounded offended and his expression said it all, so she pushed a bit more.

"The way Genesis talks about you," she gathered enough courage to look the man in the eyes. "Anyone would assume that much about you."

Andrew rolled his eyes and shook his head before he pushed off the wall and walked ahead of her. "Now, I'm turned off."

Aurelia laughs to herself at the memory of his face, he looked so confused before he covered it with that grin. Though he smiled she could tell certain words got under his skin, and it was entertaining to her to see a guy like him let the littlest words affect him. It made her want to get to know him more. What makes him tick? What makes him... him.

When he left her at the library, Aurelia did what he instructed. After the two hours passed, she ended up walking back to the house. Everyone was gone, including Jackie and her friends. Aurelia felt relieved that she was alone, but she was upset that she had to clean up everything that Jackie didn't have the decency to clean up after her mess. When she finished cleaning everything up, she went right to bed. She heard that the police didn't show up from Adrian, since he heard from his friends, who was at the party, that everyone just moved the party to Aiden's house.

The very next day, nothing. Jackie wasn't there. Aurelia was still very relieved, she had a whole day to focus on class and other work she needed to complete. The girl spent the day catching up with work and brainstorming her canvas that she still hasn't touched since Arthur's class. Once she spent hours brainstorming, she tried to call Jackie. Of course, at the time, she just wanted to see if she would pick up to finally have that adult conversation, but of course she didn't. That was Aurelia's final attempt to fix anything they had since she got to the school.

"Miss Mitchell?"

Aurelia stands up and walks towards the front desk with the papers of her housing acceptance letter and anything else she thought was important. She already explained the situation twice to two different people, and have been waiting for a while since the last person.

"Yes?"

"So," She types on her computer and sighs. "The head of student housing is on parental leave. She won't be back for a while. After reading your report of relocation or a new roommate, I understand your frustration but there's no way we can help you at this moment."

Another woman walks out of the back office, with a sandwich wrap in her hand. She wraps it back up and walks forward looking over the report Aurelia made. She shakes her head and tilts it slightly. "I see you said that you have tried to make things work, but have you tried stepping away for a while and then coming back together to have an adult conversation?"

"Ma'am, I tried multiple times as I stated in my report. It's all there." Aurelia explains calmly watching the women look at each other.

"Do you have a friend you can stay with for the time being?" The second woman suggests. "This is your three weeks here? I'm sure you have friends by now-"

"I don't." She cuts her off. "I'm in this city all alone with no friends I trust enough to live with. All I'm asking for is a new house with someone else, or even an empty dorm you can offer. I just can't live with someone who has no respect for me or my things."

"You should try to work things out more, it's not everyday a freshman is granted a chance to spend their first year in student housing." The first woman tries to state optimistically. "You got picked out of five students for this opportunity. You shouldn't be worried about fighting your roommate, you two should try to work out your differences."

Aurelia avoids their eyes before taking her report and other papers, putting it in her bag. She utters a small thank you before she exits the meeting hall. Once she is outside, she sighs deeply before walking towards the building her first class is being held at. They could've just told her there was nothing they could do rather than trying to push something that'll never happen.

She just needed to put everything on hold for the time being, right now she needed to focus on school before going to the meeting with the head of her department. Sunny. The man she talked to briefly at the event they held for newbies at the school. He sent her an email asking to speak with her, so she responded that she would.

After her first class, she rushed to the art department building, which is where her class with the famous painter, Arthur, would be teaching her class. The class she's not excited for, As she walks through the large doors, she could see Sunny walking back and forth, telling different people to do different things, or fix certain things. He looked really busy.

Sunny finishes his conversation with the woman beside him before looking up to see Aurelia standing there with her bag and canvas.

"Ah, Aurelia!" He greets, walking towards her.

"Hello, Sir." She shakes his hand and sighs.

"Please, call me, Sunny." He laughs softly before waving her over to his office. "Calling me sir makes me feel a lot older than I am."

Aurelia follows him inside and takes a seat right in front of him. "What did you want to see me for?"

Sunny chuckles and sits in his seat, folding his hand. "You're straight to the point, reminds me of someone."

He pulls out a few flyers and slides them across the desk. "These are the rooms available if you need a quiet place to study or even work on her artwork. I see that you're the freshman in Arthur's class. Congratulations."

"Thank you."

Aurelia looks over the flyers and the open spots, immediately signing her name in two different spots just in case she's not able to get one or the other. Sunny slides another printed sheet of paper across the desk.

"As you can tell, I've been rather busy preparing for Newbie week at the art gallery not too far from here. I encourage all freshmen to participate because you never know when the rich feel like spending a bunch of money on your piece." he tells her, "I saw your portfolio and I'm impressed. Especially with your piece bleeding loneliness. It's really beautiful and it could turn heads."

"Oh my god," she covers her eyes from embarrassment. "I did that piece under a lot of pressure, and when I finally finished it, my hands were sore, and I couldn't paint for a while."

Sunny snaps his fingers. "A perfect reason to enter it, each day is a cash prize winner. Enter yours on the last Friday two weeks from now, that's when the big shot artist shows up along with other rich friends. This world is competitive, but I believe you'll do well with enough motivation and focus."

Aurelia's heart swells as she hears the man's compliment. "Really?"

"Hell," he chuckles. "You don't need me to tell you that, Aurelia."

Aurelia looks down and shrugs a bit. She was not that confident in some of her pieces, she wasn't even confident that she could complete Arthur's class, but here she is, sitting in front of a man who saw the portfolio that she sent in a year before she was even a senior in high school. She used to be so confident in her work as a kid, but she could see all the flaws and brush strokes in her older work that she wishes she could fix now. How could she believe what he's saying?

Sunny sighs and taps his finger on the top of the sign up sheet. "Just think about it. It'll be a great opportunity for you. Trust me. I wouldn't have called you to this meeting and begged you to join like this if I didn't think you could really do well here."

Aurelia looks at the paper one final time before picking up the pen again, signing her name for next, next, Friday. This was the whole point of attending the school, it was to get her work out there as well as learn from others. She needed this.

"There!" He chuckles and stands from his chair. "Just bring any artwork you want at twelve noon, and then come back around six or seven."

Standing from the chair, she nods her head watching the older male walk towards his closet, but he stops before turning around. "I almost forgot to tell you."

"Yes?"

"Make sure to send your description of your work a day early, that way we can have it set up and ready the day you bring your piece." He explains crossing his arms as he thinks to himself for a second. "I'll send you a reminder if you want?"

Nodding, she smiles at the man. "That would be great, actually."

"Good!" he snaps before two people walk into his office bombarding him with questions.

She tries to contain her laughter as he scolds the two students before answering their questions separately. Sunny looks over their shoulder and nods slightly while waving goodbye to her subtly. Aurelia mouths goodbye before leaving his office, closing the door behind her. She had the flyers for the study rooms in her hand before she shoved them neatly in her bag on her shoulder.

"Aurelia!"

She looks up and smiles, greeting Adrian with a small hug. "Hey, you."

"I see Sunny convinced someone else huh?" He crosses his arms, causing her to look over his strong forearms, probably from kneading clay to use for his sculptures. She could also see the dry clay on his hand and arms as well. She couldn't help but stare since he was at least a foot and a few inches taller than her.

"Yeah," she laughs before meeting his gaze. "It could be a good opportunity for me."

"For sure," he nods and nods, motioning for her to follow him. Since she had time, she followed him across the hall from the current area they were in, and through the glass doors was where the potters and sculptors were working. "I took the opportunity my second year, since no one really noticed me freshman year."

"I'm sorry." She laughs softly.

"I mean, that's the effect of living in the shadows of your twin." He shrugs and leads her to his work area.

She's shocked at the neatness of his space. It reminds her of his car. Pristine and neat. She wishes she could be this organized with her work space, but she works best in the mess.

"This is what I'm entering," he uncovers the sculpture he is working on. It seems to be an unfinished bust, a sculpture of a human torso, the head and arms are missing, but she could tell it's intentional. The details are amazing, making her really take in his hard work for what it is.

"I still need to smooth some things out," he explains, pulling his stool up and sitting on the edge while resting his foot on the footrester. "I also need to add a few more details."

"Adrian," Aurelia admires his work further, by taking a closer look. "It's beautiful."

"I know," he laughs. "But, it could still use some touch ups."

Aurelia pushes his shoulder playfully and sighs softly. "Wow... I'm starting to envy your confidence."

He laughs again and shakes his head. "I'm only confident because I'm confident in this piece. If you were to say that when I did that,"

She looks past him seeing an angel sculpture with medium sized stone wings. Her mouth hangs open for a moment, before she hits him playfully while whining slightly. "Adrian, that looks so good, what are you talking about?!"

"I could've added more details to the hair, and hello, the arms look flat too. I hate that thing, I've been entering it since I started getting notice. Hopefully someone wants it for cheap." he sighs and looks at her again. "Anyway-"

"Adrian?" Two girls walk up, one standing rather close to Adrian while eyeing Aurelia down.

Aurelia is all too familiar with this look, this was the same look Jackie has been given her since she got to this city. "Who's this?"

Adrian looks over his shoulder, smiling widely before nodding at Aurelia. "Aurelia this is my friend, Rochelle, and Rochelle this is my friend, Aurelia. Oh, and this is her friend Becky. They are both in this department as well."

Friend?

Aurelia could tell from the way she's inching closer to the male that she is making her claim. Lucky for her, she only sees Adrian as a friend and nothing more. She just wishes she didn't glare her down like that. She clears her throat and holds her hand out.

"Nice to meet you." she politely says, causing the girl to shake her hand firmly and her friend doing the same thing. "I should let you get back to work Adrian, I'll call you later."

"See you later," he smiles at her before turning around to talk to Rochelle.

Aurelia sighs and shakes her head before walking over to Arthur's class early. It would give her an hour alone to catch up. She works best with music playing low in her ear rather than silence. She turns to one of her favorite songs from her inspired playlist, and sets her canvas on the easel. She takes her granite pencil and begins to sketch carefully. As she allowed herself to guide the pencil across the once blank canvas, she could see two figures coming together, but she wasn't sure what it was.

It felt like she was sitting there for hours, but when she used her knuckle to turn the song off, only ten minutes passed. She places her granite pencil down and wipes her hand on her cargo pants before pulling her head-phones off.

"What is this..." she whispers to herself before groaning out of frustration.

A gentle touch caresses her waist and a soft deep voice tickles her eardrums. "I think it's coming along well."

She gasps and turns around seeing the blonde male she hadn't expected to be present. He is laughing to himself before he walks closer, looking over her work. Aurelia still had a frown on her face, glaring at him.

"You can't just sneak up on me," she says, crossing her arms, but the man just ignored her, looking at her unfinished work. "I could've pepper sprayed you."

"But you didn't," he glances at her, before he gives her canvas more attention than her. "I don't know what you're talking about. If you keep working on it, I'm sure it'll turn out well."

Aurelia crosses her arms and rolls her eyes. "I could've told myself that, but I can tell it's not going to be good enough. Why are you here anyway? I thought you graduated already?"

He sighs and crosses his arms. "I was called to motivate Arthur's new students since he had an interview that he couldn't decline in another country."

She sighs and pulls a stool up to her canvas, staring at her work. Arthur's input on the new state of her piece would've motivated her enough to finally see where she is going with the art piece, but of course, a guy like that would rather prioritize his reputation than a bunch of college students thriving to live life like him.

"Great..." she mumbles. "So much for being the only freshman to make it to his class."

Elijah glances at her, his staring not going unnoticed, but she is too nervous to meet his gaze. He walks closer giving her no choice but to look at him this time. "Can I touch you?"

She can feel her breath quicken as she searches his eyes to see if he's serious. "Touch me?"

"Not in that way," he tells her, grinning slightly before shaking his head at her impure thoughts. "I want you to remember something about art."

Aurelia pulls her gaze from his and slowly nods. "Yes."

Elijah's large hands grip her wrist gently and slowly walk behind her. His lips brushed against her ear, making her heart race. "Art isn't always about this..."

He drags his fingertips up her arm, past her shoulder, caressing her jaw and cheek before tapping her temple. "If you think too much about it, your passion becomes lost in the piece. If you lose the passion, you lose the piece."

His deep whispers has her chest rising and falling at a rather slow, but quick pace. She could feel herself shiver as he brought her hand over her heart. Elijah covers her hand with his, the sound of his voice still teasing her eardrums.

"Remember where that passion comes from," he whispers, "right here, if you don't feel it, don't take that pencil or brush to the canvas until you do."

After a few seconds of silence, she can sense that he's grinning at her silence. As he appears in front of her again, she is right. Elijah had that smile on his face, that smile that made her swallow air and her race for no reason at all.

"Hopefully that helped, Aurelia." he tells her as the rest of the students begin to walk into the classroom. Elijah winks at her subtly before explaining the situation to the other students walking into the area.

Aurelia couldn't breathe. The man made it harder for her to focus. She clears her throat and excuses herself from the room. With fifteen minutes to spare, she rushes to the bathroom, finding the first empathy stall. She shuts herself in and sits there panting heavily, covering her chest.

What was that?

□

eleven

an artist sometimes lay everything out bare for the world to see, even the darkest of emotions get brought to the light.

Elijah couldn't fight the grin covering his face as he sees the timid, yet quite stubborn, girl excuse herself from the room. He just shakes his head, knowing exactly what he did will cause her all sorts of emotions. He is a tease. He loves teasing people, especially the ones who are just as stubborn as him.

"As I said," Elijah crosses his arms, not falling stranger to the stares he gets from everyone present in the room. "Arthur will be back on Wednesday, I'm just here because I had time. It's nice to see the school I've been trying my hardest to get out of."

He says sarcastically, but his tone is all amusement. It causes the students present to laugh softly before they begin to work. Elijah leans against one of the stools far from the working area so he wouldn't distract them. He still has fifteen minutes before their actual class time starts, so he decides to take his time looking over his co-workers, and employees, messages about the parlor. Of course, Adrian tells him he'll be late again, and he already informed his clients.

Elijah expected this when he hired Adrian. Sure, in the beginning, he couldn't stand Adrian. He rightfully judged him due to the nature of his brother. He thought, if Aiden got his partner hooked on drugs, and involved with them in general, who's to say that Aiden's twin, Adrian, isn't the same way? When he was cutting down to the right people for the positions, he had to spend a week with Adrian to see if he's really different. Fortunately, Adrian is the complete opposite of Aiden. In fact, Elijah realized they had a lot more in common than he expected.

Just like Adrian, he too lived in the shadows of his brother, and he technically still does live in the shadows. The famous painter extraordinaire, Arthur James, is his older brother. Even his known name is overpowering his birth name—Elijah James. Some people don't even realize that they are brothers, simply because he was the idiot art prodigy who turned down fame for a tattoo parlor, but Arthur is the art genius, who made millions on his most popular piece, joyous lust, a piece well known in the art world.

Anyway, similar to Adrian, Elijah was neglected and ignored by his mother. Not because of a different hobby, he and Arthur love art and took it seriously, and one thing his and Arthur's mother did do was encourage her sons to work hard in what they are passionate about. His mother neglected him because he came out to her. He would've never thought coming out as bisexual to his mother would cause her to treat him as if he never existed. As if he was a ghost that lingered. Even though Arthur doesn't treat him like shit, like Aiden does to his twin brother, Elijah could sympathize with him that much. So in the end, the man ended up getting the position at his parlor.

"Hey, Elijah, can you give me some suggestions?" one of the people in the room calls out to him.

Elijah slides his phone into his pocket and walks over to the male sitting at the stool and easel just a few feet in front of him. His eyes glanced over the piece, truly amazed by the skillful brush strokes and the creativity. However, he could tell there is no passion. He could also tell that he, the male who's the owner of the piece, wasn't confident in it himself.

Pulling on his signature smile, Elijah crosses his arms over his chest and leans down to the male ear. "Do you love this piece?"

The male swallows and shrugs his shoulders.

"Then there's your suggestion," he tells him. "Put your brush down and look within yourself to know what made you start this artwork to begin with. Find that passion."

The male nods and takes a deep breath before pulling his sketchbook out from his bag. Elijah continues to walk around, looking at everyone's piece carefully. It seems like his brother, Arthur, has too much impact on these people. They lost their flair, what made them good because they are trying to please him rather than please themselves. They lack a lot of confidence. He doesn't blame them though, getting in the class took a lot, and maintaining the right mindset to keep up would definitely be a lot for them to handle.

Just as he moves on to the next person, his eyes land on the girl of the hour. The only reason he's here.

He told them he was only present at this moment because his brother, Arthur, couldn't think of anyone else to fill in for him. Little did they know, he only agreed because he heard a pretty freshman with a lot of talent was in Arthur's class, and she happened to be the only freshman in his class. Being the flirtatious curious individual that he is, Elijah wanted to see if the rumor was true. Now that he knows the rumor happened to refer to the first person to ever turn him down, it made him realize they didn't give her the justice she deserved.

Aurelia is beyond the word pretty. The girl's aura alone is absolutely beautiful, and her eyes are full of passion. He could spend hours looking into her pretty dark brown eyes. He could tell that his teasing definitely distracted her, and her flustered expressions tell him a lot. Making his way toward her, he stands there beside her, watching slowly sketch out more soft lines.

He could tell from her hand slowly guiding the granite pencil across the canvas, that she wasn't certain. Elijah steps forward, tilting his head at her piece.

"You need to relax more," he tells her quietly, watching her face frown up a bit before she sighs under her breath. "I'm only giving you advice, love."

"Advice that I didn't ask for." she mumbles quietly before crossing one knee over the other and folding her arms under her breast.

Elijah lets out a sound of amusement, and looks down at his boots before shaking his head. "I am technically your professor, Aurelia."

"You are merely a substitute," she declares. "A sub that's distracting his student from her work."

"Elijah?"

The blond male turns around to see the person two easels down call out for him. He knew him, in fact he's well acquainted with the guy. He has been to his parlor a few times, but most of the time it wasn't for the tattoos. There were times where he only showed his face around for the intimacy, which he does mind. Giving the male a slight nod, he turns his attention towards the scolding girl. He could tell from her soft glaring that she didn't appreciate the attention he was giving her.

"Someone is asking for your advice," she says quietly before bringing her pencil back up to the canvas. "Why don't you go help them rather than distract me?"

Elijah laughs quietly to himself. He didn't think he was distracting, in fact, most of his actions, especially towards her, were him trying to get to know her, but she had been keeping a distance. Her stubbornness and unwillingness to get to know him reminded him of the earlier days when he first met Andrew back when he was in his junior year, here at the art college. Back then, Andrew was an attractive guy that everyone wanted.

He was known as the sophomore that had everyone hypnotized by his dancing. At the time, Elijah wasn't into the dancers, he only interested in the theater and art students. However, one big event, the event he didn't want to go to. It wasn't the typical event that you attend with company and walk around to different booths. He would be much more willing to go if the event was a normal one, but this one was created by the dance department. They would hold a dance performance to promote the department for the freshman who didn't choose a major yet, but he thought it was just their excuse to show off their best dancers.

Grace, his long time best friend, ended up dragging him to the event because she didn't want to go alone. It was at that event when he actually acknowledged Andrew. They made it just in time for the performance, and it was a typically mega performance with different dance styles having a few seconds to dance before the next group moved on to the next dance group.

It was dark and cold that night. Elijah remembered complaining quietly to Grace about it, but he stopped talking when the lights changed and three people came out. The crowd got louder, and when he saw Andrew, it left him stunned. His aura was captivating. He could tell right away why everyone was obsessed with him more than they were with him. Even if some, and by some, just Grace, told him countless times before that this love at first sight thing was just in his head at the time.

She was dead wrong though.

He's sure it was love at first sight. Otherwise he wouldn't have been so infatuated with him. Elijah didn't really dive deep in the song he was dancing to, but the song playing made him focus on him. It was like he was the only one dancing. Though the moment was short, after his group quickly moved off the stage for the next group, Elijah was just standing there still stunned. After the big performance ended, he told Grace he would catch up with her, and quickly made his way to the stage. He knew he had to be behind it, since he heard the cheering over the music playing for the event. As many people begin to walk back to the building, he spotted Andrew amongst the people.

He remembered grabbing his wrist to talk to him, and he frowned and snatched his hand away from him. From that moment, they couldn't get enough of each other. Now, watching the scolding girl made his smile slightly fade, since it brought old memories up. He clears his throat before pulling his smile back to his lips.

He turns around slowly before walking over to the guy who called him over. Once he gets to him, he looks over his shoulder and grins.

"Why do you always attract the pretty ones?" He asks, dipping his brush in the little pile of paint. "I remember the campus being slightly pissed that you ended up snatching Andrew away."

Elijah grins and crosses his arms as he looks over the male's work. "It's not like I got a leash on him, we both live in the lifestyle we are comfortable with."

"Well, I wouldn't be in an open relationship if I had either one of you." he comments, causing Elijah to see right through him. He quickly finds out the real reason he called him over.

"Is that so?"

He nods and looks over at Aurelia again. "Especially when word on the street, Andrew found him a cute painter with pretty brown eyes. Seems like you two are more connected than you think."

"We just got a good taste in women." He says with an amused tone before taking hold of his hand, and twists his wrist gently. "Now focus. Steady your wrist, it makes your lines look sloppy."

The male looks at him before looking at his hand, nodding his head before positioning his hand correctly. Elijah winks at him before moving around the room, making sure he gives pointers and advice to everyone, and when he got back to Aurelia, he put his teasing on a pause and allowed her to focus. It gave him enough time to analyze her.

He could see why Andrew would find her physically attractive, she was pretty, and not your typical pretty. Everything about her just screams pretty. Now that he thought about it, just using the word pretty wasn't enough to describe her. He would work on that, for now, he needs to work on getting on her good side.

He pulls his gaze from her and onto her work.

He could see two shapes of something coming to life, a cloud maybe, but she is still in her head with it. It's turning out a lot better than it was before, and he could almost feel the emotion she's trying to showcase.

"Are you angry?" He asks her, making her tilt her head at her work before nodding.

"How could you tell?"

"I can see it." He tells her truthfully, nodding at her canvas. "Even though I haven't seen any of your other work, I can tell you're an emotional artist, one who can really bring the emotions out through the piece. It's really amazing."

She finally looks at him, making him swallow a bit before coughing. He wasn't really expecting her to stare at him like that.

"Thank y-you..." she mumbles quietly, as if she's unsure if she believes his compliment or not. As she puts her granite pencil down she wipes her fingers on her pants, creating a dark ash color of her finger prints on her pants.

"If you don't mind me asking," he says, wanting to change the topic before leaning down just for her to hear him. "Did you ever solve what happened at that party? You know, with Aiden?"

She leans away and turns her head back to her artwork. He starts to wonder if he offended her in some way. Aurelia is fidgeting with her bracelet on her wrist.

"Did he hurt you?" He asks her, feeling a bit pissed, since he knows exactly what kind of guy Aiden is, so he was hoping she didn't have to go through what he did to Andrew.

She quickly shakes her head and nibbles at her lip before turning to look at him again, making his heart beat quicken. "Is there any way I could get a different roommate, or even a new place to stay? I know you don't attend here anymore, but I need some help."

Elijah tilts his head before he nods. "Maybe."

"Maybe?" She repeats quickly, confusion covering her face as she stares into his eyes, making intense eye contact.

"Uh... Yeah, well, kind of." He crosses his arms. "I don't know if it'll help, but I can put the word in for you. I'm sure they have a dorm or something for you."

Hope glosses over her eyes, making him clear his throat again. "Uh, just give me a call and we can go to the board when it's open."

Aurelia nods her head slowly and bites her lip again, nibbling at her smooth bottom lip. Elijah begins to walk away, trying to get out his stunned state of mind. He hasn't felt this way in a while, and the only person who had him feeling this way is Andrew. When the class ended, and Aurelia left, he felt like he could breathe again.

The effect made him want to chase after her, talk to her longer like he did Andrew back then. Now that he thought about it, he and Andrew spent most of their time teasing each other back then before they gave in and ended up forming a stronger bond.

Elijah leans back in the chair in the room and sighs. His quick moment of silence is ruined by his phone vibrating in his pocket. He digs in his pocket and pulls his phone out and answers it without really looking at the caller ID.

"Hello?"

"Can we meet up?" Andrew's voice fills the phone, making him sit up quickly. "Right now?"

"Y-Yeah," he's flustered, he hadn't expected him to call to meet up with him. He was expecting their conversation to start and finish like it always does. "Uh... I guess we could meet at-"

"Meet at the Eye Studio." He tells him the location, which is a dance studio he used to teach classes at, but he's sure he's probably only using it to dance since he's technically not allowed on the campus yet.

"Yeah, I'll be there."

Once he agrees, Andrew ends the call. Elijah stands up from the chair and pushes his phone in his pocket before walking out of the room. This would be the first time they meet in person since he has been back. He didn't know why, but he was starting to feel anxious. Perhaps he doesn't know if he could hold back if he sees him. He hasn't kissed or held him since he got back to the city. He wanted to give him the space he knew he needed, since everything went downhill for him since his friends got him hooked on hard pills.

The memory of his state when he found him at that party, unconscious on the bed. If genesis hadn't called him, he's sure that he would've...

Elijah quickly shakes the memory out of his head before quickly making his way down the stone steps to the parking lot, which wasn't that far since the long path led right to the parking lot. Once he gets to the car, he gets another call, he halts his steps to answer his phone.

"Yeah?"

"Elijah, mom wants us to meet her this weekend." His brother tells him, making him close his eyes before leaning against his car. "I know you don't want to, but she has an announcement to make."

"Arthur, you could've just texted me." Elijah says, opening his eyes before getting into his car.

"Yeah, so you could ignore my message? Calling you will leave you no choice but to show up and not go phone silent all week. Be there, I mean it."

Elijah hangs up and gets into his car, holding his head before quickly pushing that behind him, and makes his way to the studio. He just knows Andrew is going through a lot, and he knows the last thing Andrew wants from him is pity, but he needs Andrew just as much as he needs him.

That's why they fit together so well. There's no separating them.

□

Andrew Dance from the past (for those who want a visual)

https://youtu.be/VA4HwopPzOE

twelve

Art is driven by emotions, and emotions make the madness in your work beautiful.□

TW: mention of drugs usage and mention of self-inflicted injuries.

□

Not here.

Is the phrase Elijah continuously repeats in his head. It is the only thing keeping him from losing himself further into the moment with Andrew. Though his mind is telling him to stop their intimacy, stop this passionate kiss they both have been waiting for weeks to have, his body just couldn't listen to him. Or in this case, his inner conscience didn't want to stop it. Not this time. The phrase is louder, overpowering the logical one. He's no stranger to the thrills he experiences with Andrew.

When they were in their first two moments of dating, their sex drive was high, through the roof. Andrew wanted to sleep together after every dance practice, after every work shift, and even when they went to parties together. Of course, since Elijah had the stamina, he didn't mind it. He loves the thrill, he loves the thrill he gets when he and Andrew have risky moments like the one they are having now. On the wooden floor of a dance studio room. The same room Andrew had just been dancing in. The music is still on, loud, loud enough to keep their noises contained if they were to take it that far.

If Elijah allows it to go that far, He knows why Andrew pounced on him the moment he got inside the studio room. Even he wanted to pounce on him as well. Pin him against the mirror the moment he laid eyes on him. However, they have a lot to speak about, though he didn't want to talk about it here, he still believes the conversation needs to happen. They haven't seen each other until this point. The only thing he heard was his voice, and how sad his tone was over the phone. He missed dancing. He missed the university, but they blamed him for everything. They ruined the one thing he had to escape.

"Stop," Andrew complains into the kiss, while gripping the bottom of Elijah's shirt and pulling it over his head. "Fucking stop, Eli."

Elijah knows what he is telling him to stop for. He is telling him to focus on the moment, stop thinking. He couldn't though. No matter how exciting and thrilling this moment is, he has too many questions for him, questions that can ease his mind and worry less about him. Conversations that can make it easier for him to cope with this new lifestyle. One he had no choice to live now, because he knows Andrew. He's spending these days getting drunk and partying with the very people he shouldn't even be around.

Andrew pulls from the kiss abruptly, panting heavily. Their lips were swollen, their eyes dazed with lust and desire, and their heart racing quickly. His naturally wavy hair is curling from the sweat on his forehead from dancing for hours before he called him here. The mirrors her starting to fog up, from the moistness from the room. Elijah loves when he looks like this, but he really has to control himself at this moment.

Panting, Andrew stares into his eyes, leaning in to kiss him again, but he stops himself. Annoyance gleaming over his gaze, piercing them deeply into his own. He's upset.

"I told you to stop." Andrew leans back, pushing his hair back. "I hate when you do that, just focus on me. Not whatever the fuck you're thinking about."

"Andrew," Elijah says through his own heavy pants, sitting up from the hard wooden floor onto his elbows, which hurt a lot more now that the thrill is wearing off. "We have to talk... It's been nearly a month."

"Two and a half weeks is a month now?" Andrew pushes at Elijah's shoulders, causing him to fall back onto the floor before standing from his position that he had been straddling his lap.

Elijah sits up entirely this time, his head shielding himself from becoming frustrated with him. He had to choose everything he said cautiously. "Don't do this..."

"Do what?" Andrew's voice rises and his eyebrow furrows.

Elijah stands up from the floor, grabbing his shirt in the process. He pulls it over his head quickly, taking a deep breath before speaking again. "Don't shut me out. Close me off from what you're thinking about."

"I was thinking about fucking right here, and right now." He grins fakely before it drops instantly. "But you ruined it with your loud ass thinking."

Elijah runs his hand over his face, holding it over his mouth for a moment before speaking again. "You know that is not what I was getting at, you know that." He reaches out to hold his hand but Andrew pulls his hand further from his reach and glares deeply.

"I called you here, didn't I?" he snaps, walking over to the stand where his phone is plugged into the stereo. "I wanted to see you and now that you're here, you want to talk instead of fuck?"

"Don't treat me like the others." Elijah's frustration peels through his words. "I would never treat you like the people I sleep with and you shouldn't do that to me. As much as I miss touching you, and kissing you, that can wait. I'm not an animalistic beast with no sympathy and care for you."

Andrew turns around, his eyes slightly lowered, narrowed with anger. "What?"

He didn't mean to say it in that way using the tone he did, but Elijah needs him to know his limits as well, and saying things like that really does pisses him off sometimes. Those words only slip out in moments like this for Andrew, when the tension between is on a high and they are getting ready to argue again

"You know what, fuck you, Elijah." He glares at him, his eyes fill with hate, causing Elijah to realize his mistake quickly. "You are the last fucking person I want to hear this shit from."

"Andrew-"

"I knew you only showed up to play twenty-one questions with me, and find out what's wrong with me. I don't want or need your pity and since you want to know what I'm feeling, fine! I'll tell you what's wrong with me!" Andrew slams his phone down and raises his arms, both, high in his face. "This! This was the result of my own decisions. I got hooked on the happy pills and couldn't stop!"

Andrew's arms were full of scratches, ones that look self-inflicted. He's sure these were the marks of withdrawal when he was in the rehabilitation facility. Seeing them pains him, but he knew this was because he didn't choose the right words or tone.

"I did the drugs! I kept taking them over and over again! No one forced them down my throat! This is my fucking fault!" He yells in his face before looking down at his hands. "So don't give me that pity bullshit. I expect that from strangers and the people I fuck, but I not from you."

"That's not true." Elijah didn't believe that this was all his fault. "This being all on you is not true."

Everyone could tell Aiden never liked Andrew. Even though they party with the same friends group, people could tell Aiden just really didn't like him. Elijah only knew that back then because Aiden didn't like him either. When they crossed paths he would purposefully say things or bump him to provoke him, but Elijah is much more mature than he is. Aiden despises them and even after Andrew's overdose scare, he still used that time to spread rumors and throw hate in his direction.

Who's to say that Aiden didn't pressure Andrew to take those drugs, he is the one who distributes them. Most people know he sells them at his parties. This could definitely be that entire group fault as well.

"Don't you fucking start-"

"Yeah? Getting you hooked on them is a form of forcing them down your throat! They kept them around you, can't you see that? Can't you see that they are to blame?" Elijah snaps slightly, fed up with him blaming himself when the real culprits are the ones who bought and gave him the drugs to begin with. "How can they call you their friend when they kept you around that shit, pressure you to take them."

Andrew shakes his head. "You weren't there."

"Andrew, I know what kind of fucking people-"

"No!" He snaps. "You weren't fucking there, Elijah! You don't know what the hell... no, I'm not doing this."

Andrew slaps his hand away and walks to the other side of the room, gathering his duffle bag and hoodie. As he forces the hoodie over his head, Elijah walks after him, gripping his wrist, stopping him from leaving.

"Let me go!" Andrew snatches from him again, making the man frown a bit.

Elijah grips both of his shoulders and pins him against the mirror, a lot harder than he intended, but he didn't want him to leave. That was the last thing he wanted from this. Elijah presses his forehead against his, closing his eyes in frustration. He needs to calm down, hoping Andrew would use this moment to calm down as well.

Elijah wanted to talk. He did but he didn't want to talk about all of this at the moment. Not in his only place to escape reality. He didn't want to talk about this inside a dance studio, his place of comfort, but Andrew left him no choice. He planned on leaving the studio with him, bringing him back to his place, ordering food, helping him whine down before finding it comfortable to talk about his plans if the college rejects him. However, that didn't happen. He hates hearing him blame himself for this, when it's not his fault.

"Andrew, please," He says, sliding his hand down the mirror, cupping the back of his neck. "I'm sorry, okay? I'm sorry I brought all this up right at this moment, but please..."

Elijah stands up straight cupping his face with both hands, staring into his eyes. "Please stop pushing me away. I want to know what you're thinking. I want you to talk to me about everything like you used to. I hate when we fight, you know that."

Silence falls over then for a few moments, their hearts slow down to their normal pace. Their breathing returns steady, and after a few seconds more they were both calm. They weren't completely calm, it didn't magically wash away, but they were calm enough to know that all the shouting and fighting is exhausting. Andrew sighs, taking Elijah's wrist in his hand, running his thumb over his carpal bone before pushing gently at the male's shoulder. Signaling that he understands.

Elijah smiles cautiously. Of course he didn't move yet, he didn't want to. The blonde male leans forward a bit, kissing him softly. At least that was his intention. Kissing Andrew always turns a lot more passionate in moments like this. After their small spat. As they share yet another kiss, it isn't steamy and lustful as the one before. This one is a lot more tamed, calm, and slow. The passion slowly consumes for a few moments before Andrew actually pushes him away.

"God," Elijah sighs happily, leaning closely to his ear. "I missed you."

Andrew pushes him away again, turning his head before letting out a defeated sigh. "Yeah, you said that forty million times already." He picks up his duffle bag again and begins to walk to the door.

"Did you not miss me or something?" Elijah follows behind him, pulling the hair tie out of his messy hair, so he could fix it to the ponytail he had in before.

Andrew ignores him and puts his hood to his oversized hoodie on before walking through the lobby of the studio quietly. Once they are outside and making their way to his car, Elijah took this moment to watch Andrew from afar. He knows he needs a lot more time before completely opening up to him, but he's just glad their conversation didn't end over a phone call. Especially when those phone calls were about nothing.

"So, how's everything with your parents?" Elijah asks him as he walks around to the driver's seat, unlocking the door before getting inside.

As Andrew puts his duffle bag in the back seat, and sits in the front seat, leaning the seat all the way back. His silence is enough of an answer for him. He kind of figures that he has been ignoring his parents calls. Andrew's parents aren't horrible, they love him, and they loved Elijah a lot more than he expected them to. However, when the news got out that Andrew was rushed to the hospital of course Elijah called his parents. Even though that decision was the right one to do at the time, calling them resulted in Andrew hating him the moment he regained consciousness, and Andrew's parents hating him for not looking after him like he promised them he would.

"Well," Elijah says, starting the car up while pulling his seatbelt on. "Arthur called about my mom. Telling me to show up to whatever this gathering. I don't want to go, but I won't hear the end of Arthur if I don't show up."

"Then don't go." Andrew finally speaks, rocking his leg side to side. "Your mom's a bitch, no offense, and your brother is a passive aggressive asshole. I really don't see the reason for you going somewhere you don't want to go."

Elijah pulls into traffic and out of the parking spot off of the curb, and pulls up to the red light. "Apparently she has an announcement, and Arthur seemed serious about it when he called."

"If you plan on going why fucking tell me about it." He grumpily says, crossing his arms after pulling his hood further over his face.

Grinning to himself, Elijah places a hand on his knee as he drives. He just wants to stop him from shaking his leg. He knows it's an anxiety thing, or even anger, but Andrew never realizes he does it sometimes, so he would subtly stop him from doing it.

"I might as well go," he tells him. "If it is serious announcement, I could fuck up the mood by saying something stupid or just simply exist, let my mother tell it."

Andrew stifles a laugh. "Idiot."

Elijah stops at another red light, pulling his hand away from Andrew's leg and back to the steering wheel, switching hands so he could lean on his other hand. As the silence falls over them again, he turns the radio on, planning jazz, something he prefers over all and every music. On the ride back to his place, he couldn't help but think about the scars on Andrew's arms. He didn't want to bring that up at this moment.

"Are you planning on covering them? With a tattoo?" He asks Andrew. "You know I'd do it."

Andrew pulls his hood off and pulls his sleeve down. "What do you think I could put over them?"

Elijah glances over at him and shrugs. "I think you should come up with something meaningful to you, and let me know."

Andrew nods and digs into his jeans pocket and pulls out a box of cigarettes. He rolls the window down and lights one of the cigarettes he got from out of the box. Of course, he's smoking at a time like this.

"Give me one?" He asks, leaning over, eyes still on the city street. Once he stops at another traffic, Andrew puts a cigarette between his lips and lights it for him just before the light changes.

The two of them sat comfortably in silence, the drive back to his place was going to take a while, he didn't live too far but with the city's traffic, he's sure it took about an hour to get to his penthouse. Perks of making lots of money from art and his brother being awfully generous. As he parks in front of his building, Andrew gets out first, not giving him time to turn the engine off. He gathers his things and walks through the door and towards the elevator at the end of the lobby hall.

Elijah follows him, after locking his car door. As he walks inside, he greets the man at the front desk lobby and continues down the hall where Andrew is patiently waiting for him. He walks up beside him and puts his key into the elevator, causing it to open. The both of them step inside and wait for the doors to close before they are standing in silence.

"I need to shower." Andrew suddenly announces.

Not looking at him, Elijah chuckles and pushes his hands into his pockets. "Are you asking me to join you?"

When the doors to the elevator opens to his penthouse, Andrew steps off of the elevator, removing his shoes and dropping his duffle bag to the side. "I'm not asking."

Andrew walks away from him, hands deep into the pockets of his hoodie as he makes his way down the hall where the bathroom is located.

"I'll be there in a second!" Elijah tells him as he opens the bathroom door before going inside.

Elijah walks in the opposite direction, going straight to his kitchen. The penthouse wasn't huge, just the normal size. He had a loft office space for his painting, the living and kitchen was an open concept, and down the hall were doors to the bathroom and two bedrooms. He is in the kitchen to clean the few things he had in the sink. He could hear the shower running as he finished the last cup in the sink. As he makes his way down the hall, he gets a phone call.

He stops just outside the bathroom door, pulling his phone out of his pocket, looking at the caller ID. Elijah hadn't expected her to call so soon, but that didn't stop him from answering the call right away.

"Hey," He says in his playful tone. "I didn't think you would call this soon."

"Are you free saturday? We can go to the board together." Aurelia mumbles on the phone, nerves hidden in her words as if she never talked to someone on the phone before. "I have a lot to do next week, so I don't know if I'll be able to find a day to go with you."

He couldn't help but smile. How can she make his heart race like this without even seeing her. "I'm busy this weekend, but don't worry about it. I'll talk to some people that I know to see if they could help me help you. Okay?"

"I... I know I sort of asked for help, but I don't want to burden you with my problems." She says quietly into the phone, making him lean against the door frame to the bathroom, watching Andrew shower alone.

"It's really no burden, I'll try to help you out of the shit situation you're in right now." He could hear a sigh of relief from the other end making him smile wider. "I have to go now. I'll call you later, baby."

He couldn't resist not teasing her before he ended the call. Elijah could almost picture her reaction to him calling her that. Smiling to himself, he removes his clothes and steps into the shower with Andrew. As the two practically pounce on each other in the shower, Elijah couldn't shake the deepest feeling of excitement adding to their mix of intimacy.

Was it because of her?

□

thirteen

Within the fortress of anger, shielding all it touches, art emerges as a sanctuary for our reality. However, unlike anger, art chooses not to conceal but to reveal, unraveling the tapestry of emotions, ensuring that no sentiment remains hidden or untouched.

Aurelia sits at the counter in the small kitchen space. Her phone is pressed against her ear and the purple gel pen is resting on her bottom lip. She waits for the call, trying to drown out the terrible background music. It has been twenty minutes since the man on the other end told her to hold. Twenty hold minutes of the same song being played over and over again. Her arm grows tired as she waits, causing her to pull her phone from her ear and just deciding to end the call. She lets out a long sigh before scratching out the retail job number and location on her notepad.

"I got thirty minutes before my next phone interview," she murmurs to herself as she reaches for her mug filled halfway with tea. "Thirty minutes to apply for more campus jobs."

Aurelia slowly begins to search the campus website, looking through the open positions available. She didn't need the money, but it would be irresponsible of her to spend the money in her savings account for little trinkets and other things when it could be saved for something important. Her parents made sure she was comfortable with money during her college days, but they didn't want her to rely on their money.

"You never ask for money," her father said as he chopped onions to put in the soup he was making. Her mother was on her way from the hospital, since she was done with the important patients already, and her father wanted to cook since it would be the first time, after a while, since they all sat down at the expensive dinner table to eat. Aurelia was sitting at the kitchen island serving as verbal support, since her father never really taught her the ways around the kitchen.

"But since You're moving out and to another state in less than a month, I think we should have that conversation." He continued before he began to chop the other half of the onion.

Aurelia picked up half of the carrot that he chopped and bit into it. "What conversation?"

"The money conversation." Her father swiped the onions into the medium sized pot and wiped his hand after with the towel that was hanging over his shoulder.

"Your mother and I saved up a little over thirty thousand in your college funds. The school you're going to attend in a month, tuition is no joke, but the money should help you get by for your first two years." Her father began to explain. "But you need to look for jobs earlier on, because who's to say that this art thing is going to help with financial stability?"

That day, she thought it was a no-brainer that she would need to find a job, but her father seemed troubled. Like, he wanted to tell her something but couldn't find the right words.

"I know. I know I need back plans just in case my art does get me nowhere." She told him with a smile, so he wouldn't feel guilty for saying what was on his mind. "That's why I'm also taking art history, and with my degree, I can always become an art teacher. A teacher just like you, pops."

She remembered her father smiling before he wrapped his arms around her. Pulling her into a tight hug. "I don't know why I'm so worried. You're all grown up, and it's clear you have it all figured out. I'm proud of you sweetheart."

"You and mom don't have to worry anymore," she told him as she pulled from the huh. "You, mom, and my friends all supported me up to this point. I can handle the rest on my own."

Aurelia smiles to herself at the heartfelt memory with her father. She didn't think that memory would pop up at a stressful time, such as this moment right now, but she embraced it. Allowing it to consume her heart so she could feel a little less stress. Her parents made sure to embed the idea of saving the money they give her for emergencies. So, she's looking for a job to make money on the side so she can spend on whatever she wants.

As she sits there, comfortable in the silence of the home, the empty home. The home where two are supposed to share, but it seemingly became her home. That didn't last though. The front door knob twists with the lock, before the sound of the door unlocking causes her to focus on who's coming in. She honestly didn't need to look to know that Jackie is the one coming through the door.

Jackie hasn't been at home since the party she threw. Aurelia also hasn't spoken or seen her since then either. Not around campus or even at the local markets. She knows the girl is to be avoiding her, but now that she's here, there isn't anywhere for her to run off to, unless she runs out the doors again.

Aurelia watches Jackie stumble into the house with multiple bags of snacks and clothes. As they make eye contact, Jackie rolls her eyes and puts everything on the couch not too far from the front door. She's dressed in a familiar hoodie, a hoodie that she only really sees Aiden in. It's obvious that she spent all that time away at her boyfriend's place. At least she can push the worry out of her mind. Jackie wasn't very deserving of her sympathy.

"Oh," she says, crossing her arms. "You're still here."

"Unfortunately, I am." Aurelia turns around to look at her laptop again, scrolling through the website, trying to find something that's at least part time.

Jackie begins to look through the bags, pulling out three party size bags of different flavors of potato chips. "Why are you? Didn't you say you were going to the housing board or something? Why aren't you gone?"

Aurelia turns around in the stool, pulling her attention away from her task, crossing her arms this time. "I don't want to be here just as much as you don't want me here. But, unfortunately, we're going to have to deal with each other until I get some help from Elijah to get a new place."

Jackie walks over to the kitchen, putting a large two liter lemonade on the counter. She laughs, full on laugh, at Aurelia. As if what she had just said was the funniest thing she had ever heard in her life. What did she find funny? The idea of tolerating each other until she goes? Or was it because she mentioned Elijah would help?

"Elijah?" She repeats with a snooty tone.

So that's why she laughed.

"Elijah agreed to help you? And what you're giving up in return? Huh? You don't even look like the type that can handle someone like him." Jackie grins. "That's probably why he's interested. You're not giving him what he wants. Typical."

"What are you talking about?" Aurelia glares at her. "Sorry that there are genuine people here to help me with any catch."

Jackie shakes her head, crossing her arms as she laughs at her. "First you hang out with Andrew, and now you're receiving help from Elijah? You must be sleeping with them both. People are talking around the campus, you know."

Aurelia rolls her eyes and turns to look at her laptop screen, not caring what the girl had to say anymore.

"You can ignore me all you want," Jackie says, putting the lemonade bottles in the refrigerator. "But word of advice, sweetie, getting involved with those two isn't a good idea. Especially when one is well off with a famous brother and the other is a hardcore ex-junkie who used to sell what he used."

She hears a lot about Elijah in the art department, but she hardly hears anything about Andrew unless she's around Jackie and her friends. Aurelia knows that hearing stuff like this from Jackie is irrelevant, she prefers to hear something like this from the person that it's about. Now that she thought about it, she hasn't text or called Andrew since he left her in that library. That thought alone made her hold her head from embarrassment. What if he thought she didn't want to be friends, or even talk? Did she even want to associate herself with him?

"Did you not hear what I just said?"

Aurelia looks up and sighs. "I don't care about what you just said. Why should I listen to anything you have to say when you clearly don't like them? Everything you are saying right now could be lies, and you already proved to me twice that you aren't very trustworthy."

"If you didn't try to get with my boyfriend, I wouldn't be like this!"

Slamming her laptop close, she glares at the girl across the counter, trying not to raise her voice, but the girl was making it very hard. She has never been this upset with anyone, not since high school at some boy who claimed he just liked her that's why he picked her. At that time Sabrina and Cameron weren't close friends like they are now.

Aurelia was a freshman, she had just got told that her artwork is too amateurish to even be considered to put up in an art gallery. She was already in a very down mood, and the boy that just wouldn't leave her alone, no matter how many times she told him to stop, she blew up at him. He never looked so regretful before, but when she was done yelling at him, she took that art piece that took her months to finish and smashed it. Causing a huge scene in the cafeteria. That was when she finally poured everything out to Sabrina and Cameron, the two who have been by her side, but she just wasn't really comfortable to open up to them.

Here she is now, the same anger taking over her calm demeanor. "For the last time, I never tried to get with your boyfriend! For anything, Aiden has been flirting with me despite me turning him down constantly!"

Aurelia did it. She raised her voice, something she didn't want to do, but she did and she wasn't done. "You're so worried about me, someone who outright turned him down in your face multiple times, who you should be worried about is Genesis! Your best friend, the girl who has been getting at your boyfriend before I even showed up!"

Jackie's face drops, and she shakes her head. "No, he said it was a one time thing, you're lying."

"That night, at Tony's party, I was literally there to tell you that, but then you blew up at me! Made accusations about me wanting to be with Aiden, and then threatened me." Aurelia isn't holding her voice back at all. "He told me to show up at the party, telling me to let what I heard go, and not to tell you, but I didn't want to keep it to myself. I was there to tell you everything, everything! This is what I get for trying to give you the benefit of doubt! I did nothing wrong, and that's why I want to leave. I tried so hard to compromise with your lifestyle and all you've shown me is disrespect and nothing else!"

Jackie stands there, shock covering her face. She grabs her purse and pulls her phone out of her bag, dialing someone's number. Aurelia sits there panting softly after yelling at Jackie, she pushes her shaking hands between her thighs trying to calm down. As she tries to calm herself down, she flinches as Jackie screams.

"Aiden fuck you! You lying piece a shit! Tell Genesis if I see her I'm going to beat her ass!"

Aurelia starts to gather her things, to get away from her screaming because it isn't helping her calm down at all.

"Yes! Yes Aurelia told me the fucking truth! You liar!" Jackie walks away, stomping towards the door. "We're fucking done! Don't call me back!"

Jackie slams her phone on the floor screaming out before she falls to the floor in front of the door. With her laptop and other things in her arms, she stares at Jackie, watching her cry to herself while slamming her fist on her thigh over and over again.

"I hate you..." she mumbles as she hugs herself, leaning against the door.

Aurelia's alarm for her interview begins to go off, snapping her out of her thoughts. She was about to comfort her. Jackie. The one who doesn't deserve anything from her. Turning around, she walks up the stairs and closes the bedroom door, and collects her thoughts. After five minutes, she finally gets her interview phone call.

"Aurelia Mitchell?"

Aurelia clears her throat, trying to sound cheerful. "Yes. That's me."

"I'm Tasha Greene, the owner of the cafe you sent your application for, and after looking over your application, we think you'll be great for the job. How soon can you start?"

Aurelia's eyes widens as she hears the news, making her clear her throat again. "Wait, I thought this was an interview?"

"It was supposed to be an interview, but another one of our staff members just put their two weeks in, so we need a part-timer now. When I looked through the application, you are the only one who applied to be a part timer." Tasha explains nicely, her cheerfulness making her feel a lot more cheerful.

"In that case," Aurelia smiles. "How soon do you want me to start?"

Tasha hums on the other end, "Next week Wednesday at three? How does that sound?"

"Perfect!" Aurelia declares. "Is there a specific uniform you want me to wear?"

Tasha tells her to wear all black before they finish the call up. After yelling at Jackie and finally getting hired, things are starting to look up. All she needs now is a way out of this house. Aurelia couldn't hear Jackie crying, so she assumed she left, but that was until she hears a car and Aiden's voice outside.

"Jackie!" he calls out, before Aurelia could hear banging on the front door. "Jackie out this fucking door!"

"Go away! I hate you!"

Aurelia shakes her head, she wasn't about to sit here and listen to this, she couldn't. Looking around, she picks her headphones up and puts them over her ears.

"If you don't open this door, I'm going to kick this door down!" Aiden threatens loudly, and after five seconds, she could hear the muffle sound of shuffling before Jackie's voice is loud again.

"Don't touch me, again! You lied and told me that Aurelia was being delusional that she was making passes at you, but the truth is you just wanted to shut her up because you fucked Genesis! AGAIN!"

Sighing, Aurelia turns her music on and drowns them out. She was in bliss. She got a job and she finally let everything off her chest. This is comfortable for her-

The bedroom door slams open, causing Aurelia to flinch as Aiden approaches her with Jackie standing behind him, pulling his arm. Aiden snatches her headphones off her head and throws them across the room.

"Aiden stop!" Jackie screams, but he pushes her and points his finger in her face.

"Stay out of mine and my girlfriend's business, bitch! I let it slide once, but this time you're really starting to piss me off."

Aurelia is scared and she's sure it shows on her face.

"Aiden stop it! We aren't together anymore! Leave her alone-" Jackie screams as Aiden backhands her.

Hyperventilating. Aurelia is hyperventilating as he glares at her. Threatening her with his eyes and words. His attention wasn't even on her, but she was scared, shaking, wanting nothing more but to get out of this situation. One she didn't put herself in. One she tried so desperately to get out of before it got to this point. IS the universe punishing her for not trying harder to get away from this? Or was the universe telling her, she shouldn't have picked a different school.

Shaking, Aurelia thought of the only thing she could do, call the police. She uses the emergency call button on her phone, only for it to be snatched out of her hand and tossed with her headphones.

"I'm only going to tell you this once." Aiden leans down in her face. "You're on my bad side now, so you piss me off again... let's just hope you don't."

Aiden grabs Jackie's wrist and drags her out of the room. She could hear Jackie trying to fight him off, but the moment Aurelia hears the door slam close, she lets out the breath she was holding, and begins to cry. She is scared. She didn't want to be at the house anymore.

Stumbling over to her phone, she dials Elijah's number, crying silently. She doesn't know why she called him. All she knows is that she wanted to get out of the house. Aurelia didn't feel safe anymore, and he is the only one that can help her with the one thing she desperately wanted. A new place. A place away from Jackie and her friends. A place where she could comfortably attend her dream school without feeling like she has to look over her shoulders, or fear that something may happen to her in her sleep.

"Hello, pretty-"

"Help me..." Aurelia utters through heaves, trying to calm down, but she couldn't, not while fear is taking over her entire body.

"Aurelia? Help you?" He panics. "What do you mean? Where are you?"

Aurelia breaths in and out rapidly. "Home."

That's all it took. Elijah tells her to stay on the phone, his voice. His soothing voice, helping her calm down.

"That's it, baby, deep breaths." He says softly, she could hear the sound of a car door on his end, so she knew he was on his way.

As she slowly calms down, she begins to come from what she just endured. Who she just called and who she's waiting for. Aurelia shakes her head, hugging herself, questioning if she made the right decision coming this far, alone. She started to question if her dream was really worth it.

□

fourteen

In the existence of humans, our mistakes compose the harsh notes, but it is the harmonious colors of regret that paints growth and transforms the art inside our souls into a masterpiece on the canvas we call life.□

□

Aurelia has her knees up to her chest as she stares at the butterfly sun-catcher hanging from the rear view mirror of Elijah's car. The butterfly looks like the butterfly tattoo on his forearm. It was royal blue and hot pink, two colors she couldn't imagine going so well together.

"Pretty." She murmurs, turning her head to look at the male pacing back and forth outside the car.

The muffle sounds of Elijah's voice fills the silent car, as he has a conversation with someone. Someone she did not know. Someone she is curious about but not for the reason the campus may believe. She's curious if this person can help her. If this person can finally get her out of the student housing she was so excited to live in the beginning. Now her longing dream is turning into a nightmare.

Elijah ends the call, and sighs out of frustration. He turns around and knocks on the passenger side window. Aurelia presses the button down, letting the window down enough for him to lean into the car.

"Judging from your expression," she shyly leans away from him and avoids eye contact. "There's no one to help me out of this situation."

Elijah sighs again. "Not even my influence can help you get a new place."

Aurelia sighs and tucks her head into her knees, hugging herself tighter.

She didn't want to stay a night in the house. She didn't feel safe. Aurelia has nothing to do with everything that's going on with Jackie and Aiden. Judging from the way the man talked to her on the phone, assuming it was Genesis, they have done things together a lot more. Even Jackie confirmed that Aiden cheated more than once.

So why?

Why is she the only one suffering from this? She has nowhere to go, and she doesn't want to stay in the small home anymore. Aurelia could feel the tears coming again, and her mind clouding with doubts and regrets. Scary thoughts.

"Hey..." Elijah's smooth voice softly fills her ear. "Calm down. There's this senior I know, I think she doesn't have a roommate. If we talk to her, I'm sure she wouldn't mind."

Aurelia peeks from her knees, staring at the pretty male, who's smiling but his gaze is filled with cautiousness. He's more than likely thinking about his choice of words before he says them. He reaches into the car, his thumb gently brushing the tear from his cheek. "Don't cry, okay? There's no need to be afraid anymore."

"Is this even allowed? Am I allowed to move houses?" She asks quietly before looking at him with panic in her eyes. "What if the school-"

Elijah holds his finger up to his lips and shakes his head. "Don't worry about what the school would say. You want out of this situation, right? Trust me."

Trust Him? He wants her to Trust him. A guy she barely knows? Aurelia looks the other direction, trying to think over her other options. However, that quickly did not matter. She has no other option. It's either stay in the house she does not feel safe in or trust Elijah.

"Okay." She murmurs softly, her head slowly turns to look at the man once again. "When can I move?"

Elijah leans further into the passenger side window to pull his phone out of his pocket. He scrolls through it before tilting his head, causing his hair to that side. He hums quietly, his eyes focus on his phone screen as they slowly turn to uncertainty. "Maybe, a week from now."

"A week?" She repeats with a distraught tone behind it. "Elijah I don't think I can stay here for another week. I have to work next week too, along with classes and other things. I can't-"

"Baby," he utters that word again, cupping her cheek, gently caressing it. "Deep breaths."

Aurelia didn't even notice she was panting, and why she instantly calms down when he calls her that, and displays such intimate affection. Her heart begins to rapidly pound against her ribs, and her panting slows down as she stares into his eyes.

She hasn't felt like this before. This feeling is similar to how she feels when she's around beautiful art. Sometimes her best friends used to joke around when they saw her getting lost in any and every artwork they would see if they were walking in the park or even along the street where a lot of street murals are on the side of buildings and grounds.

"Who got you looking like that?" Cameron asked, pushing at her shoulder.

"No one!" She said carefully, panic ridden in her tone as she covered her face from embarrassment. "I think... This mural is really pretty. However, even though the colors are bright, you can feel the sadness coming from this."

"Brina needs to hurry up out of this Clinic because listening to you geek out over art isn't something I want to hear. I thought you saw a cute guy or something." Cameron mumbled, causing the girl to pout her lips slightly.

Her best friend noticed and rolled his eyes before wrapping his arm around her. "I'm kidding, Relia, I love seeing you get all excited when you talk about art. It's cute, and sometimes it makes me want to lock you away so now others can't see how cute you look."

She remembered pushing him away and covering her ears. Sabrina was guilty of it too, asking her what boy got her looking so in love, but she was disappointed to know the boy she had her eyes on died a hundredths of years ago, and all she could do is admire the statue of David, created by Michelangelo.

"He's not even that good looking and," Sabrina leaned down to her ear. "He's small as fuck."

Aurelia remembered turning toward her best friend with disbelief covering her face. "Brina the sculpture is huge! What are you talking about? He's not small at all."

Sabrina just laughed quietly and shook her head before they walked to the next sculpture together. Aurelia didn't know what was funny then, but looking back on that memory made her feel a whole lot better. However it just made her heart pound more as she sits in Elijah's care with the man still caressing her cheek.

Aurelia turns her head slowly and avoids his affection. "Where am I going to stay until I can move into the new place? I don't want to stay here, Elijah."

Elijah pulls his head out of the window and places his hands on his hips. The male thoughts were loud. He didn't know where she could stay, and now he's trying to figure out a solution on the fly.

"If you-"

"Me." He cuts her off, causing her to flinch as he refers to himself. She didn't even know what he meant by me. Her face is definitely full of confusion. "I mean, it'll be for a week. You can bring some of your things and stay with me until they are ready for you to move in."

Aurelia's eyes widen as she puts her feet down on the floor of the car. "You meant to stay with you? Like your place? Alone?"

He grins, holding his hand up to his mouth, trying to keep his laughter down. In his amusement filled tone, Elijah nods his head and speaks softly to her. "Yes, my place. I have a guest room, you could stay with me until then."

Aurelia's facial expression must've said exactly what she's thinking, because seconds later, the male walks to the driver's side to sit inside his car with her. He turns his body to look at her, giving her no choice but to face him instead of avoiding him. "I'm not a pervert, baby. There are two bathrooms, so you have a ton of privacy. Not to mention I have my own art space that can be shared, so you have room to work and stuff. I also spend most of my time at my parlor, so you would only see me in the morning and in the evening."

Did she have a choice? Of course she did. She has a choice, and it's as clear as day that the logical option is staying with Elijah for a week. What could possibly go wrong? He already told her that he's not a pervert, and the way he describes his place, it doesn't sound so bad.

"What do you say?" He asks again, waiting patiently.

Aurelia takes a deep breath, trying not to picture her mother's reaction to her agreeing to stay with a man. A man older than she is. A handsome man who has a pretty smile, nice hair, and eyes that can stir all sorts of emotions inside. She nods her head slowly, watching the man smile grow wider.

"Shall we get something from this place before we go, and before those two assholes show up again." He murmurs the last part, but she chooses to ignore it. She knew he was referring to Jackie and Aiden. They were very deserving of that title.

Nodding, again, she pulls the handle to open the passenger side door. Aurelia slowly steps out onto the sidewalk and quickly makes her way back to the house. She had just been happy to finally get a job, just for her mood to turn upside down once again. She wasn't one to blame others for her bad moods, but Jackie and Aiden, along with their friends, aren't very nice people. They cause a lot of drama and headaches, and she doesn't understand how they consider each other friends when they hurt each other.

Aurelia could hear Elijah following her inside, making her a bit nervous. She is already starting to regret agreeing to stay with him when she doesn't even know him, but if he was some psycho serial killer, she would've noticed something off about his behavior, but that's not alarming at all. He seems perfect. Really perfect.

It's just for a week.

"What made you call me?" Elijah asks as she walks through the threshold of the bedroom. "I mean, wouldn't Adrian have been a more rational choice? Why me?"

Aurelia grabs her empty suitcase, unzipping it slowly. "Adrian is Aiden's twin. Even though they have different styles, I would've been freaked out by his presence during a panic attack, such as the one I had."

He hums and begins to walk around her side of the room, looking at everything with his eyes, and occasionally touching a few stationary items she had on the desk in the room. "I see."

"Would..." she nibbles at her lip, trying not to sound so needy. It is already burdensome for him to show up on her behalf, and asking him to pack her art stuff downstairs would be way too much. "Nevermind."

"What?"

Aurelia shakes her head and folds her clothes that she would be bringing neatly, before placing them inside the small suitcase. "It's nothing."

Elijah crosses his arms, leaning against the tall dresser in the room. "You need help?"

She slowly raises her head, looking the man in his eyes. "Yes, but... you have already done so much for me. I don't want to-"

"It's fine." He declares, looking around. "What do you need help with?"

She points to the black tote bag hanging on the handle of one of the drawers. "Can you put my art supplies downstairs in that? I know you have your art space at your place, but I would rather use my own things."

Elijah takes the empty bag. "I'll be right back to help you carry that, alright?"

Aurelia nods her head again, something she has gotten used to since her words could not form words. They couldn't even utter a big thank you. He dropped everything he was doing to help her. Sure she's thankful, but perhaps that's the reason why she couldn't say thank you. Why? Why did he come running when the both of them can agree that they barely know each other? Too many uncertainties. So many questions.

It's not like she has never talked to a man before. She has done so comfortably a lot of times, but what made him different? His appearance? Or maybe it's that he's super sweet? Selfless? Aurelia shakes her head at those thoughts. Adrian is the same way, but she's not super nervous around him. He doesn't make her feel like she's out of breath? He doesn't make her heart go...boom.

After fitting a week's worth of clothes, and more, into the suitcase, she starts to fill the front of the suitcase with necessities. Such as, things for her hair, and other bathroom related things. She didn't want to leave anything. More so she doesn't want to make a second trip back to this place. The only time she wants to see this place is when she's coming back to get the rest of her things to move in with her new roommate. The roommate, the male haven't really told her much about it, but she'll just wait until the time is right to ask about it.

It's been twenty whole minutes since Elijah went down the stairs to get her things. She didn't have many art supplies, so what was taking him so long to come back? Putting her book bag on her back, she takes the handle of her suitcase and begins to carry it down the stairs.

As she makes the final step, she could see Elijah standing in front of her easel, looking at an unfinished art piece that she had plans on entering into the contest Sunny convinced her to sign up for. She slowly walks towards him, clearing her throat, but he didn't take his eyes off the piece.

"Wow." he murmurs, and turns his head to meet her gaze, earning a shy head tilt to avoid his eyes from her. "This is amazing. Did you leave the bottom half unfinished on purpose?"

Aurelia swallows and nods slowly. "I used oil paint, allowing it to drip naturally on its own."

Elijah walks towards her, making her tilt her head to look at him. "You still want to know why... Why do you deserve that spot in Arthur class?"

"W-Why?" Aurelia is curious, she tilts her head, watching his expression turn from disbelief to straight shock.

"Aurelia. Look at this. Your technique is amazing, and using oil paint can be a risky because if not used properly it could ruin you work, but you used it to your advantage, making something so fucking beautiful. You're really good, I have geeked out over art like this in a while." Elijah's compliments went on and on. Causing her to take the art piece out of his hand from embarrassment.

"Damnit, sorry I-"

"Let's go." she murmurs quietly, walking towards the door with her suitcase.

She didn't mean to sound so rude about it, she couldn't handle his compliments, so of course she felt shy. Elijah grabs her wrist, making her stop, but she doesn't turn around. She could hear him sigh near her ear before he gently pried her hand from the hand of her suitcase.

"I got it." he tells her softly.

Aurelia nods and continues to walk towards the front door. She opens it, holding open long enough for Elijah to grab the doorknob before she walks down the concrete stairs. As she got closer to his car, she could feel her heart beating throughout her body, filling her ears. She takes deep breaths as Cameron taught her and opens the bag door to his car to put her things inside.

She is really doing this.

She's really living with a man.

As she sits in the passenger seat, the soft jazz music, the same music he played the last time she was in his car, calms her nerves as she looks at her broken phone screen. Her headphones were fine, but her phone was shattered.

"Did he hurt you?" Elijah asks, breaking the silence.

Aurelia shakes her head. "He hurt my phone... it's completely shattered."

Elijah's eyes were on the road, so all he could do was nod.

"Honestly, from what you told me. There's nothing new with that news, Jackie's the one who decided to stay with him." He speaks like he personally knows them, and judging from their behavior from the party, he definitely seems like he knows the friends group. "What I'm trying to say is, you're the not the first person to tell Jackie that Aiden's a fucking prick and her so-called best friend is a snake. You're probably the only one that Aiden couldn't convince to keep your mouth shut about it."

Aurelia wants to know the full story, but not at this moment. She wants to ease her thoughts before she talks about them.

"Enough about them," he changes the subject, no-so smoothly. "Tell me a little about yourself."

"Now?" She questions, looking up from her broken phone.

"We are going to be roommates for a week, right? I want to know if you're a heavy sleepier or a light sleepier, a snorer?" He glances at her after saying that, causing her to roll her eyes and turn her head to hide her smile.

"I do not snore."

"Well I do." he tells her, making her laugh a bit. "I'm serious. Comes with being a smoker."

Aurelia plays with her fingers while cradling her phone. "I'm a light sleeper and an early riser."

Elijah makes an ah sound, causing her to nodding slowly. "Well, lucky you, I'm an early riser as well."

The two of them continue to make small talk. As in small talk, the small talk consists of Elijah asking a basic question, and she answers them with a short reply, but it was enough for them to feel somewhat comfortable around each other. His small jokes did help ease her mind as bit as well, but she still feels shaken up by the whole situation. Will anything change? Jackie didn't seem like she wanted Aiden to verbally attack and threaten her the way he did. She did get hit by him. Maybe now that she knows the truth, Jackie can finally apologize to her for being rude and disrespectful.

Perhaps Aurelia is being too hopeful.

Way too hopeful.

□

fifteen

Overthinking is akin to sketching the outline of a masterpiece; the ideas are vivid on paper, eager to be brought to life. However, each stroke, when pondered too intensely, can lead to bewilderment, causing one to lose their way within the piece, unsure of how to navigate back to the original vision. Just like overthinking.

Two days. It has been two days since she moved in with Elijah. So far everything he had told her was true. He spent most of his day out, and he comes back to his place late. In other words she didn't really see the man too much. As he told her, the only time Aurelia sees him is earlier in the morning when she's waking up to start her day. They would have very short conversations, while she drinks tea and eats the toast she made with the bread in his kitchen. Everything is perfect and comfortable for her, but why did she feel so lonely? It didn't feel like she did when she was living with Jackie, but it feels like she's living with a ghost. Is it too much to ask him for some quality time?

"Relia!" Aurelia looks at her laptop screen, seeing Cameron and Sabrina watching her. "Girl, are you okay?"

Right. She called her friends to let them know her situation. Aurelia had already told Cameron about what was going on a few weeks ago, but she never really updated him on it. This whole time she pretty much kept her thoughts and worries to herself, that is, until she called Elijah. Even after telling the man everything, from start to finish, he didn't seem that surprised by what she told him.

"Sorry." Aurelia apologizes to them both, watching them smile again, but she could feel their concern through the screen.

"Did you get a renovation or something?" Cameron comments on the room, the guest room she's staying in with a big window and a pretty view on her right. "Where are you?"

Aurelia looks down trying to muster up the courage to finally say what was on her mind to her two best friends. "I'm living with someone else."

Sabrina's face twists with confusion. "What do you mean? Why?"

"I already told Cameron, but I've had a lot of issues with my previous roommate, Jackie." Aurelia says somewhat confidently, watching Sabrina and Cameron nod their heads. "I went to the student housing board just as Cameron suggested, but when I went there, the board leader was on leave, so there was much for them to do with my situation."

"The fuck?" Cameron cursed, rolling his eyes before crossing his arms. "It was still early into the first week of classes for you. They couldn't help?"

Aurelia avoids their faces this time. "I wanted another week. I wanted to give her another chance, but then her boyfriend, and herself, were super rude and mean to me. So, i called someone, i met, and now I'm living with him."

"Can she fight?" Cameron asks, his anger flaring up. "Because if she can't I don't give a fuck, her and her little chump ass-"

"Him?!" Sabrina cuts Cameron off, causing Aurelia to finally look at her best friends. "You're living with a man?"

Cameron looks confused for a second before he gasps dramatically. "Word? Is he more attractive than me? Because I don't know how to feel about that."

Sabrina groans. "Cam shut up! This is serious. She's living with a man she just met."

Aurelia tilts her head a bit. "I didn't just meet him, but yeah, I'm slowly getting to know him."

She values her best friend's opinions, and so far she's getting mixed reactions. Cameron isn't saying much about her moving in with Elijah, but Sabrina seems so concerned, as if she made the wrong decision. Even though she downplayed everything she went through when telling the story, she was certain that she got the one point across. The one point that there weren't any other options besides this one.

"Aurelia, you know I'd never judge you or your decisions," Sabrina sighs, already giving signs that she's going to speak her mind loud and clear about all of this. "And I know you wouldn't make decisions like this unless you have to, so just be careful."

That's it? Aurelia was sure that she was going to get an earful from her best friend, but she's more relieved that she trusts her with the decision she made.

"Well, honestly," Cameron starts speaking again. "It's clear that this guy, whoever he is, got deep ass pockets. Look at her room. We can't even see all of it, and the design itself looks expensive. Aurelia, did you get a sugar daddy?"

"W-What?" her eyes widen as she quickly shakes her head. "I know he's well off, at least, that's what he told me, but no he's seriously just a good person, someone I'd definitely consider my friend."

Her best friend sighs again. "Whatever you say, baby. You ain't fooling me though."

"Stop teasing her, Cameron, can't you see you're giving her a heart attack." Sabrina scolds, causing Cameron to make faces making Aurelia laugh.

It seems like it's been forever since she talked to her best friends like this. She knows that they are busy, and she is too, but she would love to have more moments like this when they are all together having conversations about any and everything.

"Well, I have to go, Relia. Remember what I said okay?" Sabrina tells her. "See you Cameron, love you both!"

Camerons yawns. "I should go too, I need to sleep, I got an early class. See you, pretty princess, love you."

Aurelia says goodbye to Cameron and Sabrina before closing her laptop. A small pout forms on her lips as she tries to keep her tears down. She didn't know how much she missed her friends until now. Moments of stress, moments like the one she's currently in, she would cuddle up to Sabrina or Cameron, venting her frustrations. However, she doesn't have anyone like that here. All she has is the pillow she sleeps on at night.

"Hey," a knock on the bedroom door causes her to flinch before climbing out of the bed quickly. She didn't know why she got startled, but it made her look suspicious when Elijah opened the door. He raises an eyebrow at her behavior before smiling a bit. "I won't be back tonight."

There goes her plan to get to know him more. "May I ask why?"

The male chuckles and walks further into the room. "No need to be formal, Aurelia. You're my roommate, not my secretary."

"Sorry."

"Don't be," he shakes his head and leans against the door frame. "I find your politeness cute."

Cute?

"But, if you must know why. I'll be going out with some friends, and I don't want to come back tipsy, or drunk, I wouldn't want to scare you with that side of me." He explains, avoiding her eyes, making her think that some of what he's saying isn't completely a lie. "Not that I'm a messy drinker, but when I'm out with friends, my drinking becomes a bit heavy. If that makes sense."

Aurelia didn't really grow up around heavy drinkers. Her parents weren't drinkers at all. The most alcohol she witnessed her parents drink was wine and champagne but they always drink a glass and never showcase themselves being drunk. She had no idea what the male meant, but she still nodded her head and grip at the thick blanket of the bed she's sitting on.

"So," Aurelia says softly, causing the male to bring his gaze back to hers. "Does that mean you will be showing up tomorrow night?"

He shakes his head quickly. "God, no. I won't be working tomorrow, that's the only reason I'm going out drinking. I was going to have a few of my non-drinking coworkers open up at the same time tomorrow, so I'll be here tomorrow morning, the early afternoon at latest."

"Okay." She nods again, but it was her turn to avoid his eyes.

Elijah steps closer, sitting on the empty spot beside her. "Mind if I sit?"

"You're already sitting, aren't you?" She mumbles quietly causing him to laugh at the same volume.

"I know I haven't asked in a while, but," he leans forward, resting his elbow on his knee. It is clear he is trying to make eye contact just as he did before, but it was hard. Especially with her heart thumping against her chest as it is at the moment. She's sure the male could hear it. "How are you? I know it's still early in the week, but you're so quiet sometimes that I forget you're here. Is everything comfortable for you?"

Aurelia nods her head, slowly turning to face the man. "Yes, everything is fine."

"I can normally read people well," He chuckles. "And I have a hunch that something's troubling you."

She slowly turns her head again, focusing on the pretty bouquet sitting nicely on the expensive modern dresser just a few feet from the bed.

"Are you regretting agreeing to stay with me for a week?" He asks bluntly, his tone soft and deep, as if he has no intention of offending her. "It's understandable if you are. Living with a man you hardly know is a bit scary, and that's why I'm giving you all the space you need until you're ready to get to know me more. Okay?"

Aurelia stays quiet, the silence surrounding them causes the room energy to shift. Elijah stands slowly from the spot of the bed, not saying anything else. He walks towards the open door to the room, smiling at her before, slowly closing the door. Just before he closes the door completely, Aurelia takes the leap of faith and tells him the truth.

"It's not true!" She blurts out, watching the male slowly push the door open a bit. "It is true that I hardly know you, and that moving in with you for a week was not a normal decision for me, but I'm not regretting it. It's only been two days and having the short conversations that we have today and yesterday morning is helping me get to know you more and more. I just wish..."

Aurelia looks down at her shaken hands. "I just wish I had more time to get to know you. Especially since you've been helping me a lot recently."

Elijah's smile never falls from his face, as he stands in the doorway of the room. "Well, how about, tomorrow night? You know if you're not too tired from class and your job, we could go walk around or eat out somewhere. What do you say?"

Even though he's not wording in a way to make it sound like a date, Aurelia knew for certain this smooth talker is asking her out. After thinking about it for a few moments, she finally nods her head. "Yeah, sure."

"It's a date then." He winks at her before closing the room door.

She knew it. She knew the man was asking her out indirectly. Even though it's hours away, Aurelia is nervous. What if she is too tired to go out. Would he be upset about it? No. She shakes that negative though trite out of her head. The man has shown her plenty of times that he doesn't get mad about the trivial things like that. He seems like the type that would just reschedule or pick another day where she's not busy.

With all this thinking, she finally realized that she wasn't even thinking about the possibility of being asked out when she picked all afternoon classes, as well as the evening shift at the cafe. Good thing it's part-time and it closes at seven, she wouldn't be working too late. It is a cafe.

"What will I wear?" She asks herself as she looks at her open suitcase with the clothes spilling out on the sides. "It's just a casual thing right?"

Aurelia continues to have conversations with herself, until she gets a notification on her laptop. Since her phone is broken, she has been using her laptop for phone calls and messages. Of course this was neither. It was

Sunny, her department head, sending her reminder about the event. She hasn't really given her piece a name, and since Elijah's compliments, she couldn't look at it without replaying everything that he said to her. His words made her shy, but they also made her confident. More confident in the piece than she was when she was in the process of painting it.

Seeing the email did send a rush through her, a rush to work on her unfinished project for Arthur's class. It wasn't late, at least not to her. With no classes today, now would be the perfect time to paint, and get other things done while she's alone and her surroundings are quiet. Aurelia is in pale yellow shorts, and an oversized t-shirt. One she didn't care about getting paint on. As she slides on her houseshoes, Aurelia grabs her laptop, and walks out of the room, choosing her music as she descends down the hallway. Once she found a song, she puts her headphones over her head, while holding her laptop carefully, and walks up the stairs to the loft space where Elijah set up, himself, for painting.

Before she moved in with him, he showed her around, and she just couldn't believe he was allowing her to use his art space to paint. The area is spacious, and it was enough room for them both if one day they wanted to paint side by side. Like that would ever happen. Aurelia knows if that were to happen, she would probably get too nervous and run away. Far away.

Sitting her laptop on stool, Aurelia presses play on Simmer by Mahalia as she sets her paint up to use. Once everything is set up, she starts painting, while singing and dancing along to the songs that were on her painting playlist. Sometimes when she's really focused, she loses track of time. Just like now. Aurelia allows her pencil to guide her across the colorless canvas, her emotions dancing its way on the canvas. As she takes a step back to admire her progress, she finally pulls her eyes from her canvas and looks towards the large windows. It was getting dark a lot faster than she expect-ed. It was surely turning into the colder season by the second.

"Should I add color?" She asks herself as she stares at the canvas of two masculine figures coming together. No facial features, nor were there certain attributes. The canvas that started with two circles is now forming into something. She doesn't know what it is yet, but if she keeps at it, it'll surely be something beautiful. She just needs to be confident.

Finally coming to an agreement with herself to not add color, she starts to clean up the paint she put out. There would be no use to waste it, since she didn't use it, so she tried to salvage as much as she could. As she finishes cleaning up, she leaves the area with her laptop and walks towards the kitchen with it. She had some work to finish and she noticed it was getting dark by the second.

Sitting her laptop on the counter, as the next song plays, she walks towards the refrigerator, grabbing a water bottle to drink. As she stands in the empty kitchen, blasting music in her ear. She didn't hear the front door open. Elijah's elevator up to his penthouse had a hall that separated the elevator and the door to the penthouse, so when the front door opened and closed. Aurelia had no idea, due to the loud music in her ear.

Humming along to the song, she opens the fridge once again, grabbing the cherry tomatoes. Her music stops and a long whistle fills her ear.

"Well," Andrew grins, his hands in his hoodie pocket. "This was unexpected."

Aurelia holds her hand over her chest as she panting softly. "You s-scared me!"

He laughs, amusement oozing out as he eyes her down. "I scared you?"

He walks around the counter, approaching her slowly, causing her to walk backward, her back hitting the refrigerator. Aurelia had the tomatoes and water bottle tightly in her grip as the male trapped her between his torso and the fridge.

"Shouldn't I be the scared one here?" He asks, his tone soft, but his voice smooth and monotonic. "A stranger is dancing and singing in my kitchen. Eating my food and drinking my water."

"W-Wait a minute—"

Andrew stares into her eyes as he brings his finger up to his lips. They were so close that Aurelia forgot to breathe. The heat rising between them as the same finger that was on his lips, were caressing her arm, hardly touching it. "Shh, no need to explain, it's clear Elijah brought you here to keep us entertained right?"

"What?" She blurts out, pushing him back. "I'm here because he offered a room for a week! And by the way, I bought this stuff with my own money."

The male's smile fades a bit before a sigh pours from his lips. He steps away from her, walking towards the couch in the living area. Andrew falls back onto the couch, making himself quite comfortable.

"Well," he pulls his beanie over his eyes. From where she was standing, he seemed like he just got from the gym or something. She could tell from the beads of sweat rolling down his face when he was close to her.

"Don't mind me, Angel. Continue what you were doing." He yawns, putting his hands behind his head.

Aurelia still had the items in her hands, they were close to her chest before she placed them down. She didn't understand. She knows Jackie may have told her that Elijah and Andrew know each other, and the way Aiden spoke to Elijah that night, she's sure they were really close friends. Why didn't Elijah tell her that he lives here too?

Is there something more going on that she doesn't know about?

◻

sixteen

Whether it's the passionate hues of love, the bold strokes of anger, or the intricate patterns of frustration, art mirrors the human emotions. Each masterpiece invites you to gaze upon it, becoming a mirror to your own heart's rhythm, making it race and develop with the vivid tapestry of emotions embedded in the strokes and contours. Art, like a captivating encounter, has the power to evoke the same heartbeat, creating an intimate connection between the observer and the artistry before them.

Aurelia watches the man from the chair opposite of the couch he was sleeping on. This may look weird from an outsider looking in, but she's only curious. The man she had spoken to weeks ago is now sleeping on the couch that belongs to another man that she is slowly growing close to. She only heard a few stories, but she knows that Andrew and Elijah know each other. However, even if she heard a few mindless rumors, she'd much rather hear their story from them.

Andrew sighs, causing her to flinch slightly, almost falling out of the chair she is sitting in. "I told you not to mind me, Angel."

She pulls her hand from her chest, sighing quietly before pulling her knees up, using it to shield her embarrassment from being caught staring at him. "I thought you were sleeping. I didn't mean to stare."

"I was sleeping," He slowly sits up, pulling the hat up a bit so he could look at her. "But, I felt a pair of pretty eyes eyeing me down so I couldn't stay asleep."

She didn't mean to stare for too long, her curiosity must've blinded her from the fact that she did look weird. Extremely weird. "I'm sorry."

He tilts his head after sitting up to face her. Andrew is still covered in sweat, and his hair is poking from under his hat, even his hair looks a bit damp. "I compliment your eyes, and all you can say is sorry?"

"Thank you?" She says, but in the form of a question, not really sure if that's what he wanted to hear from her. Aurelia is already nervous seeing him suddenly after being so deep into her own world. Why is he here? How did he get in? Does he seriously live here?

"If you're here for a week," he says carefully, pulling his hoodie off his head, and yanking his hat off with it. "Does that mean Elijah told you about me, or us in general?"

Aurelia shakes her head.

"Fucking figures." Andrew pulls his hoodie off, causing her to get a quick glimpse of his toned body, making her heart thump against her chest. However, this time she tried not to stare too long or she would get caught like she did before.

"I can feel your eyes undressing me," Andrew jokes, but the comment made her shove her face in her knees, scolding herself. "Don't worry, I love attention. You should know this by now."

As she lifts her head again, he shoots a wink at her before his signature playful grin covers his lips. "This is... what? Our third time meeting. Except this time, we're alone, with no one around."

Andrew stands up from his spot on the couch and slowly approaches her, still drenched in sweat. She could feel her heart in her ears as he she watched him get closer and closer, making her throat and mouth dry. Once he is standing in front of her, he leans down, placing each hand on each armrest of the chair. Trapping her just as he did when she was in the kitchen.

"So tell me," he leans down to her ear, causing her body to tremble. It wasn't from fear, but it was definitely from some unknown emotion. Anxiousness? "What does it take for you to finally give into my charms, and let me see this facade of yours go away?"

"Facade?" Aurelia murmurs softly, trying to hide behind her knees. Andrew caresses the tip of her knee with his index finger. The manner he did it in was playful, but it made her visibly tremble, and the man noticed right away because as she shakes from being so nervous, his smile grows wider.

"When I overheard your conversation with Jackie," he slid his index finger down her shin, making her nibble at her middle finger knuckles. "I instantly became more interested in you. I wanted to know who's this pretty girl that had the guts to actually put Jackie in her place. Believe or not I think she's stuck in her immature high schooler ways. I wouldn't believe you if you told me she's a senior in college."

Aurelia's toes begin to wiggle, but only slightly, as she drags his finger up her leg, slowly, pressing into her knee body, causing her to bite her lip. "Were... W-Were you and Jackie close?"

Andrew stops his movement once she asks the question. He cock his head to the side, frowning a bit. As he pulls away from her, she knows now that the question must have upset him. Made something go off inside him in some way, somehow.

"Let's just say I wouldn't invite her to my funeral." He mumbles, crossing his arms as he looks away from her. "I never really had problems with her, but the moment her and her fucking corward of a boyfriend pushed themselves in my friend group, everything went down hill."

She watches him closely. His stance, the way he crosses his arms. The movement of his eyes as if he's watching the old memories play out in front of him. "Is that why you still go to the parties? Because your friends are still hanging out with them?"

He stares out the windows for a moment before he turns to look at her. "I don't even know why I'm telling you anything. And what's with the twenty-one questions? Huh?"

"I was jus-"

"You were just trying to get in my fucking head," he snaps, causing her to close her mouth instantly. "Look, I'm not interested in letting someone else get in my head."

Even though the words didn't seem cold, his tone was harsh. Each word made her throat get drier and drier. All she wanted was to get to know him better in hopes it'll help her understand Jackie better, but instead of saying that, it really did seem like she was interrogating him.

Andrew gathers his things and storms down the hallway. Once she hears Elijah's room door slam close, she lets out the deep breath she was holding. Aurelia rises from the couch, walking over to the kitchen, where she left her laptop, and begins to send Elijah a text from it. It was a good thing her laptop and phone were already in sync, but she doubted he'd answer. It's still early, so he's probably working, or getting ready to hang out with his friends. The man probably answered her message in the morning.

Just as she was about to close her laptop, Elijah's name pops up. Aurelia pushes the laptop screen back and moves her cursor over to the green answer button. When she sees his face, it looks like he just got out of a heated conversation, or worse.

"Hey, sorry." He instantly says, making her shake her head.

"No, I know you two are friends. I just wanted to let you know that he's here." She smiles shyly looking down at her hands. "He's in your room now. I think I might've upset him. Or said something to upset him."

"Don't pay him any attention," Elijah sighs. "Especially since he likes it... but it looks like I'll be coming back tonight. I wished he told me he was coming over today. I would've given you the heads up."

Aurelia nods her head, and looks away awkwardly. "So, um... are you okay? You seem upset as well."

Elijah wasn't wearing what he left the penthouse in. It was something fancier. His is slicked back into a low bun. Even the background didn't seem like the tattoo parlor, where was he? Will she be stepping over a boundary asking him about it?

"I'm currently at a place that I desperately want to escape right now." He sighs, running his hand over his face as he moves the camera away for a moment. "But other than that, I'm fine. Thanks for asking, Aurelia."

She tilts her head. "If you want to leave. Why don't you?"

"It's complicated." He answers quickly as if he has been ask the same thing over and over again. " I'll be there soon. Just let Andrew stay by himself for a while. Once he's done sulking, he might apologize for his outburst, but if he doesn't, I'll make sure you get one."

Aurelia shakes her head quickly, waving her hands at the screen. She didn't need an apology. Yes, he was rude, but there was no need for an apology because she wasn't offended by what he said. She also understood why he got upset, but she was just curious about him. Her mother used to tell her to let someone know that she's curious, because sometimes her blunt questions can offend someone even if it's not her attention. But that was when she was younger. Younger than she is now.

"It's fine. I was asking a lot of personal questions."

Elijah sighs. "That doesn't give him the right to yell at you, okay? No one should yell at you if you're only curious, baby."

There goes that name again. Aurelia looks away shyly, settling in a comfortable silence with the man before he breaks it.

"I'll see you two soon, okay?" He smiles genuinely, making her smile with him.

After ending the call, she walks around the counter, opening the refrigerator, looking for the cherry tomatoes she grabbed earlier and never got to eat. She was getting hungry, but she wasn't super hungry that's why she wanted something small to eat. Opening the tall cabinets for a bowl, she reaches for one of the bottom shelves, since she's too short to reach the other ones. She didn't want that many tomatoes anyway, so the small bow would do just fine.

"Should I cut them?" she asks herself as she fills the bowl with the cherry tomatoes.

Deciding not to cut them, she puts a few more in the bowl and puts the tomatoes back. She grabs the bowl and walks over to the couch again with her laptop so she could watch a lecture for one of her classes, but just as she was getting ready to play the lecture, loud music could be heard from the back. Aurelia sits her bowl down, and grabs her headphones putting them on her head. Once they are on, she plays the lecture, blasting it so she wouldn't hear the music. The song Andrew was blasting wasn't a bad one, and she knew the song.

Was he choreographing something using the song? Ever since she watched him dance once, she wanted to see more from him. He's very good and it's hard to look away when he dances, but maybe that's because he's attractive. To her, that's just a plus. His dancing is also attractive.

After watching the twenty minute lecture, Andrew walks down the hall in new clothes, sweatpants and an oversized tank top that wasn't covering anything. They stare at each other for a moment before she looks away, pulling her headphone down, and closing her laptop.

"Uh," he runs his hand through his damped hair. "You don't mind if I sit next to you."

She shakes her head and crosses her arms. Aurelia folds her legs, scooting more towards the edge of the couch, not wanting to be too close to him.

"Sorry." he mumbles, grabbing the bowl of the tomatoes.

His apology was quick, unneeded, but quick. It's clear he's not used to this but she just accepted his apology and watched him carefully analyze the bowl before putting it back down on the accent table in the middle of the living area.

"What?" She tilts her head.

He leans back against the couch, pulling his phone out his pocket, tapping away. "I thought they were grapes. You're eating tomatoes?"

"What's wrong with tomatoes?" Her tone is full of amusement, curious about what he thought about her common snack.

"Nothing wrong with tomatoes," he says, not looking up from his phone. " But eating them by themselves, like apples or grapes, is insane."

Aurelia's mouth falls open before she laughs. "Oh, so now I'm insane because I like to eat tomatoes?"

He chuckles and shakes his head. "I never said that, but if the shoe fits."

"Whatever." She mumbles playfully, hugging herself.

"Cheese, meat lover, or supreme?" He says randomly making her look at him. "Pizza. What kind?"

"Oh, uh," she shrugs her shoulders. "I'm not picky, I eat anything that isn't too greasy."

"So you're picky." he laughs, causing some of his hair to fall in his face.

She huffs. "I mean, I'm not too picky unless it's too greasy. It makes me feel sick sometimes."

"I know what you meant, Angel, I was just teasing you."

"Then stop!" She found herself rolling her eyes before she looked down, trying to avoid his eyes. "I honestly have never been this talkative with anyone since I got here. Yeah, I talked to Adrian occasionally, but since the whole thing that happened with his brother, I'm so nervous to get to know more people."

"What happened?" He asked, putting his phone down after ordering the pizza. "Did he touch you?"

"Well," she shrugs. "Not necessarily. He broke my phone screen, and threw my headphones."

Andrew sighs. "That fucking asshole."

Aurelia finally found enough courage to look at him, wanting to know the full story. Why is it that almost everyone she knows doesn't like Aiden and Jackie? Why is it that the campus spread rumors and talked down on Andrew and even Elijah at times.

"I told Jackie about him and Genesis, and he exploded... he even hit Jackie."

"That's nothing new." he mumbles. "Before Jackie and Aiden started dating, Genesis was his fuck buddy. They never were a couple. According to Genesis it was just sex, until she started sleeping with me."

Even though he's talking about it, and she's curious about it, hearing in great detail with no substituted words for the vulgar vocabulary. It's not that she doesn't use them, it's just that Andrew curses a lot, and it shocks her to hear it.

"That's when the insecure prick got jealous," he chuckles. "At one point, I was just messing around with Jackie, we never thought of each other in that way, but Aiden. He claimed her after that. Parading their relationship around, as if their relationship mattered to me. Now that I think about it, everything he did back then was to get back at me. Little did he know, I didn't give a fuck."

"Why does he hate you so much?" She asks, watching him tilt his head before he shrugs his shoulder.

"I guess it's because everyone loved me." He laughs, as if saving that is hilarious. "Believe it or not, I was untouchable. If you spent one night with me, everyone on campus would be talking you up, but those were the days when I was freshman in college. When I was in my second year, I got more serious about dancing, reducing my sleeping arrangement with two people instead of five."

Aurelia quietly listens to him talk about himself, since it seems to make him happy when he does. He wasn't lying when he said he likes attention.

"Then I met Elijah. He... He was a lot different than I expected." He leans back again, staring at the ceiling. "He did things, said things, that just made my heart ache. Not in a bad way either. He didn't treat me like this trophy, put me on the pedestal. He treated me like a human. And I love him for that."

"What happened?" She asks softly, tilting her head. "Why do everyone hate you now?"

"I..." Andrew sighs sitting up. "I don't want to talk about it. I don't know if I'll ever want to talk about it."

Aurelia took that as a sigh to let it go. She didn't want to upset him, and she's already grateful that he told her a little bit about his and Elijah's relationship. She could safely say they are together. In a relationship. Why does that bother her? Is it because they are dating or is it because she just heard some of Andrew's story? It had to be that, She had to be feeling a bit sad because he felt like everyone treated him like an object.

"So," he looks at her. "Tell me about yourself."

"It's not much to tell."

He scoots closer, making her nervous again. "Come on, Angel. You can't just be this quiet pretty girl. What do you do for fun?"

"I paint." She answers simply and quickly, leaning slightly away as he gets closer.

"That's it," He murmurs close to her ear in a teasing manner. "Angel?"

She shakes her head, closing her eyes as she listens to him speak into her ear. "I listen to music and I love long walks."

He hums softly, his lips brushing against the tip of her ear, making her quickly cover them and stand up from the couch. Her heart couldn't take it. Why are they both so good at making her heart race? One day, they're going to be the cause of her heart attack.

"Are you okay?" He asks with that smug smile on his face.

She crosses her arms and shakes her head. "I uh, I need to get something out of the room. I'll be back."

Aurelia walks quickly to the room, closing the door behind her, panting heavily holding her hand over her chest. It's happening again. Her heart raced uncontrollably, her thoughts running with so many thoughts. Why were they so good at making her feel things she has never felt before? Does she like them or something? This is what she's feeling. Developing feelings? Or is it because she has no else to talk to, and these feelings are stemming from that? She didn't have more friends, more girl friends. Being around men like this for too long will drive her crazy.

"Just calm down," she mumbles to herself. "Breath in and out."

It wasn't working, her heart was still pounding against her chest.

□

seventeen

Art, like life, unveils its true beauty when you step back from the canvas of an incomplete piece. Just as in navigating life's challenges, taking a pause allows you to reassess the situation. Stepping away creates a blank canvas in your mind, offering a fresh perspective and clarity before returning to infuse it with newfound inspiration.□

□

Aurelia walks up the steps to the art department on campus. Her heart and mind is racing uncontrollably. Now that she's finished the art piece for the show that's only a few days away, she needed time to herself to write what the piece meant to her and possibly title it as well. She couldn't do it at Elijah's place because she's now too embarrassed to face the two men. Not after what she heard last night.

Last night, the pizza Andrew ordered was delivered, and at this point it was pretty late, and they were both still waiting for Elijah to return. Aurelia nibbles at the cheese pizza crust, while watching the male again as he scrolls through his phone while sitting on the counter top. He was on his second slice of pizza when Aurelia finally broke the silence.

"Are you and Elijah close friends?"

The question was a silly one, maybe she just wanted a solid conformation rather than him dancing around the terms of their relationship. Andrew glanced over at her, chewing slowly before he swallowed the pizza down. He shoved his phone in his sweatpants pocket and raised an eyebrow at her. She could tell from his expression that the question seemed invasive.

Did he not want to share? His eyes made her believe she took it too far again.

"More than that." He finally answered, causing her to let out a small breath of relief. Not because they were more than friends, she did it because she was relieved that she didn't offend him by asking the question she was curious about.

"Why?" He asked, crossing his arms over his shoulder after sliding off of the countertop. "Did that good girl in you turn perverted after hearing my fucked of story?"

Aurelia coughed, choked slightly on her pizza. "No! I was just curious!"

He let out a quiet chuckle. "You're a very curious person."

That wasn't what caused her great embarrassment last night. No. That wasn't even scratching the surface. When Elijah got back, it was really awkward for her, but she could see at that moment what Andrew meant when he said they were more than friends. She watched them showcase affection, and not a full on kiss, she could just tell by looking at the men looking at each other that they were dating, which is more than close friends for sure.

"Did you apologize?" Elijah asked Andrew. The question caused Andrew to sigh through his nose, before sitting on the kitchen counter again. "Andrew?"

"He did!" Aurelia blurted out, so things wouldn't get awkward the moment he walked in.

Andrew grinned and looked at Elijah. "See. I apologized. Why are you always so grumpy?"

Elijah shook his head after pulling his long hair out of the neat low bun he had it in. He looked nice dressed in a nice suit. She wondered where he went, but Andrew was right about one thing. The blonde man did not look to be in the mood for anything. Aurelia wanted to ask more about it, but she could tell he wasn't ready to talk about it. Or at all. He looked very disorganized when she called him before, but that was a while ago.

"I'm especially grumpy tonight, so please," Elijah pulled his gaze from Andrew to her, making her shift in her spot. "I just need a moment."

"O-okay." she stuttered, swallowing down air as he eyes her up and down before unbuttons more buttons of his shirt.

Andrew whistled as the man turned around and walked down the hall and into his bedroom. He leaned over to Aurelia, causing her to pull her attention from Elijah.

"He's really in a shitty mood," he chuckled and tilted his head, as if it was so assuming that Elijah wasn't in the best of moods. "That means he was with them tonight. How unfortunate."

It wasn't surprising, but she was shocked to see him still upset. He seemed like the type that could bounce back to positivity with no problems, but she didn't know him that well to even assume that. These are the moments she looked at closely, because his emotions are what made him human, something Andrew was telling her before. Aurelia would be lying if she said that she doesn't notice how people put these two men up to the highest standard.

"Unfortunate for him, but fortunate for me." Andrew said, hopping off the counter. "I think I'm going to head to bed early tonight. You don't mind putting the pizza away right?"

Andrew strolled down the hallway, a small grin covering his face. At that time, she didn't know what he meant by it being fortunate that Elijah wasn't in the best mood. However, she learned quickly what he meant by that. After she put the pizza away, Aurelia grabbed her things she brought from her room back. Closing the door right behind her. As she finished up some emails and small assignments for the next day, she started to get tired.

At this point, it has been a little over half an hour since Andrew and Elijah disappeared in the room. Aurelia was putting together a small list of things she needed to do the next day, so she wouldn't forget anything with distractions. Once she was finished, she started turning down all the lights. It was when she was getting comfortable when she realized she left her laptop charger in the living area. Pulling the blankets back, she slipped on her robe, and opened the door slowly. She didn't want to wake the two men, especially when it was late.

She walked down the hall quickly, but each step was light. Once she retrieved her charger, she slowly but quickly made her way back to the bedroom. However, just before she passed the threshold of the bedroom, she heard a noise. It sounded like a mumble, and a light bump sound. Worried, she walked over to Elijah's door, pressing her ear against it.

"Quiet," she heard Elijah mumble, but he sounded different. "You're going to wake her up."

Aurelia's face twisted in confusion, her eyes squinting as she pressed her ear against the door again, wondering what was going on, until she heard it. A sound. One that she knew had to be Andrew. It wasn't a sound of pain, and she knew it was a moan. One full of pleasure. Embarrassment washed over her, but like an idiot she kept listening.

"What if she was here," she heard Elijah chuckling deeply. "Watching you get–"

Aurelia flinched away from the door and quickly walked back into the room, and closed the door slowly so they wouldn't hear her.

Now that she thinks back on the moment, the embarrassment is sinking in all over again. She couldn't even look them in the face when she woke up this morning. Aurelia clears her throat and knocks on the office door of Sunny's office.

"Come in," he calls out, causing Aurelia to open his door slowly.

"I already told you, Sunny. I'm not leaving until you fix this! My boys are constantly here–"

Sunny stands from his chair. "Your boys are grown men who can make their own decisions. Now look, Marie, I called you here because I wanted to use your grand hall for the art exhibition, not to get a lecture about your son's wanting to work at the academy they graduated from."

Aurelia stands there quietly with her art piece, feeling as though she has just walked in on something important. The woman is tall, with dark brown hair. For someone who has two grown boys, she didn't look that old. Marie, the woman, sighs and places her hands on her waist before she walks around Sunny's desk.

"Fine," she murmurs softly. "You can use the grand hall, I'll even provide the music, under one condition."

Sunny makes eye contact with Aurelia before sighing through his nose as he makes eye contact with the woman. "Make it quick, I'm still working here."

Marie looks behind her, giving her a chance to really look at her face. She kind of looks familiar, but she didn't dwell on things like that. The older woman turns to look at Sunny, laughing a bit before turning around on her heels.

"My assistant will send you the details, enjoy the grand hall, Sunny." The woman walks past Aurelia, not sparing her another glance.

Sunny sinks in his seat and takes a deep breath before releasing it through his nose. "Sorry about that, Aurelia. Have a seat."

Aurelia smiles apologetically. "No, it's okay. I didn't realize you had a meeting."

"It wasn't much of a meeting, especially with a woman like her." Sunny leans forward, pulling on his smile. "What do you need, I got your email earlier about having cold feet?"

"I'm just not sure if this is good enough, what if no one likes it?" Aurelia tells him, pulling her art piece out, showing him the canvas. "I'm just not sure–"

"You lack a lot of confidence, Aurelia." Sunny tells her, making her look down, avoiding his eyes. "You're really good, but if you continue to beat yourself down, it'll start to show in your work. If you hate your work, so will everyone else. Besides, showcasing your work in this show isn't just to win, it's to show people just how good of an artist you are."

"But–"

Sunny chuckles and takes Aurelia's completed canvas out of her hand, he walks over to the large closet area, opening up. He walks inside for a moment, and comes out empty handed. "I don't need to tell you how good you are, you need to see it for yourself. I expect the description of your work before Friday, okay? The wielding team especially asked for them on Thursday, so they can print them all on the metal plaques and have them set up just in time. However, I want yours tonight."

"Tonight?" She stands up, looking at him with anxiousness covering his face. "But, I–"

Sunny crosses his arms and tilts his head. "You need to explain what made you paint that. What was on your mind? Don't forget to include the title. You need to start having confidence in yourself Aurelia. If you don't believe in yourself, what makes you think anyone else would believe in you?"

Aurelia's whole purpose of coming in the office was to drop out, but it's clear Sunny isn't allowing her to, especially when the art show is this friday. What will she wear? What if she wins a big prize? What if she loses? A lot of what ifs and other questions are filling her head.

"Now that we're on the topic of confidence." He says walking around his desk and sitting again. "How has classes been with Elijah? I know Arthur has not come back yet, but I need to know if he's any good. Sometimes, he compares himself to his brother a lot, and he could use the same confidence lecture I give you every time you step foot in here."

She knows the older man is just joking, but thinking about Elijah at this moment, after what she heard last night, what she pictured afterwards, she couldn't think of anything without hearing those words he said. She couldn't even look at Sunny after he asked that.

"Uh," she clears her throat. "It's like working with Arthur? They are very serious and give great pointers, but..."

"But?" Sunny tilts his head as she finally finds the courage to look at him.

"Elijah is too handsome for his own good. Sometimes, people are only calling him over for help because they want to flirt with him and of course, the optimistic extroverted man himself feeds into it." She tells him honestly. "In a sense, it feels like they take Arthur a lot more seriously than Elijah. I don't know if that's a good thing at all. I think Elijah has a really good eye for art, but no one seems to care about that part of him. Which is really unfortunate."

Sunny sits there staring at her quietly, making her nervous. Maybe she said too much?

"Wow," he clears his throat, unsure to smile or ask questions. "It seems like you're disappointed in your peers' priorities when Elijah stands in for Arthur."

"No, I just wish they show him the same kind of respect. You know?" Aurelia bluntly defends Elijah, making Sunny nod his head.

"Thank you for telling me this. Now, don't forget what I told you. Also, eleven fifty nine. I expect your description and title of your piece. Okay?"

Aurelia stands from her seat and nods. "See you Friday, Sunny."

As she walks out of the office, she takes a deep breath before heading towards the entrance to the art department building. It is a pretty breezy day. The sun is still out and warm wind is still present, but with a slight bit of coolness, she realizes how summer is coming to an end. She pulls her phone out and sigh as she stares at the screen. She could get it fix with the money she has, but it wasn't her fault that it broke. It was his. It was Aiden's.

"Aurelia!"

She turns around to see Adrian jogging up to her. He's covered in dried clay, making her giggle a bit, but the closer he gets to her the more she realizes the expression on his face.

"Hey, Adrian." She spoke, but he didn't look happy at all.

"Is it true? Did Aiden hurt you?" He asks, holding her shoulder, looking over her face.

"Hurt me?"

"I tried calling you, but you haven't been answering your phone." He says, as he looks over her face. "Oh, god... did not answer because you would be traumatized because we're twins?"

"Huh?" She tilts her head. "Adrian, slow down. What are you going on about? Aiden didn't hurt me. He threatened me and broke my phone, but he didn't physically touch me."

Adrian stares at her for a moment before he sighs. "That explains why you didn't answer. Shit... what a dick."

"Yeah." Aurelia looks down. "All because I told Jackie the truth about him and Genesis."

Adrian crosses his arms for a second. "He threatened you because of that? He doesn't even like Jackie, he's only with her because... it doesn't matter. Come on. Let me take you to get your phone screen fixed."

Aurelia shakes her head. "No, you didn't break it. Aiden did. He should be the one paying for it."

"Aurelia," he sighs, rubbing his hands down his face. "You know he won't do it."

"I can't let you pay for something your brother did. He did this, not you."
She explains, watching the male take a deep breath. She can tell that not
being able to correct his brother's problem frustrates him. Aurelia just
wants the money to get it fixed, how hard could that be? She didn't plan
on going to him alone, she was going to have someone with her just in case.

"Well," he sighs. "If you aren't going to let me pay for your phone. At least
let me buy you lunch."

Aurelia locks arms with him and nods. "I would very much like that."

Adrian grins and shakes his head before leading her down the path. She's
glad she found Adrian. He's like a breath of fresh air, and he reminded her
of Cameron, someone she could lean on when she needs to. In other words
he makes her feel comfortable especially during times like this.

Once they make it to the cafe, the one she works at, she's greeted by
her work friend, Desiree. She narrows her eyes before she gasps. Walking
around from behind the counter, she hugs Aurelia tightly, something she's
getting used to.

"Aurelia, my love, didn't I tell you not to show up to work on your off
days?" She jests before she looks over at Adrian. "Who's this handsome guy?
Your boyfriend?"

Aurelia laughs before wrapping her arms around Adrian. "Yep, he's my
boyfriend."

"Yep, we're going on our one month anniversary." Adrian plays along with
her, making her smile before they both start laughing.

Desiree tilts her head before folding her arms. "Seriously? You're terrible at
lying, and he's worse."

Aurelia laughs and sighs. "He's my friend, we're in the same art department. Adrian, this is my friend Desiree."

As they greet each other, a group of people come walking in laughing. Turning around, her smile slowly fades. Adrian follows her gaze before he wraps his arm protectively around her before walking up to the counter. Aurelia didn't expect them to show up, no one would, she hadn't seen Jackie in days, and here she is, hanging out with her friends, hanging out with Genesis as if she didn't sleep with her boyfriend.

"Shit..." Jackie murmurs as she waits behind her and Adrian.

Aurelia orders tea, as usual, and a brunch sandwich, and Adrian gets the same thing, but a different sandwich. As they wait at a table close to the counter, Adrian looks at her with concern covering his face.

"Sorry." Aurelia apologizes, watching him tilt his head before shaking it.

"You couldn't have known they would be here. Let's just eat in the park, we don't have to stay here." He suggests, folding his arms over his chest while leaning in the chair.

"So, I heard from Elijah that you moved in with him," he says, sparking a conversation as they wait. "How's that going with him having Andrew around?"

Aurelia's mind instantly went to the event that she wanted to forget. "Oh, uh, It's fine. Different but I'm quite comfortable."

Adrian nods and just as he was about to stand up to get their food, Genesis walks up. "You're living with Andrew?"

Everyone who is present, looks at her and Adrian, making her anxiously swallow. "Huh?"

"You heard me."

"Back off, Genesis." Adrian murmurs quietly. "You're causing a scene for nothing."

Genesis folds her arms. "I wasn't asking you, Aiden's shadow, I was asking her. How and why is she living with Andrew?"

"If she do

Aurelia stands up and grabs Adrian's hand. She walks over to the counter and grabs their stuff, causing the male to help her. He must've understood that she didn't want to involve herself in more drama, because they both begin to ignore Genesis, not giving her the time or satisfaction.

Aurelia and Adrian decided to go to that park, and there, Aurelia lets out a frustrated groan before she hides her face in her hands. From having to move from the student housing she thought was perfect, to dealing with Jackie and her drama, this dream school was becoming a nightmare.

"Hey," he murmurs, patting her knee. "It's good that you removed yourself from the situation, because all they want is drama and nothing more."

"I just wish things were different." Aurelia looks down and leans against the back of the bench, taking a small bite of her sandwich.

"Think about it this way," he chuckles, leaning forward, resting his elbow on his knee so he could look at her. "Jackie and all of the drama is just a slight bump in your journey, you'll get right back on track with a clear mindset. Like the art show event. That would be a great restart."

Aurelia chews slowly, understanding fully what he meant. She should look at this as a learning moment, and move on with life. She can't allow this to be the defining moment of negativity. She must be a lot more optimistic and positive. Her frustration and annoyance with everything is probably the reason why she hasn't been so confident in her art lately. Her focus should be the art event.

"It's a formal event, right?" she asks him, causing him to nod while eating. "What kind of people are the judges?"

"They're different every year," he tells her. "But I heard that this year's judges are all famous."

"Oh, no."

"It's okay. We won't know when they'll be looking around. They announce the winners at the very end of the event." he smiles. "Why are you so worried? I'm sure they'll love your work. You're pretty amazing."

Aurelia shyly looks away. "I guess."

"With that talk, you definitely won't have a chance." He jokes, drinking his iced tea.

"Whatever." she laughs.

□

eighteen

Desire, Lust, and Passion are the pigments of life's canvas. Just as an artist acts on inspiration, so too must we, with brushstrokes of physical touch, bring forth the masterpiece of our emotions onto the blank canvas of existence.

Aurelia leans against the elevator wall, listening to her music as she waits for the doors to open. She hums the song as she waits, trying to prepare herself before she sees Andrew or even Elijah. She left early that day to avoid the men, especially after listening in on them. How can she face them? Anytime someone mentions their names, she replays what she heard the night before. It's going to be hard trying to pretend like she doesn't know what they were doing.

Once the elevator door opens, Aurelia steps off, taking her headphones off. The music can still be heard through the headphones as she puts the key in the door and opens it. She silently prays that neither men are present.

However, when she opens it, she sees Elijah leaning against the counter just a few steps away from the living area. He seems to be deep in thought because the man didn't even notice her come in. Aurelia pulls her headphones from around her neck and turns them off. She closes the door behind her, causing the tall male to finally snap back to reality.

"Hey," he greets softly, approaching her with a small grin on his face. "I didn't see you this morning, did you have an early class?"

Aurelia shakes her head as she takes her shoes off. "I wanted to leave early because I wanted to talk to Sunny about the event on Friday. You know, since I'm participating in it."

It was only a white lie.

She did want to talk to Sunny, but she had all day to do so. Aurelia just used that as an excuse so Elijah wouldn't start asking questions to the point she won't be able to lie about what she heard the previous night.

"Oh, right." he chuckles, running his large hands through his hair first, before guiding them down his chest. "Speaking of Friday, I have some good news from your roommate."

Aurelia swallows hard as she tries her hardest not to look at the man's bare chest, the one he had on display. The chest he could easily cover if he just buttoned the last four buttons on shirt. She could see his chest tattoo. It was a quote, but it wasn't a big font.

"French."

She shakes her head and looks up at him. "Huh?"

He pushes off of the counter and approaches her. Elijah lets out a small chuckle before opening his shirt a bit more. "My tattoo? It's French."

"Why-"

She stumbles over her words before she's silent. It is then that she realized that she was caught staring again. Here this man was trying to tell her something important and all she could do is check him out? Was she checking him out? No. He's just distracting.

"I don't mind," he steps closer, causing her voice to get caught in her throat. "How can I be upset with a pretty woman eyeing me down like that."

Aurelia takes a step back, gripping the back of the couch she was standing near. "I don't k-know what you're talking a-about. You were saying? About my new roommate?"

Elijah looks away, laughing softly before crossing his arms. "Nina. My friend, she wants to meet you Friday. After some persuasion and a deal that she would meet you first, she said you can move in with her on Saturday."

Persuasion? Did he mean, sleeping with her?

Her mind instantly went to the events that played out last night, the words Elijah mumbled in that voice. That voice. His voice. Aurelia grips the back of the couch tighter, biting the inside of her cheek. Did he really sleep with someone to get her a room? No. That can't be right. That would be just her feeding into his rumor about getting around. Right?

"Aurelia." Elijah says her name, causing her to swallow air and look him in the eyes.

"Y-Yes?"

He tilts his head and crosses his arms again. "You've been acting a bit weird since you walked in. Are you feeling okay?"

Without warning, Elijah presses the back of his hand against her forehead, and then his figure tips against her neck. She gasps and takes another step back, almost falling over the couch. Almost. The male wraps his arms around her waist, pulling her against his chest.

"I got you." He says softly. "Careful, baby."

Aurelia could feel her heart move from her chest to her throat, and the sound of her breathing gradually picking up. She is so close to him and he's holding on to her tightly. This physical moment causes her to push him back gently before avoiding his eyes. His hand is still touching her exposed waist, causing heat to rise from her toes to her head.

"Do you not want to move on Saturday?" He asks her, causing her to shake her head quickly.

"No." She says, but quickly correct her statement. "No to not wanting to leave, I mean. I want to leave. That's not why I'm acting weird."

"So you agree," he tilts his head again, pulling his hand away and crossing his arms. "You have been weird. Did something happen today? Did Aiden bother you again?"

Aurelia quickly shakes her head again. "No. Everything is fine, I just-"

"What's wrong? Did I say something-"

"I-I..."

Elijah chuckles a bit trying to lighten the mood. "You can tell me Aurelia, I promise I won't judge if it's something bad."

"It's not b-bad... well... I-" she couldn't finish her statement because Elijah kept trying to reassure her, make her comfortable, but he didn't know him saying one simple meaningless word is what caused her to be this overwhelmed, this nervous. She has never felt like this before. Was it even nervousness that got her this way?

"Aurelia, baby-"

"I overheard you and Andrew last night!" She blurts out, cutting the man off.

He looks shocked for a moment, confusion covering his face before it slowly turns to realization. Aurelia covers her mouth, realizing what she had just said, but she exposes herself. She just told this man she overheard him and his partner.

She could see his eyes change, but his expression did not. At that point her nervousness is taking over. Aurelia utters a small apology before grabbing her bag, the one she tossed on the couch when she walked in, and made a straight line to the room.

"Shit." She heard Elijah say before his footsteps followed behind her. "Aurelia, wait!"

Aurelia slams the door close, panting softly as she holds the doorknob. She knows he's on the other side, but she couldn't bring herself to speak about it. What could she possibly say? She couldn't just say she heard almost everything, because that wouldn't be true. She only heard a small portion of it before she kept herself awake all night because she couldn't shake from memory. It was her fault anyway, she deliberately went out her way to eavesdrop.

"Aurelia, I didn't even realize we were that loud." he tried to explain, but it only made it worse. It gave her more to imagine, and she didn't want to imagine it because it made her feel things. Lots of things that she could hardly explain herself.

Silence.

"How much did you hear?" he asks, but his tone seems like he's more embarrassed than she is. "Did you hear everything? Did we... shit, what am I saying."

Aurelia bites her lip before taking a deep breath. There was no point in running away. It was childish for her to run away like that. "Just... a small thing about me."

She tells him before pulling the door open. As she pulls it open, the male falls back into the room, causing her to yelp slightly. He had his hands over his face, as he lay back on the floor. Aurelia sits against the wall beside him, hugging herself as she waits for the male to speak.

Elijah finally uncovers his face and sighs before he looks over. He sits up, looking into her eyes with so much regret. "I'm sorry, Aurelia. I... I should have never brought you up while we were... Shit. No wonder why you were gone. That must've made you uncomfortable having to hear that. I'm so fucking sorry, Aurelia. I'm sorry for everything you heard."

"N-No, It's okay-"

"It's not okay, Aurelia. Especially when it made you uncomfortable." He explains, but he was wrong. She doesn't know what it made her feel, but she didn't feel uncomfortable about it.

Elijah stands up from the floor, and places his hand on hip before rubbing his forehead. "I'm genuinely sorry, Aurelia. Just... let me make a call. I'll be right back, okay?"

Aurelia nods her head and stands from the floor as well, sitting on the bed. She didn't know how to explain herself without making it worse. She really wasn't uncomfortable hearing her name, and even if she was, she would've started with that. As she waits for Elijah's return, she gets a notification from her smart watch, a message from her best friend, Sabrina. It's clear that she's checking in on her, before she could respond, Elijah comes back.

"Thanks, Nina. I appreciate it." He says puts his phone in his pocket.

"What's wrong?" She asks, tilting her head slightly.

"So," he avoids her eyes. "I think you should move in with Nina, early. She said she'd come over to meet you, and tomorrow you can move in."

"Come over? You mean today? And move tomorrow?" She stands up this time. "I can't talk to her today, not after this conversation, and I can't move tomorrow. I have so much to do tomorrow, I'm not sure If I even have time to move my stuff from my old dorm to the new one!"

Elijah sighs. "I didn't think about that."

"Are you doing this because of guilt?" She asks, feeling a bit frustrated that he wants to get rid of her even after she built the courage to even talk about it.

"We had no business sleeping together while you are standing here, I should've never agreed-"

Aurelia bites her lip, trying to not mention how she feels but it was getting hard to hold back. Something she never had issues with before. "I wasn't un-uncomfortable. Okay?"

Elijah's mouth opens to speak but it closes again when she finally tells him how she felt about the whole thing. She spent all day trying to put an image to what she heard, so talking about it would make her get rid of any feelings she has about it. Right?

"I was shocked. Yes. But, I wasn't uncomfortable, Elijah." She tells him bluntly.

The male tilts his head, and all the embarrassment and guilt that covered his face is now all gone. It's like her words washed that all away. However, it was clear that he was still concerned about it.

"But you avoided us, me, all day." He says, making her squeeze her hand in a tight fist, trying to gather more courage to tell how she feels.

"I... I know, but it's not because I was uncomfortable. It was because... I-I don't know." she murmurs, looking down at the floor.

"Did you... like me mentioning you?"

Aurelia flinched a bit, and she didn't look at him. "Did... I like it?"

Elijah steps closer, gripping her chin, tilting her head up. "Did you like what you heard, Aurelia?"

His voice got deeper, and his tone shifted. It sounds just like he did the night before. She looks into his eyes. "I-I..."

"Honey, I'm home." Andrew's voice could be heard from outside the room door, making Aurelia pull away from him and sit on the bed. "Hello?"

Andrew looks into the room and looks in between her and Elijah before leaning against the threshold. "This is interesting."

"I.. have class work to do, so please let me work." Aurelia murmurs, causing Elijah to stare at her with a serious expression before walking out of the room, pulling Andrew along with him.

Aurelia takes a deep breath before tossing herself back onto the bed, sighing out loud before turning over. Her heart is racing fast as she caresses her chin where he touched her. Did she like hearing them? She didn't even think about that possibility, was it because she denied it.

The rest of the evening she stayed locked up in the room, until she was finished with the description and title of her art piece for the Friday's event. She sends it to Sunny, hoping he would like it enough to comment on it. She stands from the bed and walks over to her suitcase and digs in it for something to wear to sleep in. As she pulls out her yellow pajamas, matching set, shorts and tank top, a knock on the room door causes her to turn around.

Andrew walks inside with a slight upset expression on his face. He sighs and walks inside, not waiting for her permission. The male sits on her bed, watching her closely as she resumes finding her things to get in the shower. His staring causes her to drop her socks on the floor.

"Sorry." He says seriously, as she bends over to get her socks.

"It's really fine. You and Elijah d-do not have to worry. Okay?" She explains, making her shrug his shoulders before nodding. He picks up her pajama shorts.

Embarrassed, she snatches them from his grasp and looks away. "W-Was that all you wanted to say?"

"Cute Pjs. I think they're too much for us to handle." He comments, causing Aurelia's heart to beat against her chest and her throat to dry. "Seeing you walk around in that, fuck... I don't think I'll be able to control myself."

"Get out!" She screams, embarrassment covering her face.

He shakes his head. "I don't think I will, Angel."

Aurelia grabs her pillow and throws it at him, but he catches it. She groans out of frustration before taking another pillow to throw at him. After the third pillow, he throws one back at her, hitting her in the chest. Her mouth falls open before she climbs over the bed with a pillow tightly in her grasp and begins swinging it at him.

Andrew moves around the room smoothly, chuckling while blocking her pillow attacks with the two pillows that he had. "Come on, Angel. You know I'm untouchable."

She laughs. "Oh please!"

Aurelia's face frowns up playfully before she kicks her feet out, tripping him as he tries to get around her. The trip caused him to fall back on the bed. Aurelia used this moment to climb on top of him, pinning him down so she could keep him from moving.

After a few seconds, she stops, panting softly from running around. She felt a lot better after running around the room with him, maybe that's really why he showed up, to make her feel better. Andrew drops the pillows and sits up on the bed. She wasn't expecting him to and she wasn't expecting him to run his hands up her waist and pull her closer.

"Do you feel better, Angel?" He asks her, making her swallow down hard before nodding her head. "Elijah wanted me to tell you that he told Nina that she'll meet you the day of an art event or something."

She nods her head. "Thank you for t-telling me."

Andrew grins and rolls them over, pinning her down on the bed. He winks at her before standing from the bed and walking towards the bedroom door. "Remember what I said, Angel. I would love to rip those Pjs off of you."

Aurelia groans and throws the pillow at him just as he closes the door. She smiles a bit, feeling a lot better after goofing off with him, but her mind went to Elijah, how serious he looked about her liking what she heard the night before. It was as if it had been something he had been pondering over. Has he?

When she finds her clothes, Aurelia grabs her shower basket and opens the room door. Once she walks out, she could hear music playing from Elijah's room, assuming it was Andrew dancing again, she walks towards the bathroom door. Before she touches the doorknob, the door swings open and Elijah is there, with his hair wet and a towel wrapped around his waist. She swallows hard as he pushes his hair back while the cigarette hangs from his lips. It wasn't lit, but it seemed like he was getting ready to smoke.

Was it because of her?

"Sorry," he says, walking around her before walking towards his room door. "Did Andrew tell you what I asked?"

Aurelia nods slightly and he turns around, but she didn't like that he told Andrew to tell her rather than him telling her himself. Did their conversation earlier bother him? Did she say something? A lot was running through her head, but she wasn't going to leave this tension like it is.

"Why didn't you tell me yourself, Elijah." She asks him, causing him to stop outside his door, towel still hanging low.

He didn't turn around to look at her, he just continued to walk, opening his door and walking inside. Aurelia frowns a bit. He could've said something, but he just ignored her? She sighs again before walking inside the bathroom and closing the door behind her. Just when her mood was a bit better, he made it worse. Did what she said really make him mad? All she said was that what she heard them do did not make her uncomfortable.

Did he want her to be uncomfortable? Did he want her to feel upset with them when she truly wasn't it. Aurelia couldn't understand him. It doesn't help that he and Andrew are quite secretive. Going through this at this moment makes her realize that living with men, especially men who make her nervous and feel a lot of things, isn't for her. At least that's what she got from all of this.

□

nineteen

Life, much like art, is subjective and open to criticism. Constructive feedback is invaluable, but it doesn't negate the validity of your emotions. Your feelings are allowed to be felt, and your opinions are allowed to be shared. Just because someone says your art is terrible or questions your worth doesn't mean you have to pretend it doesn't hurt. Embrace both the vulnerability and strength that come with expressing yourself through art and navigating the canvas of life.□

□

It's Friday and Aurelia's clearing off the final table of her shift at the cafe. As she cleans the table, her mind goes to the big event for the night. She doesn't know what's making her more nervous. The event itself or the fact that she's meeting Nina. She knows nothing about Nina, besides the fact that she's Elijah's friend.

It did feel good that she would be moving out tomorrow, but she still feels like there's a lot to be said. Elijah has been giving her that cold treatment, and since that day with Andrew, he hasn't been back to the penthouse. She spent the next day alone and confused. Aurelia replayed what went down in her head, but she still didn't understand why he's suddenly treating this way.

"What's got you deep in thought, mama." Desiree, her co-worker, asks as she wipes the counter down. "Did you have a fight with that fine friend of yours?"

Aurelia shakes her head and walks towards the counter, a slight frown resting upon her face. "How do you know for sure if someone's avoiding you?"

Desiree tilts her head and laughs. "It shouldn't be that hard to notice. They won't talk to you, try their best to not be in the same room as you. They might flat out ghost you."

"What did I do?" Aurelia whines as she sits at one of the tables close to the counter. "I didn't even say anything that would make him so cold and distant."

"So this is about a boy, right?" Desiree asks, leaning over the counter, resting her chin on both hands. "Is this about that friend of yours?"

"No. Another guy. A guy that's so confusing to understand." Aurelia tells her, watching her sigh before switching from leaning on both hands to one.

Desiree observes her carefully. "Maybe it has nothing to do with you then."

"What do you mean?"

"Perhaps he's avoiding you because of his feelings about himself," she explains, tossing the towel she was using on the side. "Basically nothing he's doing has anything to do with you. Maybe he needs time to get his thoughts together to talk to you."

Aurelia looks down at her hands, nodding as she listens to the woman talk to her. "If that is the case, I wish he would've told me he needs some time alone. The silent treatment really has me sitting here thinking I did something wrong."

"I'll see him later tonight though." She avoids Desiree's eyes this time. "I don't even know why I care so much. I can't even understand my own feelings."

Desiree walks around the counter and sits across from Aurelia. "Tonight?"

"Yeah," she sighs. "I'm supposed to be meeting my new roommate tonight at this art event. I'm just assuming that I'll see him tonight."

"Is this guy your first boyfriend or something?"

"Boyfriend?" Aurelia clears her throat and shakes her head. "No he's not my boyfriend. I mean he is attractive, and very charismatic, but he's not my boyfriend."

"Then why is this a big deal? Did something really bad happen between you two?" Desiree questions, clearly trying to get the full story, but she didn't want to tell her the details. The situation in full was private, and she didn't feel comfortable sharing that with Desiree just yet.

"It's kind of private, but I can definitely confirm it wasn't that bad, but his behavior afterwards makes it seem like what happened was absolutely horrible." She explained not exposing too much.

"Girl," Desiree says, crossing her arms. "I've been with three men in my life, and I'm only twenty-four. The first guys I dated made me chase them, and to be quite frank, they made me look so fucking stupid out here. The current guy i'm with was the only one that made me feel wanted. He chased me and after saying fuck it to being the chaser, I finally let my current boyfriend in."

Aurelia tilts her head trying to connect what this has to do with her situation. "And?"

"And—I can tell you're a cool person to be around. If this guy is not man enough to tell you straight up what's his deal, the fuck him." Her choice of words made Aurelia flinch. "He's not worth your time. Even though I don't know the full details, I can almost tell he's being a petty little shit and you should not waste your time with a guy that wants you to play mind reader—wants you to chase him."

"So," she sits up. "You want me to just-"

"Fuck it. Move on if you want me to put it simply." Desiree suggests.

Just as she was about to open her mouth and speak again, a group of people walk into the cafe, causing them to cut their conversation short. The group seems familiar, and it was cutting it close to the time she was supposed to clock out. Aurelia decided to help Desiree with these people, and then she would leave to get ready for tonight.

"Adrian texted me, he said that he was already making his way to the grand hall." a familiar saying. "I wished you offered to pick me up."

"I don't even know why you're trying so hard, Rochelle, the man has only focused on one thing since his break up with Ashley." Another familiar voice says, causing her to remember exactly who the two familiar women were.

Rochelle and Becky, the two girls Adrian introduced her to. Also the same girl who thought she was making moves on Adrian.

"Oh!" Rochelle says as they make eye contact with each other. "Hey, Aurelia! How are you?"

Aurelia smiles and clears her throat. "I'm fine, just trying to finish up with you guys so I can go home and get ready for the event."

"Oh, right, you are a part of the art department. I can't wait to see your piece." She smiles before looking at the menu. "Let's see, I think we'll all have the chocolate scones and iced americanos."

The interaction wasn't that bad, she didn't feel any disingenuous intent. After she helped Desiree with them, she left. She didn't really want to continue to talk about anything involving Elijah and Andrew. Thinking about them was hard enough considering they are the ones avoiding her, not the other way around.

The afternoon slowly turns to the evening, and she pulls the black dress she bought from the closet. It wasn't anything too fancy, just a sleeve black mini dress. The dress is the only thing that wasn't too revealing in the store, but that's what she gets for listening to Sabrina and Cameron. It took her a bit to get ready, but she wanted to make sure she looked good. Especially if there's a chance that she could win something grand.

"This is a lot," she mumbles as she eyes her chest in the mirror. Her cleavage is on display, but it wasn't out there, just a lot more than she's used to. "It's fine, don't think too much about it."

Aurelia moves in front of her laptop, where her friends were waiting to see the dress. "What do you think?"

Cameron's mouth hangs open while Sabrina squeals with excitement. "You look so cute!"

"Cute?" Cameron says, before shaking his head. "She's far from cute, the dress is short and tight."

"So?" Sabrina says. "It's not like she's dressing to capture people's attention, besides it was your idea to send her to that store."

Aurelia covers her face and sighs from embarrassment. "Are you both sure it's not too much?"

"How are you even getting there?" Cameron asks as she walks back to the mirror, and looks at the dress again, trying to build the courage up to feel confident in the dress.

Sabrina hums in agreement. "Yeah, the dress is cute, but I don't think you should go out in that without a ride. Weirdos come out at night."

She knows her friends were right. She needed to find a ride, and after overhearing Rochelle and her friend's conversation, calling Adrian was out of the question. The only person to ask is Elijah, but would he even talk to her? Would he continue to give her the silent treatment and avoid her.

"I can maybe ask Elijah."

"The roommate?" Sabrina says, but her voice is full of concern. "Didn't you tell us that he's acting weird, what if he says no?"

Aurelia groans from frustration, she didn't mean to snap at them, but what did they expect her to do. She has to go to the event, and if taking the bus is going to be the only option for her then she'll do it.

"Guys," she murmurs, sitting on the bed and turning the laptop to face her. "I know you're worried, but if I have to take a bus uptown, I will. This event is important for me and a big opportunity, I can't miss it just because I have no ride."

Cameron nods his head slightly. "We know, but we're still worried and-"

"However," Sabrina cuts Cameron off, making Aurelia smile a bit. "We trust her to make her own decisions, and we must not worry because she got this all figured out. Right, Cameron?"

The male shrugs, making Sabrina repeat herself. "Right?"

"Yeah, Yeah." Aurelia laughs softly and sighs. "Just have fun and try to take pictures if you can. I want to see some sweet memories by tomorrow morning! Got it."

Nodding, she stands from the bed and walks over to her box with her jewelry inside. She looks for her gold necklace, the one her mother gifted her at her graduation party, and the matching earrings with it. As she looks for some rings to go with it, Sabrina calls her name. Walking over to her laptop, she looks at the screen.

"Yes?"

"Make sure you wear those black knee high boots with that dress, I think it'll go perfectly." Sabrina suggests. "I also have to go, so if you can send a picture of your fit after you're completely done, I would appreciate it."

"Sorry for keeping you both here with me, I know you must be busy." Aurelia says, looking down at the rings before walking over to her shoe box, retrieving the boots Sabrina was talking about.

"It's fine, you know we'll drop any and everything for you." Cameron says, making her pout a bit. "But I also have to go, Relia."

Aurelia fully understood, she nodded her head and told them she'd talk to them tomorrow. After she ends the call, she finishes getting ready, not putting on much make-up. As she finishes, she lets her hair out of its wrap, letting her straightened hair fall down. Brushing through her hair, she runs her fingers through it trying to fix it a bit more. Once she's done, she takes her purse, with the gold chain strap, and puts her broken phone and wallet inside. As well as lip gloss and perfume. The only thing left for her to do is pull on her boots.

"Aurelia."

She flinches and looks at her closed room door. She quickly slides on the boots and stands up. Aurelia opens the door slowly and looks up at Elijah. The moment their eyes met, he adverts them down, looking her outfit over. This is the first time he spoke to her since their last conversation in the hallway.

"You look nice," he compliments.

Feeling shy, she utters a thank you before stepping forward. Elijah steps back, giving her some room to move forward. "You were going to say something?"

"Right," he clears his throat, scratching the back of his neck. "The event. I wanted to know if you would like to ride with me there?"

Aurelia took this chance to look him over, he did look nice. The black shirt underneath the blazer was button low. She saw his chest tattoo a bit more this time. His hair is slicked back but it wasn't in its typical bun, it was in his natural state. Why did he look so good, especially when she's supposed to be frustrated and confused with him? This is what she meant by him being distracting.

He was all dressed up just like she is, was he participating in the show or just watching it?

"I was going to ask you, but..." her words trails off along with her eyes. "You and Andrew have been hard to reach lately."

Elijah sighs softly, causing her to look up at him again. "Is there a reason why you've been avoiding me? Why did Andrew never come back after the day I told you about what I heard? Did I say something Elijah?"

"Look," he says, not looking at her this time. "Let's just get to the event."

It was clear he didn't want to speak about it, and she wasn't going to be pushy or stubborn. Maybe Desiree is right. Maybe she should just forget about it. He's clearly not willing to tell her anything despite not saying anything wrong. So she won't waste her time or breath.

"Okay." She says confidently, but anyone could tell she's not happy with him. Not happy with how he just brushed her off like that.

Aurelia walks past him, turning her head away from him. Before she could make it to the door, he grabs her wrist. "Aurelia, wait."

She pulls her wrist from his grip. "I don't want to hear it. Can we just go?"

Regret. His eyes were full of regret, but she didn't allow him to speak. She gave him many chances to, and all he ever did was ignore her or avoid her.

"Alright. Let's go." he murmurs, sighing deeply.

The drive to the event was silent. Elijah didn't even play his jazz music, the genre he loves so much. The only thing that could be heard was the wind brushing against the car. Inside the car she could smell hiss light cologne. The cologne she could smell throughout the penthouse, but it was overbearing and strong. He smells good. He looks good. The man is like a perfect painting but that's just her inner consciousness trying to get the best of her.

"Nina," he speaks just as he parks the car. "Will be inside somewhere. She's tall, blond braids, and a green dress."

Aurelia takes her seatbelt off and slowly gets out of the car. She could hear Elijah do the same thing, but she didn't wait around for him. She made her way towards the large doors where a lot of people were filling inside.

"Oh my god," someone in the crowd says loudly. "It's Elijah James!"

Aurelia makes sure she isn't being pushed by people as they turn around to speak with Elijah. When he told her before about being well off, she didn't think anything of it. When she found out that his brother is a famous artist, an artist she happened to look up to, she could hardly believe. No wonder everyone on campus is drawn to him. He's more than well off.

"This is why I told him to use the side door."

Aurelia turns around, quickly stopping in her tracks before she runs into Sunny. She laughs awkwardly and looks back at the people crowding Elijah. Even though he had an expressionless face just before they got out of the car, he's now smiling as if nothing happened.

"You don't think people just showed up for him, do you?" She asks in a joking way, but Sunny's face looks serious.

"Unfortunately, they are here for him. Him and his family." Sunny murmurs. "Since his family is sponsoring the event, we got more rich people willing to spend thousands on the best paintings and sculptures."

He respectfully places his hand on her upper back and guides her further inside the fancy grand hall. "Come one. I want to show you where your piece is."

"Mine?"

Sunny grins. "You didn't hear it from me, but I think yours is causing a stir. Which is good."

Of course, hearing that made her panic a bit. She didn't know if that meant something negative or positive. She was already freaking out that there were so many people present. Which also meant so many people had already seen her work. As they made their way further in the grand hall, Sunny took her up some marble stairs, and there, hanging in the middle of the room was her painting. So many people were crowding it.

"There it is, Incompletion by Aurelia Mitchell." He grins as he slides his hands in his pockets. "It's really beautiful, Aurelia. Especially the vulnerable description for it, and now I must ask you."

Aurelia is in awe as she stares at her artwork, hanging on display. "Yes?"

"Do you love it?" He asks her, causing her to look up at him. "Do you feel confident in this piece? Be honest."

She looks at her painting one more time, analyzing the brush strokes and the direction she took with the oil paint. Aurelia worked really hard on the piece, and to see it hanging up on display, she couldn't help but to love it.

"Yes." she smiles. "I do."

Sunny nods and smiles at her. "Good."

"Sunny?" Someone says softly, causing Aurelia to look over at him as he has a quiet conversation with the man who just walks up to him.

It seemed very important, and she could tell it was serious from how Sunny glances around before nodding his head. He turns back to her, making her tilt her head a bit. "Is everything alright, Sunny?"

He smiles and nods slightly. "Why don't you enjoy the rest of the event? Up here are the paintings, downstairs are the sculptures, and if you go a floor lower, it's the metal art. Refreshments are on the top floor."

"Alright."

Aurelia watches Sunny and the unknown man walk away together, though she was curious about what was going on, she quickly decided to mind her business. Tonight was obviously special, and she wanted to soak it all in. Walking closer to her painting, she could see so many people have side conversations as they view her work, she was starting to feel much more comfortable and confident.

"I don't get it."

Turning beside her, she sees Arthur, Elijah's brother. His presence alone is making everyone stir. However, his statement made her nervous. What did he mean? Did he not read the description?

"I can tell this person has not used oil paint before," he continued. "And the title is just labeling what it is–incomplete. I get this is an event for amateurs, but I expected more from the art department students. Especially since I graduated from the same art department."

It was harsh. His criticism was harsh. So harsh that all that confidence was gone.

"If I were to change this piece, I would've left it colorless and titled it something more profound. Infinite Incompletion." He chuckles, causing some people around to do the same as they glorify his harsh words. "But then again. Art is subjective. I would spend money on it though."

Aurelia bites her lip, holding back the tears that were so close to falling. Her idol. The man she looked up to just tore the piece she worked so hard on to pieces with his harsh mocking words. Is this why a lot of people don't recommend people to meet their idols?

She excuses herself through the crowd crowding her piece, well in this case, they are just crowding Arthur, and walks towards the bathroom. Once she's inside, she bumps into a girl on the way in.

With tears running down her face, she looks up and sniffles softly. "Oh god, I'm sorry."

The tall girl smiles empathetically and shakes her head. "No, it's alright. You won't be the first person to run into her with tears covering your face."

The woman turns around, her braids flowing down her back as she grabs some tissue for her. "Here you go, hun."

Aurelia utters a small thank you and carefully pats her tears. The woman walks back over to the mirror, fixing her make up a bit. Her backless green dress hugged her curves, and the slit up the side showed off her long legs. Even her dark skin was smooth, and not one mark in sight. The blonde braids really do fit her, and it ties the look all together. She looks like a model, but maybe she's just a goddess.

"I'm Nina by the way." she smiles before looking over at her. "I'm assuming you are Aurelia?"

□

twenty

◻ Misunderstandings often weave themselves into the fabric of our interactions, transforming the delicate threads of communication into a nuanced dance of interpretation. In art, where expression transcends the boundaries of language, misunderstandings become the brushstrokes that add depth to the canvas of perception. Just as shadows define the contours of light, misinterpretations cast intriguing shadows upon the landscape of artistic dialogue, inviting us to explore the nuanced interplay between intention and reception.◻

◻

Nina was nothing like she imagined. Aurelia barely had anything to go off of. When Elijah told her that Nina agreed to meet her, she just started picturing what kind of person she would be like. She was really just hoping she wasn't nothing like Jackie. Nina is tall, pretty, and judging from her speech behavior, she could tell that she holds herself up to a very high standard.

"You're Nina?" She sniffles a bit, carefully wiping the tears from her cheek.

Nina smiles and walks towards her again, the sound of her sparkling heels bouncing off the empty bathroom walls. "Indeed, I am. I'm surprised Elijah didn't tell you anything about me. Then again, I'm not too surprised, but he did tell me a lot about you."

Nina takes the tissue from Aurelia's hand and carefully pat her tears away for her. Shy, Aurelia utters a small thank you before watching the woman toss the tissue in the bin. Aurelia found it hard to believe that Elijah talked about her. He hardly talks to her and she lives with him. However, she could tell just from that smile on Nina's face, that it had to be good things he told her, right?

"He did tell me a brief description of you, and your name. That's it." Aurelia explains, causing Nina to nod before linking arms with her.

"Well," she utters softly close to her ear. "Now that we found each other, let's take a walk around the event and get to know each other. Talking about Elijah will cause great boredom within."

Her tone is dramatic and Aurelia could tell it was a playful joke. She smiles and nods, allowing the beautiful women, who made almost everyone turn their heads, guide her through the event. As they stand in front of another artist's work, Nina unlinks their arms and walks closer to the piece.

"Maneater," Nina reads out softly, she crosses her arms and reads the description quietly. "Their words are stunning."

The painting was different shades of red, but the texture from the brush and sponge technique really did look beautiful. With the different hues, and texture, there is a clear picture of a woman in the frame. Aurelia stares at the canvas in awe, wondering how they master that technique so beautifully.

"Are you an art major?" Nina asks, her eyes still on the Maneater as she waits for Aurelia to speak.

"Oh," she clears her throat a bit before nodding. "Yes. Did Elijah not tell you?"

Nina finally looks up from the metal plaque and stares at her for a moment before she smiles again. "Oh, he did, but I would rather get to know for myself and not through another person. Especially when that other person is Elijah."

The way she said his name made her wonder if she and Elijah were actually friends. Nina seems nice so far, but when Elijah is mentioned, it's like a tab bit of anger or annoyance is hidden in her tone. It made her more curious about their relationship, but at least it confirmed that Elijah did not sleep with her. Good.

"Are you an art major?" Aurelia asks as she follows Nina to the next painting titled When It Hurts.

Nina turns towards Aurelia, pushing her braids over her shoulder and placing her hand on her hips. "Do I look like an Art major?"

She panicked. She didn't want to offend her if she said no, and she didn't want to offend her if she said yes. Aurelia tries to figure out what to say, but she starts overthinking.

"Relax, hun." Nina laughs softly. "I am only teasing you. Yes. I'm an art major."

Aurelia lets out a sigh of relief, which only causes Nina to laugh again. "What kind of art do you do?"

"I do Live Art." Nina smiles as she moves on to the next piece. "I'm quite popular too, which is why I was asked to do a show later tonight. It's also the reason I told Elijah that I would meet you here."

That makes sense. Live Art is beautiful. Watching artists create art in such beautiful fluid ways. She's tall and pretty, and she is an artist on top of it all? No wonder a lot of people are fond of her.

"Nina?"

Aurelia flinches as she hears Arthur's voice. As he walks up with two glasses of white wine in his hand, all she could think of is him completely shutting her art down, making people hate it. Even worse, causing her to feel insecure about it.

"Oh god," she mumbles quietly, annoyed and discomfort covering her face before she turns around to meet the man who's slightly shorter than her. "Good evening, Arthur."

Arthur completely ignores Aurelia's presence, stepping in between her and Nina. "You look lovely this evening. I heard you're performing later tonight. I was wondering if you would like to accompany me after this for another drink?"

Nina takes both glasses and champagne and hands one to Aurelia before pulling her close. "Unfortunately, my roommate and I are going to be really busy tomorrow, so we can't be out too late. Right, hun?"

Aurelia couldn't look Arthur in the face, she kept her eyes down as she nodded slightly. "Right."

"You see, perhaps you can find some other girl to accompany you to your mother's place. Have a good evening, Mister James." Nina walks around Arthur while tugging Aurelia along gently.

Once they are near the elevator, Nina presses the lower floor bottom, and waits for the doors to open. As they both step inside, the taller woman groans from annoyance. "That man doesn't take no for an answer. I had one drink with him and shared one night, and suddenly he's in love."

"Is that why he approached you?" Aurelia asked a very obvious question, but she hoped Nina would elaborate more.

"A year ago, my junior year at this college," Nina folds her arms as they both wait for the elevator door to open. "I had just finished one of my shows, and Arthur approached me. Just as he did when we were upstairs, he asked me to have a drink with him. Then, I thought he was charming, and he is attractive, so I thought why not? As we had that drink, we talked about art and my live art performance, you know the boring stuff. Then I went back home."

The elevator door opens and Nina walks off first. Aurelia walks beside her, looking around at the different metal art. The area was slightly dimmer, so the shadows can hit each work of art perfectly. "After a month passed, he didn't contact me, but when I had another show, there he was again. However, this time, I overheard his conversation about winning the art over with some other snobby rich bastards. I told myself never again. Never again trust a man with pretty eyes and a charming smile."

Aurelia couldn't understand the situation fully, but she too had experienced the unfortunate harsh words of Arthur. Though they weren't exactly to the same degree, his words did hurt her a lot.

"I mean," Aurelia speaks softly. "He did make me cry."

"You and a few other people." Nina sighs. "He's an amazing artist, but his attitude could play catch up with the reputation of his work. In simple words, he has a shit personality."

"Aurelia?"

Both of the women turn around, staring at the male who is approaching her. Adrian looks nice in his suit and his hair in a bun. He walks up to Nina first, earning a kiss from her. He then turns to Aurelia hugging her tightly, slightly lifting her from the ground for a second.

"You ladies look nice this evening," he compliments as he shoves his hands in his pocket. "Did you all take a look around the metal art exhibit, there's some really good ones down here."

Nina sighs and crosses her arms. "No, we were too busy trying to get away from Elijah's big brother. He's an asshole to be quite frank."

Adrian chuckles and wraps his arms around Aurelia's shoulder, pulling her a bit closer, while wrapping his arm around Nina's waist. "Well, I could keep you ladies company to run all the rich and spoiled men away."

Aurelia laughs, earning a wink from the man as he leads them both to one of the bigger metal arts on the floor. It looks like an angel, the biblically accurate angels.Though it looks eerie, the art is still beautiful, so many people were looking at it, and she could tell it was the most popular thing on this level. Seeing all the beautiful art made her wonder, how the secret judges would choose a winner? Everything looks amazing.

"Nina," Adrian says, wrapping his arm from Aurelia's shoulder, and pulling Nina closer. "Are you performing tonight?"

Nina holds her hand up and pushes Adrian back gently. "I am, are you coming to watch me?"

"You know I'll watch you anytime, Nina." He flirts continuously, causing Aurelia to cringe loudly. He looks at her and laughs.

"What?" He questions wrapping his arms around her. "Can't handle my game?"

"Game?" Aurelia shakes her head. "Your flirting could use some work."

"Please," Nina sighs while walking to the next piece. "With Rochelle on his tail, twenty-four seven, and his twin being the campus tyrant, he'd be lucky if any woman walks up to him."

Adrian groans softly before he pulls Aurelia along, following Nina to the next work of art. "I can go the night without thinking about Rochelle and my brother."

"Why not Rochelle? She seems nice. I thought she was your friend." Aurelia questions, tilting her head.

Nina looks at Aurelia and laughs softly, walking towards her. "Baby, Rochelle and Adrian are exes. They only became friends because Adrian couldn't establish a clear line between broken up exes, and exes who are only interested in fucking. Right?"

"Give me a break, we were talking about old times and ended up sleeping together." He murmurs quickly, since the event chatter isn't as loud on the lower. "I already told her that we aren't getting back together, but It seems like I didn't establish that clearly enough."

Aurelia felt comfortable, it felt like she was with Sabrina and Cameron. Now that she thinks about them, she forgot to send them a picture. She holds Nina's hand and smiles. "I'll be right back, I'm going to go to the top floor."

"Where is the food at right?" Adrian says, wrapping his arm around her again. "I can go with you."

Nina sighs and walks ahead of them. "We might as well go together."

As the trio walked towards the elevator together, Aurelia felt a lot better than she did when she was alone. A lot better than she did when she left the penthouse with Elijah. She's happy, really happy that her new roommate was nothing like Jackie. In fact she was better, a lot better.

As they step onto the elevator, Aurelia leans against the far wall while Adrian and Nina talk to each other. Even though she is happy and comfortable, she could shake how hers and Elijah's conversation went. Since she got to the event, she hasn't seen the man since. She hasn't even seen Andrew in a while as well. Somehow, when she's at her highest point, she gets low again, but why. A question she's asking herself.

"Right, Aurelia?" Adrian says, as the elevator door opens.

"Yes?" she looks at him, as they step off the elevator and onto the beautiful turf. The building was so full of people. Sunny was right about the attention the event was receiving, maybe she doesn't have anything to worry about, someone will love her painting and buy it for sure, even if it doesn't win.

"There she is," Sunny says loudly from across the turf, walking over with an older gentleman by his side. "Nina."

Aurelia took this opportunity to sneak away from the two for a bit. She wanted some privacy, not to send a picture, but to perhaps call Elijah, to see where he is. She wanted to talk to him, she wanted to make sure they don't leave things the way they are.

"You look sexy tonight, Angel." A familiar voice whispers in her ear, making her flinch before turning around.

"Andrew!" She whispers before the male pulls her further in the dark corner.

"Let go." Aurelia says softly, but truly, she was happy to see him.

Andrew pulls her against him, burying his face in her neck, his lips brushing along her neck. "Fuck, I missed you."

She could smell his cologne along with alcohol. Aurelia pushes him back a bit, causing the man to place his hand above her head before running his other hand down his face. "You're killing me, Angel."

"You're drunk."

"No," he says leaning into her again, ghosting his fingertips along her and down her cleveage. "I only had a few drinks, so I'm completely sober. I know my limit, Angel, I'm not some light weight."

Aurelia breathing becomes unsteady, and her anxiousness surrounds her thoughts as different people walk past them. His public display of affection, even though they are kind of hidden, they were still outside. His touches always made her nervous, but it wasn't bad nervousness. She liked it.

"Look at you," he chuckles. "All quiet, trembling when I barely touched you. Honestly, I wish I could see what kind of face you would make when I touch you between these thighs. Would you tremble like this?"

She pushes herself off the wall. "W-Water. I need water."

Aurelia walks away, feeling hot all over, but she could tell Andrew was right behind her. She could hear him walking behind her as she walked over to one of the tables grabbing the first glass of water she saw. The man stands beside her, making her remember every word he just said to her. Andrew knows what kind of effect he has on her, but he didn't care. He just loves seeing her tremble.

"I don't think you're thirsty, Aurelia." he whispers in her ear causing her to look at him.

"Stop!"

Andrew chuckles and grabs a glass of champagne from a server who was walking around with them. He sips it a bit before looking around. "Was that Nina and Adrian you were with?"

Aurelia calms down a bit before nodding her head slowly. "Yes. They are nice. Probably the first two people I can really consider my friends."

"Ouch." he murmurs, finishing the drink before sitting it on the table. "And Elijah and I aren't your friend, Angel?"

They were different. Yes, she is comfortable with them. Yes, she has gotten to know them, but she doesn't see them as friends. Then what does she see them as? It is a question she is trying to figure out herself as she drinks the water slowly.

"There she is," Adrian walks up to her and Andrew, nodding towards him. "Andrew."

"Aiden's brother." he greets, not even sparing him a glance. "I see you have finally grown balls, you know since you never had to share yours with your psychotic brother. Barely..."

"Rather be his brother than his little bitch." Adrian bites back.

The shorter woman stands in between them both, smiling awkwardly trying to divert the attention they brought onto them. "Stop it, people are watching."

Nina finally walks up and sighs. "Andrew. I see you haven't changed."

"Nina, I see you've gotten prettier since the last time I saw you." Andrew greets with a wink before grabbing another glass of the alcohol.

"Aurelia, sweetie, don't worry about these two fighting." She grabs her hand. "But I didn't realize you disappeared until I turned around. Don't tell me you ditched me for him."

"No, of course not, Nina." Aurelia tells her truthfully, it wasn't for Andrew, though she is glad that he is at the event as well.

"Why do they hate each other?"

Nina rolls her eyes. "Same reason everyone dislikes both of them so much. Aiden."

Aurelia nods fully understanding. Adrian is related to Aiden, and they look identical since they are twins. As for Andrew, he used to hang out with Aiden and his friend group, so of course, people associated them together, but she knew even before that people didn't like him as much.

"I only wanted to find you because I have to get ready for my show downstairs, and I wanted to tell you the time you can start moving your stuff in tomorrow." Nina informs. "Anytime between twelve in the afternoon and three in the afternoon. Hopefully it isn't too much."

"No." She smiles. "Not a lot of things, I should be able to move and settle in quickly."

"Good. Then, see you tomorrow." Nina kisses her cheek and walks away, leaving Aurelia with two men who absolutely despise each other.

"Did you see my work yet, Aurelia?" Adrian asks, wrapping his arm around her shoulder, only for Andrew to grab her hand and pull her against his side.

She rolls her eyes again and pulls her hand away from Andrew. "No. I didn't, can you take me?"

"I would but you have to ditch the dead weight here." He says lowly, glaring at Andrew.

This tension was making her uncomfortable, especially when she had no idea why they hate each other when the same person they dislike is the reason for the hate they have for each other.

"Wherever she goes, I go." Andrew says, this time wrapping his arm around her waist. "Right, Angel."

Aurelia sighs and walks away from them both. She wasn't in the mood for it. All she wants to do is look at the art and wait to see if anyone wants to buy her piece at least. She also wanted to know who the winners were. As she gets close to the elevator she turns around to see them both following her. Watching as the two glance at each other, she just knew it would be a long night being with them.

Hopefully they hate each other in silence, then maybe she could enjoy the event without the commentary.

As they make it to the floor below, where all the sculptures are located, Adrian wasted no time guiding Aurelia to his work. Just as the one he keeps locked away, the stone piece is just amazing. It seems popular as well with the amount of people surrounding it. It was a bust, a torso piece, with detailed stretch marks along the abdomen. She could feel how vulnerable the piece must have been for him. Especially since he titled it, A Mother's Unconditional Love.

She didn't know much about Adrian's family, besides knowing that Adrian and Aiden do not like each other. This piece alone blows hers out of the water, he's truly talented.

"It's beautiful, Adrian." Aurelia looks at him, and he seems to be awed with his own work. "It looks completely different from the first time I saw it."

"Even though I made this piece for this specific event," Adrian sighs and walks closer to it. "A part of me wants to keep it."

"Which is normal," Aurelia rubs his arm. "I'm sure Sunny could pull some strings."

As the two of them have a moment, she could hear giggling from a few people behind them. It was then she realized that Andrew wasn't beside them anymore. No. He was talking to a group of women and a few men.

They were obviously people from campus, but seeing how they crowd him and subtly brush his arms, even though it wasn't subtle, bothers her a lot.

"Speaking of the devil," Adrian chuckles as he sees Sunny approaching them both. "Enjoying the event?"

"It's probably our biggest one yet," he sighs before looking around. "They are about to announce the three winners before they allow people to buy the works they want. Why don't you two go back up to the first floor? Rumor has it that one of you two is definitely going to win the grand prize."

Even though it was great news, she couldn't focus on it completely. Her mind was too busy on the man who was a few steps away from her, flirting up a crowd around him.

"Aurelia?" Sunny calls out, making her look at him with a smile.

"Yes, Sunny?"

"Make sure you come upstairs at fifteen," he repeats, patting her shoulder. "They're going to reveal the secret judges and the winners. Adrian, walk with me."

Aurelia watches the two men walk away, causing her to turn around and walk towards Andrew who had his arm wrapped around some random girl's waist. When he sees her approaching, he pulls away from the crowd and meets her halfway.

"What's with the long face?" he teases, pulling her close, but she just turns away from him.

Andrew chuckles and holds her wrist. "Are you jealous?"

She doesn't know why she's jealous, would she even call it that. Aurelia didn't care at that moment, she needed to get upstairs the event was coming to an end. "I'm not, I was just wondering how you do it."

He walks besides her and tilts his head. "How do I do what?"

"How do you casually flirt with people without having any feelings for them." She asks him as they walk together towards the elevator. "Do you really not feel anything?"

Andrew's silence meant he was thinking about it, and she didn't mind waiting, because the question was serious to her.

"There has been one other time, besides Elijah, that I have felt something with someone." He tells her, making her throat dry before she steps on the elevator as soon as the door opens.

"Did you and Elijah have a break?"

Andrew shakes his head as he leans against the elevator wall. "We dated her for a short amount of time, exclusively, but things didn't end well. I hate bringing it up sometimes, but to give you the short version, we just didn't click with her the way we thought."

He pushes himself off of the wall as the elevator doors slowly begin to close. "But, that was a year ago, and we found another person we feel a little something for."

Aurelia's heart begins to ache after hearing that they found someone. That's probably why Elijah was so distant, and why Andrew just was being himself as usual. It was all coming together, it was all making sense to her.

"You're quiet now, Angel." Andrew murmurs, circling as the elevator goes up.

The walls started to feel like they were closing on her, making her feel smaller as she watched the number of the elevator change. Andrew stands in front of her forcing her to make eye contact with him, and the moment he touches her chin she swallows down the last moisture she had in her mouth.

"Did the little story make you-"

The elevator dings and Aurelia steps around him, leaving him there as she makes her way to the main area where they would be making the announcement. She sees a few people on a stage, and Sunny is the one at the microphone.

"I want to thank everyone for attending this year's AAE," Sunny announces. "I also want to thank the James Enterprise for sponsoring this evening's event. We greatly appreciate your presence."

Aurelia nervously waits alone as Sunny continues to thank different people before he gets into the judges.

"We had a short amount of judges this year, three to be exact," he chuckles. "But they all did their rounds, and after a very long discussion the three of them came to a decision of this year's AAE top three winners. Before the announcement, I want to bring our three judges to the stage, and they all are well known."

Even though the event was slowly coming to an end, she couldn't shake what Andrew said to her. She could shake that both him and Elijah are into someone. Even if that was the case, did Elijah and Andrew have to treat her like they do anyone they meet?

"The James brothers and their grandfather Carson James." Sunny announces, causing Aurelia to look at the stage where Elijah is standing. He looks good but she knew from the look of his eyes he did not want to be up there.

"Arthur, why don't you announce the third place winner." He says, making her nervously stand there.

Arthur walks towards the microphone and clears his throat. "Of course, our third place is Our Angel by Greg Haste. The Metal art was very detailed, and the eeriness you feel when you look at the golden metal pieces really stood out to us. Therefore, congratulations to Greg."

Aurelia claps her hands with everyone else as Greg, the artist for the biblical accurate angel on the floor of the metal art, walks up to the stage and receives his ten thousand dollars check and flowers. She assumed that he would've gotten first place for how big and beautiful it was, but maybe the James family had other things they were looking for.

"Now, for our second place, Elijah?" Sunny calls for him, causing the crowd to use their voice this time, cheering and whistling.

"Please, settle down," Elijah chuckles in the microphone before looking around in the crowd until his eyes land on her, making her flinch before turning away. "Our second place winner is A Mother's Unconditional Love by Adrian Colton. My brother and I really loved the vulnerable emotion you feel when you view the piece. We were so blown away that this decision was hard to make between him and first place. So, congratulations Adrian."

Aurelia looks up to see Adrian walking up onto the stage, purposely trying to avoid Elijah's gaze. She knew that meant that her art did not win. Sunny told them that either her Adrian were winning something, and it was him. It is her first year participating, so maybe next year she will make it.

She claps as Adrian receives a thirty thousand dollars check and flowers. The event's first place winner was Nina. She would for her live art, which she didn't get to see because she was left with Adrian and Andrew's bickering, but she was happy for her. She looks like a pageant winner up on stage. As she receives her fifty thousand dollars flowers and a contract with the grand hall to perform whenever she wants, Aurelia sighs from exhaustion.

After the very eventful night, Aurelia decided to call it. She didn't win anything, and Sunny told her before that if someone wants to buy her piece he would contact her the next day. She was tired, confused and she just wanted to sleep. Besides, she has a lot to think about. She had to think about Andrew and Elijah.

□

twenty-one

Within the graceful steps of dance and the strokes of artistic expression, beware the shadow that frustration casts. For in the pursuit of perfection, the dance with despair can lead to a perilous choreography, where the beauty of creation may be overshadowed by the haunting steps of relentless discontent.

Andrew sits on the steps of the main building of the campus, headphones in his ear, and his foot tapping to the rhythm of the song playing. His eyes were close, visualizing and counting steps to a choreography he was making in his head. This was the third meeting he had with the board of the school. The third meeting that they called him into, the third meeting to determine if he could return to the school and finish his last year.

As he mumbles the lyrics to himself, his earbuds are pulled from his ear, causing his jaw to clench before he glances over at his father. "Didn't I tell you to wear the suit!"

"Honey, don't draw attention to us." His mother murmurs, patting his father's hand before glaring at him. "He's right. We are here to support you and you're dressed in ripped jeans and a jacket? If you don't take this seriously, how will they forgive you for what you've done? The police statement can only do so much."

Rolling his eyes, he takes his earbud from his father's hand and pushes it back into his ear. He didn't need them with him. He's an adult, he could go through this meeting on his own, but his parents finally want to show up by his side. Support him. They're only showing up because of their statues. Andrew knew they were going to attempt to use their statue to get him back into the school. His father is a very important doctor who owns two hospitals in the city, and her mother who wrote multiple books about her struggles as a young mother. Their statue skyrocketed since he made a name for himself at the university, but that was before–before he was accused of disturbing and using drugs.

"Damnit Andrew," his father snatches his earbud again. "Can't you go to another school? How about you live with your grandparents? You can attend school there–"

"I'm not moving to another country to attend one year of fucking college." Andrew snaps, standing from the chair, snatching his earbud back. He slowly watches his father's expression turn from angry to super piss.

"Why the fuck are you two here anyway? You didn't give a shit then, why now?!"

His father stands up and backhands him. "I heard enough! We took time out of our day to come to this hearing with you, and all you've done was shown us disrespect!"

"Honey-" his mother stands up holding his father's arm.

"No!" his father shouts, "We're done here. You want to live your life as a damn junkie, then fine! We're cutting you off, for good!"

Andrew still had his face turn in the direction it went when his father backhanded him. He could taste the blood on his tongue, as he looked at his father's angry expression. "Who needs your fucking money anyway, I'd rather be broke and homeless than see your face again."

"You little-"

His father raises his hand but before he could hit him again, the main doors to the board room open and the secretary steps out holding papers. Her face looks horrified at the scene but Andrew just picks his earbud off of the floor and walks towards the door. He didn't feel like dealing with his family, not now, not anymore. He just wanted the one thing that made him feel free, like his own person.

"Ah, mister Kang, why don't you take a seat." Andrew nods and turns his phone music off. He takes a seat in one of the chairs and waits patiently for the meeting to start.

"Alright," the head of the board begins to speak. "After great discussion this past few weeks, we have decided to decline your request to return to this university."

Andrew bites the inside of his cheek, squeezing his hands together as he tries to keep it together in front of the police officers, the detective, and the school's board. This is the second time they rejected him and the first time was understandable since he was still in rehab, but now that he's sober they still reject him.

"Why?" Andrew asks, watching the head of board laugh in disbelief.

"Why?" he tilts his head that stupid grin lingering on his face for a moment before it falls. "You used and sold drugs on our property, and everyone recorded what happened at the party, the party that wasn't supposed to be held at any of our student houses, and you're sitting here asking us why?"

"Not to cut you off sir," one of the other members on the board cuts into the conversation. "We have already been informed that he is not the main source of the drugs, though we found evidence of drugs being distributed in the house he was staying in, we did not find any evidence that he was the operator of the drug ring here on campus."

"We also told you the first time," the other member of the board says. "You tarnished our reputation in the media, so it's going to be really difficult to accept you back into the school."

Andrew slams his hand on the table, standing slowly, watching the cops jump up as if he was going to attack them or something.

"I've been sober since I got out of that place–"

"But you still party," the board head says. "We see you at parties and drinking online."

Andrew scoffs. "I'm twenty-four, not fucking four! I had a few drinks and went out partying with friends what's the big fucking deal!"

"You were told not to be on the property, and the student houses are on our property mister Kang."

His glare deepens as he tightens his fist. He kicks his chair back, making it fall back onto the floor before turning around to leave the room. Just before he left through the doors, the head of the board said something that made him snap completely.

"Better luck next time, Mister Kang."

Andrew turns back around and storms towards him, but the cops present were ready, already holding him back, trying to cuff him. "Are you fucking with me!? You think my life is a fucking joke?! Fuck you, you stupid fucking piece of shit!"

As he pins to the ground, the police press him down harder, cuffing him. "Get the fuck off of me!"

"If you stop resisting we'll let you up!" One of the cops tells him, making him stop thrashing so they can stand him to his feet.

"We hope you spend this time looking for another school that would accept you. Have a nice afternoon, Mister Kang."

After saying those last few words, the police drags Andrew out of the building, uncuffing him as soon as he exits the entrance doors. Andrew is panting heavily, he is just so frustrated, angry, mostly confused and devastated.

"S-Shit." he murmurs, hyperventilating, trying to calm himself down, but it wasn't working, nothing was working.

Andrew feels around his pocket for his phone, calling Elijah. He begins to stumble down the stone steps, holding onto the railings. He needs to get out of her, fuck his frustration out. "Answer the fucking phone!"

He slams his phone down on the ground. The sound caused some of the students around to look at him, and the attention didn't feel good at the moment. He pulls his hood on and squats down, picking up his phone. He didn't even sell the drugs and that night, he could hardly remember what happened and why he overdosed. Even the small clip the police made him watch didn't explain how he got like that, but would they believe him?

"Andrew?"

The male stands up, shoving his shattered phone in his pocket before looking at the woman in front of him. Genesis, someone he didn't want to see, not at this moment. "What?"

"How did the meeting go? Are you... coming back officially?" She asks him, making him step forward glaring into her soul, but she doesn't turn away.

"How the fuck did you know about the meeting?"

Genesis steps closer, making him frown as she runs her finger along his exposed chest before adjusting her duffle bag. "You told me two nights ago, when we were smoking together?"

Andrew sighs before he closes his eyes. He does remember being with her two nights ago. After they were done fucking, Genesis decided to share the weed she had. He never planned on sleeping with her, but it just happened. "What do you want from me?"

She smiles at him. "The crew missed you. You haven't danced with us since you got back, did you lose your groove or something?"

His eye twitches slightly before he tilts his head. "You saw me at Tony's party, my groove never left."

Genesis shrugs her shoulders, looking away as she crosses her arms. "Hard to say, Sean did say you struggled to keep up."

"Bullshit!" Andrew scoffs. "It was my choreography we were dancing to!"

The ginger woman grips his hand and begins guiding him in the direction of the performing art department. Andrew stares at her hand before looking around, making sure no one is paying too much attention to them. He snatches his hand from her grip and stops walking.

"Come on, drew. The family missed you. Would it hurt to at least stop by and say hello?" She pushes, making her way up the steps to the performing arts building entrance. "Don't be a fucking pussy, come on Andrew!"

Andrew stares at her for a moment before sighing under his breath. The woman cheers happily before walking up the stairs. He follows behind her, walking through the doors, keeping his head down so security wouldn't recognize him, as they walk down the hall, he could feel and hear the thumping from the bass of the music playing from the rooms. When they get to the end of the hall, Genesis opens the door.

"Look who's finally here, everyone!" Genesis announces, causing the music to stop and all the attention to focus on him.

He slowly pulls his hood off and instantly gasps and murmurs. He expected it, he expected them to react this way because he wasn't supposed to be in the room, let alone the building. After a few more seconds of silence, they all attacked him with hugs and cheers.

"Man, where have you been!" Simon says as they hug him tightly. They were someone who always had his back, but it did surprise him that they were still there. The crew continued to push him around, and the overall atmosphere felt familiar. He could definitely say he felt at home when he's in the dance studio.

"I thought you were never going to visit us." Another person, Gregory, chuckles, messing his hair up.

"I don't know, a short thirty second dance doesn't really show us much," the familiar voice, Simone, says, causing everyone to calm down and get quiet. "You haven't been here for months, who's to say that you are the same Andrew everyone here remembers?"

Genesis grins and walks over to the small cart in the room, where someone's phone is connected to the built-in bluetooth speakers in the room. She scrolls for a moment before playing a song, the song that everyone present is familiar with. Andrew chuckles and looks down at his feet before looking at Simone.

"Do you remember this choreography?" Simone asks, grinning at him when Genesis stops the music again.

"Remember?" Andrew tilts his head before zipping his jacket up complete-ly. "I made this."

Everyone starts cheering before getting into their spots. Carmen decided to pull her phone out and begin recording the whole thing. Genesis starts the music again, and this time Andrew gets ready. He closed his eyes for a moment, allowing that feeling to over take him. The moment the song starts, Andrew begins to dance. The song was fast, but he was having the time of his life, dancing with the people he knew since he started at the university. It was like he was back at the school, dancing and fucking around with them.

He felt like his old self.

When they finished dancing, everyone was panting heavily before they all started cheering. "Is he back? The guy never left! He's still our Andrew!"

Panting and sweating, Andrew laughs along with them. It really does feel like home to him. Home. As they all catch up, dance some more, and just vibe together everyone slowly begins to leave, one by one. In the end he and Genesis were the only two left in the room. She sits down beside him, patting the sweat from her face. He drinks the water slowly, not wanting to forget this moment, wanting to do this without restriction. Without sneaking around. He just wanted to dance. Desperately.

"You know," Genesis says, breaking the silence. "The crew isn't the only one that missed you, Andrew."

"Genesis, don't start."

She drops the towel beside her and snatches his water from his hand. Climbing onto his lap, straddling him. "Our friends missed you too. Sean, Abby, Jackie, Tony, and everyone else."

Andrew lifts her off of him, making her sigh out in frustration. "Are you going to attend every party we throw without talking to us once?"

"Where were my so-called friends when I overdosed in front of everyone? Huh?" Andrew shouts, glaring at her. "I don't even know what happened up to the point I took that one pill! I don't even remember how I got so..."

Andrew shakes his head and grabs his jacket, pulling it on so he can go. "I don't even know why I'm even telling you this shit. All you're going to do is run back to Aiden and tell him everything."

Genesis stops him, closing the door just as he opens it. "What are you trying to say? That I'm responsible for you mixing heavy drugs with alcohol? It's my fault that you got involved with Danika?"

His eyes widen when he hears her name. Hears the name of the one girl Elijah and he agreed to never mention her again. "What the fuck does she has to do with anything?"

"Oh don't play fucking stupid, Drew!" She whispers. "I told you, I told you Danika is bad news, especially when it was fucking Aiden who introduced you to her. Now look, look what happened three days after you and Elijah broke up with her!"

Andrew is stunned, he doesn't even remember Danika being at the party back then, besides, why should he believe anything she says. "For someone who fucks Aiden all the time, you are loyal."

"What are you talking about? Wait," she crossed her arms. "You think I'm lying?"

He shakes his head and moves her out the way so he could leave, but she closed the door again. "You know what Andrew, I may fuck Aiden and put up with his bullshit, but I'm not fucking stupid! He's spoiled! Been told all his life that he's special! Aiden believes he deserves everything in the world and if he doesn't get it, he takes it."

"I don't give a fuck about his life story," Andrew growls lowly, anger covering his face. "He took everything from me, whether you want to delude yourself from the truth or not, I took one pill that night, like every party. I'll take one! That night something was off, I know there's more to it than what he told the cops. I also know you and everyone else is lying for him because you are so far up his dick hole!"

"Fuck you, Andrew! You're just mad that you were fucking reckless! Alway on your high horse thinking you're better than any and everyone! That's why he targeted you! That's why Aiden never liked you! That's why everyone talked about you behind your back! You're an asshole!" Genesis screams, but he could see it. He could see the regret covering her face, masking over her gaze as she looked him in the eyes. Andrew knew about everyone talking shit about him; he wasn't stupid. He never called many people friends either, but he did consider Genesis and Sean friends, but now, he doesn't even know who the fuck they are anymore.

"Drew wait–"

Andrew shakes his head and finally leaves the practice room. He didn't bother closing the door, he just continued to speed walk out of the building. As he makes his way down the concrete steps, his phone begins vibrating in his pocket. He stops just at the bottom of the stairs and pulls his phone out. He couldn't really see who it was, but knew right away who it was when he saw the eggplant emoji.

"Now you call back." Andrew says, anger oozing out in each word.

Elijah sighs. "Andrew, I told you I had to help Aurelia move, remember? You sound upset, how did the meeting go?"

It floods back in, everything he forgot the moment he stepped foot in the dance practice room, the meeting. The meeting that basically declared that he would never be able to get back into the school. Aiden really fucked his life up.

"Can you come get me, please." He says, trying to stop himself from showing any sadness in public at the moment.

"Yeah, I'll be there in ten minutes."

"Make it five," Andrew covers his mouth, after pulling his hood over his head. "If I fucking cry in front of everyone, I'm going to fuck you up."

Elijah chuckles on the phone as Andrew makes his way to the parking lot, so he could wait for him. "I'm sure you would. Hang tight, I'll be there soon."

After ten minutes, Elijah drives up slowly. Andrew stands up from the curb he was sitting on, and walks towards the car. He gets inside, leaning back in the seat, feeling himself crying. He covers his face with his sleeve, and silently cries for a moment. Elijah didn't say anything, he just allowed him to cry until he was ready to speak.

"They told me no." Andrew murmurs, sniffling a bit before looking out the window. "I don't blame them, I'm a junkie, a fuck up, but I refuse to believe it was my fault."

"Babe," Elijah sighs and pulls over into a dead end alleyway. "You can still teach dance, and you don't have to attend that university. You can go to any other place."

"You sound like my fucking father."

Elijah grips his chin, forcing him to look at him, but the inside of his mouth was sore, causing him to wince when he grabbed his chin. Andrew snatches his face away, holding his face. "He hit you again, didn't he?"

"And cut me off, isn't that funny." Andrew murmurs, sighing as he closes his eyes. "Enough about me... I don't feel like talking about all this shit at the moment. How was everything with Angel?"

Elijah leans back and sighs.

"That bad, huh?" He chuckles and tilts his head. "You are the reason she hates us right now."

Elijah groans and starts the car. "Can we not talk about this right here, I need a shower, and a drink."

"Same here."

□

(here's the dance Andrew and the performing art department did togeth er.)(start at 15 seconds)

https://youtu.be/FXvfunk7Yp0

twenty-two

Much like the intricate dance of love, the canvas of life unfolds in unpredictable ways. Experiencing what you believe to be love can at times resemble your worst nightmare. Just as the world you've tirelessly built may crumble before you, akin to the delicate strokes of art and the graceful movements of dance. The frustration of watching your efforts dissipate is reminiscent of the artist who questions the worthiness of their creation or the dancer who practices tirelessly, yet still feels inadequate in the end.□

□

Andrew stands under the running water, pour down from the fancy shower head. The pressure felt right, not too hard, but good enough to leave him feeling less stressed out. As he rinses the soap from his body, Elijah is standing behind him, lathering his back with soap. The shower was intimate, but it was quiet. Typically, the two would be able to keep their hands off of each other, the actual showering would come later. However, they were truly just showering. He could tell that Andrew was having one shitty day, and sex wasn't on his mind. Though he's probably a lot more sexual than Eli, he too has days where sex doesn't help solve his anger issues or problems. Elijah turns him around, looking in his eyes before pressing a soft peck to his lips. Again, nothing too intense, that's just what he does. Reassuring him that he's there with physical touch. As he stood under the water for a moment, to make sure all the soap was off of him, his thoughts were starting to appear in his negative head once again.

"I'm going to get out now." he murmurs, causing Elijah to nod his head.

When Andrew slides the shower door open, Elijah steps forward, rinsing the soap that was on him off. As he steps on to the shower mat, the one that was placed on the floor, Andrew takes the towel from the rack, and uses it to dry his hair. His thoughts were now front and center, recalling the events of the day. His parents cut him off, which he didn't care much about. They only started being a pain in the ass since he began to make a name for himself. His parents never were the type to tell him he couldn't do things. His mother used to sign him up in almost every class a five year old could take, just to see what he liked more. When he took one hip-hop class, he fell in love with it quickly. His father used to hold family gatherings just to show off his talent to the family. However, the moment he turned eighteen and landed in his dream university, and he became the talk amongst the campus and the campus rich society, his parents began to hassle him about reputation. So, when he overdosed last year, they were disappointed.

Even before they forced him into a rehab, Andrew told them before that he didn't take whatever the paperwork was saying. He even admitted to taking one pill, just one, and it's like from that day forward, his parents distanced themselves. They no longer cared or supported him anymore. They wanted him to move to South Korea, with his grandparents, just to finish university there. He didn't want that, he didn't want to go for numerous reasons. South Korea didn't have his dream university, and South Korea didn't have Elijah. Everything was only pissing him off further,

Genesis and her attempt of trying to be in his good graces by showing him a world that he missed only made him mad further. Before, when he first started, Genesis and Sean were his closest friends, people he didn't mind hanging out with, but then they involved him with a guy that never liked him. A guy who clearly ruined his life for a reason he doesn't know, but he's sure it has a lot to do with Jackie. Everything is just getting worse for him. It's like a tornado of glass and he can not escape it. He just keeps going up and up, getting cut along the way.

He sighs from frustration.

"Shit."

Andrew dries his hair more aggressively this time before using the same towel to wrap around his waist. He was letting his thoughts get the best of him. Allowing it to just, piss him off further. The anger was only rising.

"You okay, drew?" Elijah asks as he turns the shower faucet off, stopping the running water.

"Uh," he says, looking himself in the foggy mirror before looking over at the shower door, where he sees Elijah's silhouette squeezing the water from his hair. "I'm trying to be, okay."

Elijah slides the shower door open, stepping out of the shower in his wet naked glory. Andrew leans against the counter, towel hanging low on his waist as he watches the blond male take the extra towel hanging up and wrapping it around his waist. His damped curly hair frames his face as he approaches him. Once again, he pecks his lips before tying his damped hair in a low bun.

"Are you ready to talk about what happened today?" He whispers softly, making Andrew turn his head, avoiding his eyes for only a moment before returning his gaze.

"Which part?" He asks, searching his partner's eyes as he crosses his arms across his chest and tilts his head. "The part about how fucked up my life became when i started hanging out with Genesis and Sean? Or the part that my parents are so far up the school ass that they can't see that their son is constantly being screwed by them for their own fucked up entertainment."

Elijah was tall. He had a few inches on Andrew, so when he stood in front of him with his arm crossed across his chest, it made him appear bigger. "I want to hear about what happened with your parents, and why are you hanging out on campus when you know you're not supposed to be there."

Andrew sighs and mirrors Elijah's arms, looking in the opposite direction, not wanting to look him in the eye. "You're always nagging me."

"Is it wrong to be worried about you?" Elijah questions, but it was clear asking the question made him more concerned than receiving an answer from Andrew. "You've been hanging out with them again, and I know this because you wouldn't have been on the campus that long otherwise."

"I'm sorry, i didn't know I was fucking a cop." Andrew says, making Elijah frown a bit. "Yeah, I was dancing with my old friends. Is that so fucking wrong? Me wanting to do the thing I love?"

"I didn't say that," Elijah sighs. "I just don't want you self-destructing because of all of this. Like breaking the law by being on campus. After that meeting you should've left."

"After the meeting, I called you!" He snaps watching Elijah's frown disappear. "I get it, you were helping, Aurelia, which is why I'm not mad or anything, but don't try to make it seem like I deliberately went out my way to be with Genesis. Genesis of all fucking people."

"I'm just worried about you," Elijah says, making Andrew sigh. 'I'm worried about my boyfriend, you disappear a lot and don't answer my calls. What else am I supposed to assume when you're not even texting me."

He cringed. He's not used to Elijah saying boyfriend.

"Please, please Eli," Andrew's face twists and he shakes his head. "Please just say babe or something."

"Putting babe there in that sentence, doesn't even sound right." Elijah chuckles, pulling him close again.

"Now stop changing the subject." he murmurs, pressing a kiss to his forehead. "I know you. I know you do this because you don't want to open up."

"That's because I'm tired of talking about it." He says, shaking his head as pushes him back so he could turn around to brush his teeth.

"How about you open up to me about what you said to Angel." asks him as he puts the toothpaste on his toothbrush. "What did you say to make her hate us."

Andrew was curious because it was like one day she was interested in the both of them, now she wants nothing to do with them.

He could see his face crumble from that neutral happiness to unsettle frustration in the mirror. Elijah turns around and sits on the toilet seat. "She overheard us one night, and the next day she avoided us."

"Which night again?" Andrew jokes as he brushes his teeth.

"It's not funny," Elijah's expression is serious, his eyes holding that gaze. The gaze that shows he wants to talk about it, but Andrew gotta take it seriously. "We had no business saying her name while we were fucking, Drew."

"She said she didn't care," Andrew spits in the sink, covering his mouth so his spit everywhere. "I think you're overreacting, Eli."

"Correction," Elijah stands up. "She said that she didn't know how she felt about it. I can't go through what we went through with Danika, with her.

I just don't want to feel like we're putting everything on line again. I can't experience that heart break again for fucking up."

After rinsing his mouth out, Andrew crossed his arms. "Aurelia is nothing like Danika, don't even try to compare the two."

Danika was their ex, their third.

Andrew and Elijah are in an open relationship. However, if the both of them like same person a little more than causal fuck buddies, they would agree to be exclusive to that person and each other. Thus, making the relationship close. Danika was the first person they both agreed to be exclusive with, but what felt like equal feelings, shifted to Danika only liking him. Elijah.

Even though she was only able to meet Elijah through Andrew first, Danika wanted Elijah more, which is not the relationship he wanted, they wanted together. When he first met her, she was like every party goer on campus. One night at a party he was at, after he got done just dancing in a circle full of people for fun, Danika was eyeing him, subtly.

"Who's that?" Andrew asked Sean.

Sean looked around before he finally looked in the direction Andrew was looking at. His friend laughed before and shook his head. "That's Danika, but everyone calls her Dani. She's Aiden's people, I don't know that much about her besides the fact that she's hot and fun."

At the time, Andrew didn't approach her, he thought if she really wanted to talk she would come up to him, and that night she did. He thought they hit it off well, and Sean was right, she was attractive, especially up close. Two weeks after seeing her, Andrew finally introduced her to Elijah, and unlike their first interaction, she basically threw herself to Elijah. Which made him waver if he could even like her. A month after both he and Elijah had seen her, they finally had the discussion. The discussion of whether or not they want Danika to be their third.

"I really like her, Drew." Elijah said at the time, his face look serious. "She's like everything we wanted."

"I know," Andrew agreed, before he looked away. "But I don't know. I just, been trying really hard to like her but it feels one-sided. It seems like she likes you a lot more than me."

That day, Elijah never looked so distraught. "I didn't notice, shit, I'm sorry, babe."

Andrew knew how much Elijah liked her, and it wasn't like Andrew disliked her, it just felt like she wasn't in it to be with the both of them, it felt like she was only in it for Elijah. Nevertheless, he agreed to try. He thought maybe he could get her to like the both of them, but when they started their relationship with her, the truth started to come out.

One day, when Danika went back home for the holidays, Andrew and Elijah had just come back from his mother' place. It was a Christmas party, and Eli wanted him to be there. When they got back to Elijah's place, they were clearly slightly tipsy.

Andrew and Elijah were all over each other that night, even though they were a bit tipsy the moment they saw what they did, the alcohol, and lust, was out of their system. Andrew moved over to Elijah's nightstand, where they kept all their condoms. When he opened it and slide on himself, that's when he noticed that it was a hole in the condom. Andrew thought he ripped it on accident but when he went to get another one the same thing happened,

As the both of them checked every condom they had, it sent chills down their spine. Of course, they didn't want to accuse Danika, they actually started to believe they got a faulty box. However, after the break was over,

Elijah found out that she wasn't taking her birth control. It was clear what she was trying to do at that point. Andrew had to recall everything, but the picture was very clear. Elijah's family is an important one, the city knows of him and his family. He would be considered one the richest people in the city if they had a list. From the moment she approached Andrew at the party Danika's entire plan was to trap Elijah in a pregnancy.

"Are you two serious!" Danika screamed at them, tears running down her face as she threw the condoms at her. "Why would I want to get pregnant at this time! You two know I'm trying to be a model! What agency would hire a pregnant woman!"

Elijah was crumbling, and Andrew could see it on his face, but he wasn't affected by the tears.

"So we're just fucking stupid, Dani?" Andrew snapped, watching the woman's face twisted with frustration and anger. "You stopped using birth control anymore, and our condoms were tampered with! We're just pulling this out of our asses!"

Danika screamed so loud that night. "I stopped using the birth control because my doctor recommended that I don't take the pills anymore! I set up an appointment to get a Nexplanon! The condoms have nothing to do with me! Nothing, maybe you two got a faulty box."

It was all bullshit. Andrew knew it.

"Elijah you have to believe me, I wouldn't do that to you and Andrew." She tried to appeal to him, but before Elijah could say anything, Andrew stopped him.

"No," he said, shaking his head. "Even now, at this moment when we're trying to speak to you, you're lying to us. We fuck all the time, and how inconvenient it is for us that the moment we started dating you our boxes become faulty? Just admit while we're willing, just keep this between us.

You're trying to trap us, yes us, especially Eli, in a pregnancy and for what money?"

Danika slapped him, slapped him hard and Elijah finally stepped in.

" We're done, Dani." Elijah told her that night, causing her to cry hard, and Danika never cried like that.

Since then, Elijah and he have been really closed off with adding someone new. Elijah especially. Andrew knew the night that they found out what she had been doing, broke him. Andrew was only broken up about it because he had never witnessed Elijah that way. Even with all that they went through with Danika.

Aurelia is different.

"It hurts now," Elijah says, leaning his face on his fist. "It hurts when Aurelia doesn't look at me like she used to. It hurts to know that I'm the main reason she's like this. Fuck, I haven't even taken her out or expressed this to her, and I'm starting to really like her."

Andrew closes his eyes, remembering the day he came back, the day he sat on the campus stairs with his hood up. Aurelia sat down right beside him, smiled and handed him water. She probably didn't realize it was him, but he had a good memory. Being a dancer and all. "We barely know her, but I agree. She's... different. When I'm around her I feel..."

"Free." They say in unison, staring at each other before looking away.

"It doesn't even compare to the feelings I had for Danika." Elijah says. "I need to fix this, but..."

Andrew walks out of the bathroom, with Elijah trailing behind him, he walks to the bedroom and into the walk in closet. "But what?"

"What did you say to her at the event?" Elijah asks, leaning on the threshold of the closet. "She said something to me as I was helping her move. She said that she hopes I treat our new girl better than I've been treating her. What girl is she talking about?"

Andrew tilts his head trying to recall if he ever mentioned any new girls to her that night. As he pulls on some boxer briefs, he looks over at Elijah and sighs before covering his face with his hand.

"She must've assumed I was talking about another girl."

Even though the conversation on the elevator was interesting, to say the least, she left him there and disappeared in the crowd full of people. Now that he thought about it, when he was talking it was indirectly, so of course she would've assumed it was another girl, but why?

Elijah walks towards him, his hair wavy and falling just above his shoulders. "What do you mean?"

Andrew sighs. "She asked a question and I answered honestly. I sort of mentioned that we were into her, but she must've thought I was talking about a different girl."

The man watches the other find clothes to wear himself as he shakes his head at the confession. Andrew never intended on making her more pissed at them than she already was, but nevertheless it seems like he needs to apologize to, and maybe see where they would go from there.

"Wait, Eli." Andrew pulls on some sweatpants, tying the strings in the front. Elijah drops his towel, pulling his boxer briefs on before looking over at him. "Why did you get Nina involved? She's Danika's best friend."

"She was her best friend." Elijah says, pulling on pajama pants. "Nina said after she found out that Danika was trying to trap us, me, in a pregnancy, she cut her off. You know Nina, she doesn't associate herself with people like that."

"Is that why she ignored me when I was at the event?" He was being petty, he knows that's not what he meant, and Nina did acknowledge him when he was there, but still just the wording of that made him sulk just a bit.

"Come on, Drew, not everyone hates you for what you went through. Not everyone is like Aiden and his friends. Those people are stuck in their immature mindset, and need to grow up." Elijah walks towards him and kisses his forehead. "No one outside of them will shame you for overdosing. What matters is that you got helped."

Andrew didn't want to get in at the moment, he just sighs and pulls on his shirt before walking out of the room to get something to drink. They both agreed to show and drink afterwards. However, one thing he did know, he didn't take any of the drugs that the doctor was telling him, he will figure it out. He took one thing that night, so the help was not necessary, he was not an addict.

□

<h1 style="text-align:right">twenty-three</h1>

Art has a remarkable ability to soothe the soul, to ease the burden of frustration that weighs heavily on our minds. Yet, amidst the strokes of paint, lies a subtle truth—a truth veiled by the colors of expression. We may unwittingly conceal our deepest wounds, using art as a shield against the piercing gaze of our own vulnerability. It becomes not only a balm for the soul but a mask, hiding the raw emotions we dare not confront. Thus, while art may offer respite from frustration, it also holds within its embrace the potential for deception, a delicate line between healing and disguise, between truth and illusion.□

□

Aurelia hands moves across the canvas, headphones over ears, playing her frustration playlist. Paint is everywhere. On her hands, arms, clothes, and even a bit on her face. Why is she painting? What caused her to get so in her head that she had to take it out on her paintbrushes? Andrew. Elijah. The two that have been running through her mind since the event. It's been only a week since she moved in, and the last time she heard anything from Elijah and Andrew was two days ago when they invited her out to eat. It was right after she finished up at work, they were waiting for her outside, causing a scene with their attractive appearance.

"You want to change?" Andrew asked her, in his typical get up, only this time he wasn't showing that much skin since the weather is getting chilly since it's at the end of September.

"If you two don't mind taking me back to get change." She said, walking passed them, opening the door to the back seat, settling in the seat after putting her seat belt on. Andrew and Elijah exchanged looks before getting into the vehicle. "Are we going to go?"

That moment in the car, they ambushed her with confessions.

"That day at the event, I was talking about you." Andrew confessed, causing Aurelia in present time to drag her paintbrush across the canvas roughly. "It's cute that you thought I was talking about someone else."

Cute?

Aurelia takes more paint, rubbing across the canvas, the loud song plays in her ears. She goes back to thinking about the men and what they said to her. What they confessed, what frustrated her more.

"What we're trying to say is," Andrew and Elijah looked at each other, as if they were giving each other confirmation before turning around in their seats to face her. "We are interested in you, and we were wondering if you could give us a chance to get to know you."

Interested? In her?

As the words repeat in her head, her paintbrush finally snaps, causing her to stare at the piece she did out of anger. The red and yellow hues match the emotions she feels at this moment. A soft hand touches her shoulder, causing her to turn around, unknowingly glaring at the person. Nina tilts her head before handing the cup of tea to her.

Aurelia pulls her headphones off and sighs apologetically. "Sorry, Nina, and thank you."

"Wow," She whistles, looking at the practically finished art piece, standing beside her with her own hot cup of tea. "I'm afraid to ask who pissed you off."

The piece was of a woman, the woman representing her, lying on a chunk of gray rock, floating above a black abyss. The flames and chaos are hues of fire; orange, red, yellow, white, and a bit of blue. The chaos piece. Her chaos piece.

"I'm more frustrated, if anything." Aurelia admits, sipping the hot lavender berry tea, probably one of her favorites. It's been a week and Nina has done everything to make sure she's comfortable. She also made the effort to get to know her to the point that she knows what kind of tea she likes and what kind of food she enjoys. Like cherry tomatoes and avocados.

Nina pulls one of the stools in the area beside her, and sits down, crossing one knee over the other. "Does it have to do with Arthur, and what he said about your piece at the event?"

Aurelia had told the woman the full story of why she ran in the bathroom crying, the day of the event, the second night of staying together. She told her how Arthur completely ripped her piece to shreds in front of a crowd full of people. She had yet to get a call from Sunny about her artwork from that night. She had already come to terms with herself that her piece will return to her with no buyers lined up. However, that was not the reason why she was so frustrated.

"No."

"Good," she sighs in relief, sipping her cup of tea slowly. "Because that man hardly critiques your work, he outright hates it. Art is subjective, not everyone's going to like your work, but the least he could do, as your teacher, is to give you pointers to elevate your work."

Aurelia nods to agree, but she turns her attention to her piece in front of her. "But this wasn't made because of that. I'm just frustrated with some words that were shared with me a couple of days ago."

"Such as?" Nina rests her cup on her lap, patiently waiting for Aurelia to speak.

"What would you do if you received a confession from someone," Aurelia looks down at the cup of tea she had in her hand. "But before the confession, the person had shown no actual signs that they are into you."

Nina hums, pushing her braids over her shoulder, before sitting up in her stool more. "Well, it depends on what you consider as signs of interest. For me, I know when someone's interested when they give me things, and constantly go out their way to see me."

The younger girl sits in front of her canvas, thinking about everything she week through the week of staying with Elijah. However, despite repaying the moments, there wasn't anything really anything she could think of that Elijah and Andrew did to showcase their interest. Andrew and Elijah have only shown her that they can be flirtatious, and that's with everyone. She couldn't understand, or maybe she didn't.

"Let me ask you this," Nina says, leaning forward. "Were the confessions from Elijah and Andrew?"

"How'd you know?"

Nina points to her head. "Woman's intuition."

The two women laugh before Nina shakes her head. "When getting into a relationship with someone like those two, you have to understand their relationship, and knowing how careful those two are, you should have to worry about too much."

"But," Aurelia looks down. "I hardly know them."

"Which is why there's this long period you can go through called, seeing someone, that you take to get to know someone," Nina sighs. "Well, in your case, seeing some people. You aren't in a relationship with them, but it's something you say to people so they know you are working on being with someone else, but nothing's official."

"I see," She says, looking at her art piece again. "Well, that doesn't necessarily make me feel better though. What made them like me? Why tell me now?"

Nina shrugs and stands up from the stool, pushing it back where she grabbed it from. "That's something you should be asking them. Just... put your heart first, love. If you feel like you can't handle being with them, because their baggage can be a lot, especially when they come as pairs, it's okay to step away."

"Baggage?"

The tall woman smiles, and shakes her head. "You have a lot to know about them."

Aurelia watches Nina leave the area, causing her to let out a long sigh before looking at her watch. She has yet to repair her phone, so she has been relying on her watch and laptop for everything. She had only a few minutes before class, so she needed to go. Arthur sent a class email, telling them to bring in a recent art piece. The one in front of her is the most recent, besides the one she hasn't touched in a while for the end of the semester.

As she stands from the stool, she walks towards the bathroom, letting the canvas dry in the sun shining through the windows of the work area Nina had set up for her. Aurelia walks inside the bathroom, cleaning as much of the paint off of her, so she could show up to Arthur's class without looking too crazy. She decided to put her hair in flat twists after washing the paint off of her.

"Relia, I'm heading to the campus, do you need a ride?" Nina asks, knocking on the door.

"Yeah, give me a couple of minutes." She tells her, putting little to no makeup on, just eyeliner, a little bit of green eyeshadow, that goes well with her shirt. She steps out of the bathroom, putting her favorite bracelets, rings, and necklace on before spraying herself with a subtle scent perfume and grabs her canvas and bag for class.

Aurelia walks outside, closing the door behind her and locking it. She walks up to the car, getting into the passenger seat after putting her things in the back seat. "I need to pick a day to get my screen repaired."

"Right, Aiden's rage." Nina sighs, pulling her seatbelt on before pulling out of the parking spot. "He seems to be a little more unhinged these days."

"Why does everyone hate him?"

She's curious and she didn't want to ask Aiden, because just the thought of seeing him again freaks her out a bit. That's what she gets for caring about someone who cared little about her.

"Sweetie," Nina says, sighing. "To put it simply, he's an asshole who thinks he runs everything. He got told all his life that he's the best, and no one could compare to him. His family is also the mayor of the city, and his uncle owns the school. So other than being an asshole, he's a nepo baby."

Aurelia tilts her head, not sure if that should be a reason to dislike someone, but she could tell that his behavior and how he treats people, only make people hate every little thing about him.

"That's how he gets you," she says. "He smiles, shows off his charming smile, and expects you to bend at his every command. The friends he has now are the only people who have little to no respect for themselves. They can't even do what we all did in that friend group. Cut him off."

She's starting to get the picture now, Aiden is like the commander of his friends group, and the ones who didn't want to associate with him anymore ultimately cut him off.

"Was he always like this?"

Nina shrugs. "My ex-best friend used to hang out with him a lot, but I never really talked to him, but I found Adrian more interesting than his brother."

"Your ex best friend?" Aurelia questions as Nina drives into the art department parking lot. "Where is she now?"

Nina looks conflicted, as if she didn't really want to talk about it, but she just sighs before parking the car. "She dropped out and disappeared after Andrew overdosed. I think she moved back home. I'm not sure. After what she did, I cut her off."

Aurelia wants to ask more but she didn't want to make Nina uncomfortable so she dropped it. "Well, I'll see you later, right?"

"Yeah," Nina says, getting out of the car. "I'm inviting Adrian and a couple of other friends over tonight, we're celebrating our wins at the event together because Adrian piece got sold to a big spender."

"Really?" she smiles, getting her things out of the backseat. "That's so exciting."

"I know right, that means we have to celebrate. What do you say, are you going to meet me after your class to get something cute to wear?" Nina links arms with her, deciding to walk her to Arthur's class.

"Hm," she shrugs. "Maybe."

"I'll take that as a yes." Nina jokes as they walk up the steps to the art department entrance. "I have to see Sunny, so I'll see you after your class, okay?"

Aurelia nods and unlink their arms and walks in the opposite direction the moment they make it inside the building. She walks down the hall, pushing the door open to Arthurs class. Unfortunately, he was there, but he wasn't alone. Elijah was standing there and they were arguing.

"All I'm saying is that bringing Andrew to this family event isn't wise!" Arthur snaps. "I don't care if you're in an relationship with him, but showcasing your relationship in front of dad's side of the family is social suicide for you and him!"

"Then I'm not going, it's as simple as that!" Elijah's tone was deep, and his words were filled with anger and his arms crossed over his chest. "We both know I am not showing up if it's just going to be a question about when I'm getting married, when you're the one who's older than me!"

"I'm too busy for marriage." Arthur says.

"Yeah, tell that to your two kids you are hiding from mom." Elijah tells him, causing Aurelia to sigh under her breath, hating that she overheard yet again another conversation she does not want to be involved with. She steps fully into the room and closes the door hard enough to get their attention.

"It looks like I'm early." She laughs nervously, before walking over to her spot.

"This conversation isn't over, Eli." Arthur murmurs but Aurelia heard him as clear as day in the empty room.

"Hey, baby," Elijah greets her, making her avoid eye contact as she murmurs a small 'hi'. "Woah..."

Aurelia looks up, watching him analyze her recent piece. "What is it?"

More people started to walk inside the room, and Arthur was looking down at his phone, too busy to notice the students walking in.

"I can feel the angry just by looking at it." he comments, peeling his eyes away from the board and onto her. "I can also see that it's still wet, did you just finish it?"

Aurelia shrugs before nodding slowly. "Yeah, I did."

Elijah eyes her carefully, opening his mouth to speak, but Arthur walks up behind him. "I need to start my class, can you leave? Come back later so we can finish talking about this."

The blond man rolls his eyes and glares at his brother. "No, we're done with this."

Before Arthur could say anything, Elijah was already out the door. Something in her wanted to go after him to talk about it, but she had class, maybe she could call him later.

"Alright, let's look at everyone's art piece."

After Arthur's class, Aurelia had to wait back because the man wanted to speak with her. Once everyone left, she walked up to him, her art piece in her hand as she observed him carefully. He looks like he was sending a very hateful message from the frown lines on his forehead and the line his lip forms as he hits send.

"Aurelia," he says. "Right, have a seat."

"Yes?" She says again, sitting in the seat in front of the desk, avoiding his eyes as he stands over her.

"I really loved your piece you showcased today," he compliments, causing her to raise an eyebrow and tilting her head to look at the man.

"T-Thank you, sir."

Arthur smiles, his smile looks similar to Elijah's smile. The same one that made her shy, the same one that gave her no choice but to turn her attention to an object in the room to avoid eye contact. Of course, at a time like this, she's thinking about the man.

"You know," he sighs. "I see you and Elijah, my brother, are well acquainted, right?"

Aurelia tilts her head and slowly nods. "Yes, you can say that."

"Then how about you come to my family's event?" He suggests. "Elijah is feeling quite shy about going alone, I think you should tag along so he can see his family before they leave the country at the end of the week."

She knows what the man is doing, she did overhear their conversation, ultimately the same conversation that caused Elijah to storm out of the room about moments before the class officially started. It seems like Elijah did want to go, but not if he couldn't go with Andrew.

"Well," Aurelia says, looking down at her hands. "I think it's best if I decline. I don't know Elijah that well to attend something his family is throwing. So, sorry, Arthur."

Arthur jaw clenches before he pulls a smile on his face. "Alright. Thank you for waiting after class to chat. See you on Thursdays, Aurelia."

"May I ask why?" She questions, causing the famous man to put his phone back down, looking at her with a shock expression covering his face. "You don't have to go into details, but, I would like to know why you want me to go when Elijah has other friends he's a lot closer to than I am."

The man sighs and scratches his cheek before crossing his arms over his chest. "If I'm honest, you look normal. Someone my family wouldn't mind having around. All of my brother's friends are just too much for an old traditional family like ours."

The more she sees this man, the more he becomes someone she can not stand. When she was that high school girl, admiring this man's work, she idolized him, wanted to be just like him. However, being in his class, seeing how he tears down anyone who's not up to his standard, makes her really dislike him.

"I see." She says, standing up from the seat. "Well, Mister James, those people, the people you think are too much, care a lot about Elijah. If you or your family can't handle the company he keeps around, maybe you all should take a page in your judgemental book and look in the mirror and question your own character."

"Excuse me?"

"Have a good day, sir." Aurelia turns on her foot, walking out of the room with her canvas in her hand. When she opens the door, Elijah was standing right there, exactly how she was when she was listening in on them, by accident.

The man clears his throat and steps out of the way for her to leave. Aurelia looks into his eyes for a moment before nodding, acknowledging him before she continues to walk.

"Thank you, for that." He says just before she walks off to the other side of the building to see Adrian.

Aurelia turns around avoiding his eyes again. "No one should judge someone based on their appearance, especially when you don't know them. So, there's no need to thank me, Elijah."

He crosses his arms, causing his tone hairs to flex as he watches her closely. "I'll be there tonight. Maybe you, Andrew, and I could finish our conversation that we couldn't finish."

"R-Right..." She says, remembering their confession, the same confession she just got frustrated over. "Well, I'll see you two tonight, then."

"Good."

Aurelia nods while staring at him with a small smile. She turns around and resumes her walk to the other side of the building.

□

twenty-four

The first brushstroke, like the first touch of lips, is tentative yet charged with possibility. As emotions swirl and colors dance on the canvas, there's a moment of sheer vulnerability, of surrendering to the unknown. But in the end, as the painting takes shape or the kiss lingers in memory, there's a profound sense of triumph over fear, a celebration of newfound courage and the beauty of embracing the unknown.

Aurelia looks through the dresses, tilting her head as she watches Nina pick up different dresses, and outfits she put together, making it look easy to put things together. Aurelia never really was never really into fashion, some comfortable overalls and a cute top with it was her go to. However, on rare occasions, the cases when Sabrina and Cameron would drag her to a mall or any clothing store, they would pick something out for her, and convince her that she looked good in it.

Now, she's shopping for herself with someone who is more knowledgeable on the subject than she is.

"Found anything?" Nina asks, standing beside her, looking at the clothes.

"No."

Nina looks down at her, smiling before erupting in a quiet laugh. "Girl, you can't shop for yourself?"

"No," Aurelia says quickly. "I know how to shop for myself, but I don't shop with future parties and events in mind. I just shop for things I'm comfortable with wearing."

Nina nods her head and picks up a leather top, it looks like one of those corset tops. "I think you have a nice figure for this, if we pair it with a cute faux leather skirt, and some cute heels, you would look so good."

Aurelia looks at the top, tilting her head at how sheer the top is, she never worn anything like it before, let alone a corset. However, she did want to know what she would look like, she wanted to trust Nina's judgment. "Alright."

The tall woman smiles and hands the top to her and walks over to another section of the store and picks out the skirt she was telling her about. Nina turns around and nods, "Now, let's go try these on."

"You sure this is going to look fine?" She asks again, looking at the skirt, trying to picture herself in the outfit.

"Yes," Nina laughs, linking arms with her and walking her over to the dressing rooms. "You are going to look so fine."

She teases before gently nudging her into one of the rooms and closing the door. Aurelia takes a deep breath, looking around in the small room before sitting the outfit down carefully. The top was clearly supposed to be worn without a bra, but she was keeping hers on, just in case she did not want to buy it. As she puts the top on, she looks at herself in the mirror. The top is really pretty, but would she pull it off? It was black top and really sheer, but the good thing was that the bust wasn't sheer.

Aurelia pulls her jeans off and pulls on the black leather skirt, finally looking at the full outfit. Nina is right, she also thought it looked good on her.

"Aurelia~" Nina calls out, knocking on the door. "Let me see it!"

Aurelia takes a deep breath and walks out of the room. She is shy because she has never worn anything like what she has on before, so having other people see her like this makes her want to cover up a bit.

"See," Nina says excitedly, walking towards her, adjusting the top a bit. "You look so sexy! Don't you think so?"

Shrugging, Aurelia slightly nods her head. "I guess I do."

"Have some confidence," Nina encourages, giving her a soft pat on her butt before guiding her back to the dressing room. "Now we need to find you some cute heels that go with it and then we can go back to the house and meet my girls Brooklynn and Tessa. They are already decorating the place."

"How many people are coming to this party?" Aurelia asks, as she closes the door to the dressing room to put her more comfortable clothes on. "I'm not really good with crowded parties."

"Don't worry," Nina says on the other side of the wall in her own dressing room. "It's just going to be people Adrian and I know. There's not going to be more than twenty people max there. They are all from the art department and a few people off of campus. Like Elijah~"

Aurelia rolls her eyes as she puts the clothes back on the hanger before exiting the room. "It's not like that."

Nina walks out of the dressing room stall with the clothes in her hand before linking their arms together. "Well, with time it will be like that, right?"

The both of them walk to the front of the store, paying for the clothes before leaving the store. Aurelia looks in the bag and sighs before getting in the passenger seat of the car. As Nina sits in the driver seat, she looks at her for a moment before turning around.

"I saw you talking to Arthur, when I was leaving the building." Nina mentions, making her lean on her fist and nods. "What were you talking about with him?"

"You were right about him," Aurelia says. "He's extremely judgemental and he thinks that smiling and saying a few smooth words was going to get me to say yes to him."

Nina sighs and shakes her head. "What did he want you to do?"

"I overheard," Aurelia sighs. "I overheard his conversation with Elijah, he was trying to get me to come to a family event, simply because I'm normal and I know Elijah. He was being really rude and I just didn't like how he talked to his brother about it either."

"That's what happens when you tell a kid that they're better than everyone all their life." Nina sighs again as she makes a turn. "He's hot but I wouldn't fuck him again."

Aurelia covers her face before shaking her head at Nina's choice of words. "So what shoes am I going to wear?"

"I think I have some heels I got gifted a while ago that are way too small for me. I didn't want to throw them out, and no one else could fit them. I think they'll look cute with your outfit." Nina explains, pulling into the driveway of their home.

"Come on," She smiles. "Brooklynn and Tessa are inside, I'm sure they are dying to meet you."

As she steps out of the car, Aurelia looks at the decorated front, with a big sign saying congratulation Adrian. It was silly but the idea is thoughtful, and she appreciates that it looks really creative. The two girls walk up to the door, opening it just to be greeted with r&b jams and two girls dancing with each other. One girl is just as tall as Nina, curly brown hair and freckles all over. She's in simple jeans and a cropped sweater. The other girl, with a similar hairstyle to Nina's, braids to the back, is dressed in jeans and a cropped tank top.

"We're here!" Nina announces, watching the two girls greet her by dancing their way towards them.

Aurelia looks around, seeing how everything looks elegant, with a black and gold theme. The house that she currently lives in is a lot bigger than the typical student houses. There's two floors. On the first floor is a half bathroom, living room, and kitchen. On the second floor is a full bathroom, two bedrooms, and an office space just off to the side of the stairs. The girls were currently in the middle of the once filled with furniture, living room floor.

"This is my new roommate, Aurelia." Nina smiles, pulling her close to them. "Aurelia, this is Brooklynn."

She points to the short girl with the cropped tank top on. Nina then turns to Tessa holding her hand, spinning her around, making her do a three sixty. "And this hottie with a body is Tessa."

"Nice to meet you both." Aurelia smiles before Brooklynn puts her hands around her waist.

"I know you! I've seen your work at the event!" She smiles, hugging Aurelia close. "It was so pretty! I wish I had the money to buy it myself."

"T-Thank you." Aurelia nods as Nina pulls her away, stopping her from hugging her.

"Alright, alright," Tessa says, shaking her head. "We should get ready, the food should be here in ten minutes. So, Nina and Aurelia, you two can go get ready first."

The two women walk up the stairs hand in hand, and Nina thought they should get ready in her room since she needed to get the shoes for her. Once the both of them put their outfits on, Aurelia looks in the mirror, deciding to let her hair out, fluffing it out so it can sit in an afro. Both of them look good. Nina was in a tight black dress with a gold accent, while Aurelia was in her outfit, with some gold jewelry.

This wouldn't be her first, themed party, but it was the first college theme party that she was actually excited to attend. Aurelia walks over to heels Nina set out for her and they slipped right on her feet. The shoes were a gloss heel with straps that went up to her thighs.

"Who gave you these?"

"My ex best friend." Nina says, putting makeup on, trying to hurry but also not trying to rush.

"Well, they are really pretty."

Nina smiles at her through the mirror, gasping as she looks at the full outfit. "I don't know Aurelia."

Aurelia looks down at herself, looking in the full body mirror before looking at the woman again. "What? What's wrong?"

"You're just, really sexy, maybe I should tell some people to not show up." Nina jokes. "Because the fishes won't be able to leave you alone."

"Oh my god," Aurelia groaned from embarrassment, hovering her hand over her face so she wouldn't ruin the make-up but she was still hiding behind them because she didn't want to show Nina how embarrassed the statement made her. "Stop it!"

"It's true." Nina giggles. "Just wait until everyone shows up, they are going to be talking you to death."

"I hope not."

As the night went on, the two women help the other two downstairs so they could get ready themselves, once everything was set up, the first couple of people begin to show. Nina wasn't kidding when she said most of the art department was showing up. They brought congratulation gifts for Adrian, and other things to add to the party fun. Everyone look amazing in their black and gold outfits, and Nina was right about people talking to her. Soon the part was filled with a lot of people, but still no sign of Adrian, Andrew, or Elijah. Perhaps they were going to show up together?

"So you're an art student? I don't think I've seen you around." The guy in front of her says, making her smile awkwardly. "Which wing are you in?"

"The A wing." She answers sweetly, causing the male to smile at her.

"I'm Simon, Nina's friend. You are... Aurelia, right?"

As she was about to answer the man, she looked over her shoulder to see Adrian walking inside with Grace, the girl she met when she crossed path with Elijah again. Aurelia smiles, and excuses herself from the person who was talking to her before making her way to Adrian.

Everyone cheers and congratulates him before she walks up to him. Adrian smiles down at her and whistles. "Wow..."

Aurelia smiles and pushes him. "Stop it, I already want to go up those stairs and change."

Adrian wraps his arm around her shoulder and guides her to the kitchen, as if he had been to the place more than once before this moment. "Why change, you look nice."

She knew what word he wanted to say, but he was sparring her, since she already voiced that she wanted to change. "So you're living with Nina now?"

He asked, making small talk. "That's better than Jackie one hundred percent. I just wish you would allow me to at least fix your phone screen."

"Adrian..."

"I mean my idiot brother broke it and I know for a fact he won't fix it, so let me pay for it to get fixed. If an emergency happens and you can't call your parents or something?" Adrian says, sipping from the glass he took off of the countertop. He had a point. She already had to explain to her parents that she dropped it by accident. She never lied to them before but it was a lie that was necessary to prevent her parents from worrying.

"Fine." She gives in and crosses her arms under her chest. "If you want to fix the screen, then I can't stop you. I just wish you wouldn't, especially since it was your twin's fault not yours."

"I know but still-"

"Ah ah ah," Nina giggles, "You can't have the party boy all to yourself all night, hun~"

Adrian shakes his head and wraps his arms around Nina's waist. "Oh please, you just wanted me to yourself, Nina, it's okay you can admit it."

Nina groans and pulls away from him. "Now, Now, I'm not interested. You can have him back, girl. I'm going to find Gregory."

Aurelia laughs and watches Adrian chase after her. "Why him!"

She shakes her head and grabs a class she knows that didn't have alcohol in it and walks towards the back doors. She needed fresh air, though the party was nice, she felt hot inside, so she needed a break. As she pushes open the door, she gasps when she sees Andrew and Elijah sitting there. Her heart was racing and she was happy to see them, but she could tell from their expression that they were not in the best of moods.

Andrew tilts his head and eyes her up and down. "Well, this certainly a step up from that cute dress you had on at the event."

"T-Thank you, Andrew." Aurelia swallows hard before clearing her throat. "Is everything okay? Did I interrupt something?"

Elijah crosses his arm and shakes his head. "We were just finishing the conversation."

"Like hell we were." Andrew snaps, causing Elijah to pinch the bridge of his nose.

"For the tenth time, Drew, I'd rather not take you to my family's event not because I'm ashamed of us, I just don't want to make you uncomfortable."

"Why would that make me uncomfortable?" Andrew challenges, causing the girl to look in between them, back and forth. "I want to be seen with you. So what if they talk, you know I don't shut up."

"That's not the point."

Andrew steps forward. "Then tell me-"

"Stop!" Aurelia says, standing in between them, finally saying something. "You two do not need to fight about the situation."

"What are you even-"

"Andrew," she says, looking at him before turning towards the other male. "Elijah. I think you shouldn't go because, no offense Elijah, your brother tried to convince me to go when I hardly know you. So how about we solve this by just dropping it and no one goes."

As they stand there in silence, Elijah stares into her eyes along with Andrew. The three stood in silence, making her heart race. This has happened before.

"This is what I meant," Elijah says, looking at Andrew before cupping her cheek gently. "She really does calm me down when she's around."

"Yeah," Andrew says, crossing his arms, looking at her face the whole time. "I don't want to yell at you anymore."

Aurelia knows where this is going. She knows what they are getting at, but she didn't know if she was ready. She has never been in a relationship, let alone one with two guys, how would she be able to handle this emotionally and physically.

"We'll go at your pace." Elijah says, holding her hand.

Andrew nods to agree. "You can start with going on to dates with use separately and when you're ready, we'll start doing a lot of things together including fuc-"

"No." Elijah murmurs before rolling his eyes. "We're saying let's just take our time. Take it easy."

Aurelia nods her head slowly. They were telling her they would take their time with her, go at her pace. That means she was in that phase, the seeing someone phase. Aurelia doesn't know where this would leave, but maybe this could lead somewhere good. Hopefully.

☐

twenty-five

In the canvas of reality, our emotions paint a complex portrait where love, wants, and desires blur the lines between clarity and confusion. Just as in art, navigating these tangled emotions requires courage to confront the chaos and find beauty in the midst of the whirlwind of confusion.□

□

Aurelia smiles and holds her bottle of water, but really her mind wasn't focused on the conversation she was having with Nina and Adrian. She could only focus on the two men who were talking to others on the other side of the room. Elijah is whispering to Grace, the girl she met for the first time at the cafe a while back. They seem to be having a casual conversation, she couldn't really tell from the angle she was watching him at. Her eyes slowly travel across the room where Andrew is leaning against the counter, a glass of champagne in his hand, and his eyes are on her.

She quickly turns away, causing Nina to look at her with a confused expression. "Are you okay?"

"O-Oh," Aurelia clears her throat and nods. "Yeah, I'm fine. Adrian, are you working on your next art piece?"

She tries to change the subject fast, so her observant roommate, Nina, wouldn't ask questions. However, she could tell from the holes that the taller woman is burning into her face with her eyes, that she's already forming the questions in her head.

"Nah," Adrian answers, sipping his drink a bit before shrugging. "I plan on taking a long ass break. I spent months on that thing, and I'm glad someone bought it."

"But?"

Adrian sighs. "I just wish I took it off the market, the sculpture held a very deep meaning for me."

"You know, you could've asked Sunny, he would've helped." Nina tilts her head.

Aurelia turns her head from the conversation, just to see Elijah approaching them. A lot of things were running through her mind. Specifically the part of the evening where he and Andrew basically asked her out and she agreed to it. As the man gets closer, she finally is able to take a look at his clothes. He looks nice dressed in his suit, and the black sheer shirt underneath gave her a small glimpse of his chest.

"Congrats, Adrian." Elijah says, placing his hand on her lower back, causing her to jump slightly. "My grandfather loved your piece so much that he bought it."

"Yeah," Adrian sighs. "I loved that stupid thing as well."

Elijah chuckles, lightly dragging his fingertips up and down her spine. Even with the laced corset, she felt his fingertips through the fabric, causing goosebumps up and down her arm.

"I can't believe you all gave me first place," Nina complains. "I know I'm good, but there were a lot more artists that deserved that more than me."

Aurelia stares at everyone, too stunned to move, and too speechless to form a sentence. His touch is a distraction, she's distracted from the conversation.

"You're too modest," Elijah says, guiding his hand past her spine, and moving it towards her waist, pulling her slightly closer. "You performed exceptionally well, Arthur, especially, could wholeheartedly agree."

"Why should I give a shit about what your brother thinks?" Nina says, causing Elijah and Adrian to laugh.

"Please," Adrian says, drinking from his glass again before leaning closer so only they could hear. "It's clear you prefer toxic kinds of relationships."

"I do not!"

Elijah chuckles, his eyes haven't meant hers once yet. "Remember Darrien? You two fought every night, especially during your surprise birthday trip we all decided to take to france."

Aurelia nibbles the inside of her cheek, trying to focus on the conversation rather than Elijah's large hand squeezing her waist with the corset. She could hardly breath with the corset top on now, or maybe it was just her freaking out from Elijah's physical touch.

"I'm going to go get something else to drink." Aurelia says, excusing herself, not sparing the man a glance as she tries to get out of that circle.

As she walked away, she could hear a set of footsteps following right behind her. As she makes it to the stairs, she walks up them, turning around to see Andrew right behind her. Aurelia blinks before turning around to face him. He was a step below her, she was looking down at him.

"You look stressed," Andrew says, leaning against the railing, glass in his hand as he stares up at her. "Is it because of what we said outside?"

"No!"

Andrew raises an eyebrow and grins before laughing quietly. "No?"

She shifts her wait on the other foot, holding the bottle in her hand. The party is still going on behind him, and no one seems to notice she was going up the stairs, but they did notice Andrew standing on the stairs with her, having a conversation. It was so much attention—attention she didn't really want on her at this moment.

"No," Aurelia sighs softly and looks down at her feet. "I mean... I'm fine, I just want to go somewhere quiet to collect my thoughts."

"Alone?" He questions, taking a step up, causing her to take one up as well, trying hard not to fall forward with the heels she has on.

"Y-Yes." She says, looking him in the eyes, unconsciously licking her bottom lip after swallowing down her nervousness.

His gaze lowers to her lips as he takes another step up, and she takes one up as well. Anyone who sees them talking would think they look weird, but they have no idea what she's feeling at this moment. Part of her wants to stand on her word and go up the stairs alone, and another part, one that's new to her, wants Andrew to come with her. She wants to...kiss him.

"Well," he grins, taking another step up, but this time she doesn't move, she's as frozen as a statue. Andrew leans to her ear, one hand holding his glass while the other his ghosting over her arm up to her shoulder. "I'll see you down stairs later, Angel."

Aurelia closes her eyes, confusion covering her expression as her thoughts swirl around in her head. "W-What?"

Andrew takes two steps back down the stairs, grinning up at her before he pulls on a teasing smile. "I'll see you downstairs, you know, since you asked to be alone. Unless, you changed your mind?"

She blinks a few times before shaking her head and walking up the stairs quickly. She takes large fast steps towards her room. Aurelia opens it and closes it behind her softly, sighing out before holding her hand over her chest. She's going crazy. No one ever made her feel like this before. Her heart just races like crazy when she's around the men. What's wrong with her?

She hardly knows them, yet they have a lot of control over her emotions.

"Relia?" Nina's voice could be heard on the other side of the door, making her sigh again before she opened it.

Nina walks inside as Aurelia slowly drags her feet over to her bed to sit down.

"I knew it." Nina says, closing the door. "I knew Elijah was being too touchy, should I beat his ass?"

"Huh?" Aurelia shakes her head. "No, it's fine, It's not like I hated it. Besides, that's not what's wrong."

"What's... wrong? Something's wrong?" Nina questions, sitting her glass on the accent table to the right of the door before walking over to Aurelia with a concerned expression covering her face.

"They asked me out?" Aurelia says, not sure if that's what went down. "I declined before, well... I didn't decline, I just didn't know yet, but tonight they asked and I kind of said okay."

"Okay," she says. "So, what's wrong?"

"I've never been with anyone," Aurelia admits. "I never really had a real deep crush, and I hardly give any guy the time of day. This wall I built up kind of, pushed all the guys whoever approached me wanting something more than a friendship away. Now, two obviously attractive men took interest in me, but I don't know the first thing about relationships."

"Not only am I inexperienced with relationships, everytime they are near me, brush against me, say things that sound really flirty, my heart races and my stomach tightens. I feel short of breath, and my legs feel weak."

Nina crosses one knee over the other and crosses her arms. "Aurelia, from what it sounds like, you're physically attracted to them."

"Obviously, Nina."

"No, I mean you want to sleep with them." Nina says. " You said it yourself, you don't know them, so you probably just want to sleep with them."

Aurelia couldn't believe what she was saying, but maybe she is right. Perhaps she is just physically attracted to them. Maybe going on these dates will help her find something else, besides their face and body, attractive.

"Am I that shallow?" Aurelia asks herself, mostly, but Nina shakes her head.

"Girl," Nina stands up and puts her hand on her hip. "If wanting to fuck two guys, and two guys that want you, is shallow, then half of our campus is shallow as hell."

Smiling, she shakes her head and looks away. "I guess you're right."

"Look," Nina smiles and sits down next to her again. "One thing I can tell you about those two, when they love, they love hard. I mean they've been together for a long time."

Aurelia looks at Nina for a moment and looks down at her feet. "What if their ex, the girl Andrew told me about, comes back and they change their mind about me."

Nina scoffs and rolls her eyes. "Trust me, you have nothing to worry about, love."

"Besides, I know you can take care of yourself. You just need a little more confidence and you could handle yourself even better."

The both of them laugh before hugging each other, and just when Nina was about to stand up, Tessa comes running into the room with concern written all over her face. Aurelia stands up and so does Nina.

"What?"

"Aiden showed up with Jackie and Genesis," Tessa says quickly, trying to explain, "Aiden started jeering about Adrian and Andrew and–"

Tessa's words were too hard to follow, but Nina just shakes her head and sighs before walking out of the room. Aurelia follows behind the two, walking down the stairs where she hears the once soft chatter turned completely into commotion.

"No, fuck you!" Adrian's voice could be heard overpowering the gasps and screams.

Nina pushes her way past the few people who were circling around them in the kitchen area. There he was, wiping his blood from his lip while staring at Adrian as he was being held back by Elijah and someone else. Andrew is nowhere to be seen and Jackie is clinging onto Aiden. Tessa did say Genesis was there, but maybe she's off in the crowd.

"And who invited you to my home?" Nina asks, crossing her arms standing in front of Aiden as he chuckles. The man licks the remaining of the blood from his lips and steps close to Nina.

"Nina!" Aiden greets, spreading his arms out wide, smiling at her. "I'm assuming my invite got lost along the way?"

"No," Nina rested her hands on her hip, tilting her head at Aiden. "You or your dead weight wasn't invited."

"Dead Weight?" Jackie questions, anger in her tone as she steps up, getting hostile. "Say that again. I dare you."

"And if she does?" Brooklynn challenges, frowning at Jackie as she walks up.

"Ladies, Ladies," Aiden grins, laughing right after, as if everything happening right now is a joke. "I'm just here to celebrate my brother's success. Can I not be here? I mean, he is my twin, afterall."

Adrian tries to break out of the hold the two men holding him back got him in. "Fuck you! You came here to start a fight, and now that I'm here, you want to play fucking victim!"

Aurelia takes a step forward, not trying to draw attention to herself, she just wanted to see if she sees Andrew anywhere. However, just one step caused Aiden to whistle before raising an eyebrow at her.

"Well, aren't you looking good this evening?" Aiden says making Aurelia uncomfortable.

"I'm not playing with you," Nina says. "Get out or I'll call the police."

Aiden jaw clenches before he takes a glass and sips from it. "Fine, see you around, Aurelia. And please, do come around dressed like that. You look real good."

Elijah steps up this time. "Go or I'll throw you out myself."

"Ooo," Aiden laughs. "I'm so scared. Ha... fuck off."

Aiden leans over to Elijah, whispering something before chuckling. The annoying man pushed his way through the crowd, making his way out. Aurelia could tell from the way Elijah's clenching his fist, and trying to hold that positive demeanor up, that he's bothered by whatever Aiden said to him just now.

"Ugh," Nina crosses her arms and rolls her eyes. "Can we turn the music back on, please."

"Adrian, come here!" Nina says, grabbing his hand and leading him upstairs.

Aurelia walks closer to Elijah and hesitantly grabs his clenched fist. "Do you want to step outside for a bit?"

Elijah looks down at her before nodding. Aurelia holds his hand and leads him outside, her feet were hurting from the heels, but somehow she was more worried about Elijah than herself at this moment. "Are you okay?"

The male sighs and leans against the brick of the wall of the home. "Yeah, Aiden is just really annoying. I tried really fucking hard not to punch him."

"Punch him?" Aurelia tilts her head and peeks up at him. "Why?"

Elijah sighs and crosses his arms. "Well, as you just saw, baby, he's not the most likable person."

She smiles a bit and shakes her head. "Yeah, well, that's obvious."

"You have a beautiful smile, Aurelia." Elijah says, making her swallow hard. "Sometimes, when you smile, either at me or others, I forget about the shit happening in the moment."

Aurelia could feel her throat slowly becoming drier as she stared into his eyes. "Just... Sometimes?"

Elijah pushes himself off the wall, and stands in front of her. "Well, lately it's been more than sometimes. Why? Is that a problem?"

Even though his tone held amusement, it was clear he was curious about her answer. Aurelia stares at his chest, causing the male to gently nudge her chin up, so she could look him in the eyes.

"No." she responded. "It's not a problem."

"Good." He says deeply, staring into her eyes.

The tension between them was high, but she knows that now would be the right time to halt things. "So... where did Andrew go?"

Elijah slowly steps back, and pushes his hand in the pocket of his pants. "He said that he was going to go to the bathroom, just before Aiden showed up, but that was a couple of minutes ago. He's probably inside now, why? Did he say something again?"

"No, no. I just... was wondering where he was." Aurelia says, looking down at her hands.

He nods. "You know I was going to punch him, Aiden, for talking to you like that."

Aurelia's eyes widened.

"Well, it was the other reason for why I wanted to hurt him really badly." he admits making her place her hand on his chest and shake her head.

"I'm glad you didn't, because I'm sure he wanted you to hurt him." She tells him before looking back into the party. "I'm glad it didn't turn into complete chaos–"

"There you two are," Andrew says, walking from out of nowhere. "Having secret meetings are we?"

Elijah closes his eyes, and sighs before looking over at Andrew. "No, just needed fresh air. Aiden paid his brother a visit."

"That explains the tension." Andrew says walking closer, smiling at Aurelia before looking at Elijah again. "I have places to be tomorrow morning, so I think I'm going to go."

Aurelia watches the male push his phone in his pocket before clearing his throat. She looks into his eyes and tilts her head a bit. "I'm assuming that you will stay a while longer?"

"Wait," Elijah crosses his arms. "You aren't coming back with me? Where are you going to stay?"

Andrew's long fingers combs through his wavy hair, before he grins. "You shouldn't worry, I'll be on my best behavior."

"That's not what I asked–"

The shortish male sighs. "Let's not do this right now."

Aurelia knows that Elijah is probably still on edge because of Aiden, so it's just a matter of time before he snaps on Andrew for the wrong reasons. She didn't know what to do, but she did what she thought was best.

"At least call, when you make it there. So... he can know that you are safe." Aurelia says, causing both men to look at her.

She could see it. Well, at least she assmused she could. Their eyes were showing that they were completely submitting. Maybe what Elijah was saying before was true. Maybe she was responsible for some relief, even though she had nc idea what they needed relief from.

"Okay," Andrew nods. "I can do that. I'll call and let you... both know I'm safe and sound."

The handsome man fixes his suit jacket before returning his hands to his pocket with a small grin. "Now, I'll be taking my leave."

Elijah and Aurelia watch the man walk away. Even though she wasn't all that concerned, the man beside her was definitely concerned. It was written all over his face. She just wishes she could help ease his mind, but how can she when she had no idea what was bothering him.

"I like art museums." Aurelia says, watching Elijah pull his gaze from the direction Andrew went to her. "All kinds of art, even if it's not an art museum."

He smiles a bit and crosses his arms. "How about I take you to one tomorrow, if you aren't busy."

Aurelia smiles and shakes her head.

"I'm free."

□

twenty-six

Art is a mirror reflecting the complexities of life, capturing its tumultuous waves and serene shores alike. In the strokes of a painter's brush or the words of a poet's verse, we find echoes of our own struggles and triumphs. Just as life is rife with trials and tribulations, so too is art often born from the crucible of adversity. Yet, within the very fabric of art lies a profound lesson about resilience and redemption. For just as an artist may paint over mistakes or a sculptor may mold anew from a flawed creation, so too can we, in the canvas of our own lives, find the courage to move beyond past missteps.

Aurelia looks at her phone screen, which she got fixed yesterday with Adrian, she was going through the pictures her best friends sent her. Sabrina sent her pictures of her time she spent at a beach, and Cameron sent the group chat pictures of him at the club partying. They haven't changed even though it feels like it has been forever since they've been together.

"Aurelia, baby, are you listening?" Her mother's voice speaks through the speaker of the phone, causing her to finally close the group chat and actually engage in the conversation with her mother. She sits her phone on top of the dresser before resuming her search on finding something to wear.

"Yes, ma'am." Aurelia says, looking through her drawer. "But I already told you, I wouldn't know until I get to that point."

"Relia, I told you that you need to be more organized. You need to know how much it'll cost to be in student housing for the next year." Her mother lectures, but she didn't understand that they were hardly approaching the middle of the term.

"Yes, momma." She sighs softly, pulling out a long black denim skirt. "I'll call you later, I'm busy right now."

"Alright, Aurelia. Make sure you study well, I love you."

"I love you too, momma." Aurelia says, ending the call just as Nina walks in.

Nina sighs and shakes her head. "Your momma must have forgotten you're an adult, not an adolescent."

Aurelia shakes her head and pulls out a black cropped tank top from her other drawer. "She's just worried. My momma spent most of her time working, so when I got accepted to this school, she started realizing that she hadn't really been around me that much. You know, she feels like lost time with me."

"I see." Nina walks her way, opening her drawer, looking through her clothes before grabbing her blue denim skirt, one that's similar to the black one, and replacing the top she pulled out with an off the shoulder lace top. "What about your dad?"

Aurelia watches her friend, Nina, go through her things, picking any outfit out for her. She sits down on the bed and sighs before shaking her head. "He was a teacher, so I spent more time with him than my mom."

"My dad was a professor, until word got out about the affair he was having with a student." Nina says, grabbing her ankle high leather shoes and walking the outfit to her. "My dad divorced him, I have two dads, and here I am ten years later, a beautiful, tall, and talented artist."

"I-I'm sorry, Nina." Aurelia says, grabbing the outfit for her.

"For what? That was ten years ago? I haven't spoken to my other father in years, but I still love my dad." She says, putting her hand on her hip. "Now, are you going to tell me why you're getting all dressed up?"

Aurelia smiles, appreciating that Nina felt comfortable enough to share that part of herself. "Elijah is taking me to an art museum."

"Oh?" Nina raises an eyebrow, picking jewelry out for her as well. "Just to think, last night you were having such a hard time grasping the idea of going out with the man."

She wasn't completely wrong, Aurelia was a bit nervous when she thought about going on separate dates with her, but after spending that one moment with him, she couldn't help but wonder. Was it wrong to wonder.

"I mean, It was my idea to go. He seemed on edge, so I suggested he take me to an art museum." Aurelia explains, smiling a bit before taking the clothes Nina set out and walking towards the room door. "I'm honestly curious about him too, maybe this would help him break some of those walls down he has up."

Elijah seems like an open book, but she could tell that he hides something away, but even as he hides it, his thoughts and true emotions always break through his facade whenever he's mad. Even last night, when he looked her in the eyes and said her smile helps him. No one who's an open book and people could read without a problem says things like that.

"Well," Nina crosses her arms and smiles. "I know you'd be a better person than their ex, trust me."

Aurelia watches the tall girl for a second before she leave her room, closing the door behind her. She looks at the outfit and shakes her head at how cute it was. Though she would've gone for a darker color, she trusts Nina's judgment so she doesn't mind wearing what she chose for her. Since she had been living with the woman her entire wardrobe changed, for the most part. It's not like she went out to buy new clothes, Nina just helped her style the clothes she does have to make them look different. Even though it changed, she was still comfortable with the way it made her feel.

Confidence is surely building inside her. She's also starting to find herself very beautiful.

As she walks inside the bathroom, Aurelia washes her face, since she already showered an hour before she got a phone call from her mother. When she finish washing her face, Aurelia begins undressing, putting on the outfit. She thought she looked cute, and normally she would think the clothes themself look cute, but not herself. This is the first time she believes she's actually cute. As she finishes dressing up, she walks out the bathroom hearing talking downstairs. Aurelia takes her clothes to her room before going down the stairs to see who's there. As she gets half way down, she could hear Nina snap.

"I don't care what you have to say, leave and don't even think about coming back!"

Her voice sounds so distress, and that really bother her. Aurelia walks down the stairs, seeing Nina standing at the front door, crossing her arms as she talks to someone standing outside the front door. The woman was the same height as her. She has big dark brown curls, and her style matched her mysterious vibe she had going on. Who was this? Why was Nina yelling at her?

"Nina," the mysterious woman says calmly, crossing her arm. "I told you i had to leave the city, and the night that i did leave, I also told you I'd be back. We are best friends, why are you being this way?"

Nina scoffs, holding the doorknob. "Correction, we were best friend, and best friends don't fuck with people they best friend down't like and they definitely don't fuck people over because some guy asked them too."

"Is that what this is about, Nina? I already told you, no one told me what to do. They were being over dramatic and assuming shit. All because I am friends with Aiden." The woman says, causing Aurelia to tilt her head as she approaches.

"Nina who is this?" Aurelia asks, crossing ehr arm, causing the woman to look over her shoulder.

"Oh, just a nobody, that same nobody who got five seconds before this door connects with her face if she doesn't get the fuck away from my door." Nina says looking back at the woman. "Five."

"Real mature Nina." The woman says, looking over at Aurelia. "Who the fuck are you?"

"Four."

Aurelia looks up at Nina before looking at the woman again, not sure if she should answer. "I rather not give a stranger my name, sorry."

"Three." Nina says, her voice getting lower, and more threatening. "Bitch if I get to one, I'm just going to beat your ass."

The woman sighs and shakes her head. "You know, Aiden was right about you, You replaced me and sided with them. Fuck you Nina."

Nina slams the door on her face, and groans out of frustration and walks around Aurelia and storms to the kitchen to pour herself a drink. "That girl get on my nerves."

"Who was that?" Aurelia asks, watching Nina pour herself a large glass of wine.

Nina shakes her head. "My ex best friend."

"Oh."

"Don't worry about her, she's literally butt hurt because of what happened between her and—" Nina stops herself and shakes her head. "It doesn't matter."

Nina drinks the wine, and begins to walk towards the stairs. "I'm going to do some brainstorming in my room, let me know when you leave, I don't want to be working the whole time."

"O-Oh, okay." Aurelia watches the tall woman walk up the stairs, causing a sigh to fall from her lips before putting the bottle away and resuming her task of getting ready before Elijah shows up.

After finishing up with her hair, an hour later, she gets a call from Elijah. Aurelia answers the call and presses it to her ear. "Hello?"

"Hey, baby, I'm outside." He tells her as she grab her bag and walks out of her room. "Also, I noticed that the trash outside, on the curb, is knocked over."

"Oh no," Aurelia nibbles her lip. "Uh, I'll be right out, give me a moment."

"Take your time, love. I'll be waiting." He chuckles softly, making her bite her lip at the sound of his voice before ending the call.

She walks to Nina's door and knocks before walking in. Nina is stretching on the floor, with headphones on her head. Aurelia waves a bit to get her attention, and when she does, Nina smiles and nods.

"Have fun, and don't let him hit it on the first date." She jests, but the thought of sleeping with Elijah scares the hell out of her. She wasn't ready for that, and honestly she doesn't know if she would ever be ready, this soon.

"Bye, Nina." Aurelia smiles before closing her room door and quickly makes her way downstairs, looking herself in the mirror before walking towards the front door. Elijah is standing there, beside his car, looking down at his phone. He's dressed up, but casually dressed up, not anything fancy. Sort of how she's dressed. It was getting chillier by the day, and wearing the stocking underneath the skirt was the right thing to do. The man had his hair in down, and it shaped his face nicely.

"You look nice," she compliments, and his eyes widen. "I look real good in neutral colors."

"Oh? Do I?" He grins, opening the car door for her, before taking her hand and bringing her knuckles to his lip. The whole time, his eyes were on her, making her melt inside. "Well, I think you look beautiful in everything, Aurelia."

She smiles and murmurs a small thank you before getting into the car. Elijah closes the door and sits in the driver seat. The trip to the museum felt different from when she got in his car before. Before she was much more quiet, allowing Elijah to lead the conversation, but now she's asking questions, joking around with him, and laughing.

"So," he chuckles. "Besides that, what happened today?"

"Oh," Aureli shrugs and looks out of the window. "Nina ex-bestfriend showed up and caused a ruckus, but Nina told her to leave the moment she got there."

Elijah stops the car, swallowing hard before forcing a smile. She knew it was forced because that charm wasn't there. The same charm she's used to seeing when he does smile.

"Okay," Aurelia says, folding her hands in her lap. "Who is she?"

"She's our ex," Elijah told her right away. "There's no point of keeping it from you, it's not like we want anything to do with her, but she's someone we used to be with."

Aurelia didn't want to know more, knowing that she was their ex was enough. "Thank you for telling me, I appreciate it."

Elijah smiles and parks the car on the opposite side of the museum. The both of them walk in together, and the place wasn't as crowded as it could've been, but seeing the different pieces of art made her envious. She always wanted her own little section in an art gallery or museum. Observing people's reaction when they see her work is something that she desperately wanted to experience.

"My grandfather owns this building," Elijah whispers in her ear as she looks at the painting on the wall. "He bought it out when I was seven, and he took Arthur and I here every weekend."

"Wow." she smiles peeling her eyes from the painting. "What was your favorite piece here?"

Elijah tilts his head, making a thinking face before holding her hand. The man leads her further inside, going up a set of stairs before bringing her to a large painting hanging from the ceiling. It was titled the ocean's fire creates the earth's wind. It is a huge painting of the oceans and above the ocean is a sunset, cascading the beautiful illusion of fire onto the ocean.

"This piece was hand painted by my great great grandfather, Frederick James. My grandfather used to tell me stories about how long it took him to paint the piece. He's actually the person who inspired me to do art to begin with." Elijah explains, as Aurelia just stares in awe.

"It's so beautiful, Elijah, really." Aurelia compliments the piece before admiring it some more.

"Who inspired you? Or inspires you today?" He asks, making Aurelia smile fall before looking away, walking to the next piece.

"Well," Aurelia sighs. "When I was a kid I watched a cartoon and saw a beautiful painting, and from then I loved art and wanted to make works of art on my own. When I got to high school, I followed... your brother a lot. He was my inspo and I loved his work. I never witness art like his, art that's so good that it just takes your ability to talk away."

"Really?" Elijah says, his tone changed, causing her to glance at him.

Clearly talking about his brother bothers him, and she could tell right away that he's jealous. "What about my art? Does it make you feel that way?"

Aurelia shrugs. "I never really took the time to look at your art. Maybe you can show it?

"We'll have to change that then." He chuckles leading her to the next set of art pieces. They were all so beautiful she could hardly decide which one she loved best. Elijah told her more about the pieces that he loved as a kid, giving her more details to who made them and why his grandfather picked them. It was easier to walk around and get details than she was reading it herself.

For the rest of the evening, they walked around some more before Aurelia calls the evening to end.

☐

twenty-seven

Successful dates, much like successful pieces of art, are crafted with care, attention to detail, and an understanding of the beauty in imperfection. Just as a first date can leave a lasting impression, a beloved artwork has the power to captivate the soul and evoke emotions that linger long after the encounter. Both experiences are enriched by authenticity, vulnerability, and the willingness to embrace the unknown, creating moments of connection and inspiration that endure through time.

Aurelia watched with a smile as Elijah strolled back to the car, carrying a bag brimming with food. After their museum visit, they wandered around the area, admiring the majestic pieces of art that were too grand to be confined within museum walls, instead displayed outside. They snapped photos, and for once, Aurelia didn't feel the usual shyness creeping in when being photographed.

Back in high school, Aurelia often found herself either hiding her face or avoiding participating in photos altogether. She lacked confidence and felt insecure about her appearance in pictures. However, she didn't mind capturing moments of her friends or her artwork. Being in front of the camera just wasn't her thing. But when Elijah stealthily snapped a picture of her admiring the outdoor art, she couldn't help but feel beautiful, especially when Elijah made sure she knew it.

The evening was still young, but dusk was approaching. Elijah settled into the driver's seat of his sleek gray car with a soft sigh. Aurelia glanced over at him, extending her hand to offer assistance as he adjusted himself in the seat. Despite not ordering much—she craved a chicken sandwich while he opted for a burger—they decided to share a large fry. He also grabbed a couple of bottled waters, considering Aurelia's preference for something non-sugary. As he handed her the bag, Aurelia reached into the back for his jacket, the one he had left behind when he picked her up, and draped it over her lap.

"Thank you," she murmured, smiling at the sweet gesture. "You really didn't have to, but thank you anyway."

"Well, I just thought you wouldn't want to risk getting your outfit dirty," he chuckled, taking the bag from her hand. "Here you go."

Elijah handed her the chicken sandwich first before grabbing his own burger. He placed the bag in the center compartment, positioning it between them for easy access to the fries.

"Did you always dream of running a tattoo parlor?" Aurelia inquired, unwrapping her sandwich and taking a satisfying bite, her gaze drifting everywhere but towards Elijah.

"Actually, no," he replied between bites, trying not to speak with his mouth full. "Surprisingly, my mother always pushed my brother and me towards the creative path, but she was more focused on Arthur's success than mine. It became evident pretty quickly that my mother only wanted one of us to be the family's shining star."

Aurelia winced at the revelation, covering her mouth with her hand as confusion washed over her features. This time, she looked directly at him. "What do you mean?"

Elijah grinned, brushing crumbs off his lap as he glanced down. "It means my mother preferred one son to bask in the spotlight alone; she didn't like us sharing it."

"Wow, that's... truly terrible," she says, her voice filled with genuine empathy as she watches Elijah.

"Well," Elijah responds, glancing over at her, his gaze locking with hers before he shrugs, "My mother is quite the complicated individual. Given how neglectful she was toward me when I was a child, I naturally grew rather distant from her. So, I suppose it'd be rather pathetic if I weren't used to it by now."

"What about you?" he asks, casually munching on some fries from the bag. "Did you always aspire to be an artist?"

Aurelia sighs inwardly, recognizing his attempt to divert the conversation away from his family issues. "Yes," she responds promptly, with unwavering certainty. "I've wanted this ever since I could wield a crayon and put it to paper. Art has always been my passion, in every form imaginable."

"I assume," he murmurs, his tone dampening the mood, "you never considered pursuing anything else, huh?"

Aurelia tilts her head slightly. "Why would I?" she counters. "My mom's a doctor, and my dad's a school teacher. I can't see myself fitting into either of those roles, especially considering my aversion to public speaking for teaching and my inability to handle high-pressure situations for the medical field."

He falls silent, still chewing his food. Once he's finished, he looks at her intently. "I'm not passing judgment, baby, just trying to understand you better."

"What do you mean?" she asks, echoing his initial question that started this conversation. "I'm an open book, and I'm not one to mince words."

Elijah shakes his head, visibly disagreeing with her assertion, taking a sip from the water bottle before setting it down. "Nobody's truly an open book, especially not you."

He presses on, his tone serious. "You keep a lot bottled up inside, and just when I think I've got you figured out, you throw me a curveball, straight to the face."

"When have I ever left you confused, Elijah?" she inquires, her tone a mix of confusion and curiosity.

"When we first asked you out," he says, shaking his head and averting his gaze from her this time, "we were convinced you'd say yes. We were certain that you felt the same way about us as we do about you. But you threw us for a loop when you said you didn't know, which also meant no."

Aurelia tilts her head in confusion, her face now completely masked by bewilderment, her tone rising slightly. "I didn't know you two. When I lived with you, you two were hardly there, and I didn't know. That uncertainty made me unsure if I wanted to be with you two. Where is all of this coming from? I thought we agreed to take things slow."

"We are taking things slow," he assures her, turning to hold her hand gently. "I'm not trying to upset you. We just really like you, and I don't want these solo dates to turn into something Andrew and I had to deal with in the past. In other words, I love that we are spending time together alone like this for your sake, but–"

"Your ex, right?" she interrupts, her tone softer now. "This has something to do with yours and Andrew's ex-girlfriend."

Elijah falls into an unusual silence, quieter now than he was when they left the museum, almost as if he's getting cold feet. His demeanor, usually so composed, seems to falter in the face of whatever is weighing on his mind.

"It's a long story, one that I don't feel right telling you without Andrew present," he mumbles, running his hand down his face. "I'm sorry for ruining the date. I just want to discuss important things, but I don't know what to bring up. You just make me nervous."

"I make you nervous?" she laughs softly, watching as his serious expression fades away like rain when the clouds part and the sun breaks through the gloom. Aurelia had expected this date to go more smoothly since she had only seen him become serious or upset once or twice, and never with her. Yet, here he is, vulnerable and uncertain, and it's both disconcerting and oddly endearing.

"Is that hard to believe?" he asks playfully, raising an eyebrow. "You don't think I blush when you look at me or when you smile, my heart races? One of these days, I might have a heart attack because of you, Aurelia."

Aurelia's laughter fills the space between them, her mind wandering to imagined scenes of their future together. She envisions lazy mornings, the mornings when she doesn't have class or any other work to do, and the both of them spend it tangled in bedsheets. Aurelia could almost envision the sunlight streaming through the curtains as they shared whispered compliments and dreams. She imagines painting together, laughter ringing through the office area as they work on their art pieces. And in these moments, she sees Elijah not just as the confident, smooth-sailing man she's come to know, but as someone vulnerable and real, someone she could truly build something with.

Laughing, she shakes her head, feeling a warmth spread through her chest at the thought. "You're dramatic too? That's new. I'm used to seeing the confident, smooth-talking Elijah."

He shrugs, a small smile playing at the corners of his lips as he stares into her eyes. "We all have those days when our masks fall, right?" And in that moment, Aurelia realizes that perhaps the most beautiful thing about their connection is the ability to see each other, masks and all, and still find something worth holding onto.

As the silence falls between them again, Elijah checks his watch and nods thoughtfully. "I should get you back home. Can't afford to be exhausted before classes tomorrow, right?"

Aurelia shrugs nonchalantly and nods in agreement. "I suppose so. Most of my classes start after twelve in the afternoon, so even if I get back late, I'll still have time to unwind before class."

Elijah nods, beginning to tidy up the area with her. "When Andrew was still attending, his schedule was similar to yours, but that was last year. This year would've been a lot smoother."

Her curiosity is piqued. Aurelia pauses in folding Elijah's jacket, the one he kindly offered to cover her lap. "Why isn't he attending? He would be a fourth-year student, right?" She gazes at Elijah, searching for any hint of hesitation in his response.

She had heard a few stories, whispers that danced through the halls of their shared campus, but upon reflection, none of them were ones she wanted to believe simply because she wanted to hear the story from the source. When it came to such detailed accusations and rumors, Aurelia knew firsthand the importance of hearing from the person the rumor concerned. It was a principle she held dear, one she believed in adamantly.

However, as she glanced at Elijah, she could sense his surprise, the subtle shift in his expression betraying his unexpected reaction to her question. His eyes held a hint of vulnerability, a flicker of something unspoken beneath the surface.

"You haven't heard anything?" Elijah asks, his voice tinged with a mixture of curiosity and disbelief, his head tilting slightly to the side in a gesture of inquiry.

Aurelia shrugs her shoulders and looks down at her lap, a faint furrow appearing between her brows. "I have heard some things," she admits softly, her tone thoughtful. "But who's to say they're true? As I've mentioned to you and Andrew before, people here just do not seem to like you two—less than the people who do like you. But, I've also been around those who are part of the latter group."

Elijah sighs as he starts the car, the engine purring to life with a gentle hum. "It's a long story," he says quietly, his voice carrying a weight of unresolved emotions.

"It seems like you two have a lot of stories," Aurelia observes, her gaze drifting to the passing scenery outside the car window. "Any of them you are willing to share, Elijah?" She turns back to him, her expression a mix of curiosity and frustration, but who's to say she could feel this way? If the man didn't want to talk about it, he didn't have to.

"It's not like I don't want to tell you," Elijah begins, his voice steady as he keeps his eyes on the road ahead and his hands firmly on the steering wheel. "But most of these things you want to know about don't involve me directly. They involve Andrew more than anything, and he's the one who can give you the answers you want, rather than me."

His words hang in the air, a reminder of the complexities that exist within the start of their relationship. Despite the intimacy they've created in the car, one that's non sexual, there are still boundaries to navigate, secrets to be kept, and truths to unfold.

Aurelia listens quietly, her mind racing with questions left unanswered, uncertainties lingering in the spaces between them. She understands Elijah's reluctance, respects the boundaries he's set, but the curiosity still gnaws at her, a persistent ache she can't quite shake.

"I understand." she murmurs softly, her gaze returning to the passing scenery outside the car window.

"I can tell you this," Elijah says, his voice tinged with a hint of regret as he sighs softly. "He had a big incident that happened, and because it occurred on the campus grounds, technically, he was removed from the school."

As Elijah's words hang in the air, a heavy silence envelops the car, thick with unspoken emotions and unanswered questions. Aurelia's mind races, grappling with the implications of what she has just learned. She can feel the weight of Elijah's sorrow, the burden of carrying a secret that has undoubtedly taken its toll on him.

In the midst of her turmoil, Aurelia finds herself drawn to Elijah, his vulnerability laying bare before her. She marvels at the strength it must take for him to confide in her, to share a piece of his past that is undoubtedly painful to revisit.

"I'm sorry," she murmurs softly, her voice barely above a whisper. "I had no idea."

Elijah offers her a small, sad smile, his eyes reflecting a mixture of sadness and gratitude. "It's not something I like to talk about," he admits, his voice heavy with emotion. "Especially when Andrew isn't here. I trust you, Aurelia. And I want you to know the truth, but it's really up to him. He gets sensitive about everything dealing with the situation."

The sincerity in his words touches her deeply, warming her heart with a newfound sense of understanding. In that moment, Aurelia realizes just how much Elijah values their connection, how much he is willing to risk in order to share his innermost thoughts and fears with her.

As they continue their journey home, the weight of Elijah's revelation hangs between them, a silent reminder of the bond they share. Aurelia finds herself lost in thought, her mind swirling with questions she wants to ask Andrew, if she ever gets ahold of him.

"We're here," Elijah announces as he parks the car. "Want me to walk you to the door?"

Aurelia glances at the door and nods, meeting his gaze once more before stepping out of the car. Elijah follows suit, leaving the engine running as they make their way to the front door of her home. As they reach the final landing, Elijah clears his throat, prompting her to turn towards him.

"This date started well and turned rather serious fast," he jests, slipping his hand into his pocket. "But I still enjoyed every moment we spent together, and I hope you did too."

She smiles, her gaze shifting briefly to her feet. "No, I did enjoy myself. It was fun. Really fun, and I hope we spend more time together. Thank you for the date, Elijah."

Their eyes meet once more, and Aurelia finds herself drawn into his gaze. With a sudden surge of boldness, she stands slightly on her tiptoes and plants a kiss on the corner of his lips. Before she can open the door, however, Elijah pulls her back gently, cupping her cheek as he leans in to kiss her.

At first, Aurelia is taken aback by the unexpected gesture. It's her first kiss, and she's unsure how to respond. But as Elijah guides her, she finds herself surrendering to the moment, leaning into the kiss with a mixture of surprise and desire. Just as things start to intensify, Elijah breaks the kiss, apologizing softly as their foreheads rest against each other, their breaths mingling in the cool night air.

"Sorry," he murmurs, his voice laced with regret. "I should've asked—"

"No," Aurelia interrupts, her own breath coming in soft pants. "I liked it. I liked that you surprised me with that kiss. Even though it was my first."

They share a quiet laugh before Aurelia reluctantly releases the doorknob, still locked in Elijah's gaze. He begins to walk backward towards his car, and she watches him go, a sense of longing tugging at her heart.

"Text me when you get home, okay?" she calls after him, causing him to clear his throat before agreeing with a nod.

With one last lingering look, Aurelia finally opens the door and steps inside, her mind still reeling from the whirlwind of emotions that had just transpired. As she closes the door behind her, she can't help but feel a sense of anticipation for what the future may hold, knowing that she and Elijah had just taken a significant step forward in their relationship. The relationship where she was to share her feelings with Elijah and Andrew.

As Aurelia steps inside, she finds Nina standing there with her hands on her hips and a playful smile on her face.

"Look at you, giving a kiss on your first date," Nina remarks teasingly.

Aurelia's face lights up with happiness, grateful that she didn't feel embarrassed despite Nina's comment. Her heart is still fluttering from the evening's events, but amidst the joy, her thoughts inevitably drift to the absent figure of Andrew. Even though she had a wonderful time with Elijah, her mind keeps returning to Andrew, a constant presence lingering in the background.

Despite their agreement to go on separate dates until she's ready to make a decision, Aurelia can't shake the feeling that they're leaving Andrew out. She hopes that when and if they do go on a date, she'll be able to experience the same connection and warmth that she felt with Elijah. Perhaps then, she'll be able to make her decision more swiftly, with a clearer understanding of where her heart truly lies.

Will it always be this complex?

□

twenty-eight

Like a dance under the moonlit sky, dates and kisses intertwine, drawing us into a rhythm of passion and discovery. In the embrace of another, we may find ourselves drawn to their enigmatic darkness, yet within it lies the potential for illumination. Just as in art, where shadows give depth to the canvas, exploring someone's complexities can reveal unexpected layers of beauty and truth. It's in the delicate balance of light and shadow, movement and stillness, that we uncover the masterpiece of love.

Aurelia walks outside the art department building, taking in the summer turning into autumn air. She walks down the stone stairs, meeting Adrian at the bottom. The long haired man is staring at his phone, his thumbs moving fast across the screen. Though he wasn't looking at her, she could tell that whatever he is doing is bothering him.

"Hey, Adrian." She greets him verbally, watching the male look up from his phone and towards her as she descends down the stairs.

"Hey Relia, how did it go with Sunny?" He asks, referring to the meeting she just got out of with their Major leader, or department leader.

He called her the previous night, letting her know that someone wanted to buy her piece for five thousand dollars. That's the largest, if not the only, sum she has been offered for her art. Sunny told her an older woman, a retired doctor, wanted it. The event was a few weeks ago, and Aurelia was honestly expecting to bring her work of art home with her, since no one wanted it, especially when it was not the winning piece.

"Yeah," she smiles. "Someone bought my art piece, so Sunny wanted to give me the money from the buyer."

"That's amazing," Adrian says before looking down at his phone again, his smile fading away from his lips as the confusion settles across his face. "I'm happy for you."

"Is everything okay?" She asks, standing in front of him, crossing her arms with a concerned expression covering her face as she watches him scroll through his phone as if she wasn't standing in front of him. "You seem very... bothered."

Adrian sighs and puts his phone away, running his hands down his face right after. Aurelia obviously waited for the man to feel comfortable enough to talk to her. After a couple of seconds, the two of them begin to walk further away from the art department.

"Rochelle is being ridiculous as always," he mumbles as he shoves his hands in his cargo pants, keeping his eyes straight ahead. "Now she's saying she's pregnant, all because she saw me and Nina kissing the night of my party."

Her steps halt, causing Adrian to slow down to look over his shoulder. "What?"

"Are you sure this is just her being jealous, or is she actually pregnant." Aurelia asks genuinely.

The girl did not know her, so she wouldn't talk badly about her. That doesn't mean if she did she would, but she didn't know she would judge her, but if she's actually pregnant, Adiran shouldn't take it as something that she's just using against him, he should still try to see if it's true. She remembers Nina said that Adrian sleeps with Rochelle a lot, so many during some of those times they weren't careful.

"I know she's lying, Relia." Adrian says, walking up to her, clearly upset. "This isn't the first time she tried to pull something like this. The day she met you, she tried to say that I was using you to get over her, and then... it doesn't matter, I know she lies, and I know she's lying now."

"Are you sure?"

Adrian sighs and nods his head. "I'm one thousand percent sure. I care about Rochelle but this is part of the reason why we didn't work out. She wants to move on fast, but I want to take things a lot slower than she does. It's starting to feel like she just wants in on my family's fortune."

She has no knowledge on relationships, she only has been on one date and she still doesn't know anything about dating and being with someone. "Even if you say you know she's lying, I think you should still make sure. Please."

Adrian crosses his arms and shrugs. "That is what she wants me to do, drop everything to come check on her, just so she can go down on me when I try to leave."

"Do you ever reject her advances?" She questions watching the male's eyes slowly look away.

She knew it.

"So no wonder why she's like this," Aurelia mumbles to him. "I don't know much about relationships but I do know what it looks like when you're leading someone on. If you don't want anything romantic with her then stop sleeping with her."

Her words are short, blunt and harsh.

"I tell her every time we sleep together that it's just that. We're sleeping together. I'm not leading her on, she's just refusing to move on." He explains, walking alongside Aurelia again. "It's not wrong to sleep with your ex, especially when you establish that there are no strings attached."

Aurelia looks down, stopping just at the curb of the parking lot. "Is this how complicated relationships can become?"

"There are no real perfect relationships. Even friendships are complicated. You just got to figure things out along the way. Right now, in my current situation, I'm going to tell Rochelle that I'm not sleeping with her again. That way we can solve the pregnancy scare problem and problems in the future." Adrian sighs and looks at his car parked across the parking lot. "Need a ride?"

Aurelia shakes her head and looks down at her feet. "I actually want to ask you something."

"You sound so serious, what's up?" He tilts his head. Looking down at her.

"Elijah took me out, and I can't–"

"He did what?" Adrian interrupted her, making her frown slightly at the rude outburst, but it was quickly replaced with her normal expression. "Does Andrew know? Are you like... going to be with them both or..?"

Aurelia looks around, watching people past them. She looks down with embarrassment covering her face now. The girl nods her head and crosses her arms. "I'm getting to that, but it's hard to say when I only have been on one date with Elijah, and none with Andrew. Not to mention, I'm really inexperienced with these things."

"Your first relationship will be with two people? Wow." He comments, making her roll her eyes before looking away from him.

He chuckles and wraps his arm around her shoulder and brings her in for a side hug. "I'm only teasing you, Relia."

"I know!" She says, annoyance laced in her tone. "I just wonder if going on separate dates will actually get me to... want to be with them."

"Have you kissed either of them?" he pulls a vape from his pocket, puffing away from her.

Aurelia nods slowly, and looks up at him.

The male shrugs. "Isn't kissing like confirming the relationship?"

"Is it?" She questions, playing with the rings on her fingers and the bracelet on her wrist.

"I mean if you both have feelings for each other, I guess that's confirmation." He explains looking at his watch on his wrist. "I love to help you out with your relationship problem, but I have to go. Just text me about it or call, we can talk like that."

Aurelia nods her head. "Alright. I'll talk to you later then. See you later, Adrian."

The male puts his vape away and begins to make his way towards his parked car, which is in the first row of cars. Aurelia takes this time to pull out her phone to ask Elijah for a ride, but the sound of loud music makes her turn her head towards the dance department which isn't too far from the campus parking lot.

Aurelia turns around completely and follows the music all the way to the outdoor performance stage. There were a bunch of students stretching, talking, and laughing. She's a sucker for art, so any form of it causes her to completely take it in, learn about it. Dancing is an art form, so why not watch them practice.

"Alright, you all know the drill." Genesis shouts over everyone, dressed in her pale pink colors on the stage. "If you want the top fifteen spots of the group performance follow this choreography. This will be the partner section of the group, so pay attention! Sean!"

Aurelia finds a seat in the back, watching carefully out of curiosity. She haven't seen Genesis since the party for Adrian, so seeing her serious about her class made her wonder why she's so... dramatic when it comes to certain things.

Sean and Genesis take their positions while some people partnered up with someone. All together there were six duos, meaning twelve individuals trying out.

As the music begins to play, Genesis and Sean start dancing. Aurelia watches closely, already noticing how there's no real chemistry with them. Even if they are friends, the performance seems forced and not fluid.

After they finish up, everyone looks at each other before trying to practice. Aurelia stands up, deciding to leave, since she expected better quality of the performance. As she turns to leave she hears a familiar voice shouting over the talking.

"That was decent," Andrew says, walking towards the stage. "But I know you are better than decent."

Genesis' entire face lights up before she runs to him. Andrew puts his hand up, stopping her before walking around to greet Sean. The two of them share a hug before he turns to Genesis again.

The ginger woman jumps on him, and Aurelia watches him hug her back before putting her down on her feet.

"Start the music! Andrew will dance with me to show you how the dance goes!" She informs the dancers. As the music plays again, Aurelia takes her seat and watches them perform.

As she watches the both of them, she could definitely tell it was much more fluid, smooth, and the chemistry is there. The way they move together just made the performance a whole lot better than the first. Everyone cheers along as the two of them dance, and by the end, everyone jumps on the stage to greet Andrew.

Aurelia stands up and walks closer to the stage watching Andrew laughs and smile, something she hardly sees. From the looks of it, he seems the most happy when he's surrounded by the people he spent years with.

"You got to perform with us next week Drew!" Someone says loudly, making her laugh softly at the nickname.

"Yeah! We can definitely fit a solo stage! Like old times!" Someone else shouts, but she could tell, from where she was standing, that he wasn't really happy about the suggestions. That once happy smile turned into a fake one.

"We can definitely squeeze you in, Drew. I'm sure the campus would love to see you dance with us. This is our last year here." Genesis says, clinging to his arm while everyone agrees.

Andrew pulls his arm from Genesis and looks around before his eyes land on her. She didn't know where to look, so she just glanced away before looking at him again. He sighs and nods his head.

"Alright. I'll dance with you all, just send me the details and I'll make it to the practice." He says, as he hops off the stage and makes his way towards her.

"Hey, pretty Angel." He says loud enough for her to hear before wrapping his arm around her shoulder and turning around to wave goodbye.

"Hey..." she says softly.

Aurelia awkwardly looks away, especially when she could feel Genesis' glares. She looks Andrew in the eyes and he winks at her before walking away with her under his arm. "See you all tomorrow!"

As everyone cheers him off one last time, the both of them walk away from the area.

"You liked the show," he asks, whispering in her ear, making her shyly push him back a bit. "I love it when you're like this, too shy to look me in the eyes."

"I never seen you so happy before," she says, watching the male's eyes change. "You really must enjoy dancing."

Andrew stays quiet for a moment before shrugging a bit. "That's what I decided to go to this school for, but the one thing I loved about this fucking school was ripped from me."

Aurelia stops walking, standing in front of him. She places her hand on his chest and smiles at him. "You don't need the school to do what you love, Andrew. Your passion for dance is here, not in this department. You're amazing Andrew, you don't need a school to prove it."

The male tilts his head and chuckles softly before looking down at his feet. "Well, when you put it that way, it makes me want to prove to them I'm the best thing they ever had."

"You don't need to, Drew," she teases. "You're beyond amazing."

"You're gassing me up, careful, Angel. The more you feed my ego the more I want to show off." He comments arrogantly, pulling her close. "How was your date with Eli?"

Aurelia smiles. "Good. I had fun."

"At an art museum?" He raises an eyebrow, as he wraps his arm around her shoulder and walks towards the campus parking lot. "I know five billion things we can do that's more fun than that."

Aurelia shakes her head. "Even though I love art, I'll humor you. What can we do, Andrew?"

The man grins wildly before holding her hand this time and leading her to the bus stop near the school. It's been a while since she took the bus anywhere. Aurelia would normally just catch a ride with her friends. As they wait at the bus stop, some street performers, the ones who create live music for tips. They waited for a red light before walking into the street to start performing. Aurelia holds her tote bag to herself and smiles as she watches the performers.

The wait for the bus was going to be long anyway, so she just enjoyed the music. However, Andrew had different plans. When one of the performers starts singing, Andrew starts dancing around her, causing her to laugh at him.

"What are you doing?" She watches him, laughing a bit softer.

The street performance begins to move on their side of the street, hyping Andrew up as he dances. He was right about one thing, he loves the attention. Eventually the crowd got larger, and Andrew must've got bored dancing alone. The man pulls her in the crowd.

"Andrew no! I don't know how to dance!"

He ignores her.

"Andrew–"

He pulls her closer, his hand on her waist while the other holds her hand in his. "Follow my lead, anyone can dance. All you gotta do is find the right rhythm and you'll know what to do next."

Aurelia follows Andrew lead, trying hard not to embarrass herself. She keeps stepping on his foot, but each time he spins her and pulls her in, her nerves disappear and her confidence is pushed forward with laughter and cheers from others. As their bus approaches, Andrew thanks the street performers and pays them a lot.

Of course seeing that money shocked her, but it made her more happy to see him give it to people who possibly needed it.

Aurelia pays for the bus ride and so does Andrew. They sit next to each other panting happily before laughing.

"You're not a bad dancer, Angel. You should take some private lessons with me." He grins before sending her a wink.

She rolls her eyes. "You would love that, wouldn't you?"

"I would like to, but once we're in the moment I would most definitely love it." He chuckles quietly near her ear.

She tilts her head, starting to wonder if they are talking about dancing.

"So where are we off to," she asks him, looking out the window. "I have class in two hours."

"Oops."

Aurelia snaps her attention in his direction, he wasn't even looking at her, and he wasn't hiding his grin. "What do you mean oops!? Andrew, I have to go to class."

"Live a little, Angel. Missing one class isn't going to hurt." He murmurs, crossing his arms.

"I have three classes, Drew!" She whispers to avoid attention.

"Triple oops?"

Aurelia's mouth hangs open before she looks away from him. What is she going to do? Missing three classes? Where were they even going?

"Angel," Andrew places his hand on her knee, soothing his thumb over her knee as he tries to calm her down. "You're going to forget all about those classes, trust me."

Trust him?

Aurelia nods her head and they sit side by side together for ten more minutes before Andrew requests the bus to stop at the next bus stop. He takes her hand and they get out in front of a park. The man leads the way, making, walking down the path while humming.

"Were you and Genesis always close?" She asks as they walk together to where? She doesn't know where he's taking her.

Andrew sighs. "Something like that."

"Like what though? Were you more than friends?" She pushes a little, trying to get him to open up to her.

"We weren't dating," he says, glancing at her before looking ahead again. "We were dance partners, sex partners, and now barely acquaintances."

Aurelia nods her head and looks down, trying to find the right questions to ask without upsetting him. She has done that before, and she doesn't want to upset him.

"Are you always in your head?" He questions this time, making her shrug.

"I do tend to overthink a lot," she admits. "I get so in my head that I coward away sometimes."

Andrew takes her hand and begins climbing through the bushes and trees, to some big opening. Surrounding the opening is nothing but trees, and in the middle of the opening is an abandoned building.

"What is this place?" She lets go of his hand, but he pulls her back and brings his finger up to his lips, signaling for her to be quiet.

"Spaghetti! Meatball!" He calls out, and waits, and without a second longer, two cats come running out, meowing loudly as they waste no time jumping on Andrew.

He laughs and sits on the grass and pulls four cans of cat food out of his pocket. "Did you girls miss me?"

Aurelia smiles and kneels beside him, watching Him open the first can and fluffing the food for them both before giving it to them. The cats instantly start digging in, eating the food up.

"Where did you find them?" She asks, watching from afar.

"After leaving Genesis place, back then, I heard crying in the alley, and right outside the restaurant next door, in a box that said Spaghetti and meatballs on it, they were inside. Little kittens." He explains smiling as he watches them eat. "I couldn't bring them to my dorm room, and I didn't know Elijah at the time, so I just found them a place to stay. I bring them food and water three times a day, and sometimes Spend hours playing with them."

"Andrew," she sighs happily. "That's so sweet."

"I guess." He shrugs. "I love these two, If I'm honest, they helped me through the toughest times."

"Really?" She pushes, watching him nod his head.

"I'm sure you heard about my overdose." Andrew says, glancing at her. "That overdose ruined my entire life. Sometimes, I blame myself, but now, I'm blaming everyone else. Can't even say it was an accident. I did the drugs, but that night... I knew I didn't do everything that they were saying."

Aurelia sits on her butt, giving her knees some rest. She dust her pants off and watch Andrew give them the second can. "Do you believe you were set up?"

"I know I was." He tells her while he pet the cats gently. "Hanging around Aiden only proves my point. He's the reason I'm like this. Kicked out my school, disowned by my parents. Everything."

"Then, what are you doing about it?"

"Listening around. seeing if anyone fucks up and slips that Aiden drugged me." He says, looking at her. "That's why I go to their parties, someone's bound to know what happened that night."

"I'm sorry. Andrew."

"No, they'll be sorry. So don't apologize." He murmurs, looking in her direction.

"You still went through a lot, and you are currently going through a lot." She comments, watching him closely as his eyes look at her lips before slowly looking into her eyes again.

"I am, but I always have Elijah, and, now, you also keep me at bay as well." He tells her, cupping her face. "Thank you, Angel."

Aurelia swallows hard before nodding before they both lean in for a kiss.

□

(the dance that Andrew does with Genesis for those who wants a visual)

https://youtu.be/Xass1n-anVs

twenty-nine

In the embrace of movement, we find ourselves entwined with the mysteries of passion and desire, as if the very essence of our souls choreographs the dance of our existence. It is in the fluidity of motion that we uncover the hidden depths of our being, where words fail and emotions reign supreme. For in the dance, we surrender to the music of our hearts, allowing ourselves to be swept away by the intoxicating whirlwind of sensation, where the body becomes the canvas and the dance, the masterpiece of our untamed spirits.□

□

Fire. Fire burning down below, and the heat and flames are spreading throughout her body. Even though the wind is cooler and strong, nothing could keep the rising flames at bay. This is the only way she could describe kissing Andrew. Her heart is racing, and her mind is completely clouded. It feels like she's unconscious, but she's fully aware of what's happening.

Aurelia somehow ended up straddling his thighs, while her arms wrapped around his neck. Meanwhile, Andrew's hands remained respectfully on her waist. She had only kissed one other person—Elijah—and even after kissing them both, she somehow could feel the same level of passion they put into the kiss. Their kisses to her are special. This is her second time kissing, and with people she's interested in.

A few seconds later, Andrew pulls away from the kiss. He exhales softly, his eyes closed, while he leans forward to press his forehead against hers. The two sit there, panting softly, simmering in the moment, letting the feeling of the kiss linger upon their lips. Aurelia could hear her heart beating against her chest as she tried hard no to focus on the male's strong hands, squeezing her waist.

"Damn it," she hears him curse softly, pulling away slightly and turning his gaze elsewhere, evading her eyes.

"What's the matter?" she inquires, her concern evident as she notices the conflict in his expression.

Andrew shakes his head, gradually returning his focus to her. In his eyes, she senses a restraint, a holding back from acting on whatever thoughts are swirling in his mind. Aurelia unwinds her arms from around his neck and lowers her hands, inspecting her rings thoughtfully. The tension lingers until he cups her face gently and leans in once more.

Their lips were barely grazing when he grins mischievously. "Nothing's wrong, Angel. I just adore how you tense up when I touch you, or how your breath quickens when I lean in to kiss you. You truly are something special."

Aurelia swallows nervously before shyly averting her gaze, a playful grin tugging at her lips as he chuckles softly. The two cats finally make their appearance, hopping onto her lap as she settles comfortably on Andrew's lap.

"Don't worry, she's one of the nicer people in my life," Andrew assures, gently lifting the cats off her and pulling her closer as he reclines on the grass.

"Andrew!" she laughs, playfully protesting as she leans forward, her hands resting on the grass on either side of his head. "What are you up to now?"

"Just admiring the view," he teases, lifting his head slightly to plant a playful kiss on her throat and chin. "And my, my, my, don't you look stunning."

She closes her eyes, surrendering to the sensation of his raspy voice and the warmth of his kisses trailing along her neck. It ignites a fire within her, stirring up sensations she had never experienced until she crossed paths with Andrew and Elijah. These two men had her thoughts in a clouded cycle, and her emotions entangled and shared with them equally.

"Andrew," she murmurs softly, her hand pressing against his chest as she sits up, her gaze earnest. "I want to see you dance."

He sits up as well, propping himself on his elbows and tilting his head to look up at her. "You've seen me dance countless times, Angel."

"No," she shakes her head, avoiding his intense gaze. "I mean I want to see you dance with the rest of the performance department. You seem so excited when you're with them."

"Even with Genesis?" His tone is playful, his eyebrow raised teasingly, prompting her to roll her eyes before meeting his gaze.

"You know what I mean! You appear at peace when you're dancing with them, and when you're surrounded by their love. I can almost tell... you love being around them too."

Andrew's smile falters slightly, a shadow passing over his features before he lets out a sigh and shakes his head. "Even if I wanted to, I can't dance with them at the actual showcase. I'd be escorted off the campus before I even get the chance to perform."

"Because of what you told me before, right?" she asks, referring to the reason why he's not allowed on campus grounds.

"Yeah," he replies, tapping the grass with his index finger as he avoids her gaze. "It's easier to be on campus when I'm just walking outside or blending in to avoid getting caught, but dancing in a big showcase the performance department puts on at the end of every semester isn't exactly hiding or blending."

Aurelia looks down for a moment, but then she leans forward, resting her hands on top of his as she gazes into his eyes. "Maybe I can help you."

"Angel," Andrew says, sitting up and furrowing his brow slightly. "If Elijah couldn't pull strings for me, what makes you think you could? Elijah's mother still throws a shit ton of cash at the school, and I still couldn't get back in just for being associated with him."

She simply wanted to see him happy, as he was when she witnessed him dancing among people who knew and cared about him. Maybe he was right; perhaps there was no way for her to help him. Yet, she still longed to see him dance, especially with the people she saw today. Maybe she could do something about it. But how?

"It doesn't matter," he says, assisting her off his lap and rising from the ground. "Do you have a water bottle with you, Angel?"

As Aurelia rises from the grass, she rummages through her tote bag, eventually pulling out a water bottle she had bought earlier. Andrew pours water into both cans, leaving them near the building for the cats. Once he finishes, he takes Aurelia's hand, and together they begin to leave the clearing, where the cats have already nestled in and fallen asleep. As they make their way back to the path, Andrew's phone begins to ring.

They pause once they reach the path, and Andrew answers the call. "Hello?"

"Yeah? Why would I do that? Huh?" Andrew's expression shifts to annoyance as they walk side by side, engaged in the conversation.

"How the hell did you get my number to begin with?" Andrew stops abruptly, causing Aurelia to halt as well. She reaches out to touch his forearm, urging him to step aside from the walkway as he continues his phone conversation.

He scoffs. "Funny how I'm the first person you call when you never wanted me to begin with. I bet that's why you set me up."

Aurelia soothes his arm, meeting his gaze as anger flashes across his face. She knows his frustration isn't directed at her, but it's still daunting to witness him so riled up.

"And I'm supposed to just believe that you conveniently went MIA after I was arrested and kicked out of college?" He growls into the phone. "You know what, lose my number, don't call me again."

As Andrew ends the call, Aurelia gives him a moment before gently squeezing his arm. "Are you okay?"

"No," his response is blunt, filled with anger.

Aurelia closes her eyes briefly before stopping him from walking again. "Let's talk about it. I don't want to see you angry."

"Sorry to break it to you, Angel, but I'm going to be one angry fucking person with the way my life is now screwed up!" he snaps, causing her eyes to widen in shock. She knows she's not the cause of his sudden change in mood.

"Shit," he mutters, looking down. "Shit, I'm sorry, Aurelia. I'm just really on edge and don't feel like talking about my feelings right now."

Aurelia nods her head, understanding fully, but she still didn't appreciate him yelling at her. "Whoever that was, I hope they don't ruin the rest of your day."

"She's our ex, Elijah and I." Andrew tells her right then and there, laying it on her thick. "She's a despicable person, and the prime suspect in ruining my life. She's no one to worry about, but she's also someone who's sneaky and deceiving. I don't even know how she got my number, probably from Genesis."

Aurelia wanted to ask about their ex-girlfriend, but Elijah didn't seem like he wanted to tell her the details of why they broke up. It seems serious from the way Andrew talks about it. Curiosity eats at her brain as she listens to him speak.

"Fuck, now she ruined my whole mood," he murmurs, scratching as his neck before turning away from her. "I can't even spend a chill day with you without something fucking it up."

"Andrew," Aurelia says, holding his arm, causing him to look at her. "It's okay. We can still do whatever you wanted, just take a few moments to calm down."

Andrew pulls his arm from her grasp and sigh. He nods in acknowledgement and takes a deep breath a few times before looking away from her.

"It's not like we... I didn't care about her when we were dating. I guess it hurt a lot more knowing that she didn't want us both. So I guess why it pisses me off more than it would Elijah." He explains, motioning for them to continue walking.

"What do you mean? Do you... still have feelings for her?"

He shakes his head firmly. "Hell no."

"I'm saying that my anger for her is deeply embedded because she didn't have not one ounce of feelings towards me. She only wanted Elijah, and Elijah only. I spent days stressing and crying trying to figure out why the fuck she doesn't look at me the way she did Elijah." He mumbles the last part, his tone almost giving off a vibe that it hurts for him to talk about it. "So when it turns out she was trying to trap us, specifically Elijah, in a pregnancy for the money, I snapped. Everything I held in while we were with her, came out that day a hundred times more than I actually felt."

Hearing that their ex was trying to trap them made her worry about the future, and with her possibly back in town, what does that mean for her. Should she be worried?

"Elijah took it the hardest," Andrew tells her, walking towards a steakhouse, holding her hand as he speaks about his past with her. "The breakup for him was hard, in his eyes, she meant no harm, but after he saw the signs, he completely broke. Took a while for him to come back to, but when I overdose a month after, he took that harder than ever."

Hearing about their ex and their past experiences, her heart fluttered against her chest. If both of them were interested in her, did that mean they would love her as passionately as they did their former partner? It seemed like a silly question to ponder, but it was essential to her. That's just who she was; she needed assurance before investing her heart fully. Yet, she couldn't shake the feeling that it might be too late now, especially after sharing kisses with both of them.

As they entered the restaurant, finding an empty table, Aurelia took in the cozy ambiance and the soft murmur of conversation around them. "Steak?" she questions quietly with a smile, whilst scanning the restaurant interior.

"It's my favorite meat," he replied casually, perusing the options.

Aurelia nodded, idly toying with her bracelet until Andrew's gaze fell upon her. She straightened up, clearing her throat before tilting her head inquisitively. "What?"

He grinned, mirroring her gesture. "Aren't you going to order something, instead of sitting there with that adorable expression on your face?"

"O-Oh! Right. Okay, sorry," she mumbled, picking up the menu and scanning its unfamiliar offerings.

Cooking had always been her father's domain, and throughout her life, she'd rarely encountered anything beyond his knowledge. The only time they had steak was during special occasions at home. Thankfully, the menu did feature a classic steak option her father cooked for those special events: potatoes, broccoli, and steak.

Moments later, the waiter approached their table, and Aurelia set her menu down, while Andrew continued browsing. She placed her order first, requesting just water to accompany her meal. Andrew, on the other hand, ordered his food and a beer with a slice of lemon.

Andrew taps the table softly, as if the music playing is something he could dance to, Aurelia allows the silence to linger before she opens her mouth to speak again. "Was she the first girl you two fell for?"

The male shrugs. "She was the first we were serious about."

Aurelia nods slowly already knowing about the two mens history of seeing multiple people. However, she hardly understood what kind of relationship she would have with them. "So what does this make us? Exactly?"

Andrew leans back in his seat crossing his arms. "I think Elijah should be present when we discuss that. That doesn't mean I don't want to explain it, but I think it's best when we're all together. In the same room."

She understands what he means. Aurelia also understood how careful both men were when it comes to her since all of this is new for her. "Okay—"

"Drew?"

The two at the table glanced over at the person standing beside their table, with a few people behind him. "No fucking way, Drew?! What's up, man!" exclaimed the newcomer.

Andrew's jaw clenched as he forced a smile on his face. "Calvin."

"Damn, I haven't seen you since OD at Aiden's party," the group crowded at their table, making her scoot away, holding her things, looking very uncomfortable. "Well, I did see your videos, but shit man, it has been a hot minute. How long has it been?"

Andrew kept the false smile on his face, tapping the table impatiently while keeping his eyes down. "Clearly, not long enough."

Aurelia flinched away and swatted at the guy's hand, the unknown one who just sat down right beside her when Calvin, the one who's beside Andrew, sat down.

Calvin chuckled, causing her to watch Andrew, whose eyes are on her now. She's sure her eyes screamed she wanted them to go away, but Andrew's eyes screamed that he wanted to kill someone.

"Don't be like that, Drew," Calvin leaned closer, whispering something in Andrew's ear. Whatever he said made Andrew slam his hand on the wooden table and stand slowly from his seat, towering over the male.

Calvin stood up as well, just a few inches taller than Andrew, but he didn't back down. "Fuck you, and fuck off."

"Funny you said," he grips his chin for a second before crossing his arms and tilting his head. "I'm sure we already fucked, right? Hard to keep count these days huh."

Andrew pushed his chair back with a sharp scrape against the floor, his expression tense as he strode around the table. With a gentle yet firm grip, he clasped Aurelia's hand, guiding her out of the restaurant. Once they were outside, Andrew quickened his pace, causing Aurelia to take a few hurried steps to keep up with him.

"Who was that?" she asked, trying to match his brisk stride.

Andrew remained silent, his grip on her hand tightening slightly as they walked.

"Andrew?" she pressed, her voice tinged with concern.

The man halted abruptly, turning down an alleyway and cutting through the block. "Nobody," he muttered, his tone clipped.

"He didn't seem like a nobody, Andrew," Aurelia remarked, pulling her hand away, causing Andrew to stop in his tracks and face her.

His frown deepened as he turned around, frustration evident in his movements. With a forceful kick, he sent one of the city's dumpsters — one of those large, heavy ones — skidding across the pavement. "Fuck! Just more shit after shit!"

Aurelia watched him, her brows furrowed in confusion. The encounter with those individuals had left her feeling uneasy. Despite her questions, Andrew seemed unwilling to discuss the man they had encountered. But she couldn't shake the feeling that he was deeply upset about something. "Andrew?"

"No," he shook his head, reaching into his pocket and retrieving his phone along with a box of cigarettes.

"He clearly got under your skin!" She raises her voice this time, only showcasing her concerns. "I just want to help you–"

"Well don't!" Andrew snaps, pulling the unlit cigarette from his lips. "I never asked anyone to fucking help me! Everyone's treating like I fucking need someone to depend on! Get off my fucking back!"

Aurelia holds her tote bag strap and swallows hard. She has only been yelled at once since she has been in the city, and that person was Aiden. However, that changed. Andrew changed that. He stood there, yelled at her, all because she was concerned.

"Fine."

Turning on her heel, she begins to walk away. She kept her tears from falling as she pulled her phone out to call Nina. She didn't want to see Elijah at the moment, and she definitely didn't want to talk to Andrew, not after he just yelled at her for no reason. What hurt the most was the way he didn't stop her from leaving him there.

After being picked up by Nina, Aurelia locked herself in her bedroom. She had a lot of work to finish, especially since she decided to skip class for him. Not to mention she was growing more hungry as she sat there with dry tears on her face. A knock on her room door caused her to sit up in bed and hug her pillow.

Nina walks in with a small pizza box. "I brought you pizza."

Aurelia sniffles and tosses the pillow to the side before scooting at the end of her bed to retrieve the pizza box.

"Wanna talk about it now?" Nina asks, since the whole car ride back to the house was silent.

Aurelia opens the box, and takes a small slice of pizza, folding it in half and biting into it while the tears begin to run down her face again. As she chews, Nina offers her hand to sooth her sobs, but she shakes her head and holds her hand up. She didn't want to be comforted, she needed to get over it.

"You're a mess," Nina says, "And you aren't even officially dating them."

"How did you know?" Aurelia's hoarse voice speaks, causing Nina to sigh.

"I got a lot of missed calls from Elijah, so something must've happened." Nina crosses one knee over the other, pushing her braids back over her shoulder.

"Andrew... yelled at me. For only trying to understand what upset him, so I can... make him feel better... I guess." Aurelia explains quietly. To anyone, that sounds childish, but she wasn't crying because he yelled, she was crying because of what he said while yelling. Aurelia made sure she was cautious before saying the words that came out her mouth, but apparently, not cautious enough.

"Oh, love," Nina sighs and pats her shoulder. "I honestly have no idea what to say to that. I only knew Andrew through my ex-best friend, so the only person who can help you, is you. You need to communicate that his words hurt your feelings, and you need to work that out with them. Especially when all three of you are going to be in a serious relationship."

Aurelia knows how right she is. She knows she needs to communicate, but what could she possibly say, what if that just makes Andrew even more upset than before.

□

thirty

□

Aurelia's phone is stationary on her bed. It's surrounded by school items. Her notebook, laptop, and art bag. She's pacing back and forth while nervously taking subtle glances at her phone. Her room is dim, but only because the fall weather has just started to kick in, and the gloomy pale indigo-gray days have begun.

Two weeks. It has been two full weeks. She has been avoiding them. She hasn't tried calling them at all, but her avoiding them only made her more guilty, anxious even. She didn't know why she wanted to avoid them, maybe because she couldn't form a sentence or a start to the conversation she needed to have. Aurelia wanted to be prepared for important things like this, because if she went into it unprepared she would definitely panic.

"Aurelia I'm going to get lunch with–" Nina's words were cut short when she walked into the room. "What are you doing in the dark?"

The taller woman flips the light switch. "I get it's raining but that shouldn't affect your mood like this. Did you and the boys fight again?"

Defeated, Aurelia plops down on her bed. "I haven't said anything to them in two weeks."

"My god," she crosses her arms. "Did they reach out?"

"No, they did... I just ignored them." She tells her truthfully.

"What? Why not? I thought you liked them?" She asks, sitting down beside her, causing her to lean her head against get shoulder.

"I do like them, I just... I don't know how to start that conversation up." Aurelia stands up and hugs herself. "What do I say? You both hurt my feelings, apologize?"

"That's a start, love." Nina tells her, softly. "What this situation shouldn't be doing is, making you this closed off. You hardly ever come out of this room. All you do is work, study, and sleep."

"What if they're already done with me, what if–"

Nina stands up and sighs. "You need a distraction. How about you come with me and Adrian. We're getting lunch, the art department to talk to Sunny, and then going to the performing art department showcase later to see their performance. Maybe after doing something during the day, you'll have a clear mind to finally talk to them face to face. How does that sound?"

Aurelia thought about it for a moment, and after hearing what they would be doing, she took a deep breath before nodding her head. "Okay, I'll come with you."

"See downstairs in fifteen minutes?" Nina walks out of the room, grabbing the doorknob. "Remember, this is supposed to help clear your mind so you can be able to have that tough conversation with them."

Aurelia just nods her head and begins to search her things for something to wear. She wanted it to be casual, but also really stealthy. She didn't want the two men noticing her in public. Fortunately, Andrew won't be on campus, so it'll be easy to avoid running into him, but Elijah is really persistent. If he wants to see her he would do everything in his power to. Right?

She wonders why they haven't tried just popping up out of the blue, but then she realized that they are more than likely respecting that she wants and needs space. Even though deep down she wants to kiss them and hold their hands again. She especially wants kisses that are intense and make her feel all warm inside. Just thinking about it made her embarrassed. She finds something perfect for the summer transitioning to fall weather. Since she went shopping, Nina had made it her duty to get her clothes that made her 'cute and sexy'. Then she didn't understand, but now she knows. Her choice of words just need a bit of rephrasing.

"White... can't go wrong with white." she murmurs as she looks through her clothes.

After a few minutes of putting an outfit together, she starts getting dressed. She decided to wear a white button up long-sleeve shirt with a light blue denim corset on top. She had a light blue denim skirt to go with it. She also had a pair of knee high heels she could put on to tie the outfit together. Once she had everything on, jewelry and other accessories, Aurelia styled her hair in a low puff. She really didn't feel like doing an updo style, so she settled for a slick-back puff ponytail. She grabs her tote bag and her wallet and phone before meeting Nina downstairs. Once she makes it to the last landing, she could see Adrian and Nina awfully close.

"Shit..." She heard Adrian murmur a bit too loud as he pulled away from Nina and took two steps back. "Uh, hey Aurelia! How's it going?"

Aurelia laughs quietly as she approaches them. "You aren't very good at keeping things natural and subtle. When did this happen?"

"When what happened? We aren't like... together or anything." Nina turns her nose up and push her braids over her shoulder before walking out of the door, walking out ahead of her and Adrian.

"She wants me, Relia, she just needs to convince herself that." He winks at her before following Nina out of the door. Aurelia locks the door behind them and continues to follow the two people, the ones she considers her closest friends at the college, to Adrian's car. As she settles in the backseat, Nina turns around in the passenger seat and shows Aurelia her phone.

"Look at this," Aurelia takes her phone and scrolls through the pictures and videos of people Nina's following. "The performing arts department really is going all out this year, huh?"

"Yeah," Adrian yawns a bit as he pulls off. "I heard that the whole area was going to be open to the public, so they're going to have an even bigger audience than last year."

Aurelia scrolls further, seeing a post made by Sean. She clicks the volume icon at the bottom so she can hear what's being said. "We are cooking up something special for you guys tonight. Bring your friends and tell them to bring theirs. You wouldn't want to miss this year. It's going to be big."

Nina reaches back for her phone, and Aurelia hands it to her. "What could they be up to?"

"Don't know." Nina murmurs, scrolling more through social media. "Hopefully it's good, because last year, since Andrew was gone, the performance was lackluster, wasn't even that good. I wonder what they are going to do with him gone this year too."

Aurelia stares out the window, remembering two weeks ago when she confessed to Andrew that she loves seeing him dance, and she wanted to see him dance with his class, his friends, but that was her being optimistic.

"Sorry, love, forgot." Nina's apologetic tone made her pull her gaze from the window.

"It's fine, you can talk about them, Nina. I'm not that sensitive about what's going on between us." Aurelia reassures her softly before turning to look out the window.

"Trouble in paradise already?" Adrian asks, looking at her through the rearview mirror.

Aurelia just shakes her head. "We aren't really together, just... seeing each other. But, it's hard to handle our relationship when they both are going through a lot in their lives right now. Especially Andrew."

"I see." Adrian's tone is obviously concerned and he probably feels like he shouldn't make comments on anything, which bothers her a bit. Has she given him a reason to not want to share his thoughts and or opinions? "I hope things work out then."

"Why did you say it like that?" She pushes, watching Nina put her phone down and turn to look at Adrian.

Aurelia's tone of the question wasn't aggressive or defensive. It was filled with genuine worry concerns. They don't know it, and Aurelia hardly knows it herself, but she values their opinions, especially since they've known the two longer than she has.

"Like what?"

Nina groans. "Aurelia, no. We aren't talking about them. They hurt your feelings, and you need to focus on yourself until you're ready to have that conversation. You already told me you aren't so no talking about Andrew and Elijah. Don't even mention their names."

Aurelia bites her bottom lip and shamefully turns her gaze out of the window. She did agree that she wouldn't talk about them. As well as that, I agreed to have fun and clear my mind so I'm ready to talk to both of them face to face.

As they park in front of the sandwich place, Aurelia gets out of the car, adjusting the skirt, pulling it over her butt a bit more before locking arms with Nina. Once they get inside the restaurant, it's loud with laughter and chatter. It's clear everyone present is from the campus since the place is close to it. Adrian whispers something in Nina's ear, causing her to flinch before glaring at him. The male chuckles and pat her shoulder before walking to the line at the counter.

"Adrian said he'll buy the food for us," Nina says, still making a small frown but it switches to a small grin as she sits down at the empty table closer to the door. "He's pretty observant, so he'll know what you'll like."

"If you say so."

Nina looks around, smiles covering her face, and her eyes searching every-where. Suddenly her smile falls and Aiden walks up to them.

"Wow, looking beautiful as ever, Nina." He says, sitting next to her, wrap-ping his arms around her, but she removes his arm and scoots away from him. "But your attitude is as ugly as always."

"Boy," Nina turns to look at him, holding the fork that was wrapped in the napkin. "If you don't get your ass up and walk away from our table, I'll stab you in the dick."

Aurelia covers her mouth, containing the gasp that almost brought atten-tion to herself. Seeing as the annoying man is Aiden, just movement caused him to look at her. "Well, well, well. Look who we have here. Seems like Nina found herself a pretty doll."

"You got five seconds, and if I get to one I will punch you." Nina threatens, before she starts counting down.

"Five."

Aiden rolls his eyes and stands slowly from the seat he was sitting at. He walks towards Aurelia and lean down, close to her ear. "Careful who surround yourself with. I won't hesitate to take you down with them, Aurelia."

Adrian walks up, pushing Aiden away from her, a frown covering his face. "Leave her alone and get the fuck away from my table."

His twin's left eye twitches before he grins, holding his arms. "What's with all the serious expressions? There's a big performance happening tonight! Let's have fun!"

Even though no one is aware what just happened, they all still cheered with him, but Adrian didn't move. His stance is still in front of her with his hands in his pocket. Aiden chuckles to himself before shaking his head. "It is always your own blood..."

"Fuck off. I won't tell you again." Adrian warns him, causing his brother to hold his hand ups and laugh.

"Calm down, pick up your balls," he tells him while taking a few steps back. "See you at the event, Aurelia."

"One!" Nina says loudly, standing up, but Adrian stops her, shaking his head. "Move, he thinks people are scared of him."

Aurelia hugs herself and looks down. She was in an okay mood until he had to walk up and ruin it.

"Hey, don't worry about him. If he tries anything, I'll protect you. Okay?" Adrian tells her, causing her to nod slowly before sitting down beside Nina.

After fifteen minutes of waiting, the waiter brings them their sandwiches. Aurelai had a ham and Swiss cheese sandwich with olives and black pepper on it. The other two seem to have the same turkey and cheddar sandwich. Nina was right about him being oversant, because she really did like the sandwich a lot. It is good, even on the first bite.

As the trio eats, they talk about a lot of things, including things about their future and what they plan on doing after graduating. Since she's younger than they are, she had a while before she got to that point, but the both of them were in their last year, so they were already set for the future. The time went by and people started clearing the restaurant, and that's how she knew that the event must be starting very soon. The once afternoon sunlight that was in the sky is now going down, peeking behind buildings nearby.

"We should make our way there, so we can get a good spot in the crowd, unless you girls want to stand." Adrian laughs, while wiping his mouth before standing up in his seat.

"I don't mind standing." Aurelia tells him with a smile on her face.

"Well, Nina, she'll stand and we'll get the seats off to the side." Adrian tells the tall girl as he pulls her along with Aurelia.

As they made it back to the car, Nina went on social media again, and Adrian pretty much talked to her. The ride to the main campus wasn't long, so they were there in under twenty minutes. They parked just a few blocks away, since the parking lot is full of cars, and walked to where the big stage was lighting up. Aurelia is amazed by how fast they set up the stage, because earlier, when she was on campus for class, they didn't have anything set up, but now they did, just after a few hours.

"Wow. They really went up this year, even though the stage is bigger and the lights are better." Nina compliments as Adrian wraps his arm around her, but she pushes him away and begins walking through the crowd with Aurelia trailing behind her. When they are in the middle, where the stage is in perfect condition, they realize they have chairs out, but people are standing until the show starts.

"They even have chairs." Someone behind them begins to speak. "They must be doing something boring again. Should we just go?"

"Last year they had chairs and all we got to see was contemporary and ballet, I was hoping for more hip-hop and jazz." Someone else says, making Aurelia take her seat while Adrian whispers something else in Nina's ear.

This time, she didn't look like she was annoyed, in fact, her expression looked like she was dazed as if what Adrian whispered made her weak. Nina's knees give in slightly before she turns to look at Aurelia.

"Uh, we'll be right back, we're going to see Sunny. Yeah! Remember?" Nina says, causing Aurelia to tilt her head before nodding. They didn't have to tell her where they were going, she already knew they wanted to talk to Sunny, Nina told her before they left.

As the two make their way through the crowd, or what was left of it, Aurelia waits for the show to start.

"I just wish Andrew didn't get kicked out, he made these shows enjoyable." Someone murmurs as the crowd begins to take their seat.

"He was hot too, nice to look at." A girl behind her says to her friend, causing Aurelia to roll her eyes and sink further in the seat.

When everything around them gets darker, the lights begin to lower and the crowd slowly quiets down. It was cold and she was starting to feel just how gone summer is. Aurelia pushes her thighs together and pushes both of her hands between them, trying to warm up. Soon, the loud music of a softish melody begins, catching her attention. A blue cascade over what looks to be nine people, and someone in the middle dressed in black and white is looking down. As the music builds up he slowly raises his head, and the crowd starts getting excited. Aurelia's eyes widen when she realizes it's Andrew.

Thump.

The first lyric itself is beautiful which only brought her in more as she watched him dance. Aurelia couldn't believe her eyes, she couldn't believe he's dancing when he's not even supposed to be on campus. The performance is open to the public, so does that mean staff and professors are watching? what if they escort him off—

"Relax, baby," Elijah whispers in her ear, causing her to swallow harder as she turns to look at him. "I pull some strings so... watch him, listen to the song, allow him to apologize in the way he knows how."

Aurelia nods slightly as Elijah takes a seat beside her. She turns her attention back to Andrew's performance. She listens to the song, and watches him dance, letting herself get lost in everything. As the song gets to the end, she could feel her tears building up, and she's sure everyone else could feel it too. Andrew had affected everyone with his passion and emotions he brought to the performance. At the end, everyone stands up and cheers, chanting Andrew's name. Even with everything she just watched, she could see it on his face. He enjoys it. He enjoys dancing so much and it's obvious he enjoyed doing it with his friends in front of all these people.

Aurelia watches him walk off stage quickly, and Elijah holds her hand, standing up. "Shit, come on, let's go get him."

"W-What's wrong." She asks, earning a soft smile from him.

"He's probably overwhelmed with emotions. It's been a while since he had a crowd this large watching him. Especially when he's been stressed out about what he said to you for these past two weeks." Elijah tells her, making her stop walking and pulling her hand from his grasps.

"He yelled at me... even though I tried to help." Aurelia murmurs, looking down at her feet.

"And he regretted it so much," Elijah tells her, walking closer, carefully running his hand up and down her arms. "Maybe, you should hear this from him. Come on."

As Aurelia follows Elijah to through the doors of the Art department, she could hear crashing sounds, and shouting. Elijah and her run quickly down the hall seeing Andrew throwing chairs as well as kicking them.

"Drew!" Elijah calls out, letting go of her hand, pulling him in to comfort him.

"I want to get the fuck out of here! I don't–" Andrew's words are cut short, and the moment he locks eyes with her, his face changes. He slowly walks around Elijah and approaches Aurelia.

Tears fill his eyes before drops to his knees in front of her. "I-I'm... shit. I'm sorry Angel. I didn't mean to take my anger out on you and and–"

Aurelia kneels down in front of him, shaking her head and hugging him tightly. "All I wanted was an apology, so it's fine now, Andrew. Please don't cry."

Andrew wraps his arms around her and pulls her closer, causing her heart to race more. As they pull from the hug, Andrew stares into her eyes, making her nervous. It was a good feeling though.

"Did you like the performance?" He asks, standing up, while helping her up as well.

"I loved every second of it."

□

(the dance Andrew apologized to Aurelia with)(BTWs def a Ten Stan sooooo enjoy!)

https://youtu.be/EGfPcYeXCV8

thirty-one

In life, art becomes the intricate thread that weaves together the complexities of family drama. It's the canvas where emotions are boldly expressed, where the tensions and joys of familial bonds are portrayed with raw honesty. Each stroke of creativity becomes a reflection of the intricate dynamics, the tangled web of relationships, and the colorful spectrum of emotions that define the human experience within the context of family.

Elijah shrugs on the white button up sleeve shirt, slowly buttoning each button from the bottom to the top. Jared, the one his mother hired to assist him during the preparation for events–such as the one he's currently getting ready for, helps him put on the vest that pairs perfectly with the slacks he has on. Before buttoning the vest, Elijah tucks his shirt in his slacks, making sure that it looks neat before putting the vest.

Jared steps back, allowing Elijah room to fix the outfit himself. The man looks over the personalized custom branded vest and pants that his mother requested for him to wear. It had velvet trims and the matte black color really made him look just as his mother envisioned for him. Clean, no tattoos visible, and micromanaged.

"You look handsome, Mister James." Jared compliments him, looking at him through the mirrors.

Elijah slowly lifts his head and raises his eyebrow. As the male slowly turns around to face Jared, he carefully buttons the sleeve around his wrist. The taller blond male shakes his head as he finishes the right sleeve before moving to the left sleeve. He sighs softly, pushing his hands in the pockets of the nice sleek fitted slacks he had on.

"Jared, we talked about this." He tilts his head, approaching the older, shorter man. "I hate formalities. Just call me Elijah."

Jared looks mortified as his eyes widen and he quickly shakes his head. "But, your more strictly instructed–"

"My mother doesn't control me," Elijah cuts him off, watching the scared man avoid his eyes. It was probably something else his mother had instilled in the workers head that works for her. "And when you're in my presence, she doesn't control you either."

Elijah turns around and looks at himself in the mirror again, giving himself a quick nod before turning around to step off of the pedestal they had him stand on. Literally.

He stands beside Jared, patting his shoulder. "Also, thank you for the compliment, I appreciate it."

As the both of them leave the closet area, Elijah spray his expensive cologne lightly, before sighing through his nose. "What has my mother been up to?"

Jared avoids his eyes, Elijah could tell he was hiding something. Not just anything minor. Like his mother being corrupt, or spreading false information about him to the rest of the James family. This must be major. He looks nervous, too nervous to speak.

"Jared?" Elijah turns to look at him, tilting his head. "What are you hiding? What's going on?"

Jared takes a deep breath before finally looking into his eyes. "Your mother and your former advisor, Sunny, are meeting at her private establishment on the north side of the city, after the family reunion."

Elijah froze.

Sunny? Jared had to be talking about a different Sunny. No. He said his old advisor. His mentor. Sunny. He's talking about Sunny. The Sunny he looked up to for years. The Sunny that helped him out of all his shitty situations. The Sunny he was proud to call his friend rather than his teacher is fucking his mother.

"What the fuck. How long?" Anger completely masked over the question. His tone is low and threatening. "Damnit—how long, Jared!"

"This is their second official time meeting up," Jared informed. "However, the first time they met with each other privately was a year ago."

Elijah didn't care if it had been a long time. Why has Sunny kept this from him? Elijah wasn't known to get angry easily, but his mother. Out of all the women he could've met up with, he chose his mother.

"Sir– Elijah, I promise you they are only meeting up because he asked to use the grand hall, and in exchange for the grand hall. Your mother requests for him to see her in her private penthouse." Jared explains, maybe to calm him down, but how could he calm down. Especially after hearing something like that.

"Your mother and Cornelius Willis have been fond of each other–"

"Where's my mother?" Elijah grunts out, yanking his room door open and storming across the mansion in the main hall dining room, where the family reunion will be held.

The james' family reunion isn't like a typical reunion. Though they still share the same principles; invite family to gossip, boast, and brag about who's more successful and perfect. However, it's different about how it's held. They spend two hours in silence, eyeing each other up before his mother finally walks down the stairs and makes her presence known. Since she's the most successful, she spends the next hour bragging about him and Arthur. Then they eat.

However, family isn't the only one invited. His mother invites friends, just so they can follow the same rules. But he wasn't looking for the rules. He was looking for his mother. The moment he gets in front of her room door, he forces it open, causing A gasp from his mother's assistant while his mother sits comfortably in her seat, reading her Tablet on her lap.

Only when the stylist stops working on her hair is when she finally pulls her eyes from her work to look at him.

"Hi, Eli, you look handsome–"

"Why the fuck are you seeing, Sunny!?" Elijah cuts her off, watching her eyes change, lowering slightly as she glares at him.

Jared comes in behind him panting slightly, since he was a shorter older man. "Ma'am he asked and I-I-I... y-you–"

Marie, his mother, raises her freshly pedicured finger up to her lip. "Jared. No need to explain, it's best he hears it from the person he trusts anyway."

Her words were more dismissive than her looking back down at her Tablet and snapping her fingers for the stylish to continue working.

"So you're just going to fuck my former teacher and pretend like it's not wrong!" Elijah approaches her, causing her to sigh and look at his face. "Mother!"

"You know," she says slowly, crossing one knee over the other. "This isn't the first time... Sunny and I met up. In fact, we are a lot closer than you think. Now, if you excuse me. I have a reunion to get ready for, sweetie."

She looks back down at her device, and the stylist continues to work on her hair. His jaw clenches and his fists tightened. The blond male turns on his heel and walks towards his mother's room door. Jared follows behind him closely, pleading for him to slow down. As he walks down the spiral stairs, Arthur is standing there flirting with one of the maids.

"Did you know!?" Elijah asks, causing the maid to flinch and Arthur to look at the main hall room.

"Keep your voice down," Arthur scolds. "The guests are here."

"You think I give a shit about what those fake individuals hear? We all know they are here to cause fucking problems!" Elijah snaps, his voice getting louder, causing Arthur to shush him again before crossing his arms. "Did you know about Mother and Sunny?"

"What? What about him and mom?" Arthur's words stunned him. He didn't know? Elijah was sure he knew, but it seems like he's just as clueless as he is.

"Sunny and mom are seeing each other! Behind our back, and mom just... she just dismissed it. She's basically fucking our mentor!" Elijah explains sighing as he grabs a bottle of rum, from the cart the maid was dragging to the kitchen area across the hall from the foyer they were currently in to avoid causing attention. Elijah opens the drink, and downs the alcohol slowly, trying to erase the image of his mother and Sunny together in his head.

"For how long?" Arthur asks, grabbing the bottle from Elijah's hand, downing more than him.

"According to her, they've been seeing each other longer than what Jared told me." Elijah sighs, leaning against the wall.

This is the only time, and the first time, he and his brother held a conversation this long. They normally would argue and then go their separate ways, but now—now they are sharing a drink about hearing news about their mother.

"Should I talk to Sunny?" Elijah asks, watching Jared trying to fix his hair and outfit, but Elijah pushes his hand away.

"Why should you? That fucking prick would probably lie about it!" Arthur snaps. "He probably felt so guilty about it that he kept it from us. He has known us since we were kids! That bastard."

It's true. Since Elijah could remember, Sunny has been in his life forever. He even looked at him as a father at one point. Now, he doesn't know what to do or feel. He didn't even want to be at the reunion. He already had a couple of sips of strong alcohol, if he stays, he's sure he wouldn't make it through the night.

Then his phone breaks him from his thoughts. Elijah digs in his pocket and sees that it's Aurelia calling him. He steps away from Arthur, and answers the phone call.

"Hey, Aurelia." He answers, not trying to show his emotions through his greeting. However, he's sure that she noticed.

"Are you okay, Elijah?" She utters softly into the phone, causing Elijah's heart to thump against his chest, calming his anger down.

"I'm with my family," he tells her as he leans against the wall, looking up at the decorative marble ceiling. "That should give you a wide range of how I'm feeling right now, but I know you didn't call to talk about me. What's up?"

Aurelia's silence and soft hums only made the male smile. He could almost imagine how she looks now. Biting the inside of her cheek, looking at her unfinished artwork, sitting at her easel. "I wanted to know if you would like to come over this weekend. Nina would be out of town for the weekend, and I don't want to be alone."

Elijah couldn't help but grin at the innocent invitation. Although he grinned, a laugh slipped past his lips, causing her sweet voice to ring with concern in his ear. "What? W-What's wrong?"

"Baby," his voice low, almost in a teasing tone. "Do you realize what you're asking?"

"Yes?" She says confidently. "I'm asking if you and Andrew want to spend the weekend with me."

"Overnight?" He questions, just to clarify if that is what she meant. The two men could just stay over for a while and leave later in the night. However, if it's overnight, that meant that she wanted them to stay over, in her bedroom for one night and two days.

"Yes, Elijah. Overnight. I thought that was clear. She laughs into the phone, making Elijah close his eyes. "I had sleepovers with my friend, Cameron, all the time, so this should be the same as that, right?"

Cameron?

"This is a bit different, Baby." Elijah tries to explain, looking down at his fancy shoes, while his hand is tucked in his pocket and the other holding the phone up.

"Different how?" she asks, curiosity filling her tone as she waits patiently for Elijah to answer her burning question.

"For one we're–"

"Eli! Is that you!"

Elijah flinches slightly, hearing his aunt's voice. He closes his eyes again and deeply sighs. "Baby, I'll call you back later, just let Andrew know as well."

The male didn't give her much time to respond so he hung up quickly. He didn't want her to hear anything his family had to say, because nothing they ever say is coming from a good place in their hearts and minds.

"Oh, my, God! Look home handsome you are!" His aunt says, walking up to him with her arms spread wide. She pulls him close, running her hands up his back and over his shoulders. "You have very board shoulders too! Oh–!"

His aunt leans closer sniffing him subtly. "It seems like you started the reunion before your mother came down stairs."

"It was just one drink, Aunt Macie." He lied, clearing his throat as the rest of the family begin to pour out into the main hall.

"Yeah right, Felipe! Your nephew is turning out to be a lot like your broth er..." she mumbles the last part, but it wasn't like he couldn't hear her, she was standing right in front of him.

His uncle, his absent father's younger brother, approaches him with a cigar hanging from his lips. "Nah, his wench of a mother is to blame for his... indifference towards the rest of us."

"Really, I can't imagine why." Elijah glares at him, causing his uncle to grin in his face before his aunt pats his chest.

"Oh enough, leave the poor... boy alone." She says slowly before she clings to his uncle's arm. "Arthur! How's everything going? Plan on getting married and expanding the James' family name?"

Elijah stifles a laugh before looking down at his feet. Little did they know, Arthur had two kids. Eloise and Hector. Two different women, a son and a daughter, that he keeps well fed and hidden from the rest of the family.

"No." Arthur answers confidently. "I'm way too busy with work to settle down right now."

"Is that why you still live close to your mother?" Their grandfather says, sitting in the chair the servants brough for him, so he wouldn't stand too long on his feet. "I swear, I expected Elijah to be the mama's boy, but Arthur, you're the biggest mama's boy of them all."

The room fills with laughter before a servant clears her throat. "Miss James is finished. She is preparing to come down now, so please take your seats everyone. Elijah sighs and walks towards the dining hall, trying to think of anything but the event. His mind instantly went to Aurelia, and that look in those big brown eyes of hers.

She seriously had no idea that she was inviting them to stay over, for the whole weekend. Elijah knows that she probably isn't expecting intimacy, but would he be able to control himself? The thought of her dressed in her pajamas, those soft ones she wore when she was staying at his place, the one that hugged her slightly thicker frame perfectly.

"Shit..." He murmurs to himself quietly, looking down at his lap. It was like he was back in his adolescent years, still trying to figure out who and what attracts him. He just sums it up to being extremely attracted to Aurelia, both body and heart. She's passionate, it's what attracted him to begin with. That's how he and Andrew really ended up together. He was attracted to Andrew's passion for dance and now looks at them.

"Hello, my beautiful family."

The moment his mother walks in, he just shuts her out, thinking about the different things he could and would do—with Aurelia. Elijah looks down at his lap, the slacks not hiding the obvious tent in his pants. He leans on his fist and closes his eyes trying to think of something else, but Andrew comes to mind, which only makes everything even worse. He hasn't had sex since they all agreed to take things slow. Which meant he and Andrew didn't want to do anything without her, since it felt like they were sharing their passion and intimacy without her.

"Eli, baby?" His mother says, causing him to roll his eyes before looking at his mother who's holding the glass up in the air. "Make a toast?"

"I'll pass."

His mother clears her throat. "I'm sure you all are wondering why I called for a family reunion early this year."

"Yes, why." Elijah's grandmother, his absent father's mother, says with a snarky tone. "Is one of the boys finally getting ready for marriage?"

"No..." His mother giggles. "I'm getting remarried!"

Arthur spits his drink out and looks at him, but Elijah is just as confused as him. They just found that their teacher is sleeping with their mother and now she's talking about getting remarried. Arthur is pushing thirty, and he's twenty-five. Why would she want to get remarried at her age? Granted, their genes make them look younger than they are, but, his mother isn't young at all. She's forty-five.

"I'm also proud to announce." She smiles at Elijah first before looking at Arthur. "I'll be opening another grand hall on the north side of the city!"

Elijah stands up and shakes his head. "Are you joking?"

His mother sits down, looking unphased as she sips her wine. Arthur leans back against his seat, shaking his head as he mouthed 'sit down' to Elijah.

The blond male shakes his head. "Fuck this..."

Elijah pushes his seat back and walks towards the exit of the dining hall. He couldn't be in that room any longer. His family is so full of shit that he can't even call them that. Maybe his father was smart to get out of the family when he could, but now he has to live with it. All of this was too much, and he should've left when he found out that Sunny is sleeping with his mother.

As he gets in the car, he pulls his phone out, calling Andrew. He had been drinking so he didn't want to pull out of the driveway too emotional, that'll be dangerous. He needs to calm down just a bit to make the drive back home.

"Hey, Eli, i was just going to call–"

"Drew, this family is way too much for me right now. I don't even know why I even came." Elijah dumps out on him, but Andrew is used to it, this isn't the first time he called Andrew on the verge of a breakdown.

"I already told you, Eli, you don't need them. They need you and Arthur more than anything. Just leave. You're old enough to cut them off, yeah?" Andrew tries to explain, but it's not as simple as deleting and blocking their numbers. His family are public figures, so cutting them off would just ruin everything he built as well. "Just calm down, we can talk about it more when you get here, okay?"

Elijah messes up his slick back hair, and sighs deeply, taking slow deep breaths so he could calm down and make it back home in one piece. "I'll be there soon. Have Aurelia talked to you, yet?"

Andrew chuckles for a while before he sighs. "She has no idea what she's getting herself into."

"You will behave. We will behave. She wants to spend a weekend with us, a clean, no touching, maybe a bit of kissing, weekend. Okay?" Even though Elijah and Andrew are very physical people, Aurelia is not and he doesn't want to scare her away. They agreed to go slow so that's what he'll do, until she doesn't want to go slow anymore.

"Yeah, yeah," Andrew sighs. "I know. I was only joking, but that doesn't mean I won't tease her."

"Yeah, I'm up for a lot of teasing." He grins to himself as he drives slowly, trying to make it back feeling a bit tipsy. " I'll see you soon, okay?"

"See you, Eli."

□

thirty-two

<hr>

Every brushstroke is a whispered confession of longing, every hue a reflection of the emotions swirling in the depths of the heart. In this dance of creation, lovers find themselves immersed in a world where every stroke, every line, speaks volumes of the passion that binds them together, transcending the boundaries of words to express the ineffable beauty of their connection.

The sight of Sunny patting Aurelia's shoulder, and causing her to smile so beautifully like that bothers Elijah so much. He wasn't jealous, he wasn't a jealous person. The blond male is more upset that Sunny's playing as if he didn't spend a night with his mother, who's supposed to be getting remarried. Elijah finally pushes himself off of the wall and walks towards the two. Aurelia hadn't noticed him yet, so when he wrapped his arms around her waist, she tensed up.

"Elijah," she mumbles quietly, pushing his hand away and shyly looking away from him. "You scared me."

"What are you two talking about?" Elijah asks her, but he's only glaring at Sunny, who got a confused expression on his face.

"Oh," Sunny smiles before looking down at Aurelia. "I was letting her know about the art department small event. You remember the party we threw here, on Halloween."

Elijah knows exactly what he's talking about. The party would be just with the art students in the art department. It was just another way to get close to everyone before midterms. Which is on Halloween. It's like an early Halloween party.

"Is that so," Elijah says, looking at Aurelia who's staring at his arms that were crossed over his chest. "Are you planning on going, Aurelia?"

She swallows down anxiously before shrugging her shoulders as she looks up at him. "Maybe. I-It's still a while away before that event."

He noticed. Of course he did. Aurelia is checking him out so openly, so innocently, as if it's just a normal common thing to do. Elijah grins and looks at Sunny again. "Well, we'll see you later Sunny."

Elijah wraps his arm around Aurelia's shoulder, before he begins to walk away and towards the door of the art room. As they both walk further and further away from the room, Aurelia's silence is broken when she clears her throat.

"That was tense. Did something happen between you two?" She asks, persistent as ever, but of course he doesn't want to tell her, not until he confronts the man first. He also didn't want her to dislike him because he dislikes him. Granted. His mother can see and be with whomever she wants, and the same goes to Sunny, but it's socially wrong for his former teacher and current mentor to bring it upon himself to sleep with his mother.

"Hm," he hums trying to figure out the right words to say. "Things are a bit tense, but I don't know if I want to talk about it at this moment."

He nods mentally. He likes that response.

"I see," she says, pulling away from him and walking towards another room. "I'll be right back, I want to say hi to Adrian before leaving."

Elijah follows her into the room, where Adrian has his headphones on, and is in the zone with his sculpture. She laughs softly and walks up to Adrian, poking his side before they both share a look before a look and hearty laugh is exchanged.

"Hey Relia, you off already?" He asks, wiping his hands on his clothes so he wouldn't get clay on her. "I thought you had a while to go?"

Aurelia looks at Elijah and smiles before looking at Andrian again. "Uh, I'm taking the night and weekend off from working on it. I got more than enough time to get it done."

"Oh, did uh, Nina leave for her trip yet?" He asks, scratching his chin, while looking at Elijah.

The male could tell something happened from how suspicious he was being. Avoiding his face, trying not to acknowledge his presence. Did something happen between him and Nina? Are they...

"Yep! I have tonight and Saturday and Sunday to myself." She tells him with a wide smile. Elijah's heart always stops when she smiles like that. Seeing her happy and actually enjoying her time on campus.

"Well," Elijah steps forward smiling at her before making eye contact with Adrian this time. "She won't be alone at all. Andrew and I will be with her."

Adrian tilts his head. "For the weekend?"

Aurelia nods confidently while she looks at Adrian's work in progress. "Yeah, I didn't want to be alone for the weekend so I invited them."

Adrian mouths, ' She's serious?' and Elijah nods his head with a mischievous glint in his eyes before he grins widely. "We should go pick up Andrew, so he and I can pack a bag."

Aurelia later asked if they could spend Friday night through Sunday night with her since Nina would be later Sunday. She really had no idea what she's asking her boyfriends to do. Of course, he doesn't mind just spending time with her, but there's no way she believes that they would not not tease her.

"We should get going," Aurelia says, holding Elijah's hand, squeezing it a bit before she begins to walk towards the door, leading him away. "Bye, Adrian!"

The both of them walk towards his car silently. As they get to the car, she turns around, causing him to pause his movement before looking down at her with a soft smile but curious eyes. "somethings wrong, baby?"

Aurelia looks around before staring into his eyes again. "Can we... kiss?"

Elijah tilts his head in confusion. "Only if you want to."

"No, I'm asking you if we can kiss. Right now." She says more confidently before looking away, probably embarrassed from the question.

Elijah turns around, holding his fist up to his mouth, laughing softly. The soft laughter made her look at him frowning a bit.

"I'm sorry!" He says quickly, pulling her close by the waist, feeling her tense up at the sudden touch, but she quickly relaxes into his touch as grips her chin gently.

"You're so cute, you didn't have to ask. You can just kiss me, baby."

"It feels right asking first." she explains, causing the male to lift her by the waist and sit her on the hood of his car, making her yelps of surprise only made him grin.

"Elijah your car!" She pushes at his chest, but he grips her wrist and drags them lower. "W-What... People are watching!"

Elijah quickly scans around seeing a few students whisper to each other while others ignore them. He turns his attention back to the shy girl and tilts his head. "I thought you wanted to kiss me?"

"I do- but..."

Elijah brings his long index finger up to her trembling lips. The two hold eye contact as the cool autumn winds surround them. Even though he couldn't hear it, he could feel how quickly her heart was racing with him being this close. The blond male is standing between her thighs, leaning over her on his shiny white hood. He didn't give her a chance to speak.

To be honest, he wanted to tease a bit more, but even he couldn't resist kissing her. The man slides his hand from his hood to her exposed waist, from the crop top she had on. Elijah pulls her closer, leaving no space between them.

"Hah..." she pants softly into the kiss, as their lips and breathing moves in sync. The kiss is slow, one that would leave her, and himself, breathless.

That sound alone would cause the beast he has kept locked inside to break loose. He has more self control than that. Of course he did. Elijah cups her face, kissing her slower than before as he pulls away. She grips his wrist tightly, her short nails slightly digging into his skin as she pulls him closer.

The reaction he wants, the reaction he expects throughout their entire stay. Elijah chuckles softly, pecking her lips a few times before stepping back a bit and helping her down. Dazed, she glances around before looking down at her feet.

"T-Thank you... for the kiss." She says, causing the male to shake his head at her politeness before walking her to the passenger side of his car, and opening the door for her.

When she's settled in the seat, Elijah goes around to get into his car, only to be stopped in his tracks.

"She's pretty."

Danika.

Elijah's smile slowly fades from his lips as He walks around her, ignoring her. Not trying to bring up anything from the past with her in it.

"You've been ignoring my calls." She says, as he opens the car door, making him freeze. "I thought at least you would miss me."

Aurelia looks back at Danika who's beside the car, before she looks at him. Elijah could tell from the way she stared at him from the passenger seat that her expression held a longing look of disappointment and confusion.

He steps out of the car and closes the door behind him before grabbing Danika's upper arm and pulling her from the car so he could end this. Whatever this was. She's following him and Andrew around after disappearing right after Andrew's incident.

"Eli, you're hurting me!" She snaps, snatching her arm from his grip and crossing her arms. "I didn't come here to get manhandled by you!"

"You shouldn't even be here!" He snaps, looking at the car again, worried that Aurelia may think the wrong things if he stays with her too long. "You need to back off, when we said that we're done, we're done!"

As he tries to walk away, Danika grabs his hand, making him snatch his hand from her. "I said leave me alone! Leave Andrew alone. We're not together anymore!"

Everyone around in the area saw them, but some of them didn't stop that long to be nosy, they just kept going, going on about their days. Good. He didn't want people to start talking and it gets around.

"What, you found another girl and suddenly you don't care about me!" Danika screams, but Elijah just ignores her. He gets into the car, slamming his door shut, and pulling out of the parking lot without giving it a chance to fully turn on.

The silent drive to the studio, made his thoughts grow louder. The words are Danika's words. Her words about not caring. He did care about her, that was before she tried to trap him in a pregnancy unknowingly, then only wanted to be in a relationship to be with him only, and that's not how he wanted things, how he and Andrew wanted things.

"Are you okay, Elijah?" Aurelia asks, softly, causing all the fuming anger to calm down before glancing at her.

"Yeah," He sighs and rubs his chin before leaning against his fist as he uses his left hand to drive. "I've seen worse days, baby, but thank you for asking."

Aurelia smiles before sitting back in her seat. "I'm assuming that was yours and Andrew's ex-girlfriend, right?"

Elijah nods his head.

"She's pretty." She says, looking down at her hands. "But, she obviously makes you and Andrew really upset, which makes me not like her very much. I hate seeing you both so angry."

He couldn't hide this time. He laughs at her, just outright laughs. She doesn't realize how fucking cute she can be when she make those faces, and say those things. "You really are something, baby."

Aurelia crossed her arms, her tone full of curiosity. "Why do you call me baby?"

Elijah tilted his head and thought about it. The name didn't have much meaning, it was a common pet name, but he couldn't tell her that. She would want it to mean something, it can't be common. "Hm, you have this naive innocent aura surrounding you. You're observant, and very blunt but, your words show you are still learning what life is like, like taking baby steps. So I guess that's why I call you baby?"

"I don't like that reason very much, but" she laughs softly.

"Would you preferred if I call you something else then?" He chuckles. "Princess, Honey, Peaches?"

She laughs out a bit before covering her mouth. "No, I don't like those very much."

Her laughter calms down before she looks out the window of the passenger side door. "I like it when you call me baby, when you say it softly, like baby it make me feel things."

"What?" he questions. "Hot and bothered?"

She snaps her head in his direction, causing him to take his eyes off of the road for a second to grin at her before he looks at the road again. "What?"

"Why would I feel bothered," she says, her voice seeming very genuine, as if the question is serious. "I literally just told you I like it."

"Wow," he clears his throat, holding back his laughter. "I knew you were inexperienced and didn't know somethings, but you're telling me you don't know what Hot and bothered mean. Are you really that innocent, baby?"

"I'm not innocent!" She argues. "I know that the saying has some innuendos and such. I just don't know when to use it and when not to use it."

Elijah stops at a red light. "When we kiss, it definitely gets me hot and bothered."

He wanted to give the phrase some truth to it. "I love the way you tremble and whine for more when I kiss you, it really does turn me on."

That statement alone made her quiet, and shyly kept her gaze out of the window as they continued to talk. He thought it was cute that she's avoiding his eyes, but This is only the beginning of her weekend full of teasing. He's only getting started for what's to come.

As they get to the dance studio, Aurelia gets out of the car with him and the two walk towards the entrance. Elijah holds the door open for her, so she could go in. As she walks in he walks in behind her.

"This way," he guides her to the studio room that Andrew normally rents out for the day. "Get ready? Prepare your ears, baby. The music is louder when you're inside."

Elijah opens the door, and instantly the loud music makes his eardrums ache before Andrew notices them and turns the music off. He pulls his hood off and grab the towel and wipes his sweat away. Andrew walks towards them with a wide grin. He greets Elijah with a wink before he looks at Aurelia.

'I'm almost done, I need to put the finishing touches on this choreo. You know, fix the details and such. You two can wait for me in here, or you can wait in the car."

Aurelia nods and takes her spot near the door. Elijah follows her, wanting to watch Andrew dance, because he thought he looks the most at peace when he does. Not to mention that his dancing is what made him fall head over heels from him anyway.

As the music begins to play again, Aurelia focuses on him, in awe, Elijah is kind of in the same state, but as she watches him he watches her for a few seconds before watching Andrew again. These two are, and in aurelia's case, will be his entire world. He will focus on them and only them from now on. Well, he will try. With everything going on with his family and Danika, he'll try his best to make all this work without fucking up what he has. What's making him happy?

When Andrew finishes dancing, as he said before he would leave. They all make their way back to the car, Where Andrew starts his teasing, holding her, making her tense up as he kisses her suddenly. He could tell from the way she's sitting in the passenger seat, with her thighs close together, her eyes avoiding his and Andrew's completely. She's already becoming affected by their teasing, and they weren't even starting the real thing yet.

"Are we stopping back at the penthouse?"

Elijah nods, placing his hand on Aurelia's knee, slowly dragging his thumb across her knee, massaging it. "Yeah, we need to get our things ready tonight and the weekend, right baby?"

Aurelia is staring at his hand, but she nods slowly. "Y-yes. That's right, the whole weekend."

Andrew looks at Elijah in the rearview mirror, giving each other a silent look before he continues with the drive. Elijah finally gets to the penthouse building and looks at Aurelia after parking. "We'll be up there for a few minutes, so you don't have to come up. Come on Drew."

The moment they stepped off the elevator and into the penthouse. Elijah tries his absolute best not to push Andrew against the wall for a quickie, but he refrains from that and walks to the room and begins packing his bag.

"She'll break eventually," Andrew says confidently as he folds his clothes and puts them in his own bag. "I'm surprised she's this responsive to everything we're doing. Maybe she's not that innocent at all."

"I mean of course she's not," Elijah chuckles. "But even if she knows what affection and physical intimacy takes, she's not going to understand when it happens to her."

Andrew folds the last bit of his clothes. "We never really talked about it much..."

"Talk about what?" Elijah asks while closing his bag.

"Who would be the one to take her virginity, if she's comfortable with us doing so. Of course." Andrew says, causing Elijah to stumble before feeling a bit dazed. "We're barely in the kissing zone, Andrew. Sex should be the last thing on your mind. We need to start off slow, kissing, cuddling, hell, touching, before the real thing."

"Fuck," he says annoyed. "I know that! I'm just saying who will be her first, this is the first time we fell for someone who's a virgin, and to be honest, i hardly remember my first time, I don't want hers to be like that, I want her to remember and cherish her first. So who should it be?"

Elijah sighs and looks down at his bag. "When the time comes. I believe she should be the one to decide. It is her body."

Andrew nods, agreeing with that statement. "You're right. We should go. She's waiting for us."

As they make their way back down. The question and short conversation definitely is still on his mind. The man hadn't thought about that until Andrew brought it up, but he knows that they will not be having any sex this weekend, so there was no need to worry about that at this moment and time. They'll discuss it when the time comes.

□

(Andrew's dance in this chapter)

https://youtu.be/pt8X5FvoT5A

thirty-three

In the silent dance of their relationship, his body moved in perfect harmony with theirs, yet each step was laced with unspoken longing and restrained passion. His dance was a delicate balance, a beautiful art form where every touch held back the flood of desires he dared not unleash. Every twirl ignited the fire within their hearts, and every movement told the story of their passion. In each other's arms, and the music that guided them.□

□

Aurelia squeezes his hand tightly, causing him to grin. She has grown used to holding his hand, before she would only hold it for a moment before pulling away. Andrew couldn't find any other word to describe the small action beside cute. Aurelia's cute. Not usual the type he would go for, but she's different perhaps that's why he's so into her. She really believes that this sleepover will just be cuddling and talking. Andrew's really excited to see her tremble.

"Popcorn?" She stops looking at the variety of options for popcorn, causing the hooded man to do the same. She's about his height but he was still maybe three to four inches taller than her. "Would that be okay?"

"Is that what you want, Angel?" He asks, letting go of her hand to wrap his arm around her shoulder. "You know since you're picky."

She narrows her eyes at him before pushing him away. Though her glare is intense, he could tell that her narrow stare is playful. "You keep bringing that up! I told you I don't like greasy foods that much, but that does not make me a picky person."

Andrew chuckles before leaning close to her ear. "So riddle me this,"

He sees her flinch slightly as he turns her around. Her eyes glosses over with curiosity. "What do you want right now? A kiss..?"

Andrew steps forward practically trapping her between his body and the shelf behind her with the store's goods.

"Or a hug?" He looks over her face, staring at every little detail. Watching how her eyes dance around, trying to focus on something on his face to avoid looking into his eyes. "Which one, Angel?"

"I...I.." She looks down at her hands before nibbling at her bottom lip. He grins mischievously as he places one hand on the above her head and the other raises her head so she could look him in the eye.

"What was that? I couldn't hear you." He whispers low into her ear, causing her breathing patterns to change. Instead of the normal pace. Now, she's panting a lot quicker.

"A k-kiss." She finally answers, causing him to grin.

"Oh?" He tilts his head leaning forward, teasing her a bit by dragging his lips across hers. They were barely touching, but he could tell the anticipation was killing her. "I guess you aren't picky. I see you grown to like kissing me."

Aurelia squeezes the front of his hoodie, wanting him closer so she could kiss him, but he made sure not to allow her to. "I don't see how this relates t-to anything..."

Andrew knew kissing or hugging her wasn't even related to her being picky. He just really wanted to tease her a bit, and it's working flawlessly. She's clinging onto him, practically whining for a kiss, but he's not going to give it to her, even if she says-

"Please, Drew." She begs softly, staring into his eyes so innocently as if she didn't just say anything that would cause him to have a heart attack. Andrew turns away as the groan leaves his lips. He's usually super resilient when it comes to these things, but he knows now, he would be doing a lot of controlling himself than teasing his Angel. Aurelia.

"I found the snack cakes you–" Elijah raises an eyebrow, eyeing him curiously, and the moment Andrew stands up straight Elijah notices right away what the problem was. "Oatmeal cream pies."

Elijah hands the box to Aurelia before leaning over to his ear, his tone full of amusement. "Couldn't resist, huh."

Andrew adjusts his sweatpants, and his hoodie before turning around to see how happy and excited Aurelia is to spend a couple of days with them. It made him feel... happy as well. Just to see her smile and laugh with them. Especially with them.

As his girlfriend and his boyfriend walks ahead of him, having a conversation, Andrew's phone begins to ring. He looks at the caller ID, seeing that it's Sean. One of few that he actually keeps around since his OD incident.

"Yeah?" Andrew answers, holding the phone to his ear while lagging behind so they wouldn't hear the conversation.

"Yo!" Sean says in his annoyingly chipper tone. "Drew you gotta come to this party tonight. I heard you know who will be making business tonight."

Tonight?

"I don't think I'm going to make it tonight." Andrew declines, choosing rather to spend his possibly only opportunity to stay a night with Aurelia.

"I thought you needed dirt on Aiden," Sean whispers this time, which meant he was either near Aiden, or around Jackie. "He's selling tonight. I also heard that the buyer will be here, maybe you can ask them about Aiden?"

Andrew stops walking for a moment, watching as Elijah and Aurelia get further away from him. "I'll show up. I'm in the middle of something right now."

"Now that's the Drew I remembered," Sean chuckles. "See you later, bro!"

As the call ends, Elijah and Aurelia turn around completely. "Andrew, why are you so far back?'

Aurelia calls out as he catches up to them. He wraps his arm around her shoulder, smiling a bit. "I had a phone call, I stopped to finish it so I can finish focusing on you two."

Elijah eyes him suspiciously or maybe he was concerned. "Who was the call from?"

Andrew looks at him, but not in the eyes. He shrugs his shoulders as he shoves his hands in his hoodie pocket. "My parents. Something about money, they want me to come over tonight."

Aurelia looks a bit disappointed as she stops walking and turns to look at him. "Are you not staying tonight?"

Her brown eyes were staring directly into the window of his soul. He didn't like that expression. Andrew could tell she is overthinking, overanalyzing, thinking the absolute worst. Similarly to Elijah.

Elijah arms are crossed and his gaze narrows as he stares at him. He's definitely suspicious, him being concerned is out the window. "Your parents called you about money? And they want you to come tonight? Why not right now?"

Damnit.

"I guess they are busy? I don't know babe, just I'll be leaving later but I'll be right back." He lies, patting Elijah's shoulder before looking at Aurelia whose face is covered in disappointment, he knew he would need to make her feel better. Perhaps teasing?

"It'll only be for a few hours," he chuckles, pulling her close, looking her in the eyes. "Hey, if I'm late, you can tie me up and do whatever. You. Want, Angel."

Aurelia's eyes widen before she turns away from covering her face with her hands from his suggestive words. Teasing accomplished, but now it was time for the ultimate battle. Bullshitting this to Elijah. If he finds out that Andrew's missing a little over a couple of hours of alone time with Aurelia for a party, he'll be even more pissed at him. But Andrew has to go, who's to say that they'll bring the dealer to another party, this might be the only time he could get closer to finding out what happened that night.

"I might have to," Andrew shivers slightly at the sound of Elijah's deep whisper tickling his ear drums. "You better not be late, and I hope you're being truthful."

Andrew walks a few steps ahead of them before doing a fancy footwork to turn around. "Just trust me, I won't be late."

When the trio makes it back to Aurelia's and Nina's house, Aurelia quietly begins to put everything away instantly. It was like she was in her own little world, still oblivious about what kind of sleepover they are going to have. Andrew slides on the counter and watches her closely. She was wearing Elijah's jacket still, it made her look small, but that's because Elijah's limbs are longer than theirs.

Aurelia finally looks at him, smiling at him before opening the cherry tomatoes she bought. "Do you want one?"

"Hell no." Andrew says, leaning away, a smile covering his lips. "How can you eat that?"

Elijah walks from down stairs, rolling his long sleeves up to his elbow. "Eat what?"

Andrew looks over his shoulder, nodding at Aurelia before pointing at the grapes. "How can she eat those like grapes? I barely like tomatoes on my BLTs."

Aurelia laughs to herself before popping one in her mouth. "mm..." she moans playfully. "It tastes just like grapes."

"You're really something, Angel." He comments, watching Elijah walk to her side.

The taller male silently grabs two of the small, grape sized tomatoes, and eats them both. Andrew shakes his head causing the both of them to laugh. Elijah grins before giving Andrew a subtle signal. He chuckles softly before carefully moving the tomatoes and turning his body on the counter so she's standing in between his legs.

"Shall I give it a taste as well?" Andrew says, cupping her face. The confusion covers her innocent stare before reaching for the container, but he quickly grabs her wrist and place her hand on his chest. "I meant tasting them another way."

"There's other ways to eat-" her words were cut short, Andrew closed the gap between their faces. Her kissing is still novice, but she's getting better. He liked it though, he didn't mind taking the lead, especially when it's her.

A soft moan pours into the kiss, causing him to pull away quickly, ending the kiss. Elijah stands behind her, purposely standing really close, Andrew could feel himself getting excited as he watches Elijah grip her waist. He runs his lips along her neck but he doesn't kiss her, he just turns her around and they share a kiss.

Fuck. Is the first thing that comes to Andrew's mind. He and Elijah haven't done anything in so long because they want to share moments, intimate moments with Aurelia, but they don't want to push her into it. Elijah said she has to want to do it. Which Andrew agreed with but the anticipation and the sweet sounds she make when they kiss just really sets him off.

Elijah finally pulls from the kiss and then it was his turn. Aurelia still slightly in between them watching him and Elijah kiss passionately. Andrew is glad he decided to wear sweatpants, but he's sure the tent in his pants is definitely on display. Elijah wraps his hand around the male's neck, squeezing firmly before pulling away. It was his way to establish who's in control of the kiss. Andrew bites his bottom lip as he pulls away grinning as the taller male glares at him, disapproving of his action to provoke him. He didn't care because the smallest action had Aurelia panting quietly, her eyes dancing between the both of them.

Her hand makes its way up to her chest, perhaps feeling her racing heart. She didn't know it yet, but she was definitely excited watching Elijah and him kiss like that.

"I-I... um, I'm going to get the projector from Nina's closet... y-you know for the movies? I'll be back." Aurelia stutters, stumbling back a bit before walking quickly towards the stairs.

"I think this is going to be–" Andrew's words were interrupted by Elijah's lips.

The blond male hands cups the back of his knees and yanks him forward. Andrew instantly leans into the kiss, practically grinding his front to his. He could feel it. He could feel how excited the moment got him, mostly because he initiated the provoking, but he saw the look on Aurelia's face as well. Though they both did get hard from a kiss, which isn't normal for them, especially when they weren't doing much touching before could be because they haven't had sex in awhile.

Elijah grips his neck firmer this time, tightening his grip slowly. He pulls his lips back staring at his lips for a second before staring into his eyes. Andrew could tell from his intense stare that he wanted more, they both wanted more.

"I think you went too far," Elijah pants heavily as he snaps back to reality. "You kissed her suddenly, too sudden."

A full on groan leaves his lips as he slides off of the counter. "You're overthinking, she was into it."

"You don't know that," Elijah's tone is full of concern, but he knows it's from him overthinking. "She could be up there right now–"

"You overthink too much, Eli. She's probably trying to calm down, as I said she was into it." Andrew walks around him to get a cup a water, and before he could say anything Aurelia comes down the stairs slowly, looking in between the two for a split moment before pulling a small smile on her face.

"Help please," She asks, watching Elijah approach her, grabbing some of the cords for the projector. "Thank you."

Andrew drinks the water from the cup and watches Aurelia put everything on the couch. She takes Elijah's jacket off and looks around. She pats her head a bit before clearing her throat. Before she speaks, her phone rings, and she excused herself before retreating upstairs again.

Elijah sighs and crosses his arms. "I'm going to go get our things from the car. Let her know if she asks, okay?"

Andrew nods watching the blond leave out of the front door to the house. He looked at the stairs and decided to make his way up. He sits the cup in the sink and walks towards the stairs, going up. The closer he got to the top the louder he heard Aurelia's conversation. Of course, she had it on speaker phone, she must be doing something.

"Relia," Nina's voice could be heard coming from the room with the door slightly open. "Girl, you do realize this won't be a normal sleepover right?"

Andrew leans against the wall outside the door, crossing his arm across his chest. He had intended on teasing her more, but this was much more fun, listening to her conversation about them.

"What do you mean? I mean I know we're together and we'll be cuddling and kissing–"

Nina laughs on the other end. "Relia, baby, you do realize that when you're dating two guys like Andrew and Elijah, there's definitely going to be more than just that happening."

Aurelia goes silent, making Andrew cover his mouth with his fist. He didn't want to make any sound, but he couldn't help it.

"Like what?"

Nina is silent this time before she laughs softly. "Aurelia, how about this."

"When you shower tonight," Nina hums. "How about you do some self exploring."

"Self exploring?" Aurelia's tone is full of confusion.

Nina sighs. "God, you're adorable. What I mean is touch yourself. Explore what makes you feel good before letting them touch you. When you know what feels good, then, only if you want to, you'll allow them to touch you."

Andrew grins at the suggestion. When be met Nina in the past, he thought she was stuck up, but seeing that she actually cares for his Angel, that impression of her is slowly fading. He prefers this Nina a lot more. Aurelia does have a way of changing people. Maybe...

"O-Okay. I'll do that." Aurelia agrees to the suggestion, and Andrew wonders why. "Have a safe flight Nina."

"Have a fun weekend, Relia." Nina says, giving Andrew the cue to knock on the door before entering.

"A-Andrew!" Her voice is full of shock as she holds her phone and the pajamas she must be planning on wearing later tonight. "H-How long you've..."

"What do you mean?" He says to appear more clueless before he pours out the lie. "I just got up here? Were you gossiping about me, Angel?"

Aurelia shakes her head quickly. "No, I just... just... nevermind."

Andrew didn't want to go, especially after hearing Aurelia's plans for tonight, but he had to. He needed to.

"Are you about to leave? To see your parents?" She asks, walking closer to him, making him tilt his head. "Do y-you know what time you will be getting back?"

Andrew pulls her into a hug, feeling her completely relax into his embrace. "Yeah, I should go now so I won't be there too late. You'll stay up for me yeah?"

Aurelia pulls back slightly and narrows her eyes at him. "How long are you going to be? You aren't planning on sleeping over at your parents are you?"

He chuckles and kisses her forehead. "I'd rather spend a night in hell than spend a night with my parents. It shouldn't take long I promise."

Andrew pulls from the hug and begins to walk backwards. As he gets to the threshold of the room, he smirks a bit. "Don't have too much fun in the shower, Angel."

Her face expression instantly turns from happiness to embarrassment, she grabs her pillow and tosses it at him. He catches it while laughing, but she chases him out of the room with another one. As they get down stairs, Elijah tilts his head at the commotion and before he knows it, he and Aurelia fall over the couch and down on the floor.

"You were listening!" She screams as she straddles him while swinging the small pillow at him. "You eavesdropper!"

Andrew blocks the blows with the pillow he caught before, and in one quick movement he grabs the small pillow from her hand and sits up to kiss her. She pushes at his shoulder but eventually she gives in, settling into his lap as he kisses her. Andrew glances over to the side where Elijah is watching them with an intense look. One intense look, almost as if he's trying hard not to just pounce on them both. Andrew grips her waist and presses her down on his lap. As he pulls away from the kiss, he leans to her ear, panting softly against her ear.

"You are driving me crazy, Angel." He nibbles at the skin under her ear, making her tilt her head slightly. "But I'll wait until you are ready to handle me. All of me."

Andrew helps her up before walking towards Elijah who's standing by the front door. He leans over to his ear, whispering softly. "I'll be back before eleven. I need to handle some things."

Elijah looks down at his sweatpants and chuckles. "You and I both. Go. I won't do too many things without you, we have a whole weekend."

Andrew grins and looks over his shoulder at Aurelia, sending her a wink before leaving. The moment was intense. He was close to taking her on the floor, but he controlled himself. He would be lying if he said he wasn't excited though. It has been that way since they started dating.

This is going to be a long weekend for the three of them. A long painful weekend. But, Andrew had to go to this party first. He had to get the info he needed and then he'd leave. At least that's the plan. When it comes to him, usually nothing goes according to plan. He'll just have to see how this will all play out.

☐